MW00439739

EMANCIPATION

ROAD TO THE BREAKING
BOOK 7

CHRIS BENNETT

Emancipation is a work of historical fiction. Apart from well-documented actual people, events, and places that figure in the narrative, all names, characters, places, and incidents are the products of the author's imagination, or are used fictitiously. Any resemblance to current events, places, or living persons, is entirely coincidental.

Emancipation

Copyright © Christopher A. Bennett – 2022

ISBN: 978-1-955100-06-9 (Trade Paperback)
ISBN: 978-1-955100-05-2 (eBook)

Publisher's Cataloging-in-Publication
(Provided by Cassidy Cataloguing Services, Inc.).

Names: Bennett, Chris (Chris Arthur), 1959- author.
Title: Emancipation / Chris Bennett.
Description: [North Bend, Washington] : [CPB Publishing, LLC], [2022] |
Series: Road to the breaking ; book 7
Identifiers: ISBN: 978-1-955100-06-9 (paperback) | 978-1-955100-05-2
(ebook)
Subjects: LCSH: United States. Army--Officers--History--19th century--Fiction. |
United States-- History--Civil War, 1861-1865--Fiction. | Confederate States of
America. Army--Drill and tactics--Fiction. | Women spies--Southern States--
Fiction. | Slaves--Emancipation--United States--Fiction. | LCGFT: Historical
fiction. | BISAC: FICTION / Historical / General. | FICTION / Sagas.
Classification: LCC: PS3602.E66446 E43 2022 | DDC: 813/.6--dc23

To sign up for a
no-spam newsletter
about
ROAD TO THE BREAKING
and
exclusive free bonus material
visit my website:

http://www.ChrisABennett.com

Emancipation [i-man(t)-sə-pā-shən]
noun:

1. The act of setting free from
restraint, control, or the power of
another.
2. The act of setting free from any
controlling influence (such as
traditional mores or beliefs).
3. The abolition of slavery.

DEDICATION

To
Keri-Rae Barnum,
For keeping me focused,
on track,
moving forward with confidence,
and occasionally even
talking me down from the ledge!
Thank you, Keri,
for everything you do!

Contents

"My men ... they're Indian fighters from Texas. Oh, to meet them on the street you'll never find a more polite and kindly crew—true gentlemen all ... a testament to the way their mommas raised them, no doubt. But if you cross them, they are cold, hard killers ... and that is on account of how I trained them."

– Nathan Chambers

Chapter 1. To Save the Union

"What I do about slavery ...
I do because I believe
it helps to save the Union.
... and I intend no modification
of my oft-expressed personal wish
that all men everywhere
could be free."
- **Abraham Lincoln**

Sunday July 13, 1862 – Washington, D.C.:

With a great shout, one hundred and twelve blue-uniformed soldiers leapt up, scrambled over the low split-rail fence, and plunged knee-deep into the narrow creek just beyond it, rifles thrust forward, bayonets fixed.

Through a haze of gun smoke in the dark of early dawn they forced their way, sloshing forward against the burdensome water, their captain slightly in front, his saber held aloft, shouting encouragement.

But even as the Union captain reached mid-stream, a roar like thunder rent the air, and on the far bank not thirty yards away a line of fire flashed, sending another great plume of smoke swirling skyward.

The captain clutched at a sudden hard pain in his chest, dropping his sword into the stream. He glanced down at his chest, gasping for a breath that somehow wouldn't come. A horror swept over him; his right hand had been completely torn away, sword and all, leaving a ragged stump, pumping out his life's blood. He grabbed the stump with his left hand, attempting the stanch the flow even as he sunk to his knees in the stream, no longer able to stand. And then with a sudden shock, he realized the missing hand no longer mattered; a gaping hole in the center of his chest spewed blood down the front of his blue uniform coat.

1

Everything around him began to turn black. He glanced to his sides and saw blue-coated bodies floating down the stream, in their wakes spread clouds of red. Not a man was standing. *Oh, my poor boys*, he thought, and then the rippling surface of the stream rushed up toward his face ...

"*Oh!*" Secretary of State William Henry Seward woke with a start, realizing he had momentarily dozed off in the carriage, suffering a frightful dream of war and death. His fourteen-year-old niece, Anna, had prodded him awake with her elbow, whispering, "Uncle Henry ... the president has asked you a question ..."

"*Hunh?* Oh ... sorry Mr. President, I'm afraid I dozed for a moment there ... Didn't sleep well last night. And oh, my goodness, what a horrible dream I just had."

"I'm surprised you can sleep at all in this carriage with all the bumps and ruts. I feel as if my backside were being whacked with a hammer," the president responded. But Seward noticed despite the humorous reference, the president didn't smile, and there was no levity in his tone.

"Hmm ... there's been plenty of lost sleep lately, Henry," Lincoln continued, "I should know ... Had a nightmare, did you?"

"Yes, Mr. President ... though it was so real, I wonder ... a company of our brave young soldiers was fording a stream in the midst of a battle, and they were suddenly cut down by enemy fire. It was horrific ..."

Lincoln was thoughtful for a moment, nodding his head, "Yes, it's a nightmare all right ... our own national nightmare, I'm afraid. And all too true."

"Yes, Mr. President ... I'm afraid so. You ... had a question for me, sir?" Seward asked. He thought the president looked as sad and downcast as he had ever seen him before, and that was saying a lot. *Likely not helped by this occasion, another funeral of a young child taken too soon by all the pestilence that seems to always accompany war. And only a month ago it was Lincoln's own son, Willie. This can't help but bring up painful feelings, and emotional wounds not yet healed. This good man has already suffered so much, bearing such a terrible burden for us all ... and I fear it has only just begun ...*

The president, Henry Seward, Seward's niece, and Secretary of the Navy Gideon Welles shared a carriage ride back from the funeral of Secretary of War Edwin Stanton's infant son, James. The carriage bounced along the erratically maintained roads of the nation's capital, heading back toward the White House.

Lincoln slowly nodded his head, and finally responded, still looking down toward his feet, "It was a very moving ceremony, don't you think, Henry?"

"Yes, Mr. President," Seward answered, determined to tread lightly. "I was quite touched by Edwin's brief eulogy."

The president nodded, but if he was recalling the painful recent memory of Willie's funeral, he kept the thoughts to himself.

Lincoln put his hand to his forehead, rubbing at the bridge of his nose as if suffering a headache. He stayed like this for several minutes. Seward and Welles shared a concerned look, and Anna squeezed her uncle's arm, then leaned into him. But no one spoke, allowing the president to process his thoughts in peace.

The carriage ride had smoothed out somewhat, and just when it seemed their tortured backsides might finally get a much-needed reprieve, they hit a particularly hard bump that nearly bounced them all to the ceiling.

This jolt seemed to snap the president out of his dark reverie; he suddenly sat up straight and looked around at his fellow passengers. He now had a hard, determined look in his eyes, and no longer seemed tired and haggard.

"Gentlemen ... there has been too much death, too much pain. Not just personally for those of us here, but for all the mothers who've lost sons, the wives who've lost husbands ... and the sweet young children swept away by this pestilence. And for what? *'To save the Union?'* Perhaps for those of us tasked with running the government it is a lofty enough goal to sacrifice an entire generation of young men ... but to the farmer in his field? To the merchant in his store? To the mother watching her sons march off to war? Is it enough for them?"

Seward resisted the urge to respond, knowing Lincoln well enough by now to know when to hold his tongue, and when to use it.

The president slowly shook his head again, "*The Union* ... of the United States of America ... It is by far the greatest experiment in government in the long history of mankind. Nothing the Greeks or Romans tried comes close. But to the laborer working to put bread on his table ... is it compelling enough to inspire him to go out and die for it?"

Again he shook his head. Then in barely a whisper he answered his own rhetorical question, "I think *not* ..."

Seward and Welles exchanged another quizzical look, as if to ask, *Where is this going, I wonder?*

Then the president suddenly sat up straight again, looked the two men in the eyes and said, "Gentlemen, I have come to a cataclysmic decision. This war *must* mean something more ... it must represent something every man can relate to ... something worth fighting for, something righteous, and monumental. We *must* make this war about more than two regions of the country disagreeing about their preferred form of government. We must make this a war for *freedom* ... a war for the freedom of all mankind. Gentlemen ... I have decided ... *I will free the slaves!*"

ᏂᎣᏆᎣᏯ ᏣᏏᎣᏲᎣᏆᎣᏯ ᏣᏏᎣᏲᎣᏆᎣᏯ ᏣᏏ

Tuesday July 22, 1862 – Wheeling, Virginia:

Nathan Chambers stepped up to Governor Francis Pierpont's office and knocked politely on the door frame. But when the governor looked up from his simple desk, Nathan noted that the governor's visage did not reflect his usual dauntless good humor.

This can't be good, Nathan decided. But he knew Pierpont well enough by now to know he'd likely get right to the point, for good or ill, so Nathan just said, "Good morning, Francis. You wanted to see me?"

"Yes, Nathan, and good morning to you too, though you may decide it's not so good when you hear what I have to tell you," he said, gesturing toward the chair opposite and not bothering to rise as he normally would on their first greeting of the morning.

Definitely not good, Nathan concluded, and took his seat.

"I'll get right to the unpleasantries," the governor said, gazing intently into Nathan's eyes, a habit that never failed to impress. Most men about to deliver bad news had trouble making and holding eye contact, but not Francis — one of the many reasons the two men got along so well.

"There are two serious matters I wish to discuss with you this morning, Nathan. Neither is good news, but I will start with the *least* upsetting first. With the House passing the West Virginia statehood bill, and the Senate delaying their vote until December, we'd been thinking the whole matter was on hold for a few months, and we could turn our attention to other matters in the interim."

"Yes … *but?*"

"But since the Senate voted to postpone until December, it has come to my attention, from several reliable sources in Washington, that our *own* senator, and your good friend John Carlile, has become a major impediment to the bill."

"Oh? Well, we knew he was opposed to putting anything in the new state constitution concerning slavery. I suppose he's now just miffed about Senator Willey's amendment to the bill, promising to change the West Virginia constitution to include a gradual elimination of slavery."

"That's what I'd assumed initially. But now I'm led to understand it is more than that; it seems he has become opposed to the whole concept of splitting off West Virginia into a new state. He's now actively opposing the idea in Washington."

"*What?!* I can hardly believe *that*, your honor!"

"I couldn't either, so I have double-checked with my all my sources in Washington. I'm afraid it's true. Carlile has entirely defected to the other side, it seems. The news has just reached the commonwealth legislature, and the delegates are furious. Even now they're debating a resolution censuring Carlile and demanding his resignation."

Nathan shook his head in disbelief. "This is a most bitter pill; but for the sake of my longstanding friendship with John, I will withhold judgment until I can speak with him directly."

5

"Understandable, and reasonable ..." Pierpont answered, slowly shaking his head.

Nathan was quiet and thoughtful for several moments, absorbing this troubling news. But remembering the governor had said there was another, even more upsetting topic to discuss, he looked up and asked, "And the other matter?"

"Yes ... *that* ..." Pierpont said, and sighed. "I was just making the final arrangements on your brigadier general's commission in the Loyal Virginia volunteer regiments, soon to become the *West* Virginia regiments, per our recent discussions. As usual, I sent the paperwork off to the War Department in Washington. Just routine, though for a general officer's commission there is, I understand, the additional step of running it up the hill to congress—more or less as a courtesy and formality. Congress has never yet refused the request from a sitting governor in that regard, from what I understand. Normally nothing else for the War Department to do other than file it. We never hear back on these matters, other than an acknowledgment of receipt."

"But *this* time?" Nathan prompted, a sinking feeling beginning to grow in the pit of his stomach.

"This time ... the War Department *denied* the commission."

"Denied it? *Denied it?!* Why?"

"I'm not entirely sure; their message was surprisingly vague— something about an ongoing investigation. Here, read it for yourself," he said, handing a sheet of paper across to Nathan, who took it and quickly read through the brief, cryptic telegram message.

Nathan scowled, folded and pocketed the paper, then stood from his chair, "Under *investigation* ..." he said, and snorted, shaking his head, a dark scowl knitting his brow.

Francis continued to gaze up at him expectantly, and asked, "What do you make of it, Nathan? And what do you intend to do?"

"I don't know *what* to make of it, your honor. But as for your second question, I intend to get to the bottom of this nonsense. I'll be on the first train for Washington tomorrow morning."

"But Nathan ... do you have *any* idea what this might be about? You don't seem entirely surprised. Is there something I should know about?"

"No. I am what I appear to be, Francis. I have no dark secrets, if that's what you're implying."

"Now Nathan, don't take offense. I'm on *your* side—now and always. But a man of your nature ... well, not to be indelicate, but sometimes there's a tendency to resort to *extreme measures* when called for, and those aren't always—strictly speaking—in keeping with the letter of the law, as you well know."

"Hmm ... a reasonable point. Sorry, Francis. No, there's nothing you don't already know. But as for not being surprised, I *do* have a strong suspicion who is likely behind this."

"Oh?"

"Yes. It has the *foul stench* of George McClellan all over it."

ᏰᎧᏋᏣᏋᏰᎧᏋᏣᏋᏰᎧᏋᏣᏋ

Tuesday July 22, 1862 – Washington, D.C.:

"Ah, Blair, there you are. We've just been discussing orders to the commanders in the field in regard to the Confiscation Acts ... to pass the time while awaiting you," the president said in a humorous manner intended to soften the blow of his mild scolding of the Postmaster General.

But Lincoln's expression betrayed his impatience. He had business he wanted to address with his cabinet straight away, a matter of the greatest import that he'd been struggling with in his own mind for days, before finally deciding to act. And once he'd made that decision, the wait had been galling, especially this last half hour.

Ever since he'd informed Secretary Seward and Secretary Welles of his intention to free the slaves, he'd debated the details concerning the matter with himself back and forth, over and over, around and around, nearly every hour of every day. Not about whether it was the morally correct thing to do—of that he'd never had even the least bit of doubt. No, his angst was concerning all the *other* considerations surrounding it: whether it was

7

constitutional, whether he had the authority to do it, whether it could be made to last in perpetuity or if it would simply expire or be set aside with a single stroke of the next president's pen upon his eventual exit from the office.

He also worried over its effect on the war; would it inspire the Union to greater effort and enthusiasm, giving a loftier and more meaningful reason to fight? Or rather would it cause the secessionists to dig in their heels ever deeper, and potentially alienate the slaveholding border states in the process?

And then, ever lurking in the darkest, most nightmarish recesses of his mind was the most frightful foreboding of all: could emancipation trigger a violent, vengeful uprising by the former slaves against their erstwhile masters — an unimaginably horrible bloodbath of retaliation and anger vented against men, women, and even children of the white slavers in return for all the years of wrongful bondage?

He feared such an eventuality might engender sympathy and even support amongst white northerners for their southern brethren, and turn them against emancipation, and even against the Union war effort.

It was a thought almost too terrible to contemplate — that the result of this most high-minded and moral of all acts could be a racial schism from which the country might never recover. Lincoln shuddered at the thought, but could not shake the evil images from his mind, no matter how hard he tried to reason them away.

"Sorry, Mr. President. I was delayed by ... important matters," Blair said as he took his seat, looking more than a little sheepish at his tardiness.

Lincoln gazed down at the table for a long moment before looking up and meeting eyes with each of his cabinet members in turn — Secretary of War Edwin Stanton, Secretary of the Treasury Salmon Chase, Secretary of the Navy Gideon Welles, Secretary of the Interior Caleb Smith, Postmaster General Montgomery Blair, and Attorney General Edward Bates — before finally resting his gaze on Secretary of State William Henry Seward.

"A few of you will not be surprised by what I am about to say," Lincoln began. "At least two of you have heard of it once before, though perhaps enough time has now passed since then that you expect I have changed my mind on the matter," he chuckled softly, "and truth be told, you'd be *right* about that ... I have changed my mind, more than once. But funny thing about my mind — turns out it's quite stubborn," he gazed around the room and saw smiles and nods of agreement, "once it latches onto an idea ... well, it's harder to shake off than fleas on a hound. The harder I try to shake an idea free, the more it just seems to spread and burrow in."

He paused again, smiling and slowly shaking his head as he took a deep breath, "Which is my way of saying I have finally made up my mind on the matter. I'll welcome your thoughts, but I must warn you: if I, with all my stubbornness, have been unable to talk myself out of this course, then you gentlemen, as persuasive as you may be, will have no chance at all.

"So please don't waste your time trying to talk me out of it; rather, tell me how it should be done, how it can be implemented to best effect, what consequences to expect, and so forth."

He again looked around the room and was not surprised to see looks of breathless anticipation — all knew something monumental was about to be announced. Only Henry Seward did not lean forward with eager expectation or trepidation; rather he looked thoughtful, slowly nodding his head.

"Gentlemen," the president continued, "I have decided to issue a proclamation, using my war powers as chief executive, to free all slaves held within the states in rebellion. And I mean to make my order permanent. With a single stroke of the pen, I mean to make this war have immense historic significance above and beyond the preservation of this great experiment in democracy — I mean to make this war about the freedom of all men, about fighting for the greatest of all moral causes, about something greater than ourselves or even our country. I will make this war about ridding this nation — once and for all — of the evil scourge that is slavery."

He paused, and looked around the room, but nobody spoke, so he proceeded.

"Now, I mean to read you my draft thus far and then I shall be interested in your comments … if you have any," he softly chuckled — the idea that his cabinet, made up of some of the most powerful, highly opinionated men in the country, might accept this pronouncement without comment was ironic to the point of absurdity.

Lincoln unfolded two large sheets of paper, put on his reading glasses, and read the text aloud. They could all see just how "rough" this draft was; scratch-outs abounded, and scribbles could be seen down several of the margins. And far from being a profound, poetic document — such as the Declaration of Independence, or the preamble to the Constitution — this proclamation was quite restrained, and very legalistic. And yet, despite that, no one in the room had any illusions about its ultimate significance as one of the most important documents ever to be written in the history of the young nation, if not the world.

When he finished reading, Lincoln neatly folded the papers and put them back in his vest pocket, removing his reading glasses as he did so. "Comments?" he asked.

Attorney General Bates was the first to speak. A Virginian and former slave owner, who'd emancipated his own slaves, stated that he was supportive of the proclamation in principle, but argued that it should only be issued along with a plan for the mandatory deportation of freed slaves back to Africa. He was willing to make an exception for blacks that were already freed, but he believed slaves had been held too long in a degraded, ignorant state by their masters to ever be successfully absorbed into civilized, white society.

Lincoln frowned. Though he was not surprised by Bates' statement, and knew he meant well and likely even had some reasonable arguments; still, the idea rankled.

"And would you send Irishmen back to Ireland now that the potato famine is over? Or French speaking citizens in New Orleans back to France so that they'll better fit in?" the president

10

asked. "The slave trade from Africa has been banned for so many years now that the vast majority of our black men, women, and children have been born right here in America. I would argue that makes them as American as anyone else ..."

"I don't disagree with you, Mr. President ... but you can hardly compare black slaves to Irishmen or Frenchmen. Your argument avoids the entire subject of racial differences," Bates concluded.

Lincoln thought about this a moment, then nodded, "Yes, it does. And perhaps that is for the best after all ..."

Postmaster Blair next spoke in opposition to the proclamation, but not on moral grounds, rather he was concerned about the political fallout in the North. He feared the freed slaves would threaten the good paying jobs of laborers in the North, and that could create a backlash against the Republican party at the polls.

Treasury Secretary Chase then expressed support for the initiative, but with no great enthusiasm. He feared such a "heavy-handed" approach as a presidential proclamation might do more harm than good, triggering chaos and upheaval, including Lincoln's feared slave uprising resulting in the widespread massacre of their former masters. Chase proposed a more subtle approach, where Union commanders in the field would be ordered to free and arm the slaves as they conquered new territory, and as circumstances allowed and warranted.

But when the president looked across at Seward with a questioning look, the secretary reached out his hand and said, "May I, Mr. President?"

"*What?* Oh ... oh, yes, of course, Henry," Lincoln said, reaching back into his coat pocket, pulling the papers back out and handing them across to Seward.

Seward quickly unfolded the sheets and read through the document again.

"It's good, Mr. President ... but if you'd allow me to take this home and go through it carefully, I believe I can suggest a few ... *refinements* ... that may enhance its impact and perception."

"Of course, certainly, Mr. Seward. You are a much more eloquent wordsmith than I ... I should be much obliged for your suggestions," the president answered with a nod and a slight smile.

"And no one will be surprised to hear that I am enthusiastically in favor of this move, Mr. President," Seward continued, "and I believe the signing of this proclamation will have a positive impact on our war effort on several fronts. But *only* if …"

Seward paused, and looked the president in the eye, "… only if it does not appear as an act of *desperation* on our part."

"Desperation? How do you mean, Henry?" the president asked.

"The Virginia peninsula campaign was a disaster, from which we have not yet recovered. Our army is still reeling from the aftermath, and it has allowed the enemy to take the initiative. If we were to announce this proclamation now, our enemies would smell blood and come howling … it would appear that we are grasping at any possible solution to our army's ineffectiveness. I fear it would entirely undermine and detract from the high moral purpose."

"Hmm … I see your point," Lincoln answered. "What then can we do?"

"Pray for a Union victory on the battlefield, Mr. President. Preferably in a battle that is both large and decisive. Then, and *only* then, should you announce your intention to issue the proclamation."

Chapter 2. Treachery and Violence

"Treachery and violence
are spears pointed at both ends;
they wound those who resort to them
worse than their enemies."
- Emily Bronte

Tuesday July 22, 1862 – Wheeling, Virginia:

Once his boiling anger at this latest treachery had cooled to a low simmer, and the burning desire for extreme violence had eased—somewhat—Nathan decided what he most needed in order to combat this so-called "investigation" against him was a strong ally in the War Department. Someone who could find out what was *really* going on—what he was being accused of, who had instigated it, what witnesses or evidence they had, and so on.

His first thought had naturally been General Rosecrans. The two of them had become quite close during Rosecrans' posting in the western Virginia theatre, and he knew Rosecrans would immediately disbelieve any lies being spread about him, especially if the source turned out to be McClellan as expected — that Rosecrans would stand in Nathan's defense without question or hesitation. But Rosecrans was no longer in Washington, having recently been transferred out west to serve under General Grant, who'd been having some good success against the rebels out along the Mississippi.

That left Brigadier General Rufus Saxton, recently returned to Washington now that the Harpers Ferry crisis had passed, as his next choice. And when Nathan thought about it, Saxton was probably a better choice anyway; Rosecrans tended to make too many enemies with his more brash, confrontational manner. And Saxton, being a long-time quartermaster would likely have a better feel for the overall pulse within the War Department.

So Nathan fired off a telegram to General Saxton, explaining his situation and requesting a meeting in two days' time.

His next decision was who to take with him to Washington. Of course, normally that would've been Tom, who was practically impossible to leave behind anyway. But Tom was up to his eyeballs with problems of his own—fortunately mostly of the *good* kind, for once.

"Sorry, sir. Of course I will come with you if you wish it …" Tom said apologetically, with a shrug, "But—"

Nathan snorted a laugh, "No need to explain, nor to apologize, Tom. You have a whole new family to accommodate … not to mention suddenly finding yourself a husband and father! No easy tasks, any of that, I can only imagine. You stay here and run herd on your crew. I have a mind to take Mr. Wiggins along this time, anyway. It'll give him something useful to do, and I'm sure you'll be able to rest easy knowing he has my back."

"Yes, sir. Thank you, sir," Tom answered with a grin and a slight blush.

And so, two days later, after a tiring but uneventful full day's ride east on the B&O Railroad, Nathan, Jim, and Harry the Dog stood outside an office at the War Department in Washington. Nathan knocked politely, causing the general seated within to look up from a stack of papers.

"Ah … Mr. Chambers, it's so good to see you again, sir!" Brigadier General Rufus Saxton beamed as he rose from his seat and stepped forward to greet Nathan.

"Likewise, General," Nathan said, returning the smile with genuine warmth. The two men shook hands and patted each other on the shoulder with enthusiastic affection, recalling their recent service together at Harpers Ferry.

"And *Colonel* Wiggins … you're in good health, sir, I trust?" Saxton said, turning to Jim and extending his hand, which was accepted with enthusiasm.

"Oh, yes sir, general. Never better, sir … never better, thank ye kindly for askin'."

"Excellent, excellent! And good to see you too, Harry," the general said, nodding toward Harry the Dog, who sat heavily, then gazed up at him and lolled his tongue out the side of his mouth in his usual comical manner.

"Other than the obvious matter at hand … how have *you* been, Nathan?" Saxton said, gesturing for his guests to be seated.

"Oh, I can't complain, Rufus … though occasionally I still do," Nathan answered, eliciting a short laugh from Saxton.

"Nathan, I've been digging almost non-stop ever since receiving your telegram, and I must say … I've been shocked at how surprisingly onerous the task has proven."

"Oh?"

"Gentlemen, not to sound immodest, but I am one of the highest ranking, most senior quartermaster officers in the entire Army … not to mention enjoying the favor of both the secretary and the president at the moment, for reasons you well know. Almost nothing of significance gets purchased or requisitioned in this army without my signature … which, as you can imagine, infuses me with inestimable leverage for getting things done … or finding things out. But in this case …"

"Yes?"

"I hit a stone wall—and *not* General Jackson, this time."

Nathan graced him with a nod acknowledging the play on words, but the matter was too serious for the usual banter.

"Everywhere I turned, I was told the investigation was of a highly secretive and confidential nature. That it was only being discussed with officers on a 'need-to-know' basis. Can you believe it?! Need-to-knowing *me?!* Even the secretary refused to speak with me about it, saying I ought to consider myself recused because of my previous working relationship with you at Harpers Ferry! *'Recused?!'* I argued … 'if anything I should be allowed as a character witness on his behalf.' But my arguments seemed to fall on deaf ears and were to no avail."

Nathan frowned, and rubbed at his chin, gazing down at the floor, slowly shaking his head, "Then you've come up entirely empty?"

But Saxton shook his head, "Not hardly … you should know me well enough by now, Nathan, to know I don't give up so easily. And being told to stand down by the secretary himself only made me all the more curious and determined to get to the bottom of it. I can honestly say I have pulled out *all* the stops this time—

called in favors, withheld approvals, threatened, cajoled ... and even bribed when nothing else would suffice."

Saxton chuckled, "Yes. *You*, Nathan, have the dubious honor of pushing me to discovering the very extreme limits of the leverage my position affords ... which I have to say turned out to be quite an interesting and amusing exercise ... But I digress."

"Thank you for your efforts, Rufus, I shall not forget it. But what have you discovered through all your labors?"

"Well, it's not a matter of *what*, but rather of *who* ..."

"Ah. *Who*, then?"

"Well, nobody seems to know any details, other than a vague, general suspicion of 'disloyalty,' whatever that means. But one name keeps coming up regardless of where I dig: Allan Pinkerton."

"Pinkerton? Hmph ... not surprised ... he's known to be McClellan's toady ..."

"Yes ... that is certainly rumored ... but unfortunately, he's become much more than that. His intelligence efforts, including counterespionage activities, have become invaluable to the War Department's efforts. And he has ingratiated himself with the president himself by personally protecting him from harm whenever he travels outside Washington. It is said Pinkerton's efforts have already prevented several attempts on the president's life, for which the administration is effusive in its praise and gratitude."

"I see ... so, you're telling me I should tread lightly with the man, and not just march up and put a gun to his head?"

Saxton snorted a laugh, "Something like that ..."

Nathan nodded and stood, extending his hand again, which Saxton took. "Thanks, Rufus. I'll be careful," Nathan said, and turned for the door.

ഇൠൡൠഇൠൡൠഇൠൡൠ

Nathan waited impatiently in a wide hallway at the War Department, in an entirely different wing from where he'd met with General Saxton. He'd sent Jim outside, along with Harry the Dog, to wait for him to finish his business. He figured he'd have a better chance of getting in to see Pinkerton if he was by himself—it wouldn't do to look like he'd brought a bodyguard with him, of either the two-legged or four-legged kind. Harry was agreeable to waiting outside of buildings—in fact he preferred it—especially if accompanied by one or more of Nathan's men. As long as he generally knew where Nathan was, he was content to stay out in the fresh air and wait. He seemed to have infinite patience in that regard, unlike the men.

Nathan leaned against a wall, arms folded, chewing on an unlit cigar, awaiting the return of the young officer whose job it was, apparently, to prevent anyone from getting in to see Pinkerton or anyone else having offices down the hallway. A group of men, mostly military, a few civilian, waited in the hall, hoping for an audience with one of several army officials, though most of those waiting had chosen to sit in chairs that lined the hall on both sides.

Nathan checked his pocket watch—over a half hour since the last time the officer had made an appearance, and more than two hours since Nathan had first arrived and asked to see Pinkerton. He let out a heavy sigh, remembering his promise to Saxton that he'd be civil. But he knew himself well enough to know his patience was wearing thin …

Finally, after another quarter hour, the young lieutenant returned, walking casually back down the hall. *In no particular hurry, clearly*, Nathan decided, and scowled. He'd disliked the fellow from the start—cold, snooty, and of an overly high opinion of his own worth, by Nathan's reckoning. Also likely thought himself a handsome fellow and pleasing to the ladies, with his muscular build and dark, neatly trimmed beard.

"Well, lieutenant?" Nathan asked as the man stepped up to him.

"I'm sorry, Mr. Chambers, but I have been informed that Mr. Pinkerton will not have time to speak with you today. Perhaps you should try back tomorrow … or the day after," the lieutenant answered, with a look and in a tone that was anything but apologetic.

Nathan's scowl turned to a dark frown. "No, that won't do, lieutenant. I have waited long enough. I will see him now."

"I'm sorry, Mr. Chambers, I can't allow you ..." the officer said, but Nathan stepped past him and began striding down the hall in search of Pinkerton's office.

He'd not gone three steps before he felt a firm grip on the back of his left forearm. "Sir, now I must insist you leave—" the officer began.

Nathan whirled around, seized the lieutenant by the front of his uniform tunic, lifted him off his feet, and slammed his back against the wall in the hallway, holding him there, feet dangling.

He glared into the man's eyes. That superior, even arrogant look had instantly swept away, replaced by one of shock and fear.

"Never lay hands on a man you don't know, lieutenant. Unless you're prepared for a fight!" he growled, continuing to chew on the cigar.

"Now, you've done your duty. Allow me to do mine ... *sir*," Nathan said in a milder tone, as he lowered the man to the ground before releasing his grip.

He gave the lieutenant one more hard look, then turned and continued down the hall.

He ignored the first three offices he passed; he'd seen the lieutenant bypass them when he'd gone to speak with Pinkerton before. The intelligence chief's office was somewhere past a right-hand turn in the hallway, so Nathan turned that corner before he began poking his head into doorways. If the doors were open, he looked to see who was inside, if not, he went ahead and opened the door without knocking, apologizing when he discovered Pinkerton wasn't within. Fortunately, General Saxton provided Nathan with a very precise description of the man, so he knew what to look for. It also helped that Pinkerton would be one of the few men in any of these offices not wearing an army uniform.

After the sixth, "Oops, wrong office. Sorry for the intrusion, sir," Nathan was beginning to think this might take a while and was beginning to fear the lieutenant might return with armed reinforcements before he located his man.

But the seventh office turned out to be the correct one. He opened the door and saw a serious looking man with a broad, handsome face and neatly trimmed hair and beard, wearing an expensive, dark-gray suit. So this time he stepped inside, pulling the door closed behind him.

The man looked up from a paper he was reading and said, "Yes? What can I do for you, sir? Are you looking for someone?"

"Allan Pinkerton, I presume?"

"I am. And who might *you* be ... *oh* ... Nathaniel Chambers, I'm guessing."

"Yes, you guess correctly."

Pinkerton sat up in his chair and gave Nathan a stern look. "I'm sorry, Mr. Chambers, but as I told the clerk, you will just have to come back another day. I'm too busy at the moment to speak with you."

Nathan scowled and said, "No. You will speak with me *now*, sir." He turned back toward the door, but having no key with which to lock it, he did the next best thing, grabbing a chair and wedging it tightly up under the doorknob.

When he turned back toward Pinkerton, he found himself staring down the barrel of a small revolver. But if Pinkerton thought to intimidate his uninvited guest by pointing a gun at him, he was quickly disappointed.

"I'm not here to assault you, Pinkerton, if that's what you fear. I'd just prefer no interruptions until I get what I came for. So you can either use that thing, or put it away. If your time is so precious that you'd kill a man over it, then go ahead," he said, folding his arms across his chest to await the answer.

Pinkerton frowned, then lowered the pistol and de-cocked the hammer. He slipped the revolver back into an open desk drawer, then slid it closed before retaking his seat. "Very well, Mr. Chambers," he said, gesturing for Nathan to also take a seat in the chair opposite him. "Since it seems you have successfully interrupted me—despite my best efforts—what is it I can do for you, sir?"

"You can tell me why I'm being investigated, what it's concerning, and why it's keeping me from being commissioned a general officer in the army, despite the personal request of a sitting governor."

Pinkerton was quiet a moment, gazing down at the papers on his desk. "Of course, I am unable to give *exact* details concerning an ongoing investigation concerning a matter of this seriousness."

"What *matter* is that? I don't even know what I'm being accused of ... nor by whom."

"As I said, it is a charge of the most serious nature—involving possible treason and espionage."

"Based on what evidence?"

"A young woman—a self-professed native of the Confederate capital Richmond—mysteriously appeared at Fort Monroe during the late peninsula campaign, claiming to have intelligence to the benefit of the Union. But it was determined she was an enemy agent attempting to pass on false information as part of a plot to lead our army into an enemy trap. Among other things, this woman claimed to be a close acquaintance and associate of yours, Mr. Chambers. Later she managed to escape from prison in Washington through mysterious means. A woman matching her description was then seen in your company at Harpers Ferry by one of my agents, mere days later."

"This is your so-called *evidence* against me?" Nathan asked, frowning darkly.

"As I said, this was the *basis* for the *start* of an investigation ... I cannot give details as to the findings thus far from that probe. Do you deny an association with this questionable woman, going by the presumably false name 'Eve Smith'?"

"I don't deny knowing her, nor meeting her in Harpers Ferry. But she's no enemy spy, rather a loyal Unionist, even as she claims ... and ... I feel compelled to defend her reputation and honor; in addition to her loyalty, she is brave, resourceful, and extremely capable—a true asset to our cause, and it is a damned shame her help was not only ignored, but has been spun into something nefarious.

"And further, I had nothing whatever to do with her prison escape—a prison she should never have been sent to in the first place."

"Ah! So you admit to being an associate of hers, of having personal knowledge of her doings, to having motive for helping her break out of prison, and of being in her company shortly thereafter. Surely you can see how this looks from my perspective, Mr. Chambers? Potentially very damning, I'm afraid."

Nathan scowled, "Let me tell you how it looks from *my* perspective, Mr. Pinkerton ... At great personal risk Miss *Eve Smith* provided General McClellan critical intelligence that was entirely truthful, and if he had had the good sense to have heeded it, he could have won the peninsula campaign and likely ended the war right then. But for whatever reasons—suspicion, treachery, or just plain stupidity, I know not which—McClellan chose to disbelieve her, forgoing a golden opportunity. And then our esteemed general inexplicably decided that she must be an enemy spy, despite no actual evidence to back such a serious accusation.

"And *you*, sir, are complicit by going along with him, and for continuing to do so ... because unless I am missing my mark, McClellan has also put you up to conducting this slanderous 'investigation' against me, preventing me from doing my duty for my country, to the detriment of both."

Pinkerton was now turning red in the face, "No one has 'put me up to' anything, Chambers. I am simply doing my duty."

"It's not your *duty*, sir, to serve as McClellan's bootlicker ..."

Pinkerton's face turned a darker red, but before he could respond there was a loud banging on the door.

"Mr. Chambers ... open this door, sir!" he heard a voice shouting from outside.

Nathan glared at Pinkerton another moment, then said, "I was just leaving anyway." He turned and kicked the chair out from under the doorknob, sending it clattering across the floor to bang into the far wall. The door shot open, and the same young lieutenant nearly fell forward onto Nathan, only managing to stop just inches short of crashing into him.

The officer held his palms up and backed away slowly, making clear he had no intention of laying hands on Nathan again. Behind him in the hallway stood two soldiers holding rifles, gazing into the room, looking puzzled.

The officer glanced over at Pinkerton with a questioning look, but Pinkerton just shook his head. So the officer stood aside and allowed Nathan to exit. The two soldiers in the hallway likewise stood aside and let him pass.

When he crossed out of the hallway and into a broad foyer at the front door of the War Department building, General Saxton was there waiting for him.

"How did it go with Pinkerton?" he asked.

Nathan frowned, "Hmm … not so well."

"Lost your temper with him?" Saxton said, with a knowing grin.

Nathan snorted a short laugh, "Likely *not* my finest hour, general," he answered, pulling out a cigar and sticking it in his mouth.

ಔ๑ฦಣಛಪಔ๑ฦಣಛಪಔ๑ฦಣಛ

"Damn it, Captain …" Jim Wiggins swore, gazing back toward the door of the War Department building, then out across the lawn in front of it after Nathan updated him on what had transpired within while Jim and Harry had waited outside.

"I brought my rifle along, sir … and there's plenty o' trees and bushes out across the lawn there for cover. I can wait 'til he leaves the building later this evening … take him out from two … maybe three hundred yards … easy shot. They'll never know where it come from, and ain't no way they'll ever catch me. And then … well, hell, sir … I reckon a scoundrel like that's got no end o' enemies wantin' nothin' better'n to put a .58 caliber slug clean through the rascal. They'll never connect it with *you*, sir."

Though he was still of a fiery temper, Nathan couldn't help smiling with his eyes at Sergeant Jim's very sincere offer.

"Hmm … it's a thought, Mr. Wiggins … but *no*, I don't think so."

"Well then, if you'd prefer something more subtle, I can send back for Billy. He'll find out where the fellow lives, sneak in at night and stick a knife in his gizzard. Old Pinkerton'll never know what hit him 'til he wakes up dead in the morning."

Nathan snorted, "As tempting as that is, Jim … I have been led to understand that Pinkerton *does* have some redeeming qualities, despite this apparent misconduct. So I must resist the very strong urge to do great violence upon him. Our Lord preaches that even the most dire sinner deserves a chance at redemption."

"Well, there you go, sir! I'll send him directly to the pearly gates, where he can work things out with our Lord straightaway. It'd be all for the *good*, sir!" Jim said, this time with a broad grin on his face.

Nathan grinned, patted Jim on the back and said, "Thank you for trying to cheer me out of a well-earned foul humor, Mr. Wiggins, though it's likely a wasted effort. Come on, we may as well head back to our boarding house. I believe there's a perfectly good bottle of whiskey calling my name … and perhaps yours as well."

"You'll never hear me say 'no' to that, sir," Jim answered. He then turned to Harry and said, "C'mon … you too, big feller. You heard the Captain; time to go."

☙℘ℭ℘☙℘ℭ℘☙℘ℭ℘

From all Governor Pierpont had told him, Nathan held out little hope of a positive outcome from a meeting with his old friend, now Restored Virginia Senator John Carlile. And Nathan knew himself well enough to understand that his own humor was already strained to the breaking point after the less-than-productive interaction with Pinkerton. He reminded himself to keep a tight rein on his temper, lest he lose control of it.

But despite his foul mood, for the sake of their once-close friendship, he felt obligated to speak to the man face-to-face, on the outside chance Carlile's seemingly sudden change of heart had a reasonable explanation, or had all been some sort of catastrophic misunderstanding.

So he sought Carlile out in the senate offices, and after the greetings and pleasantries were exchanged — somewhat lukewarm this time, to Nathan's thinking — he dived right into the subject at hand.

"John, I've heard some troubling news from the governor concerning your support for the new state, and I wanted to hear from your own mouth your thoughts on it," Nathan prompted.

"Oh? And what is it you wish to know?" John responded, in a tone that held little emotion, and no sign of surprise.

"I … I wish to know if it's true … that you no longer support the creation of West Virginia," Nathan answered.

"Oh, that. Well … yes, it's true. I've come to believe that it's … not in the best interests of all concerned," he answered.

Nathan frowned, *Not exactly forthcoming*, he thought.

"And why, may I ask, do you now believe *that?*" Nathan asked.

"Nathan … I've come to realize that … the war won't go on forever, and that at some point there will be a reunification. And when that happens, a divided Virginia will be a very much weakened Virginia versus her neighboring states … and I … don't believe that will be for the best."

"But, what about the ill manner in which Richmond has dealt with the counties west of the mountains? The unfair taxation, the lack of government support for necessary infrastructure, schools, and so forth? What of all the talk that we of the west were better off without the aristocratic, slave-power easterners looking down their noses at us and keeping us under their thumbs? All *your* words during the secession convention, not *mine*, I will remind you …"

"Oh … well, suffice to say all this war and upheaval can … change a man's opinion," Carlile answered cryptically. "You understand."

"No, I *don't* understand. What has happened to you, John? Something has changed in you. What is it?"

"I … don't know what you mean, Nathan."

"The John Carlile I knew before was fiery, determined, knew what he wanted, and he wouldn't back down from a fight, even from me. *This* John Carlile … I don't know *who* you are."

"Well, I'm sorry to hear you say that, Nathan. I … I am still the same man."

"No. No, you're not, it's as if …" then Nathan became quiet and thoughtful, trying to put what he was feeling into words. "It's as if you've joined the *other side* … that you are now supporting the rebels …" he gazed hard at Carlile to gauge his reaction to this divisive statement, and was surprised to see that Carlile could not meet his eyes—a thing that had never happened before between them.

Nathan sat back in his chair and looked up at the ceiling. "*That's it!* You've joined the other side, John! What did they do, threaten your family? Offer you money, land? A high position in the Confederate or Commonwealth government after the war?"

But Carlile didn't immediately answer, and still would not make eye contact with Nathan. Finally, he answered in a quiet tone, still gazing down at the desk, "Now you are just being insulting, sir. I think … I think it would be best if you just … leave now."

Nathan stared at him another moment, mouth agape. Then he pushed back his chair, stood, and walked out of the room without another word.

☜☞☙☙☜☞☙☜☞☙☜☞☙☙

"Oh my goodness, Evelyn … I can't tell you how it warms my heart to see you happy and smiling again! It has been such a long time since we've seen your light shining so brightly," Angeline said, beaming as she gazed at Evelyn over a steaming cup of tea in the Hugheses' elegant sitting room, in their even more opulent manor house in the most upscale neighborhood in Richmond.

"That goes doubly for me," Jonathan added, also smiling with obvious good humor.

"Yes … it is … hard to describe how much better I feel from just a short time ago," Evelyn answered, reflecting their happy smiles with one of her own.

"Almost as if I was dead for a time, but have just come back alive," she said.

"Understandable, understandable, my dear, after all you've been through," Angeline said. "But Jonathan will attest—though we were worried about you, of course—I knew you would pull yourself out of the doldrums and return to your old self in short order, despite all your trials and travails."

"It's true," Jonathan said, "Angeline kept insisting that I not be overly concerned; that you were more resilient than anyone knew, including yourself."

"Well ... much as I'd like to take all the credit, it was really Joseph's timely delivery of *that letter* that turned my ship around."

"Ah, yes, the letter from Mr. Chambers ... that was *most* fortuitous," Angeline said, her expression turning more serious and thoughtful. "And it is so pleasing and gratifying to know that we were wrong about him, and that he has remained faithful and entirely devoted to you, my dear. I can't tell you how much joy that has given me, and how sorry I am for passing along a painful story that turned out to be entirely false."

"No ... no fault to you, Angeline. You were only trying to do what you thought was best for me. And, it has all worked out well in the end," she said, and graced her friends with another warm smile.

"Ah ... what a pleasure to witness," Jonathan said with a chuckle. "Love suits you beautifully, Evelyn. I can almost see you sparkle and glow with an inner light any time you speak of Captain Chambers."

Evelyn nodded, continuing to smile, but could think of nothing to say in answer to this other than, "Thank you, Jonathan."

They sipped their tea in silence for a few moments, and then Jonathan, realizing he may have gone a bit too far and made Evelyn feel self-conscious, steered the conversation in the direction of its original intended purpose: to decide what their next major clandestine operation should be.

"So, Evelyn ..." he began. "Have you given any thought to what we ought to do next to lend what aid we might to the Union war effort?"

Evelyn took another sip before answering, "Well, as you might suspect … most of my attention lately has been on ingratiating myself with the first lady, Varina Davis. Though I must say, it has caused another painful episode for me, this time having to part ways with Lydia Johnston … I have really enjoyed her *friendship* … if one can call it that when one of the *so-called* friends is actually spying on the other," she said with a rueful smile.

Angeline leaned across and patted Evelyn's arm sympathetically, "I know what you mean, dear. To me it is the worst part of this whole business—knowing I am purposefully betraying ladies who believe me to be a great friend and confidant. I often wonder if we shall even be able to remain in Richmond after the war—certainly not if any of this comes out in public."

"Well, then we must make certain it does *not*," Jonathan interjected, "for *that* reason … but also … that I have a certain fondness for my own neck," he concluded, then comically mimed being strung up with a noose, which earned him a slap on the arm and a scowl from Angeline.

Evelyn laughed, though it was really no laughing matter; they all three knew if they were caught, such could very well be their fate.

"And how is it going with Varina?" Angeline asked.

"I believe it's going well, though she's a very enigmatic woman. I have a hard time determining if she truly likes me and enjoys my company, or if she is just playing a role as the president's wife—that is, feeling obligated to regularly entertain the most popular, high-class ladies in the city."

"I know what you mean," Angeline said, nodding, "Varina is a hard read. After all these months I am still trying to figure her out."

"Yes, so I am walking very carefully when it comes to inserting one of our maids into her house," Evelyn responded, "mentioning it only indirectly, proposing the idea to *other* ladies in her presence, setting it up so one of my happy 'customers' is obliged to give a positive testimonial in front of her, and so on. Oh, and subtly working her rivalry with Lydia Johnston … making sure

Varina remembers that Lydia had one of our high-end servants in her house for a time, and how much that enhanced Lydia's reputation around town."

"Good, good," Angeline responded, nodding enthusiastically.

"I have also been training someone very special for the part of Varina's maid, should we be successful. Her name is Mary Jane Richard—you may remember her, Angeline; we met her at Elizabeth Van Lew's house. She was the young freeman maid who let us in at the door. She *was* a long-time household slave of the family, and then after Elizabeth's father passed and she inherited his estate, she freed Mary, along with all her other slaves. But Elizabeth was so fond of Mary that she paid for her to be educated at Princeton, up north in New Jersey. Mary even spent some time in Liberia as a missionary there, teaching school children, before returning to Richmond shortly before the war. Elizabeth tells me that Mary excels at memorizing long passages of books or letters, which should prove invaluable in our current mission. She is extremely intelligent, literate, capable, and level-headed—in fact, my only difficulty in preparing her for this role has been to remind her to act less intellectual!

"Elizabeth was reticent about putting Mary into a potentially hazardous situation, but I convinced her it is part of the risk we are all taking in what we do. And speaking of … I understand you've been working with Elizabeth to get her more involved in our activities, Angeline?"

"Yes. We have had to be subtle about it, though, given Elizabeth's outspoken opposition to the secession, and open support of the Union." Then Angeline chuckled, "So, to combat that—with Elizabeth's permission, of course—I have started spreading it around town that Elizabeth isn't right in the head … that she's really quite mad, and so is of no concern to the authorities—just a harmless lunatic. 'Crazy Betty' we are calling her, and she is now going out of her way to act the part so as to deflect any unwanted government attention."

Evelyn smiled and nodded, "Very clever, Angeline … very clever—as usual."

"Thank you, my dear."

"Oh, and I forgot to mention that I already have an inside 'agent' of sorts in Varina's house," Evelyn continued, "though I can't expect him to do any *actual* spying.

"You will recall that Varina's favorite butler, Hank, caught me rifling through the president's desk, and he agreed not to turn me in if I agreed to help him escape to the North later, should he wish to do so? Well, I now have a new *arrangement* with him ... he has agreed to promote the idea of taking on one of our maids, should Varina ever broach the subject.

"All that being said, I don't expect any results from these efforts anytime soon. Varina is a tough nut to crack, as they say, so I am just trying to sow a few seeds now, hoping for a bountiful harvest sometime out in the future."

"That's excellent work, Evelyn—very thorough, well thought out, and well executed," Jonathan said, nodding. Then after a moment he frowned and leaned in closer.

"But meanwhile, the war rages. And with McClellan's bungling of the peninsula campaign, I fear the Confederate side will be emboldened to prosecute the war with even more vigor, especially when one considers Robert E. Lee's penchant for bold, almost reckless, offensive action," he continued.

"I fear Lee may hit hard again up in northern Virginia, even while the Union Army is still reeling from the last setback. And if he has success there, he may be tempted to cross the Potomac, and push the war on into the North. Such a bold move might very well spell disaster for our side.

"So I'd like to discuss what *we three,* here in this room, can do, if anything, to help prevent that scenario," he concluded, gazing across at Evelyn, as if expecting *her* to have the answer.

She took another sip of tea while pondering his challenge. Fortunately, she'd already been considering this question for several days now, and it pleased her that neither Jonathan nor Angeline appeared surprised when she announced, "I have already been thinking about that very thing. And I have decided ... that I must somehow get close to General Lee out in the field. And then when the moment is right ... *steal his battle plans!*"

29

Chapter 3. The Women of War

"We all have an unsuspected
reserve of strength inside
that emerges
when life puts us to the test."
- Isabel Allende

Friday August 1, 1862 – Wheeling, Virginia:

Nathan sat alone on the tiny porch at Belle Meade Farm that he ironically referred to as "the veranda." It was only just large enough for a single small table and four chairs—not even room for Harry the Dog to lay, so he typically plopped down on the grass below.

Nathan was in a foul humor, as he had been ever since his return from Washington. So foul, in fact, that everyone had taken to leaving him alone, letting him drink his whiskey and smoke his cigars all by himself. Even Tom had stopped coming around. All efforts to cheer him had been met with surliness and ill temper, so eventually everyone had just given it up. And the more he drank, and the more he ruminated on his situation, the worse his temper became.

He'd even stopped riding into town to meet with the governor, which he'd done religiously six days a week since shortly after his arrival in Wheeling—only occasionally taking Sundays off from his assumed government duties as military advisor and head law enforcement officer for the Restored Virginia government.

He knew he should be doing ... *something* ... but he was angry, and frustrated, and his heart just wasn't in anything he'd been doing previously. He was meant for greater things ... and he knew he could make a huge difference in the war—perhaps even win it, if only he were given the chance. But his enemies, for selfish reasons of their own, had conspired to prevent that, and it seemed as if there was nothing he could do about it. It was like sinking in mud; the harder you fought it, the deeper you sank.

So, he sat on the back porch, and drank. He knew he should stop doing *that* too, but then a part of him said, *Why bother? Here I sit, all my knowledge and skills wasted in this backwater, while the war rages on, and our brave young men are led to a needless death by incompetent fools like George McClellan.*

He scowled and poured another shot of whiskey. He'd filled the glass and had not yet set the bottle down when he heard the back door open behind him and the sound of footsteps coming quickly toward the table. He glanced up to see Miss Abbey. Oddly, she did not bear the sweet, kindly face he was used to seeing from his even-tempered mother. Instead, she wore a dark, angry look, and he could see she'd been crying, making him immediately wonder what could have happened to set her off.

But before he could inquire, she leaned over and slapped the glass of whiskey with her open hand, sending it skittering across the table and crashing to the decking below where it shattered. Nathan gazed up at her in shock, whiskey dripping from his face and mustache where the toppled glass had splattered him.

But Abbey glared at him and said, "Nathaniel, there's not been a day gone by since you returned from the West that I haven't been just as proud of you as a momma can possibly be. Not even when you were drunk for three days straight after Evelyn left, as I figured you'd earned the right.

"But now is the first time I'm downright ashamed of you, Nathaniel! While the country is going to hell all around us, here you sit pouting and feeling sorry for yourself like a spoiled child who's been told he can't have any more candy!"

"But I—" he started.

"So *what* if some imbecilic general and his pet detective say you can't fight?! Nobody ever gave Evelyn permission to go and do all the things she's done to help win the war; and yet she has gone ahead and done them anyway, not caring what *anyone* had to say about it—not even *you!*

"So if they won't let you put on a blue uniform and fight with the Army, then *by God, Nathaniel Chambers,* you go and find some other way to fight and stop sitting here drinking like a pathetic toad!" And though she was now nearly screaming mad, tears

31

streaming down her face, she wiped them away without ever interrupting her speech.

Then she turned and stomped back into the house, slamming the door behind her.

Nathan sat where he was, staring after her, mouth agape in his shock. *Well … I never imagined …* was all he could think of in that moment.

But then he thought about what she'd just said, and he knew she was right. *Damn me for an utter fool, but you're absolutely right, Momma. My life can't be ruled by other men's decisions; I've got to find another way to help out in the war. More than what I've been doing … but what? Hmm …*

And then he had a different thought … *Very clever of you, Momma, bringing Evelyn into it … though you never said it straight out, I know you wished me to think … How would I like for Evelyn to see me now—surly, pathetic, and half-drunken … like a damned, useless excuse for a man?*

He stood up suddenly, and pushed his chair out of the way, "No … never! *Never* that!" he said aloud, shuddering at the thought.

Then he grabbed the whiskey bottle by the neck, spun around, and threw it up into the air out over the pasture toward the river. And even as it sailed, he unholstered his revolver and fired, shattering the bottle into a thousand sparkling shards.

The back door burst open, and Megs looked out, eyes wide with fright.

"What was *that?!*" she asked, looking over at Nathan.

Nathan spun the pistol in a full circle and holstered it in one smooth movement, then walked up to her and said, "*That* was a son … obeying his momma."

Megs folded her arms across her breast and scowled at him. But as he passed her by, heading for the door, he could see that she was fighting off a smile.

℠℠℠℠℠℠

"Tom! Tom Clark," Nathan shouted as he strode down the short hallway of the Belle Meade farmhouse, "We have work to do, Sergeant!"

And as he passed the kitchen on his way to the front stairs, he saw Miss Abbey sitting there, gazing up at him, so he stopped, made a bow, and said, "Momma, I humbly apologize for my recent shameful behavior and beg your forgiveness. Every word you said just now was *true* ... and I ... I greatly appreciate you saying it, though I expect it was difficult and painful for you.

"And I also wanted to tell you that I now know what to do. Thanks to you, it has come to me, as if from the very mouth of God; I must train the freemen and escaped slaves how to fight — not just the ones on *this* farm, but from wherever they may be — so when the time comes, they will make a good accounting of themselves, and be less likely to go out and get themselves killed in the process."

Abbey nodded, tears once again streaming down her face. She smiled, and said, *"Thank you, Nathan ..."* in a voice choked with emotion and barely more than a whisper.

ജ‌ലോരുള‌ജലോരുള‌ജലോരുള

Adilida was still trying to get her bearings in her new northern home; everything about the situation was odd to her, and she felt as if her life had been a veritable whirlwind, filled with every imaginable kind of novel experience, ever since her arrival in Baltimore on the steamship less than a month earlier.

It started with her trepidation over how Thomas would react to her earth-shaking news about little Nathaniel. Her anxiety had quickly turned to joy when Thomas took to the child instantly, and announced he wished to marry Adilida straight away.

And then there was the disappointment and hurt when Thomas received a telegram from his father in Connecticut informing him that his family would *not* be coming to Baltimore to attend the wedding, and further, they wished to dissuade Thomas from marrying Adilida because "the woman must certainly have a sullied reputation due to the child being born out of wedlock."

Though Thomas had shrugged it off, and stated it only served to solidify his decision to remain with the Captain in western Virginia, she could tell that he had been wounded by it, and it took him several days to recover. In fact, he had only perked up the day of the wedding, which they held at a church in Baltimore, when Edouard placed her hand in his at the altar. When Thomas had looked down at her smiling, tearful face, his expression suddenly changed to joy, and he'd been in a good mood ever since.

And then they'd ridden on a train, an all-day trip west to Wheeling, Virginia. From there they'd ridden in a carriage out to Belle Meade Farm, home to more than a hundred people she'd never met before, the vast majority of whom were black freemen.

The first day she was introduced to so many people her head felt like it was spinning. She couldn't imagine how she would ever remember even half so many names.

She'd never lived outside a town before, much less on a farm, so everything about it was disorienting and strange. And living with Uncle, who'd been very well off since long before she was born, she'd also been used to an elegant, spacious home with only a few people occupying it. But now with the arrival of herself, Uncle Edouard, Phillipe, and Nathaniel, the already full house seemed to be simply overflowing with people. Everywhere she turned someone was walking, talking, sitting, eating, coming, or going in the cramped, modest home.

And then something had happened between the Captain and the people running the Army, and it had put him in a foul mood for several days, which had not helped matters, as it had put everyone in the house on edge. Thankfully, that seemed to have passed, and he and Thomas were now enthusiastically working on a plan to train the black men how to fight, as she understood it.

And though Miss Abbey and Megs were warm and welcoming, and to Adilida's amusement, seemed to have taken a special liking to Uncle, she did not feel like she had yet made a strong bond with them or any of the other women. When she considered it, she decided it was probably her own reticence that was causing the distance; though they had welcomed the newcomers as "the newest members of the Chambers family," she was well aware it was not truly so. Though the Captain and Thomas acted like brothers most of the time, she knew they were not even related. Thomas was clearly subservient, and was in fact in the Captain's employment, making the relationship even muddier, in Adilida's view. The whole thing made her feel unsure of where she stood in the household and what her proper place was within the new order of things.

The one bright, shining light, other than Thomas's unwavering love and affection, had been little Nathaniel; he was immediately taken in as the darling of the household. All the women, both white and black, doted on him, pampered him, and gave him no end of attention and affection.

And the men were also taken with him, carrying him about on their shoulders, rough housing with him, carving little wooden toys for him, and regaling him with all sorts of wild stories from out west, or from their prior farm called "Mountain Meadows." It was heartwarming and gratifying for Adilida, and helped lessen the sting of her awkward, unsettling new living arrangement.

But looming in the background like a dark, threatening storm cloud — seemingly every hour of every day — was the undeniable reality of the war. Adilida knew it was only a matter of time before Thomas, and all the other men on the farm, would be swept up in it. Many of them, or even all of them, might be killed.

And there was nothing she could do about it.

ळ৯୯୫ळ৯୯୫ळ৯୯୫ळ৯୯୫

Abbey was feeling irritated with Megs, and from what she could tell, the feeling was mutual. But she couldn't quite put her finger on what was causing it. There just seemed to be some kind of unspoken tension between them.

It was the middle of the morning, and Abbey was sitting alone on the back porch — what Nathan insisted on referring to as "the veranda," an ironic nod to the expansive, mostly covered veranda that wrapped around the entire Big House back at Mountain Meadows.

Abbey blew on a cup of tea, then took a tiny sip but decided it was still too hot to drink, so she set it down on the table and waited for it to cool.

She thought about why she might be feeling annoyed at Megs. Annoyed, irritated, frustrated—those were the right words for it, all right ... certainly not *anger*. Not yet, anyway. She tried to think of something Megs had done or said that had set her off, but she could think of nothing. Nor could she imagine what she might have done to make Megs feel something of the same, which seemed to be the case. Then she thought about how long she'd been feeling that way, and it occurred to her it had started right after Adilida had arrived with her young son, her cousin Phillipe, and her uncle Edouard.

Edouard ... when she thought of him, she smiled. He'd been such a pleasant surprise in the whole business with Adilida. His handsome, dignified looks, combined with a perpetually jolly expression and happy demeanor, made him someone she immediately felt a connection with ... *and an attraction for?* She shook her head slowly, the inkling of an idea beginning to form. *Yes ... I felt an instant liking for the man*, she thought, *which unconsciously turned to an attraction after a few days of being around him. He was so kindly, and funny, and attentive, it just seemed to happen naturally with no thought or effort.*

And then it hit her with a shock. He had *also* been kindly, witty, and attentive to ...

"*Megs!*" she called out. "Megs, are you in there?" she said, turning toward the back door, that'd been slightly propped open to let a little breeze into the kitchen.

Megs poked her head out the door, and said, "Yes, I'm here. You be wanting more tea, Abbey?"

"No, thank you, dear. No, I was just sitting here thinking ... well, about *you* ... and about *me*. And I ... I wanted to talk with you. Will you come join me for a moment?"

Megs frowned, then shrugged her shoulders, stepped up to the table, pulled out a chair opposite Abbey and sat.

"What you wanting to talk about?" Megs asked, with no preamble, as was her usual habit.

"Megs, I've been feeling some *tension* between you and I. And I, well, for *one*, I don't much care for the feeling. You've been my best friend for just about as long as I can remember, and I don't like it when it feels like there's something wrong between us."

Megs looked thoughtful, and her expression seemed to soften. "Yes, I reckon I know what you mean," she finally said.

"So then I was trying to think about what may have caused it," Abbey continued. "And I am beginning to think it may be Edouard."

"Edouard?" Megs asked, "What's *he* got to do with it?"

Abbey was quiet for a moment, trying to think of the right way to say what she wanted to say, so that it made sense, and so that it would not be hurtful in any conceivable way.

"Megs, when I was a young woman back in Richmond, and not yet married—but of the age for it—I attended many balls and other such gatherings where the young gentlemen might acquaint themselves with the eligible young ladies."

"Yes ..." Megs responded, with just a hint of impatience; she already knew all this, of course, but was puzzled as to where it might be headed.

"Well, my point is, I have had—in the past—quite a lot of experience with men *flirting*."

"Flirting?"

"Yes, you know ... being friendly, witty, and charming—attempting to win a lady's favor and make her interested in him."

"All right, I believe that's true. So why you telling me this now?"

"Because it has been a long time since I was around that type of thing. But now that I recall the experience, I have recognized that Edouard has been *flirting*."

"He's been flirting with you?" Megs asked.

"*Us*, Megs. Edouard has been flirting with *us!*"

Megs sat back in her chair, eyes wide. Then she gazed up at the sky for a long moment, before looking back down at Abbey. "Do you really think so? Oh, Abbey. I don't know about all that ..."

"Think about it, Megs. Think about how you feel when he talks to you, smiles at you, does nice little things for you. Think about how that makes you feel."

Megs looked down at her hands for a long moment, then looked back up and said, "It makes me feel good ... *real* good, *special* somehow." Then Megs sat up, gazing into Abbey's eyes, "Oh! You don't think ... you don't suppose ... that's why we been peevish with each other? On account o' Edouard's flirting?!"

Abbey nodded, "Yes, I think it may be."

Megs shook her head slowly as she considered this. Then she looked at Abbey and said, "Well, if that's so, then you can have him. I got no use for such nonsense anyway, and I certainly don't want to lose your lifelong friendship—no, more like *sistership*, if that's even a proper word—over it!"

Abbey smiled, and reached over to pat Megs hands, "I was going to say almost the exact same thing, Megs. But more than that, I wanted to say that I don't think either of us should be closeminded about the possibilities. Edouard is, after all, a very handsome and charming gentleman, and there can be no doubt he is a good man and a pleasure to have around."

Megs nodded, "I don't know about all that. Me and Edouard? I ain't sure the world is ready for a thing like that. Hell, Abbey, I ain't sure *I'm* ready for a thing like that."

"Well, the world is changing, Megs. When the war is over, I can't imagine there still being slavery. So then the black and white people may be able to come together ... somehow." She shrugged, then said, "But whatever happens with him—or even if it doesn't—we must make a pact to always be closer than close—like sisters—as we have been all these years, and as we should *always* be to the end of this world and beyond."

"Well, whatever else, I do agree with that *last* part," Megs said. "We must agree no matter what happens with him—or anyone else—that nothing will ever come between us."

"Agreed," Abbey said, and smiled brightly. "And if we were men, we would shake hands on it. But since we are ladies, I believe a hug would be more appropriate." And rising from her seat, she came around the table to Megs and the two of them tearfully consummated the agreement.

ᏋᎠᏋᎠᏒᏋᎠᏋᎠᏒᏋᎠᏒᏋᎠᏋᎠᏒᏋᎠᏒ

"Are you sure this is what you want to do, Ned?" Nathan asked. "I admire your wish to fight, and of course I respect and support it, but I fear … well, to put it bluntly, I fear though you and the other freemen here on this farm are more than prepared to fight, the others who'll be joining you may *not* be. And I worry that many of the white officers over in Kansas who will be leading you may also be less than ideal, and likely entirely untrained and inexperienced. I also fear they may take little care for your wellbeing once you've enlisted. Not to mention the distance—I expect it will take a full month and more of steady travel to get there, and God only knows what sort of conflicts you'll encounter along the way. For instance, you'll have to travel entirely across Missouri, which I understand has a worse rebel bushwhacker infestation than what we have here in western Virginia."

Ever since the news had begun to spread of a colored regiment being formed out in Kansas—against the federal government's wishes—Nathan had been concerned some of the freemen on the farm might decide to make the trek and get into the fight sooner rather than later. As much as he was a firm believer—and outspoken proponent—of getting the freemen into the fight *en masse*, he held a healthy skepticism for the effort currently underway in Kansas. Without the blessing and support of the federal army, and without access to its equipment and its experienced officer corps, it was more likely to end in disaster than anything he could imagine.

Ned nodded. He looked down at his bare feet where he stood across the table from Nathan on the farmhouse veranda, having declined Nathan's offer to take a seat. Then Ned looked up and they met eyes, a thing that had not initially come easy for him, and had taken many months of prodding on Nathan's part, now nearly two years past.

"I reckon you're right about them things, Captain," Ned answered. "You's the wisest man I ever met—or ever even heard of — so I don't figure on doubtin' your word now. It's just … I gotta feel like I'm doin' something, you know? Like I have this burnin' need to be out in the middle o' that big old fight … that something inside is just eatin' at me. I can't sit still no longer … can't keep farmin', like nothin's goin' on out in the world. No sir … I just can't do it no more, not one more day."

Nathan leaned back in his chair and took a long pull on his cigar, then blew out the smoke before looking back down at Ned. Then he smiled and said, "I know *that* feeling, all right, none better … yep, I know it well …"

Ned nodded, having heard that the Captain was being kept out of the Army by some fools over to Washington, for reasons he had no way of fathoming.

"So, when you figuring on leaving, Ned?"

"Tomorrow, first light, sir. Sammy, Caleb, Jack, and Sid are fixin' to go with me."

Nathan nodded. He wasn't surprised — those men were among the initial group to volunteer for Stan's rifle training back at Mountain Meadows, and some of the first to join in the fighting during its siege. But a part of him was pleased the freemen he was closest to, those he thought of as "Tony's men," including Big George, Henry, Cobb, and Phinney along with Tony himself, had not chosen to go with Ned. Nathan had asked them all, including Ned, to help train up the freemen from outside Belle Meade Farm on how to fight, and apparently they'd all decided to stay and help do that … all except for Ned.

"Well, of course I will wish y'all well, and I'll do everything I can to help you and your men on your way, though I fear it will be little enough. Of course y'all can each take a rifle, and a pistol, and as much powder and ammunition as you can bear. Oh, and I'll give you a pack horse to carry your things, if you wish, along with enough supplies to get y'all a goodly way toward Kansas, though I expect you'll have to resupply somewhere along the road."

"Thank you, sir. That's right decent and kindly of you, and ain't somethin' that's owed. Once again you done put the lie to my hatred of *all* white folks … as hard as I tried at first, by your

40

words and your deeds you done made it damned hard to hate you."

Nathan smiled, "Well, coming from *you*, Ned, I'll take that for a compliment."

Ned returned the smile, one of the few Nathan had ever seen from the man. He'd suffered a nearly fatal beating for little cause under Nathan's father, and it'd scarred him for life, both physically and spiritually, Nathan believed. But Nathan's consistent, respectful treatment of him had eventually turned him in a more positive direction. But not, apparently, positive enough to make him stay when he saw a chance to go.

☙❧❦☙❧❦☙❧❦

Unknown to Nathan, it had been a near thing for "Tony's men;" they'd had much discussion, even to the point of "heated debate" amongst themselves over whether or not to go with Ned to Kansas and join in the fight. But despite their disagreements on it, they all agreed they would leave or stay together.

They knew that the Captain, as much as he supported their wish to fight, was opposed to what was being done in Kansas, calling it premature, ill-conceived, and a "recipe for disaster." On the other hand, they knew they were more than ready and trained to fight, and that only unnecessary hesitance on the part of the federal government was keeping them out of it at this point.

Ironically, it was not the Captain's persuasion, nor the various arguments put forth during their long debates that turned the tide. Rather it was the women, Rosa in the case of Tony and Henry, and Babs, Big George's wife, who convinced them to stay. In the end, the women's arguments proved the decisive factor.

Rosa scolded both Tony and Henry for even considering going against the Captain's wishes after all he'd done for them, and after he'd put out the word he intended to train all the freemen he could so they'd be ready to fight. Both the Captain and all the other freemen needed their help, and that would likely be more important work than going out to Kansas and joining up with some half-baked colored regiment and getting themselves killed.

And Babs just took Big George by the arm one evening, walked him over to where their two little girls, Annie and Lucy, lay sleeping in their bed, and said, "George ... you gonna march off to God knows where ... some place called *Kansas* that I ain't never even heard of ... to start in to fightin', when you just got to wait a bit longer 'fore Mr. Lincoln starts signing up colored regiments right here at home? So's then you can do your fightin' right here, protectin' your own home and family?" George just shook his head in surrender; he had no answer against such a well-played argument.

ཉའཇེའཇེཉའཇེའཇེཉའཇེའ

When Ned had finished packing up his few items, in a knapsack he'd made from an old canvas flour sack, he shouldered the pack and his rifle, took one last look around the tent, shrugged his shoulders, and went out the door. Tony, Cobb, and Phinney, who shared his tent, had been up and out the door earlier, though he wasn't sure why, as it was still barely first light.

He closed the wood-framed door of the tent and stepped down from the raised platform that served as the foundation for his "home" since shortly after his arrival at Belle Meade Farm. Ned found his four traveling companions, Sammy, Caleb, Jack, and Sid were already waiting for him out front.

He greeted them with a nod, as was his habit, then gazed about to see if anyone else was out. He'd had a mind to say goodbye to anyone who might be around, though he had no intention of seeking anyone out in particular. But surprisingly there was no one in sight. *Odd*, he thought, *should be folks up and about at this hour. Well, maybe they's already out in the fields ...*

There being nothing else to do, he turned and began walking through the row of tents toward the drive, his men following. Surprisingly they saw no one, nor heard any sounds of activity in the tents.

As they passed out from the last group of tents and onto the drive in front of the farmhouse, Ned saw that Cobb had already loaded the pack horse with their supplies and had left it tied to the hitching post. He was appreciative that Cobb had gotten everything ready, but couldn't help feeling a little disappointed that he'd not waited around to say goodbye.

He couldn't resist a quick glance up to the front door of the farmhouse. He thought maybe the Captain might be up and around, that he might wave goodbye. But nobody was there either.

So he grabbed the lead of the horse, turned away toward the main road, and headed down the drive, his companions in tow. It felt good to be finally doing something, but he was surprised he also felt a sense of sadness … a nagging feeling he was leaving something behind in this place that maybe he never properly appreciated, and likely he'd never experience again. But he hardened his heart, as he always did, and increased his pace.

They'd walked about halfway down the drive to the main road — a quarter of a mile or so — when they came to a bend in the lane. It was lined with thick bushes and trees in this section where a small creek ran close to the roadway, such that one could not see what was past the left-hand turn until he was nearly back to the straight part that led the rest of the way to the main road.

As they rounded the corner and could see what lay ahead, Ned stopped dead in his tracks, mouth agape. The others stepped up next to him, and did likewise.

They saw before them all the people of the farm, both white and black, lining the road on both sides: the men on the left, and the women and children on the right. The Captain was the first in line on the left, and he stepped forward to greet them.

"Good morning, gentlemen," he said, as he came to a stop a few feet in front of them.

"G- … good morning, Captain, sir …" Ned mumbled, remembering to tip his hat respectfully. The others echoed Ned's response, and returned the Captain's bright smile with grins of their own.

"We all wished to give you men a proper Mountain Meadows — now *Belle Meade* — send-off," the Captain said. "So …" then he stepped up in front of Sid, and shook his hand, wishing him luck. He did the same with Sammy, Caleb, and Jack before stopping in front of Ned.

"Ned, take care of these men. I've grown quite fond of them … and *you* …" he said. Then they shook hands, and the Captain patted Ned on the arm affectionately.

Then the Captain turned and addressed the five men, speaking in a loud, projecting voice so that all assembled could hear, "You men are well-trained and experienced fighters, and have already proven your bravery in battle against the enemy. I have no doubts y'all will do us proud. We thank you for your service, and we *salute you* for your courage."

And with that, Sergeant Jim barked out, "Atten … *SHUN!*" and all the men, both black and white, stood to attention, and snapped a salute, including the Captain.

Ned was stunned, and felt his eyes threatening to tear up. Then he noticed the women … they had all pulled out handkerchiefs and were waving them and smiling in salute to him and his men.

Ned finally remembered his training, and returned the salute, elbowing Sid who was next to him, to do the same.

Then the Captain stepped back so he could face Ned and his men along with the rest of the people assembled.

"It is only proper and fitting, at this send-off, to invoke the word of our Lord as both a blessing and a prayer for your good fortune."

At this, the men all removed their hats, and all present bowed their heads respectfully.

"Blessed be the LORD my strength, which teacheth my hands to war, and my fingers to fight," the Captain began. "And they shall fight against thee; but they shall not prevail against thee; for I am with thee, saith the LORD, to deliver thee … Put on the whole armour of God, that ye may be able to stand against the wiles of the devil." He paused then, and looked Ned straight in the eye and said, "Be strong and of a good courage; be not afraid, neither be thou dismayed: for the LORD thy God is with thee whithersoever thou goest."

Nathan stood and gazed across the field taking a deep breath of satisfaction, a lit cigar clenched in his teeth. It was a beautiful sight, to his way of thinking. Not the idyllic green rolling fields surrounded by thick stands of trees flush with summer growth flickering in a mild breeze, only just starting to show a hint of yellow fall colors to come; nor yet the sparkling blue sky with scattered puffy white clouds sailing lazily by. No, Nathan's eyes paid little notice to these things today; what pleased his martial spirit was the beehive of activity before him out across those green fields.

Already more than three hundred men, all of dark skin, had arrived at the training field, with more arriving every hour. He watched as they marched with mock rifles on shoulders, drilled with wooden bayonets, and fired real rifles at targets.

The first men to arrive had been issued rifles and sent straight to the target range. But since rifles were in short supply—they'd brought out a hundred or so from their successful engagements on the trek north from Mountain Meadows—Nathan had ordered hundreds of wooden mock rifles built for purposes of drilling and marching. The men would have to take turns at target practice with the real rifles.

Several groups of men were selected to be trained in the loading and firing of artillery, under the expert instruction and watchful eye of Sergeant Jim. Nathan had managed to "borrow" a couple of old smoothbore howitzers that had been inadvertently left behind when General Rosecrans and his staff had left their headquarters at Wheeling. They'd been sitting in one the barns at Belle Meade for the past several months, along with a good stack of lead balls and several large sacks of powder. Nathan thought he might find a good use for them at some point, that it was not out of the realm of possibility for the rebel army to attack Wheeling eventually. He could envision giving them a nasty surprise if they came near his farm.

And most satisfying to Nathan's eye was to see much of the instruction and drilling was being led by other men with black faces, fifty-some of the freemen who'd accompanied him here from Mountain Meadows where they'd been trained to fight and had proven their metal in the long running battle north during their breakout.

He was also pleased to see Tom's new cousin, Phillipe Dubois, had joined them. He'd apparently spent time abroad as an officer in the French army under Emperor Napoleon III some years earlier, and had offered his expertise, though with the caveat that he was skeptical of training black men to be proper soldiers. Nathan assumed Phillipe's ignorance of the true—though often hidden—capabilities of these men would soon be resolved satisfactorily.

With Tom, Jim, and the other soldiers from Texas supervising and giving out tips and pointers, there was little for Nathan to do but walk around the field doling out words of support and encouragement, followed closely, as always, by Harry the Dog. And to watch and enjoy …

He also took a certain satisfaction from the poetic justice of the location he'd chosen for the training; not wanting to trample the ripening crops in his own fields, he'd decided to use his late neighbor Jesse Ward's abandoned farm for the purpose. The man had been an unabashed hater of black men, and had in fact met his well-deserved end at their hands after murdering a young freeman family. How appropriate, Nathan figured, that the man's own land would now be used to help train black men to fight. Nathan even planned to make use of the burned-out farmhouse and outbuildings in the next few days to practice siege tactics, and conversely defensive tactics, involving buildings in various states of destruction—a scenario that seemed more than likely, given the current state of the war.

ཀྵༀ

"Hey, Henry … can I talk with you for a minute?" Rosa called out. Henry stopped and turned toward the sound of her voice. He'd been going out to work the fields and hadn't seen her coming up behind him.

"Well … good morning, Rosa. What can I do for you this bright, sunny morn?" he said, and smiled. She returned the smile easily. His was a face she always looked forward to seeing, a genuine, warm, caring face with none of the awkward, uncomfortable feelings most men projected when they looked at her.

They'd figured out when they'd first met that he'd been married to her mother at a different farm, though many years after Rosa was born. She'd not seen her mother since she was a very young child, but Henry provided a connection to her past that she'd thought was lost forever.

So the feelings Henry projected toward her were both familial and fatherly. Which was, not coincidentally, exactly what she wished to speak with him about this morning.

"Henry ... I reckon you already know me'n Tony been talkin' about jumpin' the broom ... maybe right after Tony gets back from fightin' in the war with y'all ... whenever Mr. Lincoln says you can."

"Oh, yeah ... I heard about the two o' you," he said, looking thoughtful, "and I think Tony's a fine young man ... you make a right fine couple."

"Thank you, Henry. And though we been callin' it 'jumping the broom' that's just 'cause it's the old way o' sayin' it ... what we *really* want is a fine weddin' like was had back at Mountain Meadows, with a real preacher an' all."

"Oh ... well, though I wasn't there I done heard all about it later, o' course. I reckon that'd be a right fine thing, Rosa. Right fine. But what was it you wanted to ask me about anyway?"

"Well, Henry ... seein's how you was married to my mother ..."

"*Still* am married to your mother," he corrected her, "though she be far away, that don't change nothin' ..."

She smiled, "*Are* married to my mother, I meant ..."

He returned her smile.

"Anyway, what I was gonna say was, with you bein' married to my mother, I reckon that makes you sorta like my daddy ... in a way."

Henry nodded, "Guess one might see it that way ..." he answered.

"Well ... in a real, preacher weddin' the daddy of the bride walks her to the front and gives her to her new husband. So ... I

47

was wantin' to ask if you'd be my daddy ..." she said, then quickly added, "just for the weddin', is all ... you know ..."

He gazed at her a moment, and said, "Hmm ... I heard the Captain stood in as the daddy at that big weddin', for all the brides that hadn't got a daddy living at the farm. Why you ain't askin' *him* to do it?"

She looked down at her feet, and appeared to be embarrassed by the question, which surprised Henry, as it was not the reaction he'd expected. "The Captain he ... he don't feel *fatherly* to me, like he does to some o' the others ... is all ..." she answered, "not like ... like *you* do."

Henry slowly nodded his head and said, "Rosa ... it'd be my great honor to be your daddy at your weddin' ..." then he grinned at her and added, "or any *other* time you want."

She beamed at him, then stepped forward, reached up and kissed him on the cheek. "Thank you, Henry ..." she said, then paused and gazed at him a long while before adding, "... *Daddy*."

Then she turned and skipped away down the corn row. He thought he heard her humming a tune as she went. Henry suddenly had to wipe his eyes, *must be a lot of dust in the air this morning*, he decided.

৪০৪০৫৩০৪০৪০৫৩০৪০৪০৫৩

Adilida felt a growing sense of dread with each passing day as the war seemed to loom ever larger, and ever closer. Though she'd hoped and prayed every day for more than a year now that Thomas would somehow never have to fight in this war, she knew in her heart of hearts it was a fool's wish.

Thomas was a soldier, and a good one from all she'd heard and understood. There was simply no realistic scenario in which he would not eventually be called upon to fight for his country, or where he would refuse to do so when called.

In fact, she now understood he would have already joined the fight if it hadn't been for the odd circumstances surrounding Captain Chambers and his apparent feud with one of the Union generals ... some man named McClellan, who somehow was preventing the Captain from joining the army. Though she knew, from everything Thomas had said, that she should hate and despise this General McClellan, she had a hard time doing so, knowing it was likely he, and he alone, who was keeping Thomas home and safe with her and little Nathaniel.

But she had come to understand recently that she was not the only woman on the farm feeling this way — with a man they loved on the cusp of going out to fight in the war, a war from which they might never return. She had come to understand that Margaret, the Captain's sister, was in love with one of his men — the doctor named William. And that Margaret had befriended a former slave woman named Rosa, whose man, Tony, would also be fighting as soon as the black men were allowed to do so by President Lincoln, which everyone said was coming soon.

Adilida had spent a lot of time thinking about these two women, and feeling an odd envy of their relationship — that they had someone to talk to, and she didn't. But then, one afternoon, as she sat gazing out the window, she saw Margaret walking toward the path that leads to the river. And a pretty young black woman was walking beside her, talking with her. Though Adilida had never met Rosa, she knew this *must* be her.

So without a real conscious thought, or plan of action, Adilida found herself rushing down the stairs, out the front door, and across the drive in the direction the women had been walking.

When she caught up to them, they were already seated on the sturdy wooden bench on the bank of the river. They looked up as she approached, and smiled in a welcoming manner, which Adilida took as a good sign, so she decided to just dive in and say what was on her mind.

"I am so sorry to disturb you two ladies … and to interrupt your personal conversation but I … I just really need someone to talk to … someone who understands what I'm feeling … the fear, the dread … of the war … of Thomas fighting … of losing him … of being alone in the world … of … him bleeding and dying … and of …" then she found her voice choking up, and she felt out of breath. Then the tears began to flow, and she felt embarrassed, covering her face with her hands.

But then she felt a soft hand take hold of her left arm. She lowered her hands and found herself looking into Margaret's eyes. Rosa was standing next to her. Both women had serious, concerned looks.

Margaret spoke first, saying, "There's no shame in how you're feeling, Adilida. And God knows we feel the same. It is the most helpless feeling I can imagine. To love someone and know that they will soon be going into great danger, and you have no way to protect them. It goes against everything we're made of, we women. It is in our nature to take care of our families, to love and to nurture. To have our men march off to war ... it's just ... just ..."

"Just damned near unbearable," Rosa jumped in, nodding emphatically. "It makes me just wanna scream ... or cry ... or maybe break something. But nothin' helps ... and there ain't no way we can stop it from happening. Men gotta fight or they don't feel like men and then they ain't no good for nobody, 'specially themselves." She shook her head, and had a serious, thoughtful look.

Adilida nodded, wiping at her tears, but still had not recovered her voice.

"But the good news, Adilida is you're not alone. You are part of this *family* now," Margaret said.

But Adilida shook her head, and said, "But I'm *not* ... I'm not a Chambers, like you," she managed to get out, between sobs, "I'm just Thomas's wife ... and he's not a Chambers either ..."

But then Margaret looked at her sternly and said, "You listen here, Adilida ... *I* didn't start out a Chambers either. I was totally lost and alone in the world. But Miss Abbey took me in and *made* me family, and she'll do the same for you if you let her. And I can tell you one thing for sure ... If Miss Abbey says you're family, then you *are,* no matter what, and there's nothing in the world that will change that."

Rosa nodded and said, "And that goes double for the Captain. He done freed all us as was slaves and then still gave us a home away from them slavers down south. And ain't never asked for so much as a 'thank you' in return.

"And you may say Mr. Tom ain't a Chambers," Rosa continued, "but that ain't the way Miss Abbey sees it, and it ain't the way the Captain treats him. Y'all that came here from New Orleans is now as much family as the rest of us, from what I see."

Adilida smiled, and wiped back the tears. "Do you really think so, Rosa?"

"I *know* so," she answered emphatically.

"And," Margaret said, "since Nathan treats Tom as a brother, that makes you a *sister* to me."

"And to me ..." Rosa added, and reached over to pat Adilida on the arm.

Then Margaret turned back toward the bench and said, "Come, Adilida, let's have a seat. We have been dying to hear how you and Tom met, and about your travels to get here, if you would be so kind as to tell us about it."

"Oh ... all right. But please, just call me *Addie* as Thomas does."

Rosa smiled, "I like that, *Addie*. Yes, please, come tell us all about you and Mr. Tom ..."

Chapter 4. Toil and Trouble

"Double, double toil and trouble;
fire burn and cauldron bubble."
- William Shakespeare
Macbeth

Friday August 22, 1862 – near Rich Mountain, Virginia:

Confederate Brigadier General Albert Jenkins pushed his horse through the thick underbrush, into a clearing—apparently recently logged, based on the large number of stumps scattered throughout what appeared to be a camp, of sorts, an area fifty yards or so across filled with more than a dozen tents of various sizes, shapes, and colors. The general was closely followed by dozens of other riders, the vanguard of his cavalry force of some five hundred men.

Two men with rifles, in ragged clothes, stepped up to him and tipped their hats, which Jenkins accepted as a salute under the circumstances, and took as a sign that these men were Confederate sympathizers. And by the look of the camp—rifles stacked about between the tents, horses staked out in the woods— he also assumed these were guerilla fighters—bushwhackers, the very group he'd heard about and had been looking for.

"I am Brigadier General Jenkins," he announced. "I am here looking for men to join me in a raid against the Yankee invaders in western Virginia. I was told there was a large group of ... *irregulars* ... here in the woods who might be willing to fight for me."

"Oh, yes sir, general," the one on the left answered, removing his hat respectfully. "You done come to the right place, all right, sir. We's been fightin' Yankees ever' chance we get. Only ... it ain't rightly up to me to say if we's to join up with y'all or not, sir. You'll need to ask *him*," he said, waving his rifle in the direction of a large tent in the middle of the camp.

"Very good, thank you ... *private* ..." the general said, and started his horse in the direction of the command tent.

When he came close, he saw another ragged looking fellow duck into the tent, presumably to inform their "commander" of the general's arrival.

General Jenkins sat on his horse in front of the tent, waiting. In less than a minute, a strong looking fellow of about forty years stepped out of the tent and stood in front of the general. The man was surprisingly well groomed and dressed, his beard neatly trimmed, his boot recently shined. But what was most striking was his expression: serious, unsmiling, and ... somehow *odd*, to the general's thinking.

The man saluted, which the general returned smartly. "I am General Jenkins ... I understand you are in charge here, sir?" he asked. "I am looking for men to join me in a raid ... Are you and your men willing, sir?"

"Yes, general ... we are ready to kill Yankees, if that is what you're asking," the man answered. "I will just collect my sidearm and my kit, and then we will saddle up," he concluded, turning back around toward his tent.

The general thought the man strange to the point of rudeness, not even bothering to introduce himself to a "superior officer." He then noticed as the man re-entered his tent and pushed aside the flap with his left arm that it was missing its hand.

₮₮₮₮₮₮₮₮₮

Saturday August 23, 1862 – Wheeling, Virginia:

"Good morning, Nathan," Governor Pierpont said, standing up from his seat behind the desk and reaching out to shake Nathan's hand as he entered the office, Harry the Dog hard on his heels. "Thank you for coming in today. Have a seat."

"Certainly, Francis. Sorry I've been a bit ... occupied lately, and haven't spent as much time in the office as usual," Nathan answered as he took his seat.

Pierpont waved a hand dismissively, "Never mind that, Nathan ... I know you've been busy—and doing good work, I understand—getting the freemen ready to fight. Good idea … It's only a matter of time before they'll be in the thick of it. How is it going, by the way? Had many participants?"

"Yes, your honor … we've had several hundred join us … It has been most satisfying to watch; there can be no doubting their enthusiasm and motivation. To tell the truth, I would hate to be on the other side when they are finally unleashed; they will make a most formidable enemy."

"Agreed," Pierpont said, nodding thoughtfully. "That will be a grand sight to see, when it finally happens."

"True, true … But, Francis, you didn't ask me here today to discuss my training efforts …"

"No … you are quite right; though I have been curious about how it was going, so thank you for informing me on that. I have asked you here to discuss another matter … a matter of some concern, I'm afraid."

"Oh? What news have you had?"

"I received a telegram late last night, from a Colonel Lightburn, currently in command of Union forces along the Kanawha. He has received a troubling report of a Confederate cavalry force of some size, possibly as many as a thousand, moving down into the Kanawha Valley from the direction of Beverly. It is believed to be led by C.S.A. General Albert Jenkins, who has a somewhat dubious reputation. And apparently Jenkins is recruiting bushwhackers along the way to join in his raid."

"*Beverly?*" Nathan asked, sitting up. "That's just a few miles east of Rich Mountain," he said and frowned.

"Yes, why? What is troubling you about *that*, Nathan?"

Nathan was thoughtful for a moment, absorbing this news. Finally he answered, "Two things concern me, your honor. Firstly, I am remembering reading a recent report that Union General Cox was transferred from the Kanawha Valley to the eastern Virginia theatre along with 5,000 of his men, leaving Colonel Lightburn in command."

"Yes … that's correct. Why? What are you thinking?"

"I'm thinking—*worrying*, in fact—that our rebel friends may have also heard about Cox's transfer, and have sent Jenkins to conduct a reconnaissance in force to see if it's true. And when he discovers that it *is* true, and that Union forces in the Kanawha are now dangerously depleted —"

"The Confederates may be tempted to retake the valley!" Pierpont completed his sentence for him, eyes widening.

"Yes, your honor ... I fear so."

"Oh *my* ... that could be a serious blow to the formation of the new state, even as congress takes up the matter of West Virginia statehood. Losing nearly half our territory ..."

"I agree, your honor ... it would be a serious blow."

"What can we do, Nathan? Colonel Lightburn is clearly also concerned, as he has asked me to send him any available troops I have, though God knows we have but few, and those are scattered now, with the lion's share off east campaigning. The only decent sized unit I have is the newly-formed Thirteenth Infantry, which he specifically asked for ..."

Nathan thought for a moment, then said, "Send Lightburn the Thirteenth ... and every other man you can spare. Perhaps if Jenkins sees the movement of reinforcements coming into the valley, he will report that it is secure, and the rebels will reconsider attacking."

"Very good, it shall be done ... what else?"

"Hmm ... we must begin planning for the worst. I suggest you send a telegram to Governor Tod of Ohio, informing him of our fears, and asking him to send all available Ohio forces to the Kanawha as well. If the rebels succeed in retaking the valley, they'll be right on his doorstep, so he should be highly motivated to assist us."

"Good thinking, Nathan. I'll do it straightaway."

The two men were quiet for a moment, mulling over the possible outcomes of the current crisis, when Pierpont looked up and said, "Nathan ... you said there were *two* things bothering you about this, but you've only mentioned one. What else is bothering you?"

"Yes, I had not forgotten ... the other thing is more ... *personal*. Rich Mountain is where my old nemesis Elijah Walters was leading a band of rebel bushwhackers."

"Ah, and you fear Jenkins may have recruited him and his band to join in this raid?"

"The thought had occurred to me, your honor."

"Well, I will keep an eye out for any mention of his name in the dispatches …"

"Thank you, Francis. You might also keep an eye out for mention of a cruel, evil man among the rebel bushwhackers … a man who is missing his left hand."

৪৩৪৩৪৩৪৩৪৩৪৩৪৩৪৩৪৩

Monday August 25, 1862 – Terre Haute, Indiana:

Sammy, Caleb, Jack, and Sid sat in the shade of a weeping willow, leaning against its broad, gnarly trunk. The midday heat was oppressive; their clothes were soaked through with sweat, and dust from the road coated their faces. Even so, the shade was a welcome relief from the relentless sun and hundred-degree heat out on the road with its stifling humidity.

And they'd just enjoyed a cool drink from the narrow creek that trickled by next to the great tree. Now they were enjoying a brief rest from their travels. Even the pack horse stayed close by under the tree's branches without the need of hobbles as it cropped the grass, having no desire to wander back out under the hot sun.

Sammy was just nodding off when a sudden movement next to him startled him awake. He opened his eyes and saw it was Ned, who'd returned after reconnoitering a nearby farm.

Sammy sat up straighter as Ned pulled off his hat and wiped the sweat from his brow, then took a long pull from his canteen.

"What'd you see, Ned?" Sammy asked.

"Good-sized farm … corn mostly," Ned answered, then took another swig, before capping the canteen and setting it on the ground next to him.

"Talked to the farmer … nice enough fellow, I reckon … *for a white man,*" Ned said, and snorted a humorless chuckle.

"What he say?" Sid asked, now also alert and paying attention to the conversation. Caleb and Jack also leaned out to hear Ned's report.

"Well … you ain't gonna be happy to hear it, but he says we ain't quite halfway to Kansas yet," Ned began.

Caleb groaned, and leaned his head back against the tree, "Not even halfway? How long we been out on this road, anyway?"

"Long enough to be almost halfway," Ned answered. "You wanna turn back, then go … otherwise, quit your gripin'."

Caleb rolled his eyes, and leaned back against the tree, but said nothing.

"Where in creation are we, anyways?" Sammy asked.

"He says the town just over yonder is called Terre Haute … we's still in Indiana state, though he says the border into Illinois state is just beyond town. He says we black men may like Illinois, as it's where Mr. Lincoln's from … Plenty o' abolitionists there."

"Oh …" Sid said, "so, we done crossed another state … that's good, ain't it?"

"Yep … we done good so far, but our rations is runnin' short. Good news is, with the war on, the farmer's short on farmhands … all the white men's off fightin', and they don't hold no slaves in this here state. So he offered to let us rest here a bit with the roof of a barn over our heads, and regular cooked meals in our bellies if we help him bring in his corn."

"Oh, well … that sounds fair. He feed us and let us sleep in his barn, and in return we cut his corn?" Sid asked.

"That's what he said, but …" Ned paused and looked the others in the eyes with a scowl, "never forget … we ain't slaves no more … from here on we get *paid* to work. Captain says don't work for less than a dollar a day. So I said he got to pay us also, not just meals. The farmer said he'd pay us each a half-dollar a day, plus meals … no more."

"Oh … well, that seems pretty good," Jack said, joining the conversation for the first time.

"No!" Ned snapped back. "Ain't you heard a word I done said, Jack? I said we ain't slaves no more. No white man would cut corn

for half a dollar a day … not with a war on and no farmhands about … so we ain't neither. I told him we'd keep on walkin'."

"Oh," Jack said, "Damn it, Ned. Stayin' in one place for a day or two was soundin' mighty good. And cooked meals …"

Ned leaned back and snorted, "Y'all got to stop thinkin' like *slaves* and start thinkin' like *men* … when I turned to walk away, he offered a dollar a day. I said we'd work for two, and we settled on a dollar and half. And it'll take a week or so to get all his corn in."

Caleb perked back up at this, whistled, and leaned forward, grinning at Ned, "Damn, Ned … that sounds right fine … and, how'd you go'n get so smart, anyways?"

Ned snorted a laugh, and pointed at his forehead, "'Cause I go ahead and use this here between my ears, that's how."

ஐ௫௸௸ஐ௫௸௸ஐ௫௸௸

Monday September 1, 1862 – Washington, D.C.:

President Lincoln looked around the cabinet meeting at a sullen and downcast group of men. They'd been discussing the recent catastrophic defeat of Union forces at Bull Run under Major General John Pope.

General Pope had convinced the president he would secure a quick victory if given command over the entire Union Army in the northern Virginia theater. So the president, still smarting from the lackluster performance of George McClellan on the Virginia peninsula, had acceded to Pope's wishes. But Pope had proven himself a better talker than a fighter, leading to another defeat at the hands of Confederate General Robert E. Lee, despite lopsided numbers in favor of the Union side.

Unfortunately, there was no obvious, clear solution to the problem of ineffective, even incompetent command at the highest level in the Union Army, even as Lee's victorious army marched ever northward.

In the end, the president was forced to make the fateful decision he already knew would be extremely unpopular with the men gathered around him.

After he announced his decision, Secretary of State Seward would not meet his eye; he stood near the window, gazing out across the White House lawn. And Secretary of War Edwin Stanton, who was most personally and professionally impacted, hung his head in his hands, completely covering his face. The president couldn't tell if Stanton was actually crying, but wouldn't blame him if he was. It was a painful decision at best.

"Of course, I have read your ... *petition* ..." the president said, "that it is 'not safe to entrust *him* with the command of *any* Army of the United States,' ... and I appreciate that most of you have signed it," he continued in a tone that reflected the gravity of the situation.

"I want you to know that I don't take your appeal lightly; that I would not flippantly ignore your opinions, nor easily cast aside your trepidations. In fact, I share many of your concerns and reservations," he said, and paused, staring down at his hands on the table.

Then he looked back up and said, "But ... in the end, I am the commander in chief of this nation's armed forces. And as such I am required by the Constitution to provide for the common defense. I have found that this responsibility sometimes places me in a position where my heart and my head are in complete disagreement, as are my personal wishes versus my official duties."

Lincoln was not surprised that there was no further comment—he knew where they all stood on the subject, and now they knew where he did.

He shrugged, then softened his tone, "Look, gentlemen ... I recognize this seems like a case of curing the bite with the hair of the dog. But the capital itself is, even at this very moment, in imminent danger of attack by General Lee. We must use what tools we have, and there is no officer in the Army who can man these fortifications and lick these troops of ours into shape half as well as he. If he can't fight himself, he does excel at making others ready to fight.

"Given the disastrous and untenable situation we find ourselves in ... I will sign an order, effective tomorrow, relieving

Major General John Pope of command over all Union armies ... and reinstating Major General George B. McClellan as commander of same, with responsibility for the fortifications of Washington, and all the troops defending the capital."

No one spoke, but Edwin Stanton softly groaned, his head still in his hands.

ᏚᎤᏎᎣᏣᏔᏍᏙᎤᏎᎣᏣᏔᏍᏙᎤᏎᎣᏣᏔᏍ

Wednesday September 3, 1862 – near Leesburg, Virginia:

Evelyn couldn't remember ever feeling more hot, tired, dirty, and wretched than she did at this moment. And her backside ached from the relentless bouncing on the hard, wooden seat of the wagon she shared with the freeman Mary Jane and three other women. She looked at Mary, currently asleep next to her, and noted they were both so covered with dust from the great clouds kicked up by the army they followed that the color of their skin was now nearly identical—a dirty, blotchy gray with dark streaks from the sweat running off them in the relentless heat.

Evelyn slowly shook her head, wondering how she had talked herself into *this* one. *The best laid plans of mice and men ...* she thought, and smiled ruefully. She and Mary were now among the camp followers of the Confederate Army of General Robert E. Lee, rolling north after another shocking defeat of the Union Army—once again at Manassas Junction, what the Union newspapers referred to as "Bull Run."

The camp followers consisted of wives, lovers, servants, and even some slaves of the men in the army. Their official duties, such as they were, consisted of helping to serve out food, distributing blankets and other supplies as needed from the supply wagons, and generally trying to be useful in supporting the army.

Unofficially, the wives and lovers were there for conjugal purposes, or because they couldn't bear to be parted from their men, or they had nowhere else to go with their primary means of support out fighting the war.

Of course, Evelyn and Mary were there for a whole other purpose: to somehow gather intelligence on the plans of the Confederate Army and then figure out a way to pass that information along to the federals. For this operation Evelyn had taken on the role of the wife of one of the soldiers, and Mary their slave. Evelyn once again used the pseudonym "Eve Smith," though she was now playing more of a commoner rather than an aristocratic lady. Fortunately, in all the time she'd been socializing with the wealthiest and most influential women in Richmond, General Lee and his subordinate generals and staff officers had been away fighting the war. The only general she'd met in person was Joe Johnston after he'd been wounded, so there was little to no risk of her being recognized by any of the officers now.

But what had seemed like a difficult and risky operation back in Richmond, now seemed like an impossibly monumental and thoroughly dangerous task—a complete fool's errand.

For one thing, events had moved so quickly since early August, with armies constantly fighting and marching and the Confederate armies reacting in such a fluid manner, that Evelyn now doubted there were any actual written battle plans to steal, even if they could somehow manage it. She could readily imagine General Lee in his command tent, rubbing his chin thoughtfully for a moment, and then doling out orders verbally, even as they occurred to him off the top of his head.

The other problem that had become readily apparent was that she was no longer in the midst of Richmond high-society, and as such, no longer had direct access to the rich and powerful. She was now amongst the lowliest of the low; camp followers would be abandoned and left to their own devices by the army without a second thought the moment their existence became inconvenient.

Her usually effective weapons of beauty, wit, and charm were almost entirely useless in the current circumstances, with no means to bathe, dress, and fix one's hair; dressed in casual, everyday clothes and covered in dust and sweat, she had little advantage over a common street beggar. At least until they stayed in the same place for more than half a day, to give her a chance to clean up.

And the Confederate soldiers had little respect for the women in the baggage train, thinking of them as not much better than whores—which many of them were, making it also a dangerous business for Evelyn and Mary. Fortunately, Evelyn still had her tiny .22 caliber Smith & Wesson revolver up her sleeve for use in an emergency. And, of course, she also still carried the deadly, razor-sharp stiletto in its sheath strapped to her thigh. With her two secreted weapons at her disposal, Evelyn had little fear of being assaulted.

But she'd worried over Mary's safety. When she asked Mary to carry a weapon—perhaps a stiletto or other small knife such as she carried, Mary demurred. "Miss Evelyn ... I grew up a slave woman ... It's different than being a free woman ... One must *always* be on her guard and try to avoid such dangers. And if they *do* come, she must be ready to run, or to scream, or if necessary to fight with teeth, nails, and fists. But using a weapon ..." she slowly shook her head, "it'd cause more trouble than whatever one was trying to fend off, I fear."

Evelyn thought about this a moment, and nodded, "All right then, just please stay close to me so I can protect us both."

The weapons were of little use in accomplishing her mission, however. She never even saw General Lee or any of his senior officers, except very occasionally at a great distance, usually with hundreds or even thousands of soldiers in between. Getting anywhere close to them at this point was a near impossibility.

It was galling, and tiresome, but there was little she could do about it at the moment. All she could do was keep her eyes and ears open and hope for events to play themselves out in such a way as to provide her with an opportunity to act. Until then ...

And even as she was in the midst of these thoughts, the wagon lurched to a stop, causing a thicker than normal cloud of dust to waft slowly into it. Evelyn covered her mouth, trying in vain to suppress a cough from the dust coating the back of her throat. Such stops were intermittent and unpredictable, usually caused by something happening further up front—a stream to ford, a broken-down wagon blocking the narrow way, or enemy snipers forcing a counter action by the soldiers guarding the wagons. Rarely, it was even a planned stop for food and fodder, though this typically only happened at the end of the day, unless those in charge had some unknown reason to stop in a specific location.

The only thing all of these stops had in common was that those in the baggage train rarely knew the reason why. Nor did they really care; it was a chance to get out of the stuffy wagon, stretch their legs, and relieve themselves. And though Evelyn had started out the trip a modest and reticent high-class lady in that regard, after several weeks of living crudely amongst some of the lowliest of society, in the dirtiest and least civil of circumstances, she no longer cared about such niceties. She would quickly squat behind the nearest bush or tree, typically in plain sight of several other ladies doing the same.

So as soon as it was clear the wagon wasn't moving again—at least not immediately—all the women aboard quickly piled out the back, Evelyn and Mary included. And per usual, Evelyn answered nature's call straightaway.

This particular wagon stop was in a wilderness, with thick, man-high bushes crowding the narrow dirt road. So, surprisingly, for once Evelyn found herself alone, wedged between two tall bushes, as she pulled up her skirts and squatted down to ease her aching bladder. The sudden privacy seemed odd and almost luxurious somehow. She smiled at the thought of how such a simple thing had become so pleasurable.

But as she finished, stood, and took a step back toward the road, a strong arm grabbed her around the waist from behind, as a powerful hand covered her mouth and held her fast. She could see out of the corner of her right eye a gray uniform sleeve with gold trim—one of the soldiers.

The man whispered, "Don't fight, nor scream … I'll not hurt you. I just want to talk with you." She could feel the whiskers of the man's beard up against her neck and could feel his hot breath on her skin.

But Evelyn didn't believe he only wanted to talk—she knew that a man in those circumstances cared little for conversation—

but she had a pretty good idea what he *did* want. And she was determined not to give it to him.

She thrust backward hard with her right elbow, catching him mid-stomach, just below the rib cage. He grunted in pain and loosened his grip just enough for her to pull free. As she pivoted to face him, she reached up her left sleeve for the Smith & Wesson secreted there, yanked it free, cocked the tiny hammer, and brought it up to eye level, even as she'd practiced hundreds of times before.

But gazing at the man in her sights — doubled over, gasping for breath, and holding up a hand in supplication — she stopped dead. She lowered the pistol, let down the hammer, and breathed a heavy sigh.

Slipping the pistol back up her sleeve, she stepped forward, wrapped her arms around the man's neck and said, "*Joseph!* You frightened me so!"

He returned her embrace, and coughed, before chuckling, "And have paid the price for it, clearly."

"Sorry about that," she said, then she stepped back and gazed at him in wonder. His face and beard were covered in the same dust and sweat as she was. But the most startling thing was that he was fully uniformed as a Confederate soldier.

"Joseph ... what are you *doing* here?" she asked.

"Looking for you, obviously," he said, then grinned, "and also fighting a war, apparently," he concluded, gesturing at the clothes he wore.

"Yes ... I noticed."

"I joined up as a lowly private two weeks ago, but look here," he said, pointing at a yellow chevron on his sleeve, "they've promoted me to sergeant already! Next thing you know I'll be the commanding general," he chuckled.

She shook her head and rolled her eyes, "So ... once again Jonathan couldn't resist sending you out to watch over me."

But he tilted his head thoughtfully and gave her a serious look. "No ... this time it was me. I ... told him I was going after you and would brook no argument. Not that he would've given any. Evelyn ... you are too important to be out here beyond our help.

After a week with no word, I could wait no longer and came to find you."

"Well, I appreciate the thought, Joseph ... I really do, but ... despite the current unpleasant circumstances and admittedly, complete lack of success, I'm not turning back. I am determined to find a way to complete this mission ... to find a way to help win this war."

"I know."

"You do?"

"Of course. I didn't come here to bring you home."

"You didn't?"

"No. I knew if I wanted to take you home, I'd have to force you, and ..." he chuckled again, "we've already seen how well *that* would work out for me."

She grinned and shook her head in amusement.

"No ... I'm here to *help* you, Evelyn ... oh, I should say, *Eve*. Just tell me the plan, and what you want me to do, and I'll do it."

But she smiled ruefully, "The problem with the plan is ... there is no plan."

"Oh!" he said, then reached up under his hat to wipe away a stream of sweat threatening to run down into his eyes.

"But I do have a few ideas I've been ruminating on ..." she continued. "I'm happy you're here so we can discuss them, and decide on the best course of action."

"I'm entirely at your service, Miss Eve," he said, and tipped his hat.

ಏಓಔಃ಄ಏಓಔಃ಄ಏಓಔಃ಄

"Oh, by the way, if anyone asks, I'm your betrothed," Joseph said, as they made their way back to the wagons. "I told the men in my company I was going back to check in on you, though I didn't know you were here. I've looked through so many baggage trains in the last week I couldn't even tell you how many."

"Very well ... *darling*," she said, and rolled her eyes.

He snorted a laugh.

"Oh, and I have heard some important news today ... and you're *not* going to like it ..."

"What's is it, Joseph?"

"Well, you remember how pleased we were when it seemed McClellan had been demoted, with General Halleck promoted to general in chief, and General Pope placed in command of the armies in northern Virginia?"

"Yes ..." Evelyn had a sinking feeling she knew where this was going.

"Well ... after Pope's disastrous handling of the second battle of Manassas, I just heard that Lincoln has restored McClellan to command of all Union armies in the east ..."

Evelyn groaned, "How *could* he?! After how McClellan botched the Richmond invasion!" She shook her head in disgust, "I can't believe it ..." she said, in almost a whisper.

"I'm afraid it's true. All the officers were talking about it. Apparently it was in all the northern newspapers. The sad, ironic thing is that most of the papers were actually *happy* about it!"

Evelyn turned and gazed out past the wagons, a deep frown knitting her brow. "Then ... there's no point. Even if we were to somehow succeed — against all odds — in doing what we intend ... he'd never believe whatever information we might provide. He'll just think it's another Confederate trap. It's so ... so ... disheartening," she said, sinking slowly down to sit on the grass at the edge of the road, her knees pulled up under her chin.

Just then Mary stepped up to join them, "Oh, there you are, Miss Eve ... I didn't know where you'd gone." Then she glanced quickly at Joseph, but not at his eyes, giving him a quick curtsy. "Sir ..." she said, deferentially.

"It's all right, Mary. You can look up at me," he said gently.

She glanced up and met eyes with him, and a smile lit her face, "Joseph! It's *you*. I didn't recognize you in that uniform. It's so very good to see you, sir."

He chuckled, "Likewise, my dear. And I'm happy to see you looking well, though I expect this has not been the most pleasant experience."

She shrugged, "Miss Eve is a good traveling companion — cheerful and resolute, regardless of the circumstances. She inspires me to be the same."

Evelyn looked up at her and smiled, reaching out to grasp her hand and give it a squeeze. "You've been a good companion as well, Mary. Never complaining, and always trying to make the best of it. Mary ... Joseph has just informed me that General McClellan is back in command of the Union armies."

"Oh? What does it mean, Miss Eve?"

"It means this has all been for naught, Mary, I'm afraid. Our mission is a failure before it can even really start."

But Joseph sat down beside her, and gazed over at her. "I've been thinking on this problem ever since I heard about McClellan's re-instatement. Assuming we can somehow— through some miracle—gain the information we desire ... what if we could get it to McClellan in such a way as to inspire confidence in its authenticity?"

"How? The man is naturally mistrusting and suspicious, from all I've heard and seen."

"Hmm ... what if we made it seem as if his *own* people had accidentally come upon the plans? Like ... hmm ... like when an enemy position is suddenly overrun, and the officers haven't time to destroy all their papers ... something like that?"

Evelyn thought for a moment, then said, "Yes ... yes, that *might* work ... If he had no reason to suspect the source, he might be inclined to believe its authenticity—especially if it didn't contradict any of his pre-conceived notions, such as concerning the enemy's actual troop strength."

She looked up at Joseph and smiled, "It's worth a try, anyway. Thank you, Joseph. Thank you for giving me a slim ray of hope on which to proceed."

"Never mention it, my lady," he answered, and tipped his hat to her, returning her smile.

ഈഔഇൽ‌ഈഔഇൽ‌ഈഔഇൽ

The evening of Joseph's unexpected arrival, he and Evelyn discussed strategy in a hushed conversation in back of an old toolshed a few dozen yards away from the nearest tents of the rebel encampment. Mary stood guard at the side of the shed to warn them if anyone approached.

Evelyn would have preferred to include Mary in the discussion, as she had a keen analytical mind, despite a lack of military knowledge. But having her sitting next to them would hardly fit their cover story of being lovers who'd slipped away from camp for a little privacy, whereas having their "slave" keeping an eye out on their behalf, did. And besides, they certainly couldn't risk being overheard, considering the topic of their discussion.

"The officers spread the word just after supper this evening that we'd be crossing the river in the morning," Joseph announced, as soon as they'd settled themselves.

"So, it's really going to happen after all. Lee is actually going to attack the North ..." she answered, and gazed out across the hayfield in front of them.

"Yes ... into Maryland at the least, and possibly Pennsylvania as well. The word is the general believes the Marylanders will welcome our troops with open arms, as liberators, rather than invaders, and he means to use that to his best advantage. He thinks the locals will voluntarily keep the army re-supplied, and that he's like to pick up a large number of recruits along the way to replenish those he lost at Manassas."

Evelyn snorted, "Sounds like wishful thinking to me ..."

"Maybe ... but it's a border state, so there's likely a mix of sentiments ... don't forget the federal soldiers had an altercation with some locals in Baltimore early on in the war, and had to shoot several before regaining control of the town."

"True ..." Evelyn said, considering this possibility for the first time. "It could be that *we* can also make use of that, if it turns out to be even partially true."

"How so?"

"I'm not sure yet ... perhaps blending in with the pro-Confederate locals welcoming the troops in order to get closer to Lee ...?

"But let's set that aside for a moment and think about what Lee will do once he crosses the Potomac. Assuming he crosses here, at ... where *are we* anyway, Joseph?"

"*Leesburg*, Virginia," he answered.

She rolled her eyes, "Well, that's quite a coincidence, isn't it?"

"Yes, considering the circumstances," he answered. "And I understand it *is*, in fact, named after the general's family—in particular his great uncle, the Founding Father, Francis Lightfoot Lee."

"Oh! Well, that's certainly an auspicious and ironic launching point for his invasion of the very nation his great uncle helped to found."

Joseph nodded.

"Anyway ... assuming we cross over here at Leesburg ... *oh* ... I forgot to ask if there's a bridge here, Joseph ..."

"No, but there's a crossing called White's Ford that they'll likely use."

"Ah, all right, then that will put the Confederate Army somewhere in between Harpers Ferry and Washington ... just exactly where Nathan *didn't* want Stonewall Jackson to get to when he attacked Harpers Ferry this spring!"

"Yes, once across the Potomac we'll be almost exactly in the middle between those two points," Joseph agreed. "Do you think Lee will march on Washington, then, Evelyn, even as Jackson intended to do?"

She pondered the question for several minutes, before slowly shaking her head, "No ... no, I don't think so. As bold as Lee has proven, he must know that an attack on the Union capital would be like sticking his hand into a beehive. And besides, it's not his kind of fight—no room to maneuver, no opportunity to catch the enemy off guard, or to flank him. Just a head-on siege against overwhelming odds ... No, Lee will *not* go in that direction; I would bet my life on it, though he may try to convince them that he will."

"Makes sense. Where, then? What's he trying to accomplish, if not to take the capital? Wherever he goes he'll eventually be outnumbered. He can't hope to conquer the entire North. Despite what General McClellan seems to think, Lee simply hasn't the manpower ... What's his game, then, do you suppose?"

"He doesn't *need* to conquer the North to win the war," she answered.

"He doesn't? How else is he going to do it?"

"Don't forget, Joseph ... from the very beginning the goal of the South was simply to secede from the North — to become an independent nation. Subjugating the North was never the goal."

"All right then, but if he doesn't defeat the North, how does he win the war?"

"He wins it by fear."

"Fear?"

"Yes ... he believes if the people of the North begin to fear that the war will come even into their own towns ... into their own neighborhoods ... to fear that they might see enemy armies marching across their own fields ... then their will to fight must wane, and the Union will be forced to allow the secession to go forward after all. And you heard it yourself: he also expects the slaveholding border states to join with him, rather than oppose him, causing even more fear throughout the North ... fear that they might lose even more states to the Confederacy.

"With congressional elections coming up soon, he likely hopes to undermine the Republican party and get enough Democrats elected to weaken Lincoln's hold on the government, and force him to sue for peace."

Joseph pondered this for a long moment, then said, "I think what you're saying makes sense. So then, how does he do it? Where does he go? In which direction does he attack?"

"Hmm ... I'm remembering his strategy when he was outnumbered back during the peninsula campaign. He made a great show of having more men and equipment than he had ... and it worked. And now he knows he's going up against McClellan again, and that McClellan is particularly susceptible to that type of ruse."

"So ... he tries to make it seem as if he has more men than he has? How?"

"I ... I don't know ... it must be different when on the offensive ... When you're defending you can build phony fortifications, march troops in circles, drag chains to make clouds of dust, build fake artillery from logs, and light more campfires than you could possibly need. But when you're on the march ..." she shrugged, "none of those things really apply."

They were quiet for a moment, then Joseph said, "You know ... I've been doing a little reading about military strategy this past year—for obvious reasons—and remember a passage that said if a general is on the march, and outnumbered in enemy territory, he must *never* divide his forces. That only through keeping his entire strength together can he hope to survive the inevitable confrontation with the enemy on his home ground."

"Hmm ... I think you've got something there, Joseph ... if Lee is outnumbered, he must keep his entire force together. But if he comes into the North, feeling utterly confident because of his overwhelming force ..."

"Then he can afford the luxury of dividing his forces to conquer more territory more quickly!" Joseph concluded with a grin.

They looked at each other and nodded, "Lee is going to divide his army," they both said, almost simultaneously.

"And when that happens," Evelyn continued, "General Lee can no longer count on spontaneous, verbal battlefield commands to control his army. He will have to resort to—"

"Written orders!" Joseph finished the sentence for her, with a wicked grin spreading across his lips.

"Yes ... and if *he* can write them, *we* can steal them!" she concluded, returning his grin.

Chapter 5. Special Order 191

*"Let your plans be dark
and impenetrable as night,
and when you move,
fall like a thunderbolt."*
- ***Sun Tzu***
The Art of War

Saturday September 6, 1862 – Frederick, Maryland:

Evelyn, Joseph, and Mary continued their planning as the Confederate Army of Robert E. Lee moved further into the North after crossing the Potomac, setting up camp in a grove of trees outside the town of Frederick, Maryland.

After witnessing the enthusiastic reception given the Confederate army in Frederick, Evelyn decided to change her clandestine "role" from a camp follower to a pro-secession local in hopes of getting closer to General Lee.

So she and Mary checked into a local boarding house, giving the story of a mistress and her slave arriving from out of town to witness the glorious arrival of the Confederate army. They quickly cleaned themselves up and went out to join in the festivities, mingling with the crowds lining the streets to welcome the arriving army.

And at first their strategy seemed to be paying off; even as they stood on a street corner, gazing down the lane through the cheering, chanting crowds they saw a Confederate Army column marching toward them in parade formation. And Evelyn's heart skipped a beat when she recognized General Robert E. Lee himself, astride his magnificent gray horse, leading the parade. Lee held his hat in his hand and bowed and nodded to the adoration of the people lining the roadway.

Evelyn took out her handkerchief, waving it and smiling enthusiastically along with the other ladies gathered there, as men waved the official Confederate States flag, or more typically the Confederate *Battle* flag, with its blue X filled with white stars on a red background.

As Lee and his army approached, Evelyn saw that Lee was closely followed by a group of a half-dozen officers on horseback, after which marched a long column of foot soldiers, rifles on their shoulders.

When Lee came closer, she was able to catch his eye as she smiled her brightest smile and waved her handkerchief with great vigor. Lee returned the smile and nodded, before turning his attention elsewhere.

It's a start, Evelyn decided. Perhaps Lee was not immune to her charms after all, despite his growing reputation as some kind of latter-day saint throughout the South.

She then gazed at the staff officers following Lee to see if she could possibly make another connection that might prove useful. But her heart stopped, and she suffered a terrible shock as she met eyes with one of the officers. She immediately looked away and ducked back into the crowd.

The officer had been wearing a major's parade uniform—light gray with butternut trim and brightly polished brass buttons— and she knew him instantly—Ollie Boyd, her best friend Belinda's husband, and a man she'd known well for years!

She moved quickly back through the crowd, Mary hard on her heels, until they made it back to the storefront lining the street, immediately ducking into a doorway.

Mary was wide-eyed and frightened by Evelyn's sudden action. "What was it, Miss Eve?" she whispered, still struggling to catch her breath.

"One of Lee's officers ... I know him from Richmond ... he ... he may have seen me," Evelyn said, slowly shaking her head, a dark frown knitting her visage.

"*Oh!* That would be ... that *could* be very bad for our plans ..." Mary said, also becoming thoughtful. "What now, Miss Eve?"

Evelyn didn't immediately answer, gazing at the floor. She chastised herself for not thinking about Ollie before; he'd been one of General Joe Johnston's staff officers before Johnston was wounded and replaced by Lee, so it stood to reason he was now on Lee's staff. But Evelyn had failed to think of that connection until now, and it had very nearly proven disastrous.

But after a moment she shook her head, looked back up, met eyes with Mary, and said, "We carry on ... and hope he didn't recognize me ... or perhaps ... he will doubt his own eyes, as he would not have expected me to be here."

Mary nodded, but could think of nothing to add, so the two of them headed back out the door and immediately returned to the boarding house to start working out their next plan of attack.

⁁⁂ ❧

C.S.A. Major Oliver "Ollie" Boyd had been pleasantly surprised by the reception they'd received in the "Northern" town of Frederick. Clearly, General Lee was feeling the same, as he immediately ordered a parade march of several regiments down the main street of town even before his camp was completely in order.

And Lee had decided to lead the parade himself, which meant his staff officers, including Ollie, would ride with him as they always did on such occasions.

It had been a joyful, heady experience for Ollie, equaled only by a parade through the streets of Richmond he'd ridden in under General Johnston back at the start of the peninsula campaign. *This is even better than that one*, he decided. *Here we're being greeted as heroes and liberators in a town that the Yankees think they own.*

And then as he slowly rode down the street, thronged by cheering crowds, something about one of the ladies caught his eye, and he looked at her. She returned the gaze, then quickly ducked away. His heart skipped a beat, *Evelyn!* he thought. *What are you doing here?*

But then she was gone. He stood in the stirrups and looked around, but the woman was now lost in the crowd, and they were moving past where she'd been. He sat back down, and now his happy expression had turned dark and thoughtful.

"What is it, major?" the captain riding next to him asked, having noticed his sudden change of expression.

"It was … nothing … nothing, I'm sure … I just thought I recognized someone in the crowd. But it must be only a coincidence. *That* lady is still back in Richmond."

The captain nodded, and said, "It happens to me all the time, major. I see someone who reminds me of home and it's a shock until I realize it is only a touch of homesickness."

Ollie nodded, "Yes … yes, I'm sure you're right. Thank you, captain." He turned and looked back the way they'd come. *But she sure did look exactly like Evelyn. And why did she immediately turn away from my gaze? Hmm …*

℠℠℠℠℠℠℠℠℠℠℠℠

C.S.A. First Lieutenant Jubal Collins, of the Twenty-Seventh Virginia Infantry Regiment, "The Bloody Twenty-Seventh," part of the famous Stonewall Brigade, marched next to his commanding officer, Captain Bob Hill. They had the honor of being the first formation following General Lee in the hastily organized parade down the streets of Frederick town.

Jubal was feeling buoyed up by the joyous reception they were receiving: men waving flags, young boys singing, and women waving handkerchiefs. *This almost makes all the marching and fighting worthwhile … almost,* he decided, and chuckled quietly.

He looked over at Captain Hill and they exchanged a smile, "It's a good feeling, isn't it, Jubal?" Hill asked as they marched briskly along behind the horses of Lee's staff officers.

Jubal nodded, "Yes, sir … I was just thinking it almost makes up for—"

But Jubal now stared off to the side into the crowd, Captain Hill forgotten. He'd had the briefest glimpse of a face in the crowd, before it had turned away suddenly and disappeared in a swirl of long blonde hair. He raised up on his tiptoes, gazing out through the crowd. He sighted the woman again, hair streaming out from beneath a fashionable hat, before the view was blocked by a black woman following behind. Then the blonde woman was completely lost from view.

"What is it, Jubal?" Captain Hill asked, "You look as if you've just seen a ghost."

Jubal looked back at him, and slowly shook his head, "I ... I don't know, Captain ... maybe I have." Then he gazed back out at the crowd, *Evelyn ... Evelyn dearest ... why are you here?* he wondered. The unanswered question followed and haunted him for many days to come, until desperate battle drove out all other thoughts.

ଈଓଈଠ(ଷ(ଷ୫ଓଈଠ(ଷ(ଷ୫ଓଈଠ(ଷ(ଷ

Thursday September 11, 1862 – near Clarksburg, Maryland:

Union Captain James Hawkins, of the Seventh Loyal Virginia Regiment, felt a growing sense of frustration and anger as he marched at the head of his company, part of a miles-long column of Union soldiers in General Sumner's Second Corps, a third of the greater army under the command of Major General George McClellan. It was the latter who continued to fuel Hawkins' ire.

Scouting reports claimed that the rebel army under Robert E. Lee was marching through Maryland like they owned the place, even staging a parade to cheering throngs through the main street of Frederick town just to the north of the Union army's current position—a galling embarrassment to the Union from Captain Hawkins' perspective.

But despite this glaring affront, General McClellan moved his army at an overly cautious snail's pace, in Hawkins' mind. The army would camp in position for days at a time, and when they finally did move, they'd progress only five or so miles in a day before once again making camp. This when Hawkins knew full well that the army, which had faced little to no opposition thus far, was capable of marching more than twenty miles in a day, even carrying full packs.

Hawkins was experiencing a growing sense of dread, a sinking feeling that Lee was once again outsmarting and outmaneuvering McClellan, leading him at his leisure into a trap of the Confederate general's design. By moving ever so cautiously, Hawkins believed McClellan was allowing Lee to dictate when and where the battle would ultimately take place, giving the rebels every possible advantage. He only hoped the Union army's greater strength in men and materiel would be enough to offset the enemy's obviously superior generalship.

But probably most galling of all was that nobody else seemed to share Hawkins' concern. Most of the other officers chided him for being "in a hurry to get shot at"—they argued that General McClellan would use them carefully and frugally, rather than throwing them pell-mell into the fray, thus limiting the number of casualties and ensuring the integrity of the army's fighting capabilities.

But to Hawkins this was no more than delaying the inevitable confrontation—allowing the enemy to take the initiative. Nothing good would come of it; of that he was certain.

And not for the first time or the last, Captain James Hawkins wished that an intelligent, competent, capable officer, such as Nathan Chambers from western Virginia, was in command of the Army of the Potomac instead of George B. McClellan.

ೞೞೞೞೞೞೞೞೞೞ

Evelyn and company figured their opportunity would be coming soon; Lee must move quickly if he wished to prosecute his plan of dividing his forces, and that would mean issuing written orders to his various generals before sending them off to perform their various assigned tasks. They had no way of knowing if Lee would write one order that would include the assigned actions of all his generals—obviously the most ideal for their purposes—or rather a separate order for each general. Either way, getting their hands on such a document would be a major coup for the Union.

After much discussion, they decided against trying to steal the orders at the source. For one, there was now the concern about Major Ollie Boyd; he may not have known what to think of seeing Evelyn in the crowd—if he indeed had—but he would certainly know her if he saw her up close near Lee's headquarters, and could not help but be suspicious.

Additionally, General Lee's command post, where the orders would be written out and then distributed, would be the most closely guarded, and the chain of custody of the written orders

77

most closely monitored. Better to make their attempt on the other end, where the orders would be delivered to the field commanders, who'd likely have less stringent procedures in place and many more distractions ... such as the threat of actual combat.

They decided to target Major General D.H. Hill, simply because he was in command of the division of the army they were currently embedded with, and as such it would make their task more manageable—his command tent was within sight of the field where Joseph's company was bivouacked, and so he'd be able to better monitor comings and goings of the general and his staff.

But targeting General Hill turned out to be a bad decision, and Evelyn chastised herself afterward for not doing her homework on the personalities of the various generals under Lee's command.

The plan had been relatively simple: to clean Evelyn up—she'd smuggled a reasonably nice dress along for the purpose—and have her continue the role of a Confederate sympathizer, infatuated by the uniform of a high-ranking Southern officer. She intended to take advantage of the long-standing tradition among the upper class in the South that deemed a good deal of flirting to be acceptable, even between people who were married—but not to each other—to pass the time. She would use her charms to distract the general and get him away from his command tent in the evening after his staff had departed. Mary had worried that the general might try to take advantage, but Evelyn argued that once she'd lured the general outside, there would be little fear that he'd attempt to push things too far—not in the midst of a camp teeming with soldiers.

Once Evelyn led General Hill out for a moonlight stroll, Joseph would surreptitiously keep watch as Mary slipped into the tent and looked for the appropriate papers. If necessary, Joseph would distract any guards who might be about by acting drunken and belligerent.

They'd debated whether to have Mary try to memorize the document, or quickly write out a copy, but neither option seemed feasible. So, in the end they just decided to just go with good old-fashioned pilfering, on the assumption that the victimized general would not be able to admit to the loss of such a vital document, and would be forced to carry on as if nothing had happened to it. Meanwhile, they could make their way to the Union lines, and figure out a way to make it look as if McClellan's men had found the thing on their own.

They waited a day, to give Lee time to write out and distribute his orders, before executing their plan.

But General Hill proved a hard case for Evelyn. When she presented herself at his tent, all scrubbed and dressed up, and summoned up her most potent and charming Southern Belle act, he greeted her politely, but never smiled, and seemed completely disinterested. He quickly thanked her for her support of the Confederate cause and wished her a good evening, summarily dismissing her suggestion of "a walk in the moonlight that the general might get some much-needed fresh air," arguing that he'd had a long day and was overdue for some much-needed sleep. He nodded politely, then turned and re-entered his tent, closing the flap in her face.

Well, that didn't work out so well, was all her bewildered ego could come up with in response to this cold, hard rejection. She turned and walked away feeling utterly defeated, and more than a little bit humiliated.

Then she scolded herself for becoming entirely too used to being treated like gold by gentlemen, even when she didn't deserve it. It was a good reminder to stay humble and not become overconfident when using whatever gifts God had seen fit to give her.

It wasn't until the next day, asking a few pointed questions of some of the Confederate soldiers, that she learned General Hill was a devoutly religious man who never smoked, drank, or was seen in the company of loose women. He was also devoted to his wife and family—in other words, he was quite likely the worst possible target for their scheme. *Another lesson learned the hard way,* she decided.

ΕʋʂɔᴄᴙᴄʂΕʋʂɔᴄᴙᴄʂΕʋʂɔᴄᴙᴄʂ

Thursday September 11, 1862 – Frederick, Maryland:

The next morning, General Hill's command pulled up stakes preparing to depart in the midst of a light, gloomy drizzle that had started with a drenching downpour late in the night.

And from what Joseph could learn, the other Confederate commanders were doing the same—even as Evelyn and Joseph had surmised, the entire army was now splitting up and moving off in different directions.

Evelyn had to make a quick decision about what to do next—to follow Hill's army, and hope for another opportunity, or to perhaps try infiltrating one of the others. But after only a few moments' thought, she came to a very painful decision, "Joseph … Mary … I'm afraid the time has come that we must admit defeat, and return home. I'm so sorry … but if we carry on with the army from here, we risk getting swept up in an extremely dangerous situation from which there may be no escape—very likely, a tremendous battle is imminent. Under such circumstances we shall have almost no hope of doing anything useful, but a very high risk of suffering injury or even death. Better we live to fight another day, as they say."

Joseph gave her a serious look, but nodded. Mary looked like she was going to tear up, and turned away, covering her eyes. Neither spoke for several moments.

Finally Joseph said, "Y'all should have no trouble collecting your things, and preparing to leave town. No one will try to stop you. I, however, will have to slip away later on the road, get out of this uniform, and sneak back to you, so I don't get rounded up for a deserter.

"I will meet up with you later—I hope this evening—back by that old barn where we discussed plans two nights ago. Until then, ladies …" he said, tipping his hat, then turning and trotting off toward where his company was already packing up their tents and other gear.

Evelyn put her arm around Mary, and they headed back toward the wagons to collect their things. They walked on the grass at the edge of the roadway as the road itself was now clogged with marching soldiers headed in the opposite direction—out to the northwest, out to fight the war. Evelyn felt a deep sense of melancholy, thinking, *all these bright young men, many with no uniforms or even shoes, marching unquestioningly out to a brutal, violent death. And for what? To preserve slavery? Or for some abstract concept of "States' Rights"? Or for their country? And which country would that be, pray tell?*

She shook her head sadly as she walked along, pondering these dark thoughts. But Mary suddenly grabbed her arm and shook it to get her attention, "Miss Eve … we must move!"

Evelyn looked up and saw what Mary had just seen; a troop of cavalry soldiers, also moving along in the grass at the road's edge coming straight at them, passing by the infantry soldiers at a fast trot. Evelyn realized she had looked up too late; they would never have enough time to move out of the way before being trampled. She raised her hands to cover her face and braced herself for the impact.

But the officer in the lead raised his right hand and shouted for a halt, bringing his horse to a bouncing stop, only a few yards short of Evelyn and Mary. His entire troop of some twenty or more riders, did likewise, skidding to a stop; apparently well trained to obey their leader's commands almost instantaneously.

Evelyn lowered her hands and looked up at the man gazing down at her from his saddle. She had expected an angry look from a startled officer, in a hurry to carry out his duties, and annoyed by the unexpected and hazardous halt caused by a careless and inattentive civilian.

But what she saw instead was a look of amusement mixed with curiosity from a *very* handsome man in his early thirties, with a dark red beard, and piercing blue eyes. And he sat on his horse as the very image of a storybook prince, decked out for war in all his finery: a light-gray colored felt Hardee hat with gold hat band, rakishly pinned up on one side, an ostrich plume on the other, serving as the exclamation mark on the man's elegant livery. The fanciful gold embroidery up the sides of his gray uniform coat, sparkling with brass buttons, and butternut trim, marked him as a major general in the Confederate Army. And the red velvet cape over his shoulders, thigh-length leather boots, and glittering sword at his hip, marked him as a man of means and style, who wanted to make sure everyone knew it.

Evelyn experienced a startled intake of breath at the sudden recognition; this could be none other than Major General James Ewell Brown "Jeb" Stuart, the commanding general of all Confederate cavalry forces!

And more than that, he was well known as a flamboyant latter-day cavalier, who'd famously embarrassed McClellan during the late Virginia peninsula campaign by galloping his cavalry forces in a complete circle around the Army of the Potomac as it marched—the furious Union general helpless to prevent it.

He also had a reputation for being a charming ladies' man with a taste for music, poetry, and carousing, even while on campaign—and despite being a married man. In short, he was the perfect antithesis to General D.H. Hill.

Meeting him in person, she now understood the appeal to the ladies; with his dashing good looks he was certainly impossible to ignore. And it occurred to her that he and Nathan were of a similar age, and that there was some innate spark of self confidence in their demeanor that immediately set them apart from other men. But she decided this man could not compare to Nathan in at least one sense—Nathan did not need to dress in finery to attract her eye. She remembered that the first time she'd seen him he was dressed as a common farmer, and even so she'd been completely smitten when their eyes met.

The general tipped his hat to her, continuing to gaze into her eyes with an amused look, "My lady ... I apologize most sincerely for frightening you," he said, in a deep, melodic voice.

"Oh, no, general. The fault was all mine. My eyes were distracted at the sight of all these brave and heroic young men marching out to do battle against the enemy on our behalf."

Stuart grinned, "Well, who could blame a fine, Southern lady for *that* ... for do I not denote, from the beautiful tones of your speech, and the eloquence of your words, that you are from Virginia, my dear, and perhaps even from our very own most beloved city of Richmond?"

She returned the general's smile, gracing him with her very most dazzling one, "You are correct, sir, I *am* from Richmond, born and raised.

"And, my dear general ... I see your reputation for gallantry has not been exaggerated in the least ... for am I not correct in assuming I have the honor of addressing Major General James Ewell Brown Stuart, commanding officer of all our valiant cavalry forces?"

At this question, Stuart beamed, sweeping off his hat, and bowing stylishly from his saddle, "At your service, my dear lady. But you have me at a disadvantage, my dear ... for I have never before had the *great pleasure* of your acquaintance."

Evelyn curtsied, "Miss Eve Smith, good sir. Honored to make your acquaintance."

"Oh ... but the honor is all mine, Miss Eve ... and the delight." He turned to the officer next to him and said, "*By God*, Von Borcke ... have I not always said that the ladies of Richmond are by far the loveliest on all the earth?!" to which the man nodded and grinned, but made no reply.

"And you will please excuse my forwardness, Miss Eve, if I say, that here before me stands the very living proof of my assertion."

She bowed again, and smiled brightly, "Now you are simply flattering me, general. But I thank you for the compliment."

"Nonsense, my dear ... I do not flatter, I merely speak the truth. Your beauty is ... simply beyond compare."

"I thank you again, general. And ... I would like to wish you all the best on your current mission ... I shall pray for you, sir ... *wherever* it is you may be going today ...?" she ended the statement questioningly, hoping against hope the general might let slip something of his current orders. It wasn't what they'd come for, but it might be *something* ...

But the general smiled brightly, "Oh, we're not headed out just yet, my dear. The cavalry must serve as the rear guard for the army and won't be leaving Frederick for a day or two yet.

"And speaking of, Miss Eve, I am hosting a ball, of sorts, at the Landon place over toward Urbana this evening for all my officers as a farewell from this lovely city before we depart. And we are inviting all the fine ladies as a thank you for their gracious hosting of our men during our stay.

"And now that I have met you, Miss Eve, my heart shall verily be broken asunder should you not be in attendance."

"Oh, but I very much doubt *that*, general! I'm sure a man of your gallantry and charm will be simply overrun by handsome young ladies. And besides, being so long away from home—visiting my dear invalid Auntie here in Maryland—I'm not sure I have anything appropriate to wear for such an august occasion …"

"Nonsense, my lady … beauty such as yours has no need of such adornments. Even in the simple, casual attire you now wear, you surpass even the most elegantly dressed of ladies."

"Thank you again, your honor," she answered, curtsying another time, this one looking down demurely.

"Then I shall see you there, Miss Eve. I will not take 'no' for an answer," he concluded.

"Until then, my lady," he said, this time leaning down, taking her hand in his, and gently kissing it. And though he wore long, leather gauntlets, even these were of the finest make—butternut colored, and soft as silk.

Then Evelyn and Mary stepped to the side to allow the cavalry to pass. Stuart tipped his hat to Evelyn and smiled rakishly, then spurred his horse forward, his men following at a fast trot.

"What was *that* all about?" Mary asked, after the cavalrymen had passed.

"*That*, my dear … means our *game* is back on," Evelyn said, and they shared a conspiratorial smile.

☙ℰ☙ℭ℟☙ℰ☙ℭ℟☙ℰ☙ℭ℟

As she'd been taught by Harriet, her mother, Evelyn arrived later than when most people might typically be expected at a formal ball. It was the way to make "an entrance" which would be noticed by the gentlemen.

She was ushered into the large, elegant ballroom at the private Landon residence, fancifully decorated with the unusual combination of various Confederate regimental battle flags and freshly cut roses. And she could not help but notice General Stuart—if anything dressed even more elegantly than earlier in the day. At the moment, he was almost completely surrounded by ladies, laughing and chatting amiably with him as he shared some humorous tale.

Though Evelyn had made protestations of not having the appropriate dress for the occasion, it was not entirely true. She wore the same gown she'd worn during her abortive attempt to distract General Hill, and though the dress wasn't anything too ostentatious, it had a simple elegance that accentuated her God-given attributes—slim waist, long legs, and a plentiful bust that never failed to catch the gentlemen's eyes when she exposed just the right amount of cleavage. And for this occasion she'd also employed her secret weapon: the French makeup her mother had taught her to use when that little extra bit of help was needed.

So when she entered the room, though she was clearly not the best-dressed woman there, she had a confidence that shone through to anyone watching. As she moved across the hall to take a seat she could feel many eyes on her, both of the gentlemen and the ladies.

And as she sat, a butler stepped up in front of her with a silver tray. He was a black man, neatly dressed in a dark suit. She looked up and smiled at him when she accepted a drink, which seemed to startle him. But he briefly returned the smile, before quickly stepping away.

Evelyn took a sip—warmed brandy, and excellent—then looked back toward where the general was chatting with the ladies. In the midst of a bout of laughter he glanced in her direction and their eyes met. He immediately stopped still, turned to his audience, made a quick statement, then turned and walked across the room directly toward her.

She put down her drink and stood to greet him, curtsying in the formal manner as he stepped up in front of her. And it wasn't lost on her that the proper obeisance gave the gentleman a tantalizing view of the lady's cleavage.

"Dear general, I have come, even as you *commanded*," she said as she stood, gracing him with a teasing smile.

"Ha! That was not a *command*, dear lady, that was a most heartfelt pleading!"

Then he bowed, looked up and said, "I can't tell you how very pleased I am to see you again, Miss Eve. May I join you?"

"Of course, general," she answered as she retook her seat and he pulled up a chair next to hers.

"But sir … I believe you have offended your audience of a moment ago on my behalf," she said, nodding her head in the direction of the group of ladies the general had been entertaining. Many were still standing in a group, and Evelyn detected any number of surreptitious looks in her direction, and could imagine the conversation; *Who is she? How does the general know her? No, I've never seen her before. She's not from around here. Look at her dress, very common … She's not that spectacular …*

Stuart chuckled, "Well, I'm sure their wounds will heal in due time. Miss Eve … I have been breathlessly awaiting your arrival. I feared … I may have come on a bit too strong at our first meeting, and frightened you away. I find I sometimes have an effect on ladies that is … *not* what I intend."

"Oh, how so?"

"Well, I am a great admirer of the more elegant gender, and sometimes I am a bit too free with my speech in that regard. I fear at times I may be taken for the worst sort of cad. But I am actually a gentleman, in the classic sense of the word — a gentleman in both word and deed."

"That I can clearly see, sir. But I can't believe anyone would take offense at your speech. For instance, which words did you say to me earlier today that you would now take back?"

He smiled brightly at this bold question, "Not a *word* of it, Miss Eve! And I will say it again; you are the very vision of loveliness. If I have ever seen a more beautiful lady on this earth, I can't recall when."

"There you go again with the flattery, sir," she answered, returning his bright smile.

"No, my dear … as I said earlier, it is but the simple truth."

And though she was only playing a role, and this man was a war leader of the enemy, she had to admit a part of her was pleased to hear him say those words.

ಙಲಙಾಞಞಙಲಙಾಞಞಙಲಙಾಞಞ

As the evening wore on, any doubts Evelyn may have had that General Stuart was feeling a particular and very strong attraction for her were completely dispelled. He danced with her nearly every other dance, and in between dances would sit next to her and never took a seat elsewhere, though he did feel compelled to move about the room and chat with the guests from time to time, and told her so—apologetically. But as flattering as his attentions were, the most satisfying aspect of it was, to her mind, how it played into her developing plans to get ahold of his battle orders.

Clearly the other ladies had noticed the general was paying her an unusual amount of attention, to their own detriment. And a few of them weren't shy about saying so, and gave her a grilling about who she was, where she was from, why she was there, and so forth.

But fortunately, Evelyn was now well-versed in playing a role for the purpose of espionage. She already had a backstory prepared—the name of her poor sick aunt in Maryland, her illness, which town and neighborhood she lived in—not something local that someone might know well. And details about how Evelyn had come to be in Maryland—when she'd arrived, how she'd traveled, how she'd avoided the fighting, how long she planned to stay, why she was in Frederick, and so on, and so on. She smoothly answered every inquiry, but not *too* smoothly ... one didn't want to sound well-rehearsed—there always had to be just the hint of annoyance at being queried, as any normal person would feel.

Stuart had become more comfortable with her, and began treating her with more familiarity. At one point when she addressed him as "General Stuart" as she'd done all evening, he said, "Please, Miss Eve, I beg of you ... just call me *Jeb* as all my closest friends do."

"I'm honored … *Jeb*. And since we're becoming such close friends, please just call me *Genevieve*, as all *my* close friends do."

"Genevieve … yes, it suits you … beautiful name for a beautiful lady," he said. "Why shorten it, when it rolls off the tongue so?"

She shrugged, "People like shorter names, don't they? Like Jeb, made up from the initials of your full name."

"True. But when you have such an unruly collection of names such as I have, a shortening is most definitely called for," he said, and laughed.

She laughed with him. And as the small orchestra started another waltz, he stood and extended his hand, "If you're not too done in yet, *Genevieve* …"

"Certainly *not*, Jeb—I would be happy to join you," she answered, taking his hand and standing.

And as the dance was ending, he leaned in close and whispered, "I would have a word with you in private, Genevieve. Will you accompany me to my quarters for a few moments?"

Her mind raced, and she didn't immediately answer. It seemed clear what kind of "word" he wanted to have with her, so her immediate thought was to say "no." She was willing to lie, steal, and even kill for the cause, but she wasn't willing to give herself to a man for it.

But without Mary or Joseph here to help, she needed to find out where he was quartered if she wished to have any chance of stealing his battle orders. And having a chance to reconnoiter his room to get an idea of where he may have hidden the plans might prove the difference between victory and defeat, not just for her scheme, but quite possibly for the entire Union Army.

So, she decided to gamble that Stuart *was* a gentleman, even as he claimed, and trust that she could shame him out of doing what he very likely wanted to do—in the worst way. And, if worse came to worst, she still carried her secreted weapons.

"Very well, Jeb. I know you are a proper gentleman … so I will put my trust in your hands," she whispered.

"Thank you, my dear. Have no fear … I promise I *am* a proper gentleman, even as I've professed. But perhaps we should not be seen departing together … people *will* talk. I will walk out first, telling anyone who inquires that I am in need of the … *water closet.* Then a few minutes later you may follow. I will find you in the outer hallway …"

"All right, Jeb," she answered, as he made a slight bow and headed for the door. She moved back to her seat, then watched him have a word or two with several of his officers and a few more with some of the ladies before departing.

Evelyn waited a minute or two before standing and following. She was surprised that she was trembling as she walked. *Get a hold of yourself, Evelyn! You've killed men before … this should not frighten you so …*

And at the thought of having killed before, she reached down and softly patted the stiletto, strapped to her thigh beneath her gown. *Razor sharp courage … in a leather sheath*, she decided and felt her trembling begin to ease.

ᔕᕓᘓᖇᘓᔕᕓᔕᕓᖇᘓᔕᕓᔕᕓᖇᘓ

When they were alone in his room — on the second floor, four doors down from the back stairwell, on the right, she reminded herself — he gestured across the room, saying, "Welcome to my humble abode, lady, courtesy of the kindness of the Landon family."

"It's very nice, Jeb. This is a beautiful home, and it's a blessing they have opened it up for housing you and your officers."

"Yes, they are true patriots, there can be no doubt," he answered.

But she thought, *Oh, yes, there can be!* but returned his smile brightly, and nodded.

Then he stepped closer to her, took her hand in his, and held it up to his face to kiss it.

"Genevieve … you may think I am a man who uses ladies like playthings … but nothing could be further from the truth. I will admit I enjoy the company of ladies, and the more beautiful they are, the better, in my mind. But I never press my advantage, though you can imagine I have had plenty of offers …"

She nodded, but said nothing, curious how he was going to propose what she was pretty sure he was working up to proposing.

"But though I will admit I greatly appreciate the beauty and charm of the ladies, they never touch my heart ... only my eyes. And my eyes are easily overridden by my heart ... and my iron will.

"But then ... I saw *you* this morning, out on the road ... even as I very nearly trampled you to your death. The fright of it, and the sudden recognition of a beauty beyond compare—a beauty that was nearly lost to the world by my own hand ... I must confess it touched me deep down inside, and I felt *something* ..."

"Jeb ... perhaps it was just the shock of the moment ..."

"No ... it was like a thunderbolt from the blue. I've never felt the like before. I may have seemed calm to you in the moment, but I promise you, my heart was racing such that I thought it might burst from my chest ...

"I have promised to be a gentleman ... and I will keep that promise if you wish ... but I ... I would dearly love to kiss you ... if you'd be willing ..."

Evelyn considered for a moment ... she'd kissed Joseph to distract the Confederate soldiers on the pier in Richmond ... and she'd kissed Nigel when he was dying. It was only a kiss, after all, and might make him more trusting of her ... and besides ... hadn't Nathan kissed the doxy rebel spy? And if she refused, her opportunity to reconnoiter his room might be lost, and her mission might fail.

So she nodded, and Jeb leaned in, touched her beneath the chin, and gently pressed his lips to hers. She decided it felt nice ... despite him being a strong, powerful man, a war leader, a killer, a man other men feared ... he was also ... soft and gentle, and for a moment it felt good just to be held in that way by a man ...

Then he leaned in closer and wrapped his arms around her and pressed against her. She felt his manhood arousing, and thought, *Oh no ... not this ... not now ... not with this man ... oh no ... Nathan ... help!*

She pushed away, and said, "*General* ... you are certainly a handsome and charming man ... but ... are you not *married*, sir?"

He continued to hold her by the wrists, though he was no longer pressing himself against her.

He snorted a laugh, but nodded in acknowledgment. "It's true, Genevieve ... I *am* a married man. But when I first laid eyes on *you*, I felt a spark I couldn't resist—like a moth to the flame. And who am I to deny what my heart so clearly desires?"

Evelyn couldn't begin to imagine how to respond to this statement. The man was proving himself the worst sort of cad; despite his flowery words, she had no illusion that she was anything more to him than another in a long line of casual conquests. Then a sudden strong inclination to feel for her weapons began to grow inside her; she would *not* be taken advantage of by this pompous general, not even for the good of the Union!

She smiled demurely as if considering his suggestion, and gently pulled her wrists free from his grasp, taking a short step back. She briefly considered using her weapons on him, trading her life for his—that her life might be well spent if it were sacrificed for the sake of depriving the enemy of one of its most important generals. But she immediately shuddered at the thought—self-defense was one thing, but cold-blooded murder? She knew she could *never* do that.

Happily, she was spared from her dilemma by a sudden, urgent knocking at the door.

"General! General Stuart, sir! The Yankee cavalry attacks our videttes at Hyattstown, and they are hard-pressed! The men are mounting up in the drive, sir. Your horse is ready, and your presence is requested, general!"

Stuart stood, gazed into her eyes, and said, "I must go, Genevieve. But have no fear; it is far too soon for the enemy's main column to have arrived—likely this is but a skirmish, which I shall deal with in short order. Then I'll ride straight back to you ... promise me you'll be here when I return."

She gazed up at him and nodded. It wasn't the first time she'd lied to someone who thought of her as a friend. And sadly, it wouldn't be the last, she had to believe.

ℰℐℐℰℐℐℰℐℐℰℐℐℐℰℐℐ

After spending the evening with the man, Evelyn was not surprised that Major General Jeb Stuart made a great show of his departure, leading his men off to fight the enemy straight from the ballroom. First, he saluted the ladies, bowing and waving. Then he turned and looked directly at Evelyn, made a flourishing bow, the ostrich plume on his hat sweeping the gravel of the drive, before he turned, raced toward his horse and leapt onto its back in a single bound.

He immediately swept out his sword and spurred the horse forward with a shout, his men following suit and thundering after him. The whole squad was soon lost from sight in the darkness.

Evelyn returned inside with the others, but only made curt, necessary conversation with anyone who approached her. Her mind was racing … with Stuart suddenly gone, likely for several hours at the least, it was the perfect opportunity to search his room for Lee's battle plans. But she knew she must act calm and defray any possible suspicion of her.

So she accepted another warmed brandy offered by the butler—who smiled *first* this time—then casually sipped it as if she hadn't a care in the world.

After several minutes, she excused herself to use the water closet. But once out of the hall she retraced her steps to the room that was, *on the second floor, four doors down from the back stairwell, on the right*, she remembered.

ℰℐℐℰℐℐℰℐℐℰℐℐℐℰℐℐ

After a cursory look turned up nothing, Evelyn began a systematic, intensive search of General Stuart's room, starting with the desk. From working with Jonathan, she knew exactly what to look for: false bottoms or false backs in drawers, odd unused space that had no apparent access via doors or drawers, trim pieces that were not perfectly aligned or fastened, subtle scuff or scratch marks on the surface where there shouldn't be any, and so on.

But after a thorough, meticulous search, she concluded this desk did *not* contain any hidden compartments, and there were no papers in any of the normal places. Fortunately, none of the drawers were locked, though she'd also been practicing how to pick locks if needed.

So she moved on to the bed. *Surely he wouldn't have just stuck it under the mattress?* she wondered. But she shrugged, and checked it anyway, not surprised to find nothing there. Then she went over the entire frame of the bed, inch by inch. It was a heavy, simple frame made of a dark hardwood—walnut most likely, the same as the dresser, though the rest of the furniture in the room, the floorboards, and the paneling was of a lighter wood like cherry, and much more decorative and elegant.

Again, she searched the bedframe for any signs of odd seams, cracks, scratches, hollow places, screws or nails where they weren't needed, and so on. Finding nothing, she moved on to the headboard, conducting the same careful search of that. Nothing.

The room was wrapped in bookshelves, mostly empty. But there were several dozen old, leather-bound books scattered about in a seemingly haphazard fashion. She sighed, and began going through the books one at a time—pulling each down off its shelf and quickly leafing through it—a hollowed out book being an excellent hiding place for something small like a folded document. She made careful note of how each book was positioned and made sure to put it back exactly as it was, thinking there may be some intentional pattern to their arrangement; if so, someone might notice they'd been moved.

It was a time-consuming process, and in the end, she found nothing in the books. She was beginning to feel a growing sense of urgency; though Stuart was unlikely to return for several more hours, someone else might come—a maid or a butler to clean the room or freshen the bedding. But she forced herself to remain calm and moved to the dresser.

The dresser, like the bed frame, was of a dark wood, simply finished—utilitarian, rather than decorative. But the same exhaustive search turned up nothing.

Perhaps Stuart had just kept the orders on his person, not trusting to leave them anywhere unguarded, she thought. But then she realized she hadn't found *any* papers at all—not a personal letter, not a requisition … nothing. *Odd,* she thought. *He'd not carry all of his papers with him; from what I've seen and heard, army generals are fairly besieged by paperwork, mostly of the mundane type from the quartermaster or the War Department. Perhaps one of his subordinates is keeping his paperwork for him,* she thought.

But the more she thought of that, the less sense it made. Maybe for the mundane stuff, but something as important as the battle orders from General Lee would not be trusted to anyone else. The commanding general would be personally responsible for keeping such vital information secure.

But she'd checked everywhere she could think of, and was now at a loss—totally perplexed. There being nothing more she could do; she had to admit defeat. After one last look around the room, she sighed heavily and started for the door. But then she stopped, and gazed around once again. Something was nagging her about this room … but *what?*

Then it came to her: this was not supposed to be a bedroom. It had no window, for one, and the walls were decoratively paneled and lined with bookshelves, though most were empty or nearly so, at the moment. She decided that this room had originally been a library. It was clearly being used for a bedroom as an overflow, likely caused by all the Confederate officers being housed here currently. That would explain why the bed and the dresser, dark wood of a simple design, didn't match the desk and the bookshelves, lighter wood and much more decorative. And having a large desk and so many bookshelves, it made for fairly cramped quarters compared to an ordinary bedroom. Then she realized the room had no closet nor even an armoire—no place to hang clothes.

Then in a sudden epiphany she thought, *Why would they house their most important guest in the least comfortable room? It has to be*

*that there is something about this room that he specifically requested —
like … a secret hiding place? It's not in the furniture, it's something built
into this room!*

So she began her search anew, her emotions a nerve-racking
jumble of excitement and ever-growing anxiety. First, she
carefully searched the floor, including under the bed, looking for
anything unusual about the floorboards. She realized there was
no rug in the room, as a bedroom would typically have — another
sign she was on the right track. But she found nothing unusual
about the floorboards.

Then she stood up and gazed around at the bookshelves. It
was then she noticed one bookcase in particular stood out: slightly
more than man-high and three feet wide, it was the perfect size
for … a door? *Surely not a hidden room behind a bookshelf?* she
thought. *That'd be just a little too trite — like something out of a fairy
tale.*

But she looked around at the side of the bookcase and could
see a slight gap between the trim and the wall, *hmm*. She tried
pushing and pulling it to either side, but though it moved
slightly — more than a normal built-in bookcase should — it
wouldn't open. Then she pulled out the books one by one, once
again, this time looking for any kind of latch or device that might
release it. Finally, on the third shelf from the bottom, behind one
of the books on the far-right side, she noticed the head of a nail
sticking out about a half inch from the back of the bookshelf, as if
it had worked its way loose over the years. She reached in,
grasped the nail head and pulled. It moved stiffly at first, but then
something gave, and she heard an audible *click*.

She sucked in her breath, stepped back, and pulled on the
frame of the bookcase. It swung easily toward her, revealing a
dark room behind. She grabbed the oil lamp from the dresser and
stepped inside. It was a simple, bare, tiny room with a single
unadorned table and two straight, unpadded chairs. And in the
middle of the table, she saw a sight that caused her heart to pound
in her chest — a fine leather satchel, with a gold buckle, like the
kind used to carry important papers!

When she sat to examine the satchel, she noticed it was of fine, soft black leather, and the brass buckle was elegantly engraved with the initials J.E.B.S. *Of course it is*, she thought and smirked.

She opened the buckle, reached inside and pulled out a stack of papers, about half an inch thick.

She looked through them one at a time—the first four were requisitions for horseshoes, fodder, additional horses, ammunition, and all sorts of other military equipment, some of which Evelyn didn't recognize or know its purpose.

The next was a letter from the general's wife, and Evelyn had to strongly resist the urge to read it.

Then she leafed through several confirmations of brevet promotions of officers, or requests for same. So far, nothing of value ...

Then she pulled out a document of two pages, and her heart skipped a beat when she read the signature section at the bottom of the second page: *"By command of General R.E. Lee, R.H. Chilton, Assistant Adjutant General."*

She knew Chilton was Lee's chief of staff. She quickly flipped back to the top of page one and read, "(Confidential) Special Order 191 ..." and her excitement grew.

But the first two items on the document were extremely mundane: an order concerning the proper treatment of the townsfolk of Frederick ... followed by an order for a Major Taylor to transport the Confederate sick and injured back to Winchester, Virginia. She was starting to fear this document was nothing more than a series of general instructions to the army. But the next line read, *"The army will resume its march tomorrow, taking the Hagerstown road ..."* and she held her breath as she skimmed through the remainder ... orders for General Jackson ... then for General Longstreet, General McLaws, General R.H. Anderson, General Walker, General D.H. Hill, and finally General Stuart, each ordered to move in a different direction.

Her eyes went wide, *It's a dream come true ... orders for the entire Confederate Army of Northern Virginia, describing exactly where each general is going and why! With this information, even McClellan can't fail to secure the victory. He'll be able to attack each of the scattered*

Confederate forces piecemeal, never allowing them to re-consolidate their strength, she concluded, nodding her head and smiling in grim satisfaction.

She quickly glanced through the remaining papers to see if there was any other document of interest. Finding none, she neatly folded the two pages of Special Order 191, and slipped them up her right sleeve. She quickly returned the remaining papers to the satchel and closed it, re-positioning it on the table exactly as it had been when she'd entered.

Then, with heart pounding in her ears, she retraced her steps, closing the bookshelf door with another satisfying *click,* then setting the lamp back on the dresser. She made one last look around the room to make sure nothing was amiss or suspicious looking. With any luck the general wouldn't notice the missing document for some time, if at all. His own instructions from General Lee in Special Order 191 were relatively simple, so Stuart would have no particular need to look at the document again, unless he wished to know something specific about one of the *other* general's instructions.

She slipped out of the room, quietly pulled the door closed, and turned to head back toward the stairs. But she pulled up short with a start—a well-dressed, middle-aged civilian stood not five feet away gazing straight at her. She recognized him as the owner of the residence, James Landon.

"Oh! You startled me, sir," she said in all honesty, taking a moment to catch her breath and still her pounding heart.

He frowned at her, "What were you doing in General Stuart's room, may I ask, miss?"

And though his sudden appearance when she was attempting a discrete exit had caught her by surprise, his question hadn't— she'd already decided on a story to spin if she were caught. And the beauty of it was, the story would incentivize the listener to keep quiet about her intrusion.

"Oh, good sir ... when the general was ... ahem ... *entertaining me* ... in his quarters earlier, I inadvertently dropped my silk scarf," which she lifted off her shoulders as evidence. "It wasn't until the general had departed for the fight that I realized it was missing. So, I have taken the liberty of retrieving it, not knowing when the general might return."

"Oh … I see …" he said, a thoughtful expression replacing the earlier frown.

"My good sir, I beg of you … as a patriot … don't speak of this to anyone … the general is a married man … but he's a great and invaluable leader in our war effort. It would not do that he become embroiled in a scandal because of a … simple indiscretion."

Landon thought about this a moment, then nodded, and said, "Very well … I will agree, but … I believe it would be best if you leave this house now." His frown had returned; clearly, he did not approve of loose women, and didn't care to have one in his home.

"Thank you, sir. Thank you very much, and I was already leaving …"

ༀ☘ঙ☘ༀ☘ঙ☘ༀ☘ঙ☘

The happy and celebratory mood of the evening before, when Evelyn had returned to the barn with the precious document, had changed to dread and trepidation by mid-morning when Joseph returned from reconnoitering the town to report his findings.

"Rebel cavalrymen are scouring the town, going house to house, business to business, asking after a beautiful blonde woman named Eve Smith … or *Genevieve* Smith," he said, as he sat down next to Evelyn and Mary on the straw of the barn floor. "And the word they are spreading is that this woman stole something personal of great value from General Stuart."

She nodded, "So … my hope that he'd not discover my theft has clearly not come to fruition. Evidently, he's … *unhappy* with me …"

"'Wrathful,' is the word the soldiers have been using to describe their commander's disposition," Joseph said. Then he looked Evelyn in the eye and said, "What I don't understand is where the name 'Genevieve' comes from …"

Evelyn blushed, "One of my aliases—a name that also sometimes employs 'Eve' as a shortening. I used it to become more … *familiar* … with General Stuart."

"Ah ..." he responded, grinning wryly.

"I have *not* done anything immoral, if that's what you're thinking," she responded with a frown.

"*That* would never occur to me, dear lady," he answered, this time with a more serious look. Then he chuckled. "Ah ... but now I better understand the venom of the general's ire; a lover scorned?"

"Something like that ... as if stealing his battle plans wasn't bad enough," she answered, shaking her head.

Mary patted Evelyn's knee from where she sat on the barn floor next to her. "Miss Evelyn ... whatever happened with the general—or *didn't*—you have achieved a great victory for our cause."

"Yes," Joseph agreed, "but now we must figure out how to survive our victory. I think if we stay here, they will soon find us ... it's likely someone saw us either coming or going, or in the neighborhood. We'll not be safe now until the Union Army arrives."

"But when will the Union Army arrive, do you think?" Mary asked.

"They should have been here by now ... I can only imagine it is more of General McClellan's dithering," he answered.

"That's not difficult to imagine," Evelyn said with a scowl.

"I don't think we can wait for them," Joseph continued. "I think we must try to sneak out of town in the direction of the advancing Union Army as soon as possible, and hope to meet up with them on the road."

"Agreed," Evelyn said, "please ... lead the way, Joseph."

ഇരുന്ന

For the first several blocks everything went smoothly, with Joseph scouting a half block or so ahead, dressed up in his typical "vagabond" disguise. This time he leaned heavily on a walking stick, and had a pronounced limp, designed to keep either side from rounding him up for a recruit or a deserter.

At each corner Evelyn and Mary would wait and watch while Joseph walked most of the way to the next corner, before giving them the signal to follow.

They'd gone three blocks in this fashion with no incident, nor any sign of General Stuart's cavalrymen, and Evelyn was starting to feel more confident that they would make good their escape.

Evelyn and Mary turned the latest corner and stepped out into the street, after Joseph had just given them the latest "all clear" signal, when they heard a sudden loud noise behind them.

Evelyn flinched and looked back. Mary screamed; a cavalry soldier was spurring directly at them, now only a few dozen yards away, and they had nowhere to hide. As Evelyn turned to run back toward a storefront at the side of the street, the rider pulled to a stop in front of her, leaned down, and seized her by the upper left arm.

"Gotcha!" he said.

She squirmed and pulled against him, feeling his grip beginning to slip from her arm. But then he seized her again, this time just above the wrist. She realized with a sudden anguish that the hidden pistol holster up her sleeve had been her undoing; it had given him something to grasp when she'd started to slip free.

And now, with his iron grip on her arm, she could no longer reach the pistol to pull it free.

But then she remembered the stiletto. She reached down through the slit in her dress above her right thigh and pulled the six-inch, razor-sharp blade from its hidden sheath. Then she reached up and stabbed him in the arm.

He gasped and released his grip on her. But she'd been pulling so hard that with the suddenness of his release, she lost her balance and fell to the ground in the road.

The soldier held up his bleeding arm, gazing at the blood oozing out, and said, "*Damn!* You've poked me, you witch!" then he reached down with his other hand, unholstered his pistol and said, "Let's see how feisty you are with a bullet hole in you; I'm sure the general will happily use whatever's left of you."

She covered her head with her hands, the stiletto still clutched in her fist, as he pointed the pistol at her. A gunshot sounded sharply, and she flinched. Then ... nothing happened ... no shock ... no pain.

She looked up and saw the soldier wide-eyed, a bullet hole in the center of his chest. His pistol slipped from his lifeless grip as he looked down at her, then coughed up blood, slumped in his saddle, and toppled off into the road. His horse shied, turned away and trotted off.

Evelyn looked toward the sound of the gunshot and saw Joseph running toward her, his smoking pistol still held out in front of him.

When he got to her, she was already on her feet, and ready to embrace him for saving her life. But he moved past her and fired off two more quick shots, before turning and grabbing her arm. She glanced back and saw more cavalry troopers coming down the street toward them. Mary rejoined them, having scrambled out of the way when the rider had grabbed Evelyn. They turned the corner of the street and sprinted for the other side.

But before they could reach safety, another rider rounded the corner and fired his pistol at them, kicking up dirt at their feet and shattering a pane of glass in a store on the far side of the street.

"Keep going," Joseph urged. He turned to face the riders and fired his pistol again.

But Evelyn could not abandon Joseph ... not even to save her own life. She dropped the stiletto, pulled out the small Smith & Wesson pistol, and turned to stand with him. Mary also stopped and turned. Stooping to retrieve the stiletto, she stepped up behind them.

The Confederate cavalrymen pulled their horses to a hard stop in the middle of the road, unholstered their pistols and began firing. But to Evelyn's surprise, the enemy pistols were no longer aimed at them. And before she could respond, she heard a thunderous volley of gunfire coming from down the road behind them, mixed with the sound of galloping hooves.

Evelyn saw a young Confederate cavalryman in front of her, with long blond hair, of not more than twenty years, take a bullet in the face that tore his hat off, along with the top of his head, in a great splatter of blood. She screamed at the horrific sight.

But even as she screamed, she saw another young soldier take a gunshot to his wrist that snapped the bones in his arm, sending his gun spinning away. And then another man took a bullet in the neck and clutched ineffectually at the wound as blood spewed out onto his gray tunic before he tumbled from the saddle. The remaining Confederates turned their horses and raced back the way they'd come, with more bullets kicking up dust in the road around them as they rode.

Evelyn felt sick and shocked at the carnage she'd just witnessed in the space of a few seconds. Inexplicably, she thought of Nathan in that moment, realizing more clearly now all the horrors he'd witnessed in his life as a soldier. And yet somehow, he'd remained a decent, honorable, kindly man.

She turned to see hundreds of riders galloping up the street toward them, all dressed in blue with gold trim on their hats, most with drawn sabers or pistols in their hands.

The Union Cavalry had arrived at last.

Chapter 6. Pyrrhic Victory

*"One more such victory
and we are undone."*
- *Pyrrhus of Epirus*

Sunday September 7, 1862 – Wheeling, Virginia:

Nathan returned to Belle Meade farm in the early afternoon from an unscheduled meeting with the governor at the Customs House in Wheeling.

Nathan was a firm believer in the sabbath, so he did not typically attend to work on Sundays—a fact which the governor knew well and respected. So when a courier sent by the governor arrived, shortly after the Chambers family had returned home from church in the morning, and requested Nathan's presence, he knew it must be something important.

Nathan dismounted and tied Millie to the hitching post in front of the Belle Meade farmhouse. Harry the Dog plopped down in the shade of a large bush next to the house, panting heavily. The weather was still bright and hot, showing no signs yet of autumn approaching, and Nathan could feel the sweat soaking through his own clothing as he approached the house.

He took the front steps two at a time, crossed the short porch and entered the house. But rather than head straight ahead to the kitchen and sitting area as he normally would, he immediately turned left and headed up the stairs, calling out, "Tom! Tom Clark! Are you up here?"

"Here, sir …" he heard Tom answer from a room down the hall.

Nathan walked down the hall and entered a bedroom, which had been taken over by Tom's new family, Adilida and little Nathaniel, along with Tom himself.

Nathan removed his hat and nodded to Addie, "Hello Addie," then he looked down at the boy and said, "and hello to you, too, Nathaniel."

The little boy looked up at him and smiled, holding out a small wooden horse he'd been playing with on the rug. "Horsey!" he said.

"Yes, I can see that," Nathan answered, "and a very pretty one, too!"

The boy beamed, then returned to crawling along the floor, bouncing the toy as he went.

"Good afternoon, Nathan," Adilida said and smiled brightly, standing and giving him a quick bow.

Nathan returned her smile, then turned to Tom and said, "Tom, sorry to interrupt, but the rebels have launched a major offensive down the Kanawha Valley. The Union commander, Colonel Lightburn, is sorely outmatched. And although he's an intelligent and reasonably competent fellow—from what I've been told—he has little experience under such dire circumstances."

"Hmm … I assume then, that our presence is requested?" Tom asked, trying his best to fend off a smile, for Adilida's sake.

"Governor Pierpont and I discussed the situation at length, and have concluded there's little else we can do at the moment; both he and Governor Tod of Ohio have already sent Lightburn all the troops at their disposal to counter the threat; but I fear it is not nearly enough. The reports are rebel Major General Loring has sent somewhere between five and eight thousand men down the Kanawha Valley, fully equipped with artillery. Lightburn will be lucky to pull together half that number, and those are spread throughout the length of the valley, him not knowing exactly where the enemy might strike until now.

"Of course, the governor has telegraphed the War Department for help, but it's unlikely there'll be any aid forthcoming anytime soon. With General Lee running amok in Maryland, pursued— ever so slowly, of course—by our old friend *George McClellan*," Nathan couldn't help but scowl when he said *that* name, "it looks like we are on our own out here in the west."

Tom nodded. "Well, the good news is, sir … we're always pretty much ready to go on a moment's notice. Jim and the men live for a fight, as you well know, and are always prepared—guns

104

cleaned, and kits packed. I assume at this point taking the first train from Wheeling in the morning is the quickest route, though that means losing the rest of the day?"

Nathan nodded.

Then Tom gave Nathan a serious look, and asked, "But ... what about ... the *others*, sir ...?"

Nathan returned the look, then gazed up at the ceiling for a moment. Finally he nodded and looked back at Tom, "Bring them—Tony and his men. It's time for them to fight. Hell ... I'd bring *all* the freemen if we had enough horses, but we must ride a good portion of the distance, once we run out of rail line—so we can only take those few."

"Yes, sir!" Tom said, and this time grinned brightly. "Now that the Union Army has sanctioned recruitment of black soldiers down in the South Carolina islands, and by General Butler down in New Orleans, I can't see how anyone could object," Tom said.

"True enough, Tom—though at this point I'd risk it anyway. After all ... what can they do to me at this point?" he asked with a rueful grin. Tom shrugged.

"And speaking of New Orleans," Nathan continued, "let's go ahead and invite Phillipe too ... if he wishes." Nathan wanted to include the young Cajun in their actions and was also curious how he would react to the freemen coming along with them. Phillipe had expressed a good deal of doubt about their capabilities and potential during their recent training exercises, and as far as Nathan knew, had not changed his mind on the subject.

Nathan didn't have long to ponder the question, as Phillipe came to see him a few minutes later, not long after Tom left to go muster the troops.

"Captain Chambers ... a word if I may ...?" Phillipe said as he approached Nathan where the latter sat on the back porch, cleaning several Colt revolvers.

Nathan gestured toward the seat across the table from him and said, "Certainly, Phillipe ... please, be seated. What is on your mind, sir?"

"Captain ... with all due respect—you being a man of great military experience—do you think it's wise to bring the black freemen with you into a potentially violent and deadly engagement?"

Nathan left off cleaning the pistol he'd been working on and set it down on the table, looking Phillipe directly in the eye.

"Is there something *specific* you are concerned about concerning the freemen, Phillipe?" he asked mildly. He had expected something of the sort, and had already steeled himself not to overreact. Phillipe, after all, was now part of the extended family—for better or worse—him being Tom's wife's cousin and now a resident at Belle Meade.

"To be blunt, sir ... I am concerned that these men may not have the intelligence and fortitude to stand firm in the face of heavy enemy action," Phillipe answered.

"Ah ... you're saying you think they're too stupid or too cowardly to fight?"

"Well ... I should not put it so crudely, sir, but ... essentially, *yes* ... such is my concern," Phillipe answered. "In battle your life is dependent upon the man next to you, and one must be able to trust him implicitly. I can't see how one can, in good conscience, extend such faith to these simple black men, regardless of their obvious good intentions and loyalty, sir."

Nathan nodded, sat back and reached into his pocket for a cigar, which he proceeded to light. He took several puffs, gazing at the smoke as it drifted slowly into the sky, before once again meeting Phillipe's eyes.

"But I *do* have complete faith in these men, Phillipe. In fact, I would put my life in their hands and still sleep well at night, secure in the belief that they would protect my back, not only with their very lives, but with great fighting skill and courage.

"So, to answer your initial question: yes, I do think it's wise to take the freemen along into battle. In fact, I'd take more of them if I had enough horses. So, I suppose you will have to decide if you wish to join us ... or stay home."

Phillipe turned red in the face, but Nathan didn't know him well enough yet to determine if it reflected anger or embarrassment. "You ... *misunderstand* me, sir," Phillipe said, "I have every intention of coming along, and of fighting. My concern was not for myself … I have no fear of the consequences of the coming fight, come what may. My only concern was for your own safety, sir—you being the most important person on this farm, and quite possibly in the new state being built here."

Nathan nodded, and said, "I thank you for your concern, Phillipe, but I am certain I shall be well protected by *all* of my men in battle. You included, if you still wish to go."

"Of course, of course," Phillipe answered, waving his hand dismissively.

"Good. Then I will trust that upon our return, we shall sit back down at this very table, and you will tell me whether or not the freemen have changed your mind on this topic."

Phillipe looked up thoughtfully, then nodded, "Very well, Captain. I will agree to that."

After Phillipe departed, Nathan went back to cleaning his pistols. But after a few minutes he was visited again, this time by Phinney.

"Hello, Phinney … come join me and have a seat, if you wish," Nathan said, gesturing toward the same chair Phillipe had just vacated minutes before.

"Thank you kindly, Captain, sir," Phinney said, "Don't mind if I do."

The two men sat quietly for several minutes as Nathan continued cleaning, finishing his second pistol and picking up a third, still puffing on the cigar.

"Captain … I don't want to be left behind, sir," Phinney finally said, a serious, concerned look on his face.

"Left behind, Phinney? Behind *where?* What do you mean?"

"Tony said y'all are fixin' to ride out and fight rebs somewhere down south o' here. But he says I can't come on account o' my missing arm," Phinney answered, gesturing toward his empty right sleeve. "But Captain, I been practicin' real hard, and now I can load a rifle or a pistol with only one arm—and my teeth and feet when I have to—pert-near as fast as I done before."

Nathan again set down the pistol he was working on and met eyes with Phinney. "Phinney … I hear you, and I know you've been working hard to do everything you used to, and I admire you for it ... but what Tony says makes sense ... you lost that arm fighting the enemy ... defending this very farm. You've given more than anyone could ask already ... there is no need for you to do more, and there's certainly no shame in staying home this time."

Phinney nodded, then said a thing that struck a deep chord with Nathan and immediately ended the argument in the freeman's favor, "Captain ... if *you'd* lost an arm fighting ... would *you* stay home tomorrow?"

Nathan gazed at Phinney a moment, then slowly shook his head, and smiled. He chuckled at Phinney, then said, "All right, Phinney. All right ... you win."

ಶುಭೋ೦ಶ೦ಶುಭೋ೦ಶ೦ಶುಭೋ೦ಶ೦ಶ

Wednesday September 10, 1862 – Charleston, Virginia:

The day-long train ride from Wheeling to Parkersburg, by way of Grafton, was uneventful, only interrupted by a discussion of the route they should take toward where the battle raged along the Kanawha Valley. The rebels were known to be advancing downstream in a northwesterly direction, toward the heavily defended Union fort at Fayetteville, Virginia, out to the east of the major Kanawha Valley city of Charleston.

The most tempting option, from Nathan's perspective, was to debark the train early, at Pennsboro, and take the road south directly toward Fayetteville to join the battle there. If they could arrive in time, they might aid the Union forces in beating back the Confederate assault and prevent them from advancing any further down the Kanawha.

The risk, however, was great; if they arrived too late and the rebels had already overrun the fort, they might find themselves cut off behind enemy lines. If that happened, they could still aid the Union side by fighting a guerilla action against the enemy rear, but they were too few to greatly impact the outcome in that manner.

So Nathan decided on the safer route: to stay on the train all the way to Parkersburg on the banks of the Ohio River and spend the night there. From Parkersburg they would ride first to Charleston, and then continue down the valley to meet the rebel advance moving toward them.

When they arrived in Charleston, they were relieved to find the fighting had not yet reached the city, though rumors were running wild of an imminent rebel attack. It was difficult to get any reliable reports, with everyone they asked telling a different story, mostly based on rumors they'd heard. The one thing that all seemed to agree upon, however, was that the Union fort at Fayetteville had come under attack from multiple rebel regiments and heavy artillery, and that Union forces were now falling back along the river.

So wasting no more time in Charleston, Nathan and company rode out toward Camp Piatt, nine miles further upstream. There the Union commander Colonel Lightburn had reportedly set up his headquarters.

They arrived at Camp Piatt just as the sun was setting on the tenth of September, passing the Union sentries on the strength of Nathan's intimidating personality alone, his men wearing no uniforms other than blue army caps—less any insignia—but all heavily armed, including the freemen. These received some surprised looks, though if the Union sentries had an opinion on the subject, they wisely kept it to themselves.

Tom took charge of locating a spot within the crowded fort where they might bed down for the night while Nathan went immediately to see Colonel Lightburn in the log cabin that served as his command office. Harry the Dog followed after Nathan, as usual. The Colonel welcomed Nathan cordially, having been told to expect him by Governor Pierpont via a telegram the previous afternoon.

After a brief introduction and handshake, Nathan wasted no time on pleasantries, asking, "What's the situation, colonel?"

"Dire, I'm afraid, Mr. Chambers," the colonel answered, with a concerned look. He seemed a pleasant, well groomed, and sincere young man—of a similar age as Nathan—and from all reports was highly intelligent and a reasonably competent officer. But for someone with the auspicious name of Joseph *Andrew*

Jackson Lightburn, he'd unfortunately never served in the military before the war. Even so, Nathan was willing to give him the benefit of the doubt—up to a point.

"Reports are the rebels march ten thousand or more, and plenty of artillery," the colonel continued. "Our forces are much less than half that, and spread out all along the river. Though I am told they fought bravely, our men at Fayetteville, under Colonel Edward Siber, were outmanned and are now retreating in our direction. I have ordered them to destroy any Union supplies they can't bring with them and any facilities that may aid the enemy along the way.

"We may hold them here for a time … or possibly at Charleston, but ultimately I believe our only hope in saving this command is to retreat to the Ohio and cross over to Point Pleasant; there we can defend with the wide river to our front."

Nathan scowled, but did not immediately respond. Instead, he reached into his pocket, pulled out a cigar and lit it, taking a few puffs, before saying, "Colonel, reports of the enemy's strength are almost always exaggerated, so I would take that with a grain of salt if I were you. But assuming it's true and you *are* forced to pull back … what's your plan of action, if you don't mind my asking?"

"Plan? It's a *retreat*, Mr. Chambers … we must try to keep ahead of the enemy and not be overrun … I suppose …" he ended lamely, his last sentence sounding more like a question than a statement.

Nathan scowled, "Wrong answer, colonel. The most important thing to do during a strategic withdrawal is to attack!"

"*Attack?* I … don't understand …"

"Colonel, if you turn your back and run, the enemy will come howling after you like a pack of wolves on the scent of a wounded deer. It will quickly become a panicked rout; your men will be slaughtered, and your entire command will be destroyed or captured.

"By contrast, have you ever seen a pack of wolves attack a grizzly? Even in retreat the grizzly will turn every few paces and attack the leading wolves, killing them if he can, maiming them at the least. He will repeat this maneuver over and over again until the wolf pack begins to fear coming too near and eventually breaks off the attack.

"This is what *you* must do, colonel. You must be the bear, *not* the deer. Make the enemy fear to come too close, make him fear he will be counter-attacked, fear that if he comes on too fast his men will be cut off, flanked, ambushed, and destroyed. Make him cautious and careful, giving you time to move your valuable assets—equipment, supplies, and men—out of harm's way as you *slowly* withdraw in stages, *fighting* all the way. Only in this manner can you hope to survive to fight another day."

Lightburn looked down with a thoughtful expression, then nodded, "Yes ... yes, I can see the truth in what you're saying, Mr. Chambers ... and the wisdom. But ... how do we do it?"

"Hmm ... if I'm not mistaken, colonel, from what I've heard, even now you have forces withdrawing from Fayetteville under Colonel Siber, do you not? And you are even now *hoping* they are able to make it here to relative safety before being overwhelmed, so that you may consolidate your forces here at Camp Piatt ... am I correct?"

The colonel nodded.

Nathan was thoughtful for a moment, taking several more puffs on the cigar, before continuing, "Well, from my experience, sitting back and *hoping* for a thing is not a very useful strategy. I would suggest you send a large contingent out to meet Siber and hit the enemy as hard as they can ... a full regiment if you have one ready to march, with as much artillery as they can bring with them. But speed is of the essence—send whatever forces you can *now*, within the hour; don't wait for reinforcements to arrive."

The colonel gazed at him wide-eyed, but didn't immediately answer, finally managing, "But—"

"Look, colonel ... I know it seems the opposite of what you *should* be doing—sending men out *toward* the enemy when you are trying to gather them all back here—but believe me, it's the best way ... very likely the *only* way, to protect your forces. Remember ... be the bear, not the deer."

"The bear ... yes ... yes, it makes sense. I will order it. Thank you, Mr. Chambers. But what will *you* do, sir? Will you stay and help me organize the retreat?"

"No. Firstly, I'm not yet convinced you *will* have to retreat. We shall see about that. But secondly ... you'll find I'm not much good at sitting still while there's fighting going on. My men and I will ride out with your regiment to meet the enemy. I wish to see for myself just what General Loring is sending against us."

ಬಿಡಿ೫೧ಬಿಡಿ೫೧ಬಿಡಿ೫೧

When Nathan located his men, Tom shrugged apologetically and said, "It's the best we could do, sir," as he gestured toward the corner of a makeshift corral where the men had tied the horses and were preparing to bed down on the ground next to them.

But Nathan laughed, "Well, then I have good news for you, Tom ... it turns out we'll *not* have to sleep here tonight."

"Oh, that sounds good," Tom answered, brightening up. "Why? Did the colonel offer you some better accommodations?"

"Yes, as a matter of fact ... we'll be spending the night in the saddle riding east. Turns out our day's not yet done," Nathan said, and then turning to the men he said, "Sorry, men ... but we need to saddle back up. The Union forces out east toward Fayetteville are falling back and are hard-pressed by the enemy. We must ride out with whatever men the colonel can muster to do what we can to aid them."

And despite the lateness of the hour, and that they'd already spent a full day in the saddle, Nathan was not at all surprised when there was no grumbling, nor even any sour looks. Instead, he saw nods and shrugs, followed by a very businesslike preparation to depart.

Stan even stepped up to him and grinned broadly, "Finally we kill rebs again, eh Captain?"

Nathan returned the grin, "Yes, Mr. Volkov ... very likely. And likely as many as we please ... and more."

"Is good, Captain ... is *very* good," Stan said, then stepped over and threw his saddle over his stallion Groz's broad back with a single sweep of his huge right arm. Nathan just shook his head in wonder. The tremendous strength and indominable spirit of the gigantic Russian never ceased to amaze him.

Moments later, they led their horses to the gates of the fort where a large contingent of Union soldiers had formed up — what appeared to be four or five hundred men, and a half dozen small, single-horse howitzers.

While the men stood by, Nathan met Colonel Lightburn at the front of the column. Lightburn introduced Nathan to Lieutenant Colonel Augustus Parry of the Forty-Seventh Ohio Infantry.

"Colonel Parry, well met, sir," Nathan said, and then as was his habit, he cut right to the heart of the matter. "How many men have you mustered colonel?"

"Four companies, Mr. Chambers — just under four hundred men, plus half an artillery battery, as you can see," Colonel Parry answered, gesturing toward his formation. Colonel Parry was younger and slightly shorter than Nathan, but also darkly handsome and neatly groomed, with mustache and a thin, pointed patch of chin whiskers underneath, a beard that was sometimes called a "goatee." The man was quick to smile, had a twinkle in his eye, and a confidence to his step that caused Nathan to take an immediate liking to him.

Colonel Lightburn shrugged apologetically and said, "Sorry, Mr. Chambers ... it was all we could muster on such short notice. We will send other companies forward as we can get them ready to march. Unfortunately, even the Forty-Seventh is split into two groups at the moment, and the other under its commander Colonel Elliott is still away out to the north and has not yet arrived at camp."

Nathan nodded, "It will have to do, colonel; at this point, speed is more important than numbers. The good news is the enemy doesn't yet know our manpower ... if we do our job rightly, he'll think we're more than we are. And we must assume Colonel Siber's men can still fight — if turned about to face in the proper direction. Let us pray it shall be enough to stem the tide, gentlemen."

߭߭߭

Tony was beginning to understand that most of soldiering wasn't in the fighting, but rather in the packing, loading, marching, and riding in *preparation* for the actual fighting. He feared when they finally did get to wherever the fighting was he'd be too exhausted to raise his rifle. But he also knew when the time came, the blood would be up and all weariness would leave him, giving him that restless twitchiness, like bugs crawling over his skin, that he'd felt on past occasions when he'd been called upon to fight.

And not only did they *not* enjoy a comfortable night's sleep, but the evening started with a fording of the frigid Kanawha River in the dark by the Forty-Seventh Ohio and the Captain's men. Camp Piatt was on the north side of the river, but the word had come down that Union Colonel Siber was retreating along the south bank, closely pursued by the slaver army, so they had to cross over to engage the enemy and aid their own side.

The river was more than waist deep in places, giving all the Captain's men a good soaking up to the midsection, despite sitting on horseback. Tony felt sympathy for the foot soldiers who'd be even more sodden, likely up to their armpits. But they would at least dry quicker due to their long, forced march, and the evening was still quite warm, following a hot, dusty day.

After an all-night-long, dark, weary ride, with the foot soldiers trudging along behind in long lines trailing off out of sight in the darkness, they finally arrived at a place where the road wound around a thickly wooded hill. The sun was beginning to lighten the eastern sky, threatening to rise above the horizon at any moment.

Someone said the place was called Cotton Hill, though Tony couldn't imagine why—there was no way anyone could grow cotton on such a thickly wooded and sloping piece of ground. Colonel Parry, riding at the front on his pure-white horse, signaled the column to halt, and it was then that Tony noticed Billy Creek had arrived at a gallop, pulling up in front of Colonel Parry and the Captain. Billy talked and gestured as the two men nodded. Though Tony could not catch any of the words, given Billy's usual activities, he assumed it was a report on the movements of the retreating Union army followed by the advancing slavers.

Within moments they were ordered to dismount, and Tony and the others were led by the officers up into the woods of the hill. Fortunately, there were game trails, presumably made by deer and elk, so it was possible to make their way between the dense trees without great difficulty, even leading their horses. Looking back, Tony saw that the foot soldiers of the Forty-Seventh were following, dragging their artillery pieces with them, so he assumed the officers had decided this was the place where they would have their fight.

Tony was relieved they'd not have to ride any further this night ... or day, whichever it now was. When they reached a place on the hillside where the trees had been thinned, they could see out along the road heading further east. In the farthest distance he could make out soldiers on horseback heading toward them — the leading elements of the Union army, he assumed.

But before he had a chance to get anxious about the coming battle, the Captain told them to start digging in and cutting logs for a makeshift breastwork. *No rest for the weary*, Tony decided. He looked over at Big George and shared a rueful grin. Hard work was one thing they knew well, and never shied from. So he went over to his horse and pulled out an axe from where it'd been strapped to the saddle and got to work.

᚜᚜᚜᚜᚜᚜᚜᚜᚜᚜᚜

A half hour later, Colonel Edward Siber, commander in charge of the Union forces that had been forced to withdraw from Fayetteville, stood on Cotton Hill next to Nathan and Lieutenant Colonel Parry, gazing out along the road to the east through a pair of binoculars. Nathan did the same with his brass spyglass, while Parry looked on.

Colonel Parry didn't need an enhanced view to see what was coming: the rebel army, thousands upon thousands, marching in step along the road in long columns, bayonetted rifles on their shoulders, regimental flags flying, and bands playing. It was an awesome and terrifying sight.

But when Nathan lowered his spyglass and looked over at Parry, he was pleased to see the man showed no sign of fear, and even gave him a rueful grin, saying, "Well, Mr. Chambers — what say you *now* to the rebel advance? Still think their numbers may have been exaggerated?"

Nathan snorted a laugh, as Colonel Siber lowered his binoculars and looked their way, "I count six regiments at the least, possibly seven, though it's difficult to tell as the sun has not yet risen high enough to light their entire column," Siber said. He spoke with a heavy German accent, and he too showed only a businesslike demeanor — no sign of trepidation despite the lopsided numbers.

At that moment, a young officer in a captain's uniform stepped up to the colonels and snapped a salute, "Good morning, sirs," he said, grinning broadly.

"Good for men like *you* who love a fight, Captain," Siber answered, returning the salute and the grin, "I believe you will be getting more than you may be wishing for today, my good sir."

Then Siber turned to the other men and said, "Colonel Parry, Mr. Chambers, this is Captain Luther Vance, Fourth Loyal Virginia."

They shook hands, and Nathan said, "Ah, one of ours … Captain, I am Nathan Chambers from Governor Pierpont's office. Happy to meet you, captain."

"Oh … Mr. Chambers … well met, sir! Your reputation precedes you, of course. We in the Loyal Virginia regiments — soon to be *West* Virginia regiments, I understand — are well aware of the good work you've been doing up at Wheeling getting our troops organized, supplied, and trained for the fight, for which I for one thank you, sir."

"Thank you, captain … just doing what I can, though truth be told I'd much rather be wearing *your* uniform right now," he answered with a frown.

"Oh … certainly *not*, sir. From what I've heard they've slated you for a brigadier general at the least, sir, once you've got the new state properly launched and all."

"Thank you for saying so, captain."

Captain Vance then turned to Colonel Siber and asked, "What are your orders, sir? Do you wish for the Fourth to continue in the van, or shall we turn and engage the enemy now that we have reinforcements?" And though Nathan could see the man was clearly tired and his uniform soiled from days of non-stop fighting and travel in the hot, dusty weather, he betrayed no sign of reluctance to perform whatever duties were asked of him.

But Colonel Siber did not immediately answer, once again turning to gaze out at the advancing rebel army, now less than two miles distant. He breathed a heavy sigh, then turned back to the others and answered, "No, captain ... as much as my heart burns to turn and smite the enemy, we are still too few. My responsibility is to preserve this command. I must continue to fall back."

Then he looked at Colonel Parry and asked, "How long can you hold this hill, colonel?"

"However long you need us to, colonel," Parry answered evenly, and snapped a salute.

ЪJԤJЪJԤJЪJԤ

An hour later, Lieutenant Colonel Parry stood behind the log breastwork, raised his sword, then swiped it downward and shouted, *"Fire!"*

The thunderous sound of four hundred rifles firing at once echoed down the valley, and smoke curled up thickly through the trees hanging overhead.

Parry immediately pointed his sword further back and up the hill, at the lieutenant in command of his artillery battery, and made a swiping motion toward the enemy. The artillery immediately erupted, six guns firing a booming volley of high-explosive shells, grapeshot, and cannister at the approaching enemy.

Then Parry cupped his hands to his mouth and shouted, "Reload at the double-quick men, like you never reloaded before!"

In moments, he repeated the order to fire, and once again the Forty-Seventh Ohio and Nathan Chambers' small company of

Texans and freemen unleashed another deadly rifle volley at the advancing enemy.

And once again the musketry was followed by the deafening cacophony of the howitzers.

Then Parry rose up and risked a quick look over the breastworks, then popped back down and shouted, "Reload ... but *hold fire!*"

He turned to Nathan, who was standing next to him, reloading his own rifle, and said, "Well, Mr. Chambers ... that's seems to have taken some of the starch out of them. They're falling back."

"Good ... it'll give us a breath. But they'll soon regroup and come again."

Parry nodded but seemed unconcerned, calmly reloading his revolver. Nathan realized Parry was one of those rare individuals who was born for this type of work; when the fighting was thick and the blood was up, he managed to stay calm and cool, and seemed to even thrive on the action.

Nathan looked in the other direction and saw that his own men seemed similarly unconcerned, reloading their rifles in a very smooth and businesslike manner, preparing for the next assault. Harry the Dog sat next to him, his only sign of excitement was a heavy panting, leaving a long, sticky strand of saliva hanging down from the side of his mouth.

ಬಿಎ೧ಿ೩೮ಬಿಎ೧ಿ೩೮ಬಿಎ೧ಿ೩೮

Two hours later, and so many rifle volleys he'd lost count, Tony glanced over and saw Billy Creek talking with the Captain and Colonel Parry. He hadn't even noticed until this moment that Billy had been missing, but now that he thought about it, he realized Stan had also been absent during the battle. *Out scouting again, as usual*, he decided.

Moments later, the word came down to move out, and then they were falling back, moving through the woods downhill, back the way they'd come toward the road to the west.

As they marched, the Captain turned and gave them a quick update, "Billy was watching our flank to the left and observed a large enemy contingent—several thousands—working their way around the hill. Though he killed a few to slow them, they would have soon flanked us, and we'd have been overrun. So we are falling back. The good news is we've given Colonel Siber a nice head start, and it'll be several more hours before the rebels are sure we've completely deserted the hill. By then, we can set up some unpleasant surprises for them along the road."

ಬಿ೫೧ಶ೮೩ಬಿ೫೧ಶ೮೩ಬಿ೫೧ಶ೮೩

For the rest of the morning, Nathan's men and the Forty-Seventh Ohio served as the rearguard for Colonel Siber's withdrawing army. And when they weren't ambushing and counter-attacking the advancing rebel column, they were cutting trees to throw across the roadway, and lighting fires to any buildings close by to cause a nuisance—Nathan and Colonel Parry used every trick they could think of to slow the enemy and buy more time for the army and its long column of supply wagons to reach safety.

Their withdrawal finally brought them to a place called Montgomery Ferry, which featured a large, flat-bottomed ferry boat that Siber had already used to float his wagons and nearly half his force to the north side of the Kanawha.

There on the south shore, within sight of the ferry landing, they once again met up with Captain Vance of the Fourth Loyal Virginia, who greeted them warmly. The Fourth was once again serving as rearguard for Siber's army, protecting the ferry during the evacuation.

"Good morning, gentlemen ... or rather good afternoon, I should say," Vance said, glancing at a pocket watch he pulled from his pocket, "as I see it is now noon. I trust you've had a pleasant journey thus far ..."

They gave Captain Vance a quick update, after which he relayed the latest orders from Colonel Siber, "Colonel Parry ... Colonel Siber left me to guard the ferry until your arrival, at which point we were to prepare to withdraw from this place. Once the Forty-Fourth Ohio completes their crossing on the ferry, they have orders to destroy Gauley Bridge where it crosses the Gauley River on the north side of the Kanawha and then serve as rear

119

guard for the Colonel's column on *that* side of the river, destroying any remaining Union facilities and supplies in the area as they go.

"And as you can see, only about half of Colonel Siber's column has made it across, so the remainder will continue to fall back along the south bank. My companies and yours are to serve as rear guard. If we march all night, assuming not too many heavy engagements, we should reach Brownstown across the river from Camp Piatt sometime tomorrow morning. Hopefully they'll have arranged a way for us to cross over from there ..." Then he shrugged as if it was of little significance one way or the other.

ຂຍ໑ດຌຉອຂຍ໑ດຌຉອຂຍ໑ດຌຉອ

After a brief nap ordered by the Captain, Tony and the other men spent the remainder of the afternoon and evening in the same way as they'd spent the morning—marching, fighting, cutting trees, lighting fires, marching, and fighting some more.

And all the long night was more of the same. By the time the sun was rising in the morning, Tony could feel his exhaustion down into his bones. But any time he felt like lying down and quitting, he'd look over at Big George, or Henry, or one of the other freemen. Though he could see they were as tired as he, he could also see their determination and fortitude, and there was no way he would let them down. So he kept going, forcing one foot in front of the other.

When the sun peeked over the hills to the east, Tony saw they were coming to a town. And it seemed they would finally get a rest; all the remaining Union forces, several thousands, seemed to be finally stopped and staying in one place for the first time in days.

Then the Captain came and told them to get some rest while they could. So far, the rebel army had *not* arrived—though they'd never been far behind all the previous day and night. So the men caught a little sleep, staking their horses out, then rolling their blankets out on the ground in a grassy field after eating a quick, cold breakfast from their packs.

When they were awakened by the Captain a few hours later, he told them that this place was called Brownstown and was just across the river from the Union fort called Camp Piatt where the Union commander over all of western Virginia was stationed. That seemed like good news to Tony—maybe now that they were joining up with all the Union forces in western Virginia, they could turn the rebels back for good. The Captain said the army would be crossing over to the camp from here by steamboats, which would likely take all that day.

Shortly after they'd re-stowed their packs, it began to rain. At first, they enjoyed the respite from the hot, dusty weather they'd endured the last several days, but as the rain continued and gradually increased, accompanied by a cool breeze, they quickly changed their minds, crouching under the eaves of a barn. They'd have preferred to go inside the building, but it was already crowded to overflowing by Union soldiers attempting to stay dry as they waited their turn to board a steamboat for the north bank.

But as evening drew closer to sundown, and the town seemed to have mostly emptied out, the Captain came and announced they'd *not* be getting on a steamboat yet; the companies of the Fourth Loyal Virginia Regiment under Captain Vance had been ordered to stay and guard the town to prevent the rebels from using it to bombard the fort across the river. And the Captain said if the Fourth was staying, they were too.

Tony looked around at the others, Big George, Henry, Cobb, and Phinney—who'd never complained nor shirked, despite his missing arm—and they shared grim, determined looks.

Up 'til now, they'd not had as much trouble from the white Union soldiers as he had expected—only a few sideways looks, and a few sarcastic remarks, but nothing serious. He wasn't sure if that was on account of the Captain's intimidating presence—or maybe Big Stan's—or if it was because they'd shown they could fight. Whatever the case, he was determined not to show any weakness now. He wanted to prove that the freemen were every bit as tough and determined as the white soldiers from Texas. And despite his exhaustion, he felt a twinge of pride that they'd held up their end … so far.

Just before midnight, Captain Vance of the Fourth stepped up to where Nathan sat on the bank of an earthen berm the Union Army had hastily thrown up to protect Brownstown. Nathan had spent the last hour gazing out into the darkness with his spyglass, looking for any sign of enemy movement in the moonlight. But he'd seen nothing, and Billy had also reported in that he could find no sign of the enemy in the immediate vicinity. So Nathan was taking a break to enjoy the warmth of a cigar on an evening that had finally cooled off from the previous day's heat.

He stood to greet Captain Vance, but resisted the strong urge to share a salute, remembering his own lack of military status. "Captain," he said, and extended his hand instead.

"Good evening, Mr. Chambers," Vance responded, taking the proffered hand and shaking it firmly. "I have a bit of good news, finally; I've received orders to withdraw to Camp Piatt, effective immediately, given the dearth of activity by our rebel friends. There's a steamboat awaiting us at the river."

"Seems reasonable ... and more than a little welcomed. I don't know about your men, but mine are nearly done in by the non-stop fighting and marching of the past few days. Odd though ... that the rebs have suddenly gone quiet. Wonder why ..."

"Well," Captain Vance answered with a grin, "perhaps they're also done in, sir. After all, we *have* given them all holy hell the last few days on the march."

"True ... could be ... could be."

Then Nathan turned to the side and called out, "Tom ... Jim ... let's pack it up. We're finally bugging out of here."

After an uneasy and watchful steamboat crossing, Nathan and his men rode slowly in through the gates of Camp Piatt, which was full to overflowing with Union soldiers, most sleeping on any available patch of ground. But the thing that immediately caught Nathan's attention was a long line of supply wagons, fully loaded, and preparing to depart to the northwest continuing the long retreat.

He heard a groan, and turning to his right saw Tony rolling his eyes. "What's the matter, Tony? Don't like the look of this camp?"

"It ain't the camp Captain, it's the wagons. If they's all leaving, it means we will be too. I was hoping we'd finally stop and put up a fight. Getting tired o' all this hiking about and am ready to put a stop to them slavers. Right here seems a good enough place to do it."

Nathan snorted a laugh, "I can't disagree with the sentiment, Tony … I much prefer a fight to all this marching around. But this camp wasn't built to withstand a siege against overwhelming numbers. More of a staging area than a fort. Oh, we could put up a good fight, all right. But with the numbers coming against us, I'd not give us very good odds on the outcome."

He thought about it another moment, gazing about the camp, envisioning the action in his mind's eye. He slowly nodded, "Yep … we'd put up one hell of a fight all right … and then we'd all be dead."

Tony frowned, but nodded. He knew better than to argue military matters with the Captain.

ɮʊ๑๏ʗᴈɮʊ๑๏ʗᴈɮʊ๑๏ʗᴈ

They received the good news and the bad all in the same set of orders, relayed to Nathan by Captain Vance. The good news was, because they'd been the last to arrive at Camp Piatt, the Fourth would be the last to depart, allowing them nearly a full night's sleep for once. The bad news was, because they'd be the last to set out, they would once again take on the difficult and dangerous task of serving as the rearguard for the entire army, charged with holding off the enemy throughout the day's march.

But Nathan suspected it had more to do with the competence with which Vance had performed up to now, and that Lightburn knew Nathan and his men would stay with them to assist.

In any case, for the first time in several days Nathan and his men got several much needed solid hours of sleep, though they were already up and ready as dawn lit the eastern sky.

Captain Vance had also been given orders to destroy the camp and any supplies left in it before their departure, so the Mountain

123

Meadow's men and the soldiers of the Fourth Loyal Virginia Regiment set fire to everything that'd been left behind in camp, after commandeering anything useful they could carry. The supplies to be burned sadly included thousands of pounds of food, fodder for horses, hundreds of new uniforms, shoes, hats, and everything else required for a fort of soldiers.

Nathan stepped up next to Tony in the doorway to a storage room, inside of which were stacked hundreds of pairs of new shoes. Tony stood gazing open-mouthed at the site, holding a burning torch in his right hand. He gazed about the room in awe, then looked over at Nathan and said, "I ain't owned but a handful of shoes my entire life ..." Nathan nodded, and they shared a rueful grin.

Then Tony looked back at the shoes, shrugged and threw the torch in, saying, "Reckon it's better to burn 'em than give 'em over to the slavers."

Nathan just patted Tony on the back and nodded his agreement, as the fire quickly spread across the floor of the room.

ༀༀༀༀༀༀༀༀༀༀༀ

When they marched into Charleston at midday, Nathan was dismayed to see the change in the city from what they'd seen just a few days before. The streets were clogged with panicked civilians, carrying away their goods in every imaginable manner — on wagons, carts, horseback, or boats on the river. Many others carried only their children, heading up into the surrounding hills to avoid the imminent battle. Nathan shook his head in mild annoyance when he learned it was Colonel Lightburn who had issued a warning to the civilians of Charleston to abandon the city in order to avoid getting caught up in the battle that was sure to come.

Though he couldn't disagree with the sentiment of making sure civilians were out of harm's way, the colonel's premature warning was now causing his own army to be impeded and delayed from arriving in the city; whereas if he would've waited to issue the warning, these same civilians might well have impeded the rebels instead. And since this was disputed territory, the rebels were no more likely to want to endanger civilians than the Union army was.

When they caught up with the rest of Lightburn's army, they were pleased to see Lieutenant Colonel Parry of the Forty-Seventh Ohio once again taking up primary guard duty, having dug in behind a fence line in the middle of town. This time, when Nathan and Captain Vance approached Parry, he was accompanied by a full Colonel, whom Parry introduced as his commanding officer, the man in charge of the entire Forty-Seventh, Colonel Lyman Elliott. Elliott was taller and more serious looking than Parry, with a full dark beard but no mustache—friendly seeming, but more inclined to smile with his eyes than with his mouth.

And after a brief conversation it occurred to Nathan that Elliott and Parry seemed a perfect complement to each other, much as he and Tom were. Where Parry was enthusiastic, daring, and bold, Elliott was cool, thoughtful, and seemingly unflappable, the type of person who might keep a clear head even as the world came crashing down all around him. It seemed the Forty-Seventh Ohio, either by good fortune or good planning, had ended up with an exceptionally competent set of commanding officers. Nathan thought it likely this was why Lightburn continued to assign them the most difficult and dangerous duties.

Colonel Elliott gave them a quick update on the disposition of Union forces; Colonel Lightburn had moved his main column across the Elk River via a suspension bridge just north of where that river joined the Kanawha in downtown Charleston. All his wagons were now making their way across, but that would take several hours to complete.

The Forty-Seventh was to remain on the east side of the Elk River, to form a forward line of defense to slow and harass the rebel advance as they entered the city in order to give the wagons time to make it safely across the Elk River.

Then Elliott relayed Captain Vance's marching orders from Colonel Lightburn; the Fourth Loyal Virginia was to cross the Elk River via the bridge, then take up position to the far north of the Union line to protect the Union left flank and to use their artillery and rifles firing across the river to also protect the left of the Forty-

125

Seventh in their advanced position on the east side of river. The Forty-Seventh's right flank could then be anchored on the Kanawha River.

Upon hearing these instructions to Captain Vance, Nathan turned to Tom and Jim and said, "Gentlemen … as much as I wish to support the Fourth Loyal Virginia—they are our own troops, after all, and Captain Vance has proved himself a stalwart officer who deserves our aid—I think we should remain on the front lines with the Forty-Seventh to aid as we may in the most forward defense. This seems to me the best opportunity to slow the rebel advance.

Tom and Jim nodded their agreement, so they said their goodbyes to Captain Vance, wished him well, and re-joined the ranks of the Forty-Seventh Ohio.

ಬಬಬಬಬಬಬಬಬಬಬಬ

The first line of hasty breastworks thrown down by the Forty-Seventh was next to a house called "Rosedale" that someone said belonged to a colonel, though nobody seemed to know which side he was on. The house featured a solid log barn and split rail fence that looked like it might form a good foundation for their defensive position, so a hasty breastwork was thrown together. And at first that seemed to prove true; the first advance by the rebels was repulsed by a strong volley of rifle fire from the Forty-Seventh, along with Nathan's own small company.

But when the Confederates set up an artillery battery on a low rise on the south side of the Kanawha and began a bombardment of the position, it quickly became untenable. So Colonel Elliott ordered a fallback.

But even as Nathan and his men were moving back toward the new position, keeping low to prevent enemy sharpshooters from targeting them, a high explosive shell burst off to Nathan's left, knocking him to the ground with the force of the blast.

When he picked himself up, his ears were ringing and he was covered with dust, but was otherwise unhurt. He turned to his right and saw that Tom had also been knocked down, but was likewise sitting up—stunned but apparently unharmed. Harry the Dog lay on the ground, rubbing his paws against his ears — likely the ringing had affected him even more, but he didn't appear to be bleeding anywhere.

But off to the left, closer to where the shell had burst, all of Nathan's men had been knocked to the ground. Nathan and Tom scrambled in that direction to check on the others, even as enemy rifle fire continued to impact around them and zip past over their heads.

Jim was already up, and the freemen were also stirring, along with Jamie, Georgie, and Zeke. Billy and Stan were nowhere in sight, but that wasn't unusual; they were likely out somewhere guarding their flanks.

But then Nathan saw William bending over something, and his heart sank. Someone was wounded.

Nathan scrambled over and looked to where William knelt. Phillipe was there, gazing upward with a glazed, unseeing look, a deep gash oozing blood from the right side of his head.

Then another shell burst overhead, this one slightly further away, but the force still knocked them all flat to the ground and covered them in a cloud of dust.

"How bad is he?" Nathan shouted at William, once the dust had settled again, and his ears had stopped ringing.

"I can't tell, Captain … it may be bad. He can't walk, that's certain."

"Well, we can't stay here … we've got to move or we're all dead," Nathan said.

"I got him," a deep voice said, and before Nathan could answer, Big George, the largest of the freemen, knelt down and scooped Phillipe up in his massive arms. He grunted as he stood and hefted the wounded man's weight. Then without another word he turned and trotted after the retreating Union soldiers. The rest of Nathan's men immediately followed.

The Forty-Seventh set up a new line of defense several hundred yards further west than the first one, this time in a more densely built-up part of town, where they'd be less vulnerable to artillery fire.

Big George laid Phillipe down carefully on the ground, and William immediately went to work on him, examining and probing his wound, then wrapping a bandage around his head.

When Nathan came and gave William a questioning look, the latter said, "I think he'll be okay—seems he was hit a glancing blow by a piece of shrapnel. When we're out of the direct firing line I'll need to stitch him up, but for now he'll be all right. Not bleeding too badly. But he'll have one hell of a headache and may be a bit wobbly on his feet for a while."

Nathan nodded, and thanked William for his efforts. Then Nathan leaned over Phillipe and saw that he was conscious, and seemed to be focusing his eyes better. "How you feeling, Phillipe?" he asked.

Phillipe nodded, then said, "Never better, Captain ..." in a raspy, wavering voice and smiled, then closed his eyes. Nathan thought he might have passed out, but Phillipe opened his eyes again and said, "your freemen ... they can fight ..."

Nathan nodded and smiled, "You take it easy now, Phillipe."

₪₪₪₪₪₪₪₪₪₪

The new line of defense proved more durable than the first. And Nathan's initial impression of the two commanding officers of the Forty-Seventh was soon reinforced in spades; Lieutenant Colonel Parry boldly rode his white horse back and forth along the Union lines, encouraging the men and daring the rebels to shoot him from his saddle, shaking his sword at them and taunting them. And even in the thick of the fighting, the rebels could be heard to curse at him, even as his own men cheered him on as he rode past.

And Colonel Elliott proved as cool as Nathan had suspected he was, calmly walking up and down the lines, handing out cartridges and encouraging the men as they ducked behind the breastworks, bullets zipping past.

At one point, the colonel's hat was shot off his head. He calmly reached down, picked it up, briefly examined the bullet hole before placing it back on his head. Then he continued down the line as if nothing unusual had just happened.

But there came a time when the firing became so intense from both sides that even the Forty-Seventh's two colonels were forced to lie flat on the ground, as bullets tore through the air like angry bees. Anyone standing would've been immediately cut down.

Nathan, lying flat on his back to load his rifle, looked to his left and saw Stan loading his own rifle. Stan's eyes were squeezed shut to keep out a steady rain of splinters falling on his face from incoming bullets impacting against the top of the log breastwork above him. But Stan finished loading, swiped his hand across his face, then rolled over, slipped the rifle barrel into a chink in the logs, and fired. He immediately rolled back over, then glanced over at Nathan and grinned, "Is much fun, eh, Captain?"

Nathan shook his head, then rolled back over and fired his own rifle. Harry the Dog crouched next to him, and for the first time did not seem inclined to get up and move around, as if he too understood that any movement at this point would likely mean instant death.

Then there was a short respite; the incoming rounds from the rebels had suddenly ceased. A moment later, Nathan heard a great wailing shout: the dreaded rebel yell!

He looked to his left and saw Colonel Parry stand up and look out. Parry immediately shouted out, "Company will stand to, and prepare to fire on my command!"

The men of the Forty-Seventh all stood to their feet, and those whose rifles weren't yet reloaded worked feverishly to finish the job. Nathan looked out and saw what Parry had seen; a hundred yards out and coming fast was a row of rebels — an all-out assault, left, right, and center, intending to overrun the Union lines once and for all.

"Aim at their waistbelts, boys, then reload faster than ever you have. And if they get close, give 'em steel!" Parry shouted, *"Ready ... Aim ... Fire!"*

The Union rifles erupted, eight hundred strong. This was quickly followed by the bellowing of artillery fire, as the Forty-Seventh's artillery battery also let loose at the rebel charge with grapeshot and cannister.

"Company will fire at will!" Colonel Parry shouted out. Union rifles continued to pop in a steady stream as men loaded and fired as rapidly as they could.

But after a few moments it became increasingly clear to Nathan that it was *not* going to be enough—that the rebels' charge would sweep over their position before the attack could be stopped, and then it would be hand-to-hand with bayonets. To make matters worse, the Confederates were now too close to the Union lines for the federal artillery to target them without risking hitting their own men behind their makeshift breastworks.

Nathan turned to Tom, and shouted, "Have the men drop their rifles and pull their pistols," and even as he said it, he was already following his own orders, letting his rifle fall as he immediately pulled two pistols from holsters at his hips. "Have them target anyone out front, but fire off every round they have—don't hold anything back!"

Not waiting for an answer, Nathan raised up over the breastwork and began firing. In a moment the other pistols of his tiny company roared to life off to his right. Each of his men had at least two, six-shot revolvers, and several of them carried four. And though the pistols were of a smaller caliber than the rifles, and terribly inaccurate at any distance, with two pistols each man could fire off two shots per second versus two or three rounds per minute from a rifle. Nathan understood the math; fifteen men firing twelve or more rounds a piece in just over six seconds was the equivalent of having an extra two hundred men with rifles firing off a close-range volley.

With the rebels quickly closing the distance, the rapid fire of the revolvers worked to devastating effect. Colonel Parry looked over at the noise, saw what was happening, grinned, then turned to fire off all six from his own revolver, as quickly as he could cock the hammer and squeeze the trigger.

After Nathan had emptied both his Colts, he glanced over to see how his men were doing. Billy, Stan, Georgie, and Jamie were still firing off shots, but everyone else had emptied their revolvers and were starting to reload.

Even Phillipe had risen up and fired his shots before slumping back to a sitting position on the ground, looking pale and drained, the white bandage around his head beginning to show a red stain where the blood was oozing through. Nathan was not surprised to see William standing next to Phillipe, gazing down at him with a concerned look. But he *was* surprised to see Big George stood just on Phillipe's other side, and he too gazed down at their wounded companion with a furrowed brow.

Then Nathan glanced further down the line past Tony, Cobb, and Henry, and saw Phinney staring back at him. They met eyes and Phinney beamed. Phinney held up his empty Colt and blew a twisting trail of smoke off the barrel before holstering it. Nathan returned the smile, and nodded. With only one hand Phinney had emptied both of his revolvers, nearly as quickly as the others had done it using two hands.

When the smoke cleared, the rebel charge had faltered; those still standing were falling back. Union rifle shots continued to target them as they attempted to make their way back to the safety their own lines, dragging wounded comrades with them. Finally, Colonel Parry called for a ceasefire and immediate reloading.

Then, in the relative quiet, Nathan heard a more distant popping of rifle fire. Looking back across the Elk River over his left shoulder he saw puffs of gun smoke drifting up from the far side of the river. The Fourth Loyal Virginia had also opened up on the rebel attack from the west side of the river, doing their part to blunt the attack. *Thank you, Captain Vance,* Nathan thought.

But even as the gun smoke drifted lazily away through the hot air, Nathan thought he saw a familiar figure making his way back toward the enemy lines. The man was stout of build but vigorous, and unlike the others, was making no attempt to rescue any of his wounded comrades. And though he couldn't be sure through the thick haze of smoke, Nathan thought the man might be missing his left hand. He turned and grabbed Tom's sleeve, "Look, Tom ... there!" he said, pointing out across the field.

Tom gazed out toward where Nathan gestured, but saw only indistinct forms of the enemy moving away from them through the thick, swirling smoke. "What is it, sir?" Tom asked.

But when Nathan looked again, the man was gone. He scowled, emitting a low, wordless growl. "A man ... tall but stocky ... and seemingly missing his left hand ..." he finally said.

"*Walters?!* Here?! Are you sure, sir?"

"No ... no, I'm *not*, Tom. But from now on I'll be keeping a close watch out for him ... and I'd appreciate it if you'd do the same."

"Oh, you can count on *that*, sir. I would dearly love to put a bullet in that mean old bastard."

"You and me both, Tom. You and me both ..."

ഇൽഇൽരുരുഇൽഇൽരുരുഇൽഇൽരുരു

The back-and-forth gun battle continued throughout the morning and into the early afternoon. Shortly after noon, the sun broke out, and the battleground became steaming hot, adding even more discomfort to an already uncomfortable situation for the Union forces on the front lines.

Finally, a courier arrived from Colonel Lightburn ordering Colonel Elliott to withdraw, burning all Union facilities as he came.

As bullets continued to fly, Colonel Elliott stepped up to the front lines and called out, "Attention, Forty-Seventh Ohio! By companies, to the rear. Into line, parade march!"

Nathan was astounded; in the heat of battle, Elliott would not allow his men to turn and run, rather he forced them to file out neatly in parade formation. "Show some pride, gentlemen," Elliott called out, "don't give them the satisfaction of showing any fear," then he made a show of laughing aloud, holding up his hat with the bullet hole through it, and flapping the tails of his uniform coat, showing where a bullet had passed through it near the pocket. "See, men ... these damned rebs have been shooting at me all day and can't ever hit me!" for which he received a resounding cheer from his men as they marched past, heading to the rear.

Nathan exchanged a look with Tom, who shook his head and said, "The man clearly has cast iron testicles."

Nathan snorted a laugh and nodded his agreement, "Come on, men … time we also made our exit," Nathan called out.

In leapfrog fashion, the companies of the Forty-Seventh Ohio fell back toward the bridge, with half the companies providing covering fire as the other half stood and calmly marched to the rear, as if at inspection on the parade ground back at camp. And as they reached the center of town, torches were put to the remaining army stores, touching off a conflagration that threatened to burn down much of downtown Charleston.

Then, even as Nathan and his men along with the last four companies of the Forty-Seventh led by Colonel Parry approached the bridge across the Elk River, the rebels launched an assault with a full regiment across a cornfield north of the bridge—a last-ditch effort to cut off the Forty-Seventh and annihilate them. But the Fourth Loyal Virginia rose up from their positions on the far side of the river and unleashed a tremendous, withering barrage of rifle fire, followed by a volley of artillery that forced the rebels back, allowing the Union forces to make good their escape.

And as Nathan and his men crossed the suspension bridge, they could see that the stays had already been cut, and men were standing by with axes to cut the cables. When Nathan rode across he could feel the bridge deck swaying sickeningly beneath Millie's hooves.

Lieutenant Colonel Parry, astride his white horse, was the last man to cross. When his horse's hooves hit solid ground, the men started swinging their axes, even as rebel sharpshooters began to target them from the far side of the river. But the cables proved stubbornly resistant to their efforts, and their job was quickly becoming dangerously risky as bullets kicked up dirt all around them.

Colonel Parry jumped down from his horse, strode over to a cannon positioned next to the bridge, and ordered the artillery men to aim it at the bridge cables. He shouted for the axe wielding soldiers to fall back, to which they quickly complied. Parry then stepped up to the cannon, took hold of the firing lanyard, and yanked, creating the spark that ignited the explosive charge of powder. With a roar and belch of smoke, the great gun sent a load of cannister shot hurling toward the bridge, ripping through the cables holding it. In seconds, the entire structure crashed into the river, leaving only the stone columns standing on each side of the gap.

Colonel Parry remounted his horse and doffed his hat to the cheers of his men.

ಚಿ೮೧೦೩೦೪೪೪೦೪೪೮೩೦೪೦೩೦೪

As a reward for their efforts holding back the rebels, Colonel Lightburn gave the Forty-Seventh Ohio the "honor" of leading the withdrawal, which was also a way of giving them a break from the heavy day of fighting they'd already endured, as he did not expect there to be any fighting at the front of the column during its march to the Ohio River.

And Lightburn had ordered his wagon train of some seven hundred wagons to depart Charleston at 2:00 p.m., taking the road north toward Ravenswood, Virginia on the banks of the Ohio, where they were to ford the river and cross over to a more defensible position on the Union-controlled side.

In the meantime, a gun battle raged across the Kanawha River to the south, and the Elk River to the east, with neither side able to gain any great advantage. While the rebels held the high ground, from which they could pound the Union forces with artillery, the Union forces had plenty of good cover behind which they could dig in and present limited targets for the enemy. And if the Confederates tried to cross the river, the Union forces would rise up and drive them back with devasting rifle and artillery fire.

Colonel Lightburn's goal in the battle was now simply to hold the rebels at bay long enough for the wagon train to escape to the north, with its thousands of tons of supplies, worth millions of dollars to the Union cause. After that, the army itself could be systematically withdrawn. But when Nathan and the Forty-Seventh's colonels arrived at the rear of the wagon train at 3:00 p.m., it was standing still, despite Colonel Lightburn's orders to the contrary.

Colonel Lightburn was there in a heated discussion with the trainmaster when Nathan and Colonel Elliott arrived.

134

"Colonel Lightburn, why isn't this wagon train moving, sir?" Nathan asked. He could feel a great weariness settling in, and knew his patience was wearing thin, so he reminded himself to keep his temper in check.

"I … I'm not quite sure," Lightburn answered, tentatively, "I've ordered it started, but I … I can't seem to get it going …"

Nathan reached in his pocket, grabbed a cigar, stuck it in his mouth and bit down hard.

"Well, I sure as hell can," he said, then turned to Colonel Elliott and said, "let me borrow a company of your cavalry, Colonel, if you would. Have the rest of your men ready to march in fifteen minutes." Elliott gave him an amused look, and nodded, giving the order to the cavalry captain next to him to accompany Mr. Chambers.

Nathan then turned his horse, spurring down the line, headed toward the front of the train to see what was causing the holdup. His men followed in his wake, along with the cavalry company of the Forty-Seventh. And as they went, they witnessed a disheartening chaos that raised Nathan's ire: army wagons loaded with civilians' personal effects, or whole families of civilians, teamsters who'd stopped their wagons to feed themselves, blocking those behind them, others actively dumping their loads so they could make a quick escape should the rebels attack. At each point where something was amiss, Nathan dispatched several of the cavalry soldiers to whip things into shape — sometimes quite literally if the teamsters were resistant to their orders.

Fifteen minutes later, Colonel Elliott smiled broadly at Colonel Lightburn as the wagons ahead of him suddenly lurched into motion.

"Colonel … I'll see you at the Ohio River, sir," Elliott said, snapping a salute to the commanding officer, who returned it smartly.

₧₧₧₧₧₧₧₧₧

After getting the wagon train started, and saying their goodbyes to Colonels Elliott and Parry of the Forty-Seventh Ohio,

Nathan and his men returned to where the Fourth Loyal Virginia Regiment was still dug in at the very north end of the Union line along the Elk River. It was a happy but subdued reunion with Captain Vance and the other western Virginia men, as the Fourth had once again been given rearguard duty for the impending withdrawal.

So they hunkered down and endured a long day of trading volleys with the rebels. Despite the almost non-stop gunfire, remaining in one place for several hours in the relative safety of a well-dug-in and fortified position allowed William the opportunity to properly treat Phillipe's wound. He removed the bandage, cleaned out the wound with whiskey—which to Phillipe's credit he never complained about—then stitched it up and replaced the bandage with a clean one. After which Phillipe said simply, "That was neatly done, Mr. Jenkins. I thank you."

Late in the afternoon, the Confederates attempted another crossing of the Elk, this time in boats, hoping to finally dislodge the stubborn western Virginians. But once again the withering rifle fire from Captain Vance's men and Nathan Chambers' small company forced the rebels to call off the attack.

And as evening turned to night, Captain Vance realized they could not see from their position whether all the Union forces had already made good their withdrawal. So he asked Nathan if he would send Billy out to reconnoiter. A half hour later, Billy returned to report the Union forces were all gone, leaving the Fourth all alone against the entire rebel army! Captain Vance immediately ordered a withdrawal, to which his men and Nathan's happily complied. With torches in hand, they set fire to several buildings along the road as they pulled back, to discourage the rebels from following, should they have a mind.

But the fires they lit had the unintended consequence of illuminating their march, dangerously exposing them to rebel sharpshooters as they withdrew. Fortunately, they suffered no further casualties that day, despite dodging intermittent gunfire.

⁕⁔⁖⁗⁕⁔⁖⁗⁕⁔⁖⁗

The next day, when Nathan and the Fourth Loyal Virginia had finally caught up with the tail end of the withdrawing Union column, Tony was surprised to find a large number of civilians following in the retreating army's wake, including several hundred black men, women, and children, both freemen and runaway slaves, none of whom wanted to be left to the mercy of the advancing rebel army.

He spoke with several of them as they rode past, meeting wide-eyed stares and plenty of gawking from black faces when they noticed he and the other freemen were fully armed as soldiers.

"How'd y'all get them guns, anyhow?" one incredulous young man asked.

Tony thought for a moment and then answered, "I reckon we *earned* them." He turned and looked at Big George who nodded his agreement and smiled.

ᔕᗞᗢᑫᯤᔕᗞᗢᑫᯤᔕᗞᗢᑫᯤ

Tuesday September 16, 1862 – near Ravenswood, Virginia:

"Colonel … Colonel Lightburn … a moment of your time, if you please, sir," Nathan said, as he pulled Millie up in front of the Union commander, where he stood with several of his staff officers on a grassy bank at the edge of the Ohio River, watching the men of the Forty-Fourth Ohio Infantry wading across the wide ford.

"Ah, Mr. Chambers … Good morning, sir. Good morning, *indeed* … and it seems we shall finally have a good *day*; in moments we will have completed our escape into Ohio."

"Yes, colonel. And congratulations to you on that. It is … a great accomplishment and you deserve much praise for it, but—"

"Oh, but much of the success of this endeavor has been thanks to *you* and your valiant men, Mr. Chambers. From the moment you arrived, you have set the tone for our fighting retreat … with emphasis on the *fighting* part. Without *that* … well, I can only imagine the disastrous rout that may have occurred."

"Thank you for saying so, colonel, but I came here to speak with you about a matter of concern …"

"Oh? What is *that*, Mr. Chambers?"

"I am wondering about the civilians, sir …"

"The civilians? What about them?"

"Well, I see the Forty-Fourth has nearly finished their crossing, and they are the last of your command. But we have several hundreds of pro-Union civilians yet on *this* side. Once your men have departed, these people will be entirely without protection and subject to deadly reprisals from the enemy, should the civilians either stay, or try to ford the river.

"My scouts report that various elements of the enemy, both regular and irregular, have been shadowing our movements as we have approached the river. I fear once your men's presence has been removed, it may go ill for our civilians …"

Lightburn looked back toward the field where the civilians had gathered as the Army crossed the river. He sighed, "I sympathize, Mr. Chambers, of course. You know that throughout this campaign I have done everything I could to aid them — warning them when battles were imminent, assisting them with transport when possible, and so on.

"But now my orders are to get the army across the river, and then march them to Point Pleasant post haste. General in chief Halleck is concerned the enemy may choose to attack there next, and we may not have a moment to lose. We *must* have our defenses in place and ready before the enemy arrives.

"Though of course I can't *order* you to do anything, I *recommend* you and your men do likewise, Mr. Chambers. The civilians, I'm afraid, are not the Army's problem."

Nathan scowled, and said, "Colonel, I am an official of the Restored Government of Virginia … and these are fellow Virginians … and fellow Americans. They may not be the Army's problem, but they *are my* problem. Good day, sir!"

Without waiting for the colonel's reply, he pulled hard on Millie's reins, and spurred back toward where his men waited at the edge of the woods.

"What's the word, sir?" Tom asked as Nathan pulled up to a hard stop and dismounted.

"The word is, the civilians are not the Army's problem; they are on their own," Nathan answered, with a dark frown.

Tony stepped up and said, "But, Captain sir … we can't just leave them here … they'll be slaughtered for sure, or worse …"

Nathan gave Tony a hard look, "You ought to know me better than *that* by now, Tony …

"Georgie, Jamie, and Phinney … go get the people organized and moving toward the river—all that wish to go. Let them know we'll provide them with protection, but they must move *now*, and move quickly, taking only the barest essentials. We'll likely be outnumbered, and outgunned, so we can't hold the enemy off indefinitely. Get the people across as quick as may be, then we'll follow as best we can.

"The rest of us … tie the horses here by the riverbank, saddled and ready to make a hasty retreat once the civilians are across. Then we'll move off into the woods there, past the field where the civilians are camped, and set up a defensive perimeter. I am assuming Billy will find us and report back as he can.

"Let's move!"

༄༅༂༃༄༅༂༃༄༅༂༃

"The enemy comes," Billy said as he leapt over the log Nathan and Tom were huddled behind, slipping in next to them. Tom immediately handed him a loaded rifle, and Billy said, "Thank you, Sergeant Clark.

"There is a large company of bushwhackers—fifty at the least, with rifles. No regulars, though. Less than two hundred yards out, coming along the road. They move cautiously, spread wide. It seems they know we are here, or suspect it …"

Nathan looked at Tom and said, "If it's Walters … we've fought him too many times … He's smart … and likely he's started learning our tricks."

Tom nodded, but said nothing.

Billy tipped his hat at the Captain, then crawled off to their right to inform Stan and his group of the enemy's arrival. Tom did the same to the left where Jim was posted, returning after a few minutes.

"It's a good defensive position, sir," Tom said, "They'll have to squeeze by this point to get at the civilians ... but *fifty?!* We are only twelve ... not very good odds."

Nathan nodded, but said nothing. There was nothing to say. They had no choice but to fight, regardless of the odds, if they wished to save the civilians.

And then something hit hard against the log in front of them like the blow from a hammer. And a split second later they heard the distinctive *pop* of a rifle shot in the near distance. The battle was on ... and Nathan had a sudden sick feeling in the pit of his stomach; he'd forgotten to quote a Bible passage before the engagement, as he'd always done in the past. He feared that might be a very evil portent ...

ဆဝ ဿဝ ဿဝ ဿဝ ဿဝ ဿဝ ဿဝ

An hour later, what seemed like days, Nathan peeked out over the top of a grassy berm, his eyes gazing down the sights of his rifle. He saw several puffs of rising gun smoke in the woods, but seeing no actual enemy, he quickly dropped back down. He dared not waste a shot at this point, without a clear target. They were running dangerously low on balls and powder.

This was their third fallback point since the battle had begun, and still the enemy pressed them, trying to either overwhelm them from the front, or flank them to one side or the other. But Nathan's men were experienced fighters and not easily outmaneuvered, so the battle waged on, despite the lopsided odds.

Nathan risked a quick glance back over his shoulder toward the river. He saw the water was now clear of human traffic for the first time since the enemy's arrival; the civilians had finally all made it across. *Time to go,* he thought, ... *but how?*

If they made a run for it, the enemy would simply shoot them down as they made their way across the wide river, forced to move slowly, with no cover and no means to return fire. Not a very appealing prospect.

Then Jim called out, "Hey, Captain ... there's a cannon over here ..."

"What?!" Nathan called out.

"Looks like it was left behind 'cause the carriage is busted ... but it's still loaded ... looks like grapeshot."

"*Grapeshot?!* I'm coming," Nathan said, slipping his rifle onto his back by the strap, and scrambling on all fours toward where he'd heard Jim's voice. His mind was already racing with the prospect ... grapeshot was the artillery equivalent of a shotgun; rather than a single, iron ball, it consisted of dozens of smaller balls the size of large grapes that spread out after firing, ripping through anything in their path. It was a foot soldier's worst nightmare. *If we can give them a taste of that ... they'll not be wanting any more, that's certain,* Nathan thought as he crawled.

But when he got to where Jim crouched, he saw the cannon was indeed as Jim had described: primed and loaded with grapeshot, though the firing lanyard was missing so they'd have to set it off with a match. But it was all for naught; the wooden undercarriage was completely shattered, apparently having been hit by an incoming lead ball. The barrel of the cannon lay on the ground, with one good wheel sticking up, the other completely broken, laying in pieces underneath.

Nathan looked at Jim and shook his head, "There's no way we can fire it without the carriage, Jim."

Jim eyed him for a long moment, then nodded. Nathan thought it was the first time he detected even a hint of fear or defeat in the eyes of the man who'd been fighting Indians since before he'd had to shave. But they were badly outnumbered and nearly out of ammunition, with no clear avenue of escape. Their prospects were quickly dwindling.

"I will lift," a voice said.

Nathan looked to his other side and saw Stan crouching there, gazing over at the cannon.

"*What?!*" Nathan said, "The thing must weigh nearly half a ton ..."

Stan shrugged, "I will lift ... you and Sergeant Jim roll log under to hold. Then we fire ... kill many rebs ... is good."

Nathan gazed at Stan, opened mouthed. Then turned to Jim, who just shrugged. So Nathan turned back to Stan and said, "Okay ... let's do it."

"Company will lay down covering fire, then prepare to withdraw to the river ... on my command," Nathan called out, in a voice intended to reach his men but not to carry to the enemy.

Jim, who'd been looking around for something to put under the carriage, said, "Here, sir ... a piece of a log that may serve ..."

Nathan scrambled over and took one side, while Jim hefted the other. "One, two, three ..." Nathan said, and the two of them groaned as they lifted the piece of tree that was a foot and a half in diameter and nearly four feet long, sawed evenly on one end, but broken and jagged on the other.

Nathan called out, "Company, commence firing!" as he and Jim staggered toward the cannon, dropping the log a few feet from the shattered carriage wheel. Steady gunfire erupted from Nathan's men on both sides, which was returned three-fold by the enemy. Nathan and Jim rolled the log closer along the uneven ground, gasping from their efforts as bullets zipped overhead.

Stan then stepped up, stooped, seized the cannon barrel in both arms, and heaved. Nathan watched from behind, as the muscles of the big man bulged; his back seemed to expand as he strained against the impossible load. At first nothing moved, and Nathan was sure the weight was just too great, even for Stan's tremendous strength, and he was about to call out for Big George to come and assist. But then there was movement, subtle and slow at first, but gaining speed. With a tremendous groan the huge piece of iron was upright once again.

Nathan and Jim immediately shoved the log underneath the carriage. But the ground was sloping, so they had to hold it in position. With another loud grunt, Stan laid the broken right-hand side of the carriage on top of the log.

The whole thing listed badly to the right, and Nathan feared it might slip off. But a moment later, it still held.

Jim jumped up and eyed along the barrel, as Nathan dug in his heels and pushed with all his strength to keep the log from rolling away. "We need 'er about twelve degrees right, to target the enemy," Jim said, looking over at Stan, almost apologetically.

Stan's face was a dark red from the strain and he was too out of breath to speak, but he nodded, reached down, gripped the barrel once again, braced his legs, and pulled hard, and pivoted the gun to the right. Then he collapsed into a sitting position on the ground next to it, gasping for air, but covering his ears in anticipation of what would come next.

Jim looked again, "That ought to do 'er, Captain," Jim said, and hopped back down to hold the log in place.

Nathan stood, reached into his pocket, pulled out a match and struck it. He leaned forward and touched off the powder, turning his face away and covering his ears with his hands as the powder went off with a tremendous flash and a *roar* like the very end of the world.

❁❁❁❁❁❁❁❁

Nathan and his men pulled their horses forward in the waist-deep, murky waters of the Ohio as they slogged their way toward shore. Gratefully, the river bottom was a gravel bar in this spot, so their boots and the horses' hooves didn't sink into the muck as they otherwise might have. Upon reaching shore, they found Georgie, Jamie, and Phinney waiting for them, and they all shared a happy, relieved reunion.

Though hungry and exhausted, Nathan felt a sense of satisfaction that the army and all the civilians had now made it across to Ohio. And none of his men had been killed in the process.

When they'd secured their horses in the woods up away from the bank and had a moment to rest, leaning their backs against the trees and gazing back across the river, Tom said, "Well, despite the long retreat, and the enemy retaking the Kanawha ... for some reason this *feels* like a victory ... we've saved all of the Union formations, hundreds of civilians, and likely thousands of tons of equipment."

Nathan nodded, then said, "Yes … this was a *victory*, all right … but to quote Pyrrhus of Epirus, of the *pyrrhic victory*, 'One more such *victory* and we are undone.'"

Tom snorted a mirthless chuckle.

Then Nathan suddenly rose to his feet, gazing at something on the far side of the river. He reached down and grabbed his brass spyglass from his pack and held it to his eye. "Damn!" he said, "It's Walters … staring right at me … quick, Tom, hand me a rifle!"

Tom grabbed his own, but found it unloaded, then he scrambled over to where Nathan had leaned his against a tree, but it was also unloaded. And he knew they'd already used the last of their rifle balls.

"We're all out of ammunition, sir," Tom said.

Nathan lowered the spyglass, and unholstered his pistol. He looked down at the cylinder, and finding he had one round remaining, he raised the weapon, cocked the hammer, aimed across the river, and fired. A loud *bang* rang out, and a puff of smoke drifted off in the gentle breeze. Nathan raised the spyglass back to his eyes and gazed through it. "Gone," he said.

"You hit him, sir?!" Tom asked.

But Nathan snorted a laugh, "Not likely, Tom … a pistol shot from this distance?! Not very damned likely …" Then he turned and gave Tom a half smile, half scowl, and said, "But it was worth a shot."

Chapter 7. The Package

*"Good things come
in small packages."*

- Aesop

Saturday September 13, 1862 – Frederick, Maryland:

While the rebels had controlled Frederick, Maryland, Evelyn had the impression that the entire town was supportive of the secessionists' cause. But now that the Union Army was once again firmly in control of the city and its surrounding environs, it had become readily apparent such was *not* the case. Though loyalties were clearly divided, it was now obvious that the majority of Frederick's residents remained enthusiastically supportive of the Union, and these citizens had just been laying low during the recent Confederate occupation.

Upon the investment of the town by the Union Army, the atmosphere immediately changed in a dramatic way. The soldiers in blue were welcomed as liberators; as the troops marched through town, women waved handkerchiefs and men raised United States flags that'd been hidden away just the day before.

To the young soldiers, this was a heady reception, and they responded to the civilians' warm welcome with great enthusiasm, cheering and chanting with great vigor, as their regimental bands blasted out martial music.

And young ladies seemed to be everywhere. Clearly starved for the attention of young men, they roamed around in groups, waving tiny flags, singing patriotic songs, and flirting shamelessly with the soldiers.

This atmosphere made it much easier for Evelyn, Joseph, and Mary to conduct their particular business, as they were no longer in fear of being captured as spies. Yet, ironically, they still needed to conduct their business in secret, due to the need to convince General McClellan that Special Order 191 was authentic. And it was necessary to change boarding houses, as Evelyn had played a Confederate sympathizer before, and might be subject to a severe backlash now that the Union was in charge, and pro-Union residents were no longer constrained.

But this was ideal, as it allowed Joseph to change roles and dress as a gentleman, playing her husband, with Mary being their freeman maid. This allowed them to meet in much more comfort, in the rooms of the boarding house.

Evelyn felt a sense of urgency; they must get Lee's orders to McClellan within a day of his arrival in the city if the theory of it being somehow mislaid during the hasty Confederate departure was to be deemed plausible.

So they wasted no time plotting how best to get the document to McClellan without it looking suspicious. They quickly decided it should be "found" by a common soldier, ideally a private, rather than an officer. And it must appear to have been inadvertently dropped and left behind, ideally in a field where rebel forces had been bivouacked. They decided on the camp of General D.H. Hill since that was where Joseph had been camped while he was posing as a Confederate sergeant, and so he'd be most familiar with the terrain.

"But with all the activity in town, soldiers marching about everywhere, I fear that a random sheet of paper or envelope on the ground will simply be ignored and trampled into the mud," Evelyn said.

"What if we attach the document to something a man would notice and want, such as a bottle of whiskey?" Joseph suggested.

"Or wrapping it in money?" Mary suggested, but then thought better of it, "No, that won't work; Union soldiers won't care about Confederate money, and a Confederate soldier wouldn't carry Union money."

Evelyn pondered this for a moment, "Attaching it to something valuable is a good idea, but it needs to be something that's not too obvious, or it'll seem suspicious, like we are setting out bait—which, of course, is exactly what we are talking about doing. And if it's something *too* interesting, like a bottle of whiskey, the soldiers may disregard the document in their enthusiasm for the object of their desires."

They were quiet for a moment, each trying to think of the object that would best suit their needs. Incongruously, an image of Nathan appeared in Evelyn's mind. It was back during her time at Mountain Meadows, and he was standing on the veranda, looking out over his farm with a look of great satisfaction, contentedly smoking on a—

"Cigar!" she said. "It should be a cigar. No man will fail to bend down to pick one up, but it's not so valuable as to be suspicious. And if it's partially visible but wrapped in the document, then the man should be curious enough to see what's written on the paper."

"That sounds right," Mary said, "… except … a cigar is not very big, and it's the same color as dirt … what if they simply don't see it on the ground … or wherever we put it?"

"Easy," Joseph answered, "put several cigars together to make it more visible. The lighter color of the paper will catch their eye, and the cigars will ensure that they pick up the package. We can even tie it together with a brightly colored ribbon—red, or something."

"Yes …" Evelyn said, picturing the image in her mind's eye, "Yes, I think that should work … Let's get 'the package' ready, and make the drop first thing in the morning so there's no chance of it being overlooked as the evening wanes and darkness falls."

🗼🗨ℒ🗼🗨ℒ🗼🗨ℒ

"Hey, Bart … how'd you like that breakfast?" Private Frank Evans called out as he tramped across the field toward where Private Barton Mitchell was stacking the regiment's rifles into neat little pyramids, each containing eight rifles, their bayonets overlapping on top. Private Sam Johnson was currently helping Barton unload the rifles from a supply wagon that was parked next to them in the field.

"Oh my God, Frankie … I think if I'd o' ate another bite I'd o' burst!" Barton shot back. "Nice o' you to come lend a hand, by the way … you lazy bastard!"

Frank snorted a laugh as he stepped over to the wagon and grabbed an armload of rifles. "Never mention it, Bart ... always happy to help out my friends," he said with a grin.

The three young soldiers of the Twenty Seventh Indiana Volunteer Infantry Regiment were already sweating profusely under a sun that'd not yet reached its zenith in a nearly cloudless sky. The rising temperature was making Barton consider if he'd prefer a return to the drenching rain they'd endured on the march two days earlier.

But for their present hardship, such as it was, they had been more than compensated by the festive, holiday-like atmosphere that'd pervaded in the town of Frederick ever since their arrival. The parades and boisterous celebrations of the night before had given way to a Fourth of July-type feeling this morning, with civilians streaming out of their homes to treat the soldiers to hot meals, home baked bread, pies, and various sweet pastries. And despite his stomach still feeling uncomfortably full, Barton was looking forward to more of the same come evening, once their duties were over for the day.

And even as they labored to set up camp, along with thousands of other soldiers across the field all around them, civilians, dressed in their finest, came out and strolled the fields to greet the men and offer them thanks, along with cold drinks, and more libations.

"Funny to think there was rebs doin' this very same thing in this very same field not more'n two or three days ago," Barton said as he carefully leaned the rifles against one another, making sure not to let any tumble to the ground, toppling the whole stack he was working on.

"Yep ... that *is* a thought, ain't it? Wonder which bunch it was in this-here field," Frank answered, as he also steadied his stack.

"The fellow serving out breakfast said it was General D.H. Hill's corps," Barton answered.

"That a fact?" Frank said, scratching his head as he stepped away, watching to make sure his rifles were going to stay up. "Wish I knew the spot where the general had pitched his own personal tent, so I could go take a piss on it!"

They all shared a laugh.

"Hey, lookie here fellas," Sam said, nodding with his head back toward the road.

Barton looked up and saw three civilians walking toward them across the field, a gentleman and a lady, very nicely dressed, followed a few steps behind by a black maid, also nicely dressed—whether slave or freeman it was impossible to say in Maryland, where there was such a mix of both kinds.

"Are you seein' what I'm seein'?" Sam added, this time more under his breath as they came closer.

At first Barton didn't understand what Sam meant by it; there was nothing unusual about civilians walking across the field today—it'd been going on since shortly after first light in the morning.

But then as the trio came closer Barton understood what Sam was talking about—it was the lady. She wore a fine, lacy dress, which came down in a tantalizing V in front, and a fashionable hat tied on with a ribbon, from which strands of long, blonde hair hung down around her shoulders. And when Barton gazed upon her face, he realized she was extraordinarily beautiful, such as he'd never seen before up close in person.

He briefly met eyes with her as she approached, and she smiled at him. He immediately looked away, unable to maintain eye contact. Her gaze was ... too dazzling, he realized ... *like looking straight at the sun* ... he decided.

The couple stepped up to the three soldiers and stopped. The man tipped his hat, and the lady performed a short curtsy.

Barton removed his cap respectfully, and elbowed Frank to do the same. Sam also removed his.

"Good morning, my good sirs," the gentleman said, with a warm smile. Barton decided there was nothing unusual about the man; he was clearly much older than the lady, likely in his forties, and not especially handsome, though he did keep his beard neatly trimmed, and wore the finest, most fashionable suit and neat bowler hat. It flashed through Barton's mind to wonder what the fellow had done to attract such a lady.

"Good morning, sir. Good morning, miss," the three soldiers answered. Barton found he could meet eyes with the gentleman, but still had trouble looking straight at the lady. But then he realized by trying to avoid eye contact, his eyes had strayed to her bosom, and so he quickly looked back up at her eyes—and saw an amused look, so he immediately looked down at his shoes. *Oh, damn, Bart,* he thought, *that was embarrassing!* He could feel his face becoming hot, and this time not from the sun.

"Good morning, gentlemen," the lady answered. "Mr. Smith and I wanted to come out here to personally thank you for your heroic service to our nation, and especially for saving our town from the ravages of that horrid rebel army," she said. Barton thought her voice perfectly matched the rest of her: a soft, sweet, melodic sound with just the hint of a southern accent.

The other two privates just nodded, obviously tongue-tied, so Barton forced himself to answer, to fill the embarrassing silence, "Uh … you're most welcome, ma'am, though … me and the fellas … we ain't done much actual fightin' … yet."

"Oh, never you mind about that," she said with a bright smile, "Just seeing your brave faces here in Frederick has boosted the morale of our town beyond measure. And I can tell from the look of you fine, strong, young fellows that you will acquit yourselves most commendably, when the time comes to face the enemy."

"Yes, ma'am," Barton answered, suddenly realizing he was crumpling his hat and forcing himself to straighten it back out. "Thank you, ma'am. We'll … do our best …" he concluded, feeling slightly foolish and at a loss for words.

"I know you will, and I shall pray for you," she said.

Then the gentleman tipped his hat and said, "Godspeed and good luck, my good fellows. We must now go greet some of the other brave soldiers …"

"Thank you, sir," they all three answered.

"Good day, gentlemen," the lady said, then graced them with a smile that stuck in Barton's mind for the rest of that day, and for many days after.

ಶಾಶಿಞಞಶಾಶಿಞಞಶಾಶಿಞಞ

Barton was still thinking about the encounter with the fine couple a half hour later as he walked back toward the wagon for another armload of rifles. For the hundredth time, he thought about the beautiful young lady ... and he still cringed with embarrassment when he thought about her catching him staring at her bosom.

He decided to get out of the sun for a moment and have a quick drink. He grabbed his canteen from where it hung by a nail on the shady side of the wagon, and sat down in the grass, leaning his back against the wagon wheel.

He had a short rest and took several good swallows from the canteen, enjoying the relative coolness in the shade of the wagon as he watched Frank and Sam working on their stacks.

But just as he was rising to get back to work something in the grass caught his eye—an unknown object of a bright pink color. He stood up to investigate, taking two steps to where the thing lay, partially hidden by the tall grass. Gazing down at it, he saw a small package containing three cigars, wrapped in a piece of paper, tied together with a pink ribbon.

Hello! Must be my lucky day ... and some reb officer's unlucky one, ha! he thought, as he picked up the cigars.

He untied the ribbon, thinking to share out the cigars with Frank and Sam, when he noticed the paper had writing on it. He unfolded it and saw that it was in fact two sheets of paper, with writing on each. A letter of some sort, he thought. But when he saw the signature at the bottom of the second page, his heart skipped a beat; he read, *"By Command of Gen. R.E. Lee."*

He flipped back to the first page and began to read ... and then stopped and whistled softly. *"Sweet Jesus ..."* he muttered under his breath, just as Frank stepped up to the wagon.

"Now who's the lazy bastard?" Frank said, as he stepped up behind Barton, then looked over his shoulder to see what he was gazing at. "Hey ... what you go there, Bart?"

"These ..." Barton said, waving the cigars at Frank, "and this ..." he said, holding up the papers. "Found the cigars in the grass wrapped in these papers, all tied up with a ribbon."

"A letter?"

"No … it's … it's … oh, hell—you ain't gonna believe me if I tell you, so just see for yourself," Barton said, and handed Frank the papers.

Frank started reading. *"Oh!"* he said, after he read the heading at the top of the first page. He'd gotten only halfway down the sheet when he stopped and flipped to the second page to see who'd signed it. *"Mother of God!"* he exclaimed, "Ol' General Lee hisself!"

"Yup … toldya you wouldn't believe it …"

They walked back over to where Sam was just finishing his latest stack and showed him what Barton had found. He too was shocked and amazed. They all three agreed Barton must take the document straight to their company commander, First Sergeant John Bloss, who was just across the field supervising the erection of a row of tents.

"Just hand me one o' them cigars before you go," Frank said.

But Barton shook his head, "No … can't do it, Frank. This here's evidence … the generals will want to see the whole package so's they can decide on how the thing got here, who dropped it and so on …"

Sam nodded, "Yep … much as I hate to admit it, he's right, Frank. They's gonna want to see the whole thing, just as Bart found it."

"Oh damn the luck," Frank said, "too bad for me I got stuck stackin' rifles with two such honest rascals."

But Barton just smiled, folded the paper, then rolled it back around the cigars as it had been when he found it, so he could show the sergeant. "I'll just run this over to the sergeant, then I'll come straight on back," he said.

"Oh, yeah, sure …" Frank said, "just another excuse to be lazy," but he smiled when he said it, and Barton returned the smile before turning and trotting off across the field.

༄༅ཀ༈ཉཀ༄༅ཀ༈ཉཀ༄༅ཀ༈ཉཀ

At 11:43 a.m. on September 13, 1862, Private Barton W. Mitchell of the Twenty Seventh Indiana Infantry, part of the Union Twelfth Army Corps bivouacked just outside Frederick,

Maryland showed the papers he'd found, along with three cigars, to First Sergeant John M. Bloss. Sergeant Bloss took Private Mitchell straight to see Captain Peter Kopp.

Captain Kopp thanked them, took the package and immediately trotted over to where the Twenty-Seventh's headquarters were being set up, and showed the document to regimental commander Colonel Silas Colgrove.

Colonel Colgrove personally carried it to Twelfth Corps's headquarters, under the command of Brigadier General Alpheus S. Williams, and gave the package to Williams's adjutant, Colonel Samuel E. Pittman.

Pittman's eyes widened when he recognized the signature of R. H. Chilton, Lee's assistant adjutant general—whom he'd known well before the war—below Lee's name at the bottom of the second page, further proof of the document's authenticity.

Pittman showed the document to General Williams.

Williams took out a sheet of paper and pencil and wrote:

> Genl. McClellan,
>
> I enclose a special order of Genl. Lee Commanding Rebel forces—which was found on the field where my corps is encamped. It is a document of interest.
>
> Brig. Genl. A.S. Williams.

Williams placed the message to McClellan, along with the found order, into an envelope and sealed it. Williams then gave the envelope back to Pittman who had a courier carry the documents to McClellan's headquarters. General Williams kept the cigars.

The courier reported directly to General McClellan's adjutant, Brigadier General Seth Williams. Williams carried the dispatch straight to General McClellan's tent, where he interrupted a meeting between McClellan and Brigadier General John Gibbon.

Once Williams handed McClellan the document—telling him he believed it to be urgent—McClellan immediately read through the special order, his eyes widening as he read.

When he'd finished, he looked up at the two generals and exclaimed, "Now I know what to do! Here is a paper with which, if I cannot whip Bobby Lee, I will be willing to go home!"

But despite Major General George B. McClellan's enthusiasm for this miraculous piece of intelligence, and his belief that it was entirely authentic, he did not order the Union Army to advance for another eighteen hours.

৩৩৩৩৩৩৩৩৩৩৩

Later in the afternoon of the day Mary had dropped the "package" into the grass a dozen feet or so behind where Evelyn and Joseph chatted with the Union soldiers, Joseph returned to the site. This time he went in his "vagabond" disguise, complete with his walking stick and profound limp. He also took a swallow of whiskey and poured a bit on his shirt, so he'd have a strong odor of alcohol about him.

To round out the ruse, he did a little begging as he limped along, holding out his hat to soldiers he passed. A few actually responded positively, such that when he reached the spot, he congratulated himself that he'd already had pocketed several dollars off the outing.

When he reached the place where they'd made the drop, he easily identified it by the stacks of rifles, the prominent wagon wheel tracks, and even the trampled down grass where the soldiers had gathered to look at the cigars and to read the document wrapped around them.

He made a show of coughing and staggering as if out of breath or drunken, giving him a reasonable excuse to be gazing down at the ground. After a quarter hour of reconnoitering the site, Joseph was satisfied the package had in fact been found by the soldiers, so he returned to the boarding house to report the good news to the ladies.

"Then our plan has worked, Joseph," Evelyn exclaimed, clapping her hands together in her excitement, and sharing a congratulatory smile with Mary. "Now we can only hope and pray that McClellan accepts the document as authentic."

"Yes ... and then acts upon it as he should ..." Joseph added, to which Evelyn nodded, frowning slightly in agreement with Joseph.

"Anyway, whatever happens from here is out of our hands, so our job here is finished," Evelyn said. "Well done, both of you! And thank you so much for all your endeavors, and all the risks you've taken on behalf of the cause."

"Thank you, too, Evelyn. After all, it was your plan and your leadership that made it all come together," Joseph answered.

To which Mary added, "Yes, Miss Evelyn ... we just followed your directions, and everything worked out beautifully."

"Well, let's just say we make an excellent team.

"But, Joseph ... I never thought much beyond *this* point, focusing all my thought on how to actually accomplish the mission. Any idea how we might get home from here?"

Joseph nodded and smiled, "Yes, as a matter of fact. Even before I left Richmond, I arranged an escape plan with the Employer, knowing whatever else happened we were going to need that at some point.

"He has pre-arranged for our transportation from wherever we may end up. All we have to do is send a specific innocuous telegram—that includes our present whereabouts—to a certain fictitious individual in Boston, and then someone will arrive to pick us up in a carriage. Our driver should arrive in a day or two, depending on where he's currently located. I will change back into my gentleman's garb now, and send that telegram straight away."

༄༅༅༄༅༅༄༅༅

The carriage sent by the Employer arrived much earlier than expected, pulling up in the alleyway behind Evelyn's boarding house in Frederick shortly before noon the day after Joseph had sent the telegram.

Once within the privacy of Evelyn's room, where Joseph and Mary joined them around a small table, the driver explained that he'd tried to anticipate the call to action, so had been following along in the wake of the Union Army's advance—at a safe distance. He'd spent the previous night in Hyattstown, Maryland, just thirteen miles away on the road to Washington.

And Evelyn felt surprised, and more than a little honored, when the driver introduced himself as Ben *Smith*—of course—but then told her and the others that his real name, which he would not repeat again on their present journey, was Benjamin *Hughes*.

"Hughes? As in Nigel Hughes and—" Evelyn began, but Benjamin cut her off.

"Yes ... the *Employer* is my cousin, and Nigel was my younger brother."

And after he said this, she immediately noticed the family resemblance. Though Benjamin was older than Nigel, he had the same dark hair and lean, good looks as his younger brother, with a neatly trimmed beard and hair that flowed out from under his hat.

"Oh! It is such a pleasure to meet you, Benjamin. And thank you so much for coming. I feel honored that a member of the family has once again come to my rescue."

"Thank *you*, Miss Evelyn, and the honor is all mine. I have heard nothing but glowing reports about you and all you've done for our cause. So, when the Employer asked us to provide you with a driver, I insisted on going myself that I might meet you and thank you personally.

"And the honor goes for you too, Joseph. You are something of a legend in the family, and it is so very good to finally meet you."

"Likewise, Benjamin. The Employer speaks very highly of you, often referring to you as the head of the family—North."

Benjamin chuckled, "Well, I don't know about that ... but I do try to keep everyone moving in the same direction, I suppose."

Then he turned toward Mary, "And I would be remiss if I didn't also say it is a pleasure to meet you as well, Miss Mary. Though I've not heard as much about you, I understand the Employer is very pleased that you've recently joined in our efforts. He tells me that he has very high expectations of you."

"Thank you for saying so, sir," she answered, with a slight curtsy.

"Benjamin, before we discuss business, I must tell you how sorry I am for your loss," Evelyn said, now with a serious expression. "Nigel was ... everything *good* in a man: courageous, loyal, intelligent, kindly. We became good friends during our time together and I ... *I miss him dearly* ..." she finished, beginning to tear up at the thought of the young man who'd given his life trying to help her get back to Richmond.

"Thank you, Miss Evelyn. Yes, Nigel was unique ... and ... and every day I miss him ... more than I can say," he became quiet for a moment, gazing down at his own hands, resting on the table, as if suddenly immersed in a memory.

Then he looked back up, smiled, and said, "But thankfully today is a happier day. In fact, I have some *very* good news for all of you: that your efforts have been an unmitigated and most spectacular success! Our sources in the War Department tell us that General McClellan has reported finding Lee's lost orders, and is proceeding under the belief that they are one hundred percent authentic!"

"*Oh!*" Evelyn exclaimed, jumping up from her chair, and clapping her hands over her mouth in her excitement. Joseph and Mary also came to their feet, and the three of them shared embraces and smiles, and then exchanged enthusiastic handshakes with Benjamin, who beamed at their joy over the good news.

ℰᏫℰᏝᏳᏻᏱℰᏫℰᏝᏳᏻᏱℰᏫℰᏝᏳᏻᏱ

After a celebratory lunch in the boarding house common room, they returned to Evelyn's room to discuss their next moves.

"Benjamin ... how will we be getting back to Richmond? Can you tell us? I have been going over the various options in my mind, but with the whole area in such upheaval over the fighting, it isn't clear to me how we should proceed."

But Benjamin didn't immediately answer, and gazed up at the ceiling for a moment, as if searching for the right words.

"Miss Evelyn ... to be honest ... the Employer hasn't discussed that *specific* matter with me."

"He *hasn't?!* Then how does he expect us to get home?" she asked.

"He ... he doesn't intend for you to return home straightaway, is the short answer," Benjamin answered.

Evelyn raised an eyebrow at this, but said nothing, allowing him to elaborate.

"You see ... he has another mission in mind for you before your return. I'm to take you to Washington, where he wishes for you to perform a very specific task for our cause."

"Oh? And what task would that be?" Evelyn asked.

"He wants you to *kill* a man, Miss Evelyn," Benjamin answered.

They were all quiet for a moment after this shocking announcement.

Then Evelyn finally asked, "Why would the Employer wish for us to murder a man in Washington? Who is he, anyway?"

"Perhaps I should tell it from the beginning, and then you will better understand his request.

"Several months ago, one of our people in the Confederate War Department noticed a series of encrypted communications were coming in regularly to a specific officer. Through great risk and daring, he managed to make copies of several of these letters and forwarded them to the Employer, who had some of his best and smartest men work to decipher the messages. I understand it was very challenging work, and took them several weeks to accomplish.

"But when they completed their task and examined the resulting messages, it became clear that the source was a high-ranking civilian official in the Union War Department."

"Oh my!" Evelyn exclaimed, "That is *dire* news ..."

"Yes ... we had always suspected they had their spies, even as we had ours, but this proved it beyond doubt, and at a much higher level than we'd ever suspected. But the problem was we still didn't have a name. It took more than a month of probing and digging before the identity of the individual was finally unearthed. Needless to say, he is a great threat to the Union's military efforts and needs to be eliminated."

"But, then why not just turn over the evidence to Mr. Pinkerton and have him arrested for a spy? Why must we murder him?"

"It's a fair question; and believe me that option was discussed at length. As one might expect with an important official, he has many powerful friends, and it kept coming back around to there being no way to prove our case without disclosing how we came about the information. That would compromise our own people, exposing them, and either eliminating their effectiveness to our cause, or putting them in grave danger, or both.

"So the Employer reluctantly decided the only course was to have the threat eliminated … quietly and permanently."

Evelyn thought about this a moment, nodding her head, then looked up and said, "But … but I am not a *killer*, Benjamin."

"*Oh?* I was led to believe that you were one of our most reliable agents in that regard … 'equal parts beauty, brains, and deadliness,' I believe the Employer has said."

She slowly shook her head, beginning to wonder what people were thinking of her and saying about her … or maybe what she was becoming.

"Is it untrue then, Miss Evelyn? I was told you have already killed several vile men in the course of your duties."

"Well, yes, it's true, but—"

She glanced over at Mary, who was staring back at her wide-eyed; no doubt to her this was a shocking revelation about her seemingly mild-mannered traveling companion.

But Joseph did *not* show any surprise. Likely he'd been privy to such discussions about her in the past, she decided.

"I have killed men in self-defense … or in defense of others, when I had to. But I'm no assassin. You can't just tell me to murder some stranger in cold blood … I can't do it … I *won't* do it."

"Interesting … and why not, may I ask?"

"Because … murder is immoral … it's … well, for one, it's a great sin against God. *'Thou shalt not kill,'* the commandment says."

Benjamin was thoughtful for a moment, then asked, "Then would you say it is immoral for a soldier to kill an opposing soldier in battle? Or that it is immoral for a general officer to order his men to attack a group of enemy soldiers, knowing many will be killed on both sides?"

"Well, *no* … but …"

"Then if that killing is *not* immoral or sinful—and I submit to you many of the young men who will be meeting their end in that scenario are innocents, forced to take up arms for their country, forced to fight, even possibly against their own will—why is it immoral or sinful to kill a man whose intentional acts, in this case acts of espionage, are intended to ensure that those very soldiers get killed when the battle rages?"

"It's … well …" Evelyn snapped her mouth shut and frowned. She thought back on the many philosophical discussions of this very nature she'd had with her father growing up, recognizing this as one and the same with those.

"You are making some interesting arguments," she finally replied, "but there is a difference, if not in the grand scheme of things, then at least to the individuals involved—both the killer and the killed. A soldier in battle, even if there involuntarily, at least has the means to fight back, to resist, to attempt to preserve his own life. And he has a reasonable expectation that he may very well be killed in the action at any given moment.

"A man working in an office building, strolling home from work in a city, suddenly stabbed in the back by an assassin, has no means of fighting back, and has the expectation of arriving home safely to his hearth and home, regardless of what sort of nefarious dealings he may have been a party to at his office.

"But more to the point—especially considering our current circumstances—is the effect on the would-be assassin. Killing a soldier across the battlefield with a rifle, or even up close with a bayonet, may be morally repugnant to many, but it cannot be compared with putting a bullet through the brain of a man who is calmly strolling down a peaceful city street on the way to greet his wife. A person with any sort of conscience might never recover from a thing like that …"

Benjamin nodded and smiled, as if enjoying the debate. But before he could respond, Evelyn added, "And besides … even as

160

we've talked, I've already thought up a better alternative. One that will not only eliminate this one particular snake, but if we're lucky, may uncover a whole nest of vipers."

ℰᎧℰᎧᏣᏏ ᏣᎧℰᎧᎧᎧᏣᏏ ᏣᎧℰᎧᏣᎧᏣᏏ

Ollie sat up straight in shock and surprise. Then he leaned back down and re-read the message he'd just deciphered to make sure he'd understood it correctly. He slowly shook his head in disbelief, and immediately pulled out a clean sheet of paper, and repeated the deciphering again, just to be sure he'd not made some mistake.

But a half-hour later, when the message had turned out the same, he snatched up the papers, and hurried out of his tent, headed straight toward the tent of General Lee.

When he entered, Lee was dictating a letter to his adjutant, Lieutenant Colonel Robert Chilton. Both men looked up at the unexpected interruption, and Ollie came to attention and snapped a salute, which the two senior officers returned.

"Sorry to interrupt, sirs ... but it is a most urgent matter ..."

Chilton's eyes widened. Ollie was Lee's intelligence officer, so when he said something was *urgent* ...

Chilton stood, and said, "I shall return shortly to finish the letter, sir, if it pleases you."

"Yes ... thank you, Robert. I will send for you when Oliver and I have finished the current business."

Once Chilton had departed, Lee gestured Ollie to take a seat.

Ollie sat and immediately dived into his explanation, as he knew General Lee would wish. "Sir ... a civilian turned himself into the sentries this morning, saying that he was a messenger sent from Washington by certain individuals loyal to our cause, with a most critical document for General Lee. The sentries brought him to me, and the man handed me a message, written out in cipher. I recognized it as one of our very highest-level ciphers, used only by our own war department, sir, and only for messages to you alone and no other general."

Lee's eyes opened wide at this news; they occasionally received such messages from Richmond, but had never received this type of cipher from Washington or anywhere else.

"Go on …" Lee said.

"Yes, sir. I interrogated the messenger, as is my duty … and I was not gentle with him … even threatened bodily harm against him should he prove to be an enemy agent. But … he held fast to his story. I believe he is what he says he is, and that he does not know where the message originated, or what it contains. His only instructions were that it must get to General Lee in Maryland at all cost and that it was a matter of the gravest national importance."

"I see … and the message? I assume you've deciphered it?" Lee asked.

"Yes, sir … twice … to make sure I'd got it right. Here, sir … both copies …" Ollie said, handing the pages over to Lee.

The general laid the sheets out side by side, and pulled an oil lamp close as he put on his reading glasses.

He quickly glanced from one sheet to the other to verify they were identical copies. He looked up at Ollie and nodded, then tucked one sheet under the other and began to read.

After a moment, he removed his glasses and pushed his chair back from the table, gazing up at Ollie with a serious look.

"Well … this a bitter pill, Oliver …" he said.

"Yes, sir," was all Ollie could think to say.

Lee gazed up at the tent ceiling for a long moment, before looking back down. "So … McClellan has gotten his hands on a copy of my battle orders. The cipher references 'Special Order 191,' so there can be no doubt of its authenticity."

Lee slowly shook his head, "Found lying in a field by Union soldiers near Frederick, no less. Casually cast aside, seemingly — as if it were of no more import than a requisition for fodder. This is … unconscionable carelessness by … someone? Hmm … I wonder who, though I suppose at this point it doesn't much matter. The question is what to do now …"

Ollie knew it wasn't his place to even *suggest* battle strategy to General Lee, even if he had any ideas — which he didn't. He had become a good intelligence officer, quickly learning all the various ciphers, and taking charge of various clandestine intelligence-gathering operations for Lee's army, but he had never taken much interest in how to fight a battle. He felt completely out of his depth when such details were being discussed among any of the other staff officers. And General Lee ... he was their greatest strategist by far, at a whole *other* level.

"Hmm ... George McClellan ... *what will you do?*" Lee said, again gazing up at the ceiling. He sat there quietly for several moments before sitting back up and again meeting eyes with Ollie.

"Oliver ... we must keep this between the two of us for now ... until I tell you otherwise."

"Yes, sir. Of course, sir. But ... may I ask what you intend to *do* now?"

"Yes, certainly, Oliver. You've done good work here, and have earned the right to know.

"If it were anyone other than McClellan, I should be obliged to call off the offensive and retreat back to Virginia immediately. But ... he has had the document for, what ... three days now? And yet there is no perceptible increase in the speed of his advance, and no sign he moves to attack my divided forces piecemeal.

"No, I think we will continue on, though we must increase our pace so that our forces are consolidated before he arrives. The one thing we can count on from McClellan is he'll move cautiously, even now that he knows the deployment of our forces.

"We must change our plans only in subtle ways so their spies will not know that we know McClellan has a copy of my orders. Oliver, send one of your trusted men to General Jackson, telling him I have said it is a matter of the most urgency that he completes his capture of Harpers Ferry at least ... hmm ... two days earlier than the original timeline we had discussed previously. If he can't accomplish it, he must abandon the effort. In either case, he must then march with all haste to meet us and the rest of the army at ..."

Lee leaned behind him, rummaged through some rolled up papers, picked one out, and unrolled it on the table. He gazed at it a long moment—Ollie could see it was a detailed map of

Maryland. "… here," Lee concluded, "Near this town named *Sharpsburg*. Tell him to meet us in the area south of this stream here … *Antietam Creek*, by September sixteenth at the latest. There we shall have a large loop of the Potomac to guard our rear and flanks and the creek to our front."

"Very good, general, I will arrange it immediately. What do you expect will happen at Antietam Creek, sir, if you don't mind my asking?"

Lee nodded, and said, "There I expect to turn and give battle to McClellan, with all the forces at my command. And if God is merciful, we shall carry the day and end the war right then and there."

Chapter 8. Nest of Vipers

*"A nation can survive its fools, even the ambitious.
But it cannot survive treason from within."*
- **Marcus Tullius Cicero**

Monday September 15, 1862 – Washington, D.C.:

Sergeant Major Patrick Murphy of the Twelfth New York Volunteer Infantry Regiment, currently commander of the guard at the Old Capitol Prison just across from the Capitol building in Washington City, sighed heavily as he stepped carefully down the stone steps of the prison, on his way home for the evening.

On each step he felt the familiar twinge of pain in the middle of his back where the shrapnel had embedded itself, now more than a year ago. The jagged piece of metal, no bigger than a penny, had ended up so close to his spine that the surgeons had dared not attempt to remove it. But Murphy had just enough stubborn Irish pride not to show any sign of weakness, so he manfully resisted the urge to wince or betray any pain or discomfort.

He stood tall and straight, and endured the pain today, same as he did every day. As he turned and headed down the street toward home and his wife Colleen, it occurred to him his was one of those "lucky wounds" soldiers always spoke of, the kind that would allow you to return home to your family for the remainder of the war without completely crippling you.

But he'd not felt so lucky this past week as he watched his regiment move out with General McClellan for a showdown with the rebel commander Lee. The guilt of watching his fellows march away, standing there at attention, thinking he surely looked like the worst sort of shirking coward, still haunted him, despite the regimental surgeons forbidding him from anything other than light, home-front duty.

The sun had already set, and it was beginning to get dark as he approached the intersection with Constitution Avenue, a block north of the prison. He looked down the street to his left to ensure there was no traffic. Then, as he looked to the front, someone stepped out from the corner to his right and came to a stop, looking in his direction and blocking his way.

Murphy stopped as well, and was surprised to note from the thin shape and flowing skirts that this was surely a woman, though she was nearly as tall as he. He could not make out her features in the failing light, as she wore a long cape with a hood pulled up over her head, hiding her face in the shadow.

He gazed at her a moment, before saying, "Yes? Is there something I can do for you, miss?"

He heard a soft chuckle, then the woman reached up and flipped open her hood, revealing her face. Murphy gasped.

"Why, yes ... in fact there *is* something you can do for me, Sergeant Murphy," she said, and smiled brightly.

"Miss Eve!" he exclaimed. "What are you doing here?!"

"Looking for *you*, Sergeant ... obviously," she answered, still smiling brightly. "And I must say it *is* such a truly great pleasure to see you again, sir."

He returned her smile, but then turned and looked back down the street to see if anyone was coming. He looked back at her and said, "You shouldn't be here, Miss Eve. If someone sees you ..."

"I agree, Sergeant, but I had to speak with you. Will you come with me to a place where we may ... converse more privately?"

There was a moment's hesitation as he struggled between what he'd been told about Miss Eve—that she was a deadly and nefarious rebel spy, who'd been spirited away from his very prison by her fellow Confederate spies—versus what she had personally told him, and what his own instincts had seemed to confirm: that she was actually on the Union side and had been falsely accused and imprisoned by a feckless Union general.

She looked him hard in the eye and became more serious, "Have no fear, Sergeant ... I am still the same person your heart told you to trust back when you saw me every day and knew me well ... and *not* the evil traitor a certain general tried to make me out to be."

He met eyes with her a long moment, once again gauging her sincerity as he'd done on this very same street months ago after her attempted escape. Then he nodded and said, "All right … lead on, Miss Eve."

"Thank you, Sergeant," she answered, then turned and headed back in the direction from which she'd come. He made another quick look down the street toward the prison, then turned and followed.

After two blocks, she turned right onto Third Street for another half-block, then left into an alleyway. She led him to the back door of a house, which they entered, immediately going up the stairs to a long hallway. She took out a key and unlocked the first door on the right and ushered him in. He cringed to think what his wife would say if she ever heard about this!

When he entered the room, he noted there was a bed, a small table, not much bigger than a desk, and two chairs, one small and simple with no padding, and the other larger and more comfortable looking, padded with soft leather upholstery. She immediately took the simple wooden chair and gestured him toward the more comfortable one.

He hesitated; it was impolite for a man to take the nicer chair rather than allowing the lady to take it.

But she smiled up at him, and again gestured toward the padded chair. "Please, Sergeant, sit. I would have you comfortable; you've certainly earned it … I know what you've sacrificed on behalf of our country, despite your commendable efforts to hide it."

"Is it that obvious?" he asked. "And all this time I have foolishly prided myself in putting on a stoic front in spite of the pain."

"No … it is *not* obvious, Sergeant Murphy … and you have admirably disguised your discomfort. But I am, after all, in the business of finding out things about people … including my friends. Please … sit, sir."

He slowly nodded his head, then moved over and sat in the chair, letting out a heavy sigh as he did.

He looked up at her and grinned, "It *is* very comfortable. Perhaps I should get one for my office at the prison."

She smiled back brightly, "Indeed you should, indeed you should, sir."

"And ... it is a relief not to hide the ... *discomfort* ... for a few moments, anyway," he added to which she just smiled and nodded.

"Sergeant, I will get right to the heart of the matter, after which, if you wish, I will be happy to satisfy your curiosity over what happened to me after we last parted."

"Yes, please; I have to admit to a *great deal* of curiosity concerning the matter, Miss Eve," he answered.

"Oh ... speaking of *Miss Eve* ..." she said, and again adopted the thoughtful, sincere expression she'd had earlier, "as a small token of my complete faith in you, Sergeant, I wish to share with you my *real* name, under the promise that you will never betray that to another living soul."

He nodded, and she said, "My real name is Evelyn Hanson. I was born and raised just outside Richmond, Virginia on a farm which owned several slaves, though my Daddy had inherited them and was very conflicted about their circumstance.

"Then when I was grown, I met a man and fell in love, and we are now betrothed. This man had also inherited slaves—hundreds of men, women, and children—but he was *not* ambivalent about them and was already making concrete plans for their emancipation, which he has since carried through with. Shortly after that he moved them all with him to a new farm in the North.

"From him I learned to hate the very idea of slavery and to love the great Union of these United States and all that it stands for. And even before the war began, some people in Richmond recruited me to help runaway slaves escape to the North as part of the Underground Railroad. Then as the secession was looming, these same people convinced me to help spy on behalf of the Union once the anticipated civil war broke out. And that is in fact what I have been doing to this day, as I have told you before."

Murphy nodded and gazed at her face as she told her tale, then continued to look into her eyes for a moment after she'd finished. He finally said, "Once again my heart tells me to believe every word you say, Miss Evelyn. God help me if I'm wrong ..."

"You aren't, Sergeant," she answered, mirroring his intense, serious expression, "you have a good heart, and it serves you well."

"Very well, then since we are now such trusting friends you must just call me Patrick."

She smiled so brightly at this, he couldn't help but smile back, "Thank you so much, Patrick! That is *truly* an honor, sir."

He shook his head, "No need to thank me, Miss Evelyn ... it is only my name, after all."

She chuckled, and they shared another smile before she once more took on a more serious tone. "Now I must tell you why I've brought you here, beyond a very sincere desire to see you once again; I have never forgotten how kindly you treated me during some of my darkest days, and how you tried to defend me against what we both believed was a very villainous Union officer ..."

He nodded as he recalled the incident, but allowed her to continue.

"I actually have a very simple request of you, and it may turn out very well for all concerned. Of course, there is always the chance it may *not* work out well, or that it may even turn out very badly."

"I'm listening, go on ..."

"I simply want to borrow a cell at the prison, so that some men I work with can bring in a prisoner for interrogation. These men are Union officers—*real* officers this time, and really from the War Department, though they won't be using their actual names, and their uniforms will not include their usual regimental insignia."

"I see. And the prisoner ... who is he?"

"He is ... a high-ranking civilian official working in the War Department. Our people have uncovered him as a spy for the Confederacy, and they wish to interrogate him in a secure place away from the War Department. The officers will have all the proper paperwork—though neatly forged, I will confess—so there is little threat of any negative repercussions for you should things go badly."

"Hmm ... it all seems pretty straightforward. I see no problem with any of that."

"Good, good. I was hoping you'd say that, Patrick. Thank you.

"*Oh!* And there is one more thing ... and it is extremely important," she said.

"Yes?"

"The room they use for interrogation *must* have a window overlooking the gallows in the prison yard."

"*Oh!*" he said, raising an eyebrow in curiosity.

ജ്യ‌ന്‍‌ര‌രോ‌ജ്‌ജ്‌ന്‍‌രോ‌ജ്‌ജ്‌ന്‍‌രോ

Union Intelligence Service chief, Allan Pinkerton, hurried down the steps of the War Department, eager to get home so he could prepare for his planned journey. With Robert E. Lee marching through Maryland, the president and secretary were desperate for intelligence on Lee's current troop dispositions, his movements, and his anticipated fighting capabilities once McClellan engaged him in earnest.

So Pinkerton had decided he would go himself, there being no substitute for seeing something with one's own eyes. He'd infiltrated the Confederate Army before, in the guise of a C.S.A. major, and planned to do the same again. It was a risky business, of course—if they caught you, you would surely hang—but he found he enjoyed the thrill of the risk and of the adventure, the straightforwardness of taking action personally. It was a refreshing change from the tedium of dealing with generals and politicians, all day, every day, for months on end.

But as he walked down the street, two Union officers—a major and a captain—approached, and stopped in front of him, as if they wished to speak with him.

He stopped and tipped his hat to them and said, "Good afternoon, gentlemen. Is there something I can do for you?"

"Good afternoon, Mr. Pinkerton," the major said. "I am Major Smith, and this is Captain Jones. We work in the War Department, sir."

"Good to make your acquaintance," Pinkerton answered out of politeness, trying not to sound annoyed at the interruption, but eager to be on his way.

"We wish to speak with you but a moment, sir," the major continued, "it is of a most urgent nature ..."

"I see ... then why did you not meet me in my office, good sirs?" Pinkerton asked, feeling irritated that these officers had met him on the street in order to circumvent the protocols of the War Department that would've been required for them to meet him in his office in the usual manner.

"The matter is ... of the utmost delicacy and requires a level of discretion that is simply not possible *inside*," the major said, nodding toward the War Department building.

"Will you come with us to a place where we may converse in private?" the major continued.

Pinkerton sighed, "Very well, major ... lead on."

The major and the captain led Pinkerton a few blocks north from the War Department building before turning into an alleyway. Pinkerton reached into his pocket and felt the handle of the small revolver he kept there. He knew it was always possible that enemy agents might try to eliminate him due to the importance of the intelligence-gathering work he was responsible for, so he always took certain precautions.

But the major led him through the back door of a house, and into a small sitting room, which held several comfortable chairs. After gesturing Pinkerton to enter, the captain closed the door behind them.

"Please, be seated and at your ease, Mr. Pinkerton," the major said, gesturing toward the chairs. "Would you like some tea, sir?"

"I thank you, but no ..." Pinkerton answered, as he chose a chair with its back to the wall and facing the door.

The major and the captain took seats facing him.

"We know you're a busy man," the major began with no preamble, "so let us get straight to the subject at hand, shall we?"

"By all means, major, please do so."

"In addition to our regular duties, the captain and I have certain acquaintances ... private citizens who are actively working on behalf of the Union of their own initiative ... in much the same line of work as yourself, Mr. Pinkerton."

"Gathering intelligence?" he asked, now frowning. "And are you two officers providing them with that intelligence?"

"No, sir," the major answered, shaking his head, "it flows in the other direction; these individuals provide *us* with information concerning the enemy's activities, both political and military. Some of it is gathered from the very highest levels of the Confederacy."

"I see ..." Pinkerton answered, noncommittally, continuing to frown.

"Some of this information has actually landed upon your desk, sir," the captain added, joining the conversation for the first time.

"Oh? And you were saying these friends of yours ... they are in Richmond? Otherwise, how would they have access to these rebel officials?"

"Yes, sir, they are in Richmond, though they are secretly loyal Unionists and long-time opponents of slavery."

"I see ... but neither of you sounds like a Virginian; in fact, I'd say you are from New England, likely Boston, by the accent. How is it you know these *private citizens* in Richmond?"

"You are correct, sir, we are indeed from Boston — very perceptive of you. And to answer your question, before the war we worked for a certain enterprise in Boston which is run by a family with relatives running a related business in Richmond. The two sides of the family are quite close, and all originated in Boston, so the Northern influence is the stronger. The individuals in Richmond have managed to infiltrate the rebel government, their military, and even the households of key C.S.A. officials. The information they gather is then passed to us, and depending on its nature, we either disseminate the intelligence directly to certain Army officers, or provide an anonymous report to your department, sir."

"Ah ... interesting ... and why have you not come to me earlier? I assume you now wish to connect me directly to these operatives in Richmond?"

The major exchanged a look with the captain, then turned to Pinkerton and said, "We ... we are not authorized to do so at this juncture, sir ... though that may be offered at some future point ..." he answered, shrugging apologetically.

"Oh! Well ... then why have you told me of this business, if you don't wish to include me in it?"

"Ah, now we get straight to the heart of the matter, sir," the major answered, leaning forward and looking intently into Pinkerton's eyes. "We have apprehended a certain high-ranking civilian official in the War Department whom our people in Richmond have uncovered as a rebel spy."

"Oh! And who might this person be?"

"He is Assistant Undersecretary of War Silas Baldwin," the major answered.

Pinkerton leaned back in his seat and gazed up at the ceiling for a moment as he absorbed this news. "Hmm ... yes, I can see it now ... a Virginian ... I suppose we should have known ..."

"Not to be contrary, sir," the captain interjected, "but I might remind you that there are *many* Virginians who have remained loyal to the Union, including most of the western half of that state."

"Yes, yes ... I meant no disparagement toward Virginians, per se ... It only serves to establish a connection. But Baldwin is well connected here in Washington ... you'd better have some rock-solid proof of what you say, gentlemen, else the water may get very hot, very quickly ..."

The major again shared a look with the captain, then looked back at Pinkerton and said, "The evidence is conclusive, sir. I have seen it myself, and it is indisputable. But ... unfortunately we can't present it to you, sir."

Pinkerton looked from one to the other of the officers in complete bewilderment. "Then ... why are we here, gentlemen? I can do nothing with an unsubstantiated accusation against an important official with no actual evidence." And then Pinkerton cringed as he thought of Nathan Chambers ... where he'd done exactly that—on the word of General McClellan alone. *But that was ... different ... General McClellan's word makes it a whole different matter*, he decided. *Besides, we've not arrested Chambers nor accused him of anything specific, only launched an investigation ... which has so far turned up nothing. Hmm … perhaps it's time to bring that episode to a conclusion.*

"It's a reasonable question, Mr. Pinkerton. We can't present the evidence for public—or even department—consumption, lest it expose our friends in Richmond, and even ourselves, for our involvement in the investigation. That would eliminate the future effectiveness of this valuable espionage resource as well as open up its individuals to possible reprisal by the enemy."

"Hmm … yes, I can appreciate that, but then …"

"We wish to enlist your help, Mr. Pinkerton, in extracting a full confession from Baldwin, along with convincing him to expose any other persons operating alongside him."

"You think to force him to confess? Gentlemen, I'll not be party to any torture. Not that I'm especially squeamish in that regard, but from my experience a man in extreme pain will sign anything you put in front of him to make it stop. There is no way to know if the information is valid or not at that point."

"We couldn't agree more, Mr. Pinkerton. We intend no violence toward him," the major said.

Then the captain grinned and added, "But we *do* mean to employ the *threat* of great violence …

"And … if we are successful, it is our intention to give you and your department full credit for uncovering the rebel agent and his entire spy network, keeping us and our friends completely out of it."

"Hmm …" Pinkerton said, thinking of the potential coup from exposing a whole den of spies in the very midst of the War Department. It would be a huge boost to his reputation, helping to offset some of the lingering negative effects from the failed Virginia peninsula campaign in the spring.

"All right … you now have my full attention … Tell me what you have in mind, gentlemen," he said, smiling for the first time since meeting the two officers on the street.

☙ℰ☙ℭℜ☙ℰ☙ℭℜℭ☙ℰ☙ℰℭℜℭℜ

Silas Baldwin sat on a bed in a cell of the Old Capitol Prison, gazing at two Union officers standing there, a major and a captain.

They'd introduced themselves as Smith and Jones, respectively — false names, he assumed, especially considering they had not mentioned their regiments, nor did their uniforms have any identifying badges beyond their rank.

And though they'd told him they had concrete evidence against him, so far they'd stated nothing specific, and hadn't produced incriminating documentation. He was beginning to think this was a fishing expedition only, and that these were not real officers at all ... If he just kept his mouth shut and denied everything, eventually they'd have to let him go for fear of his powerful friends in Washington. Then he'd burn everything and slip quietly back to Richmond where he'd be welcomed as a hero. So he ignored their questions and merely gazed at them with a smug look.

And then a tough-looking sergeant stepped up to the outside of the iron bars of the door and unlocked it, opening it for a man to enter. As the man stepped into the light of the oil lamp in the cell, Baldwin's heart sank. He immediately recognized the serious visage of Allan Pinkerton, chief of Union intelligence. *So ... this is his operation. Still,* he decided ... *best to just say nothing.*

Pinkerton stepped past the officers and went straight to the bunk opposite Baldwin and sat down heavily. "Long day, Baldwin. I find I'm tired to the bone, and ready to head home for a little shut eye. But we have this ... *matter* to attend first."

Baldwin just gazed at him and said nothing.

Pinkerton returned his gaze steadily, a bland expression on his face. "So, Baldwin ... the evidence against you is indisputable ... the only question that remains is ... how this turns out for you."

But Baldwin decided to continue his silence to see what Pinkerton would do about that. It was then he noticed a loud banging sound coming from the prison yard outside.

The major said, "Well ... *that's* annoying. What the devil?" he turned toward the door and shouted, "Sergeant! Sergeant Murphy!"

In a moment the sergeant appeared outside the door, "Yes, sir?" he asked.

"Sergeant ... what is that horrible racket outside? That noise is making it most difficult to conduct our interrogation."

"Sorry ... orders, sir," the sergeant answered.

"Orders for what, and by whom?" the major asked.

"Orders from Mr. Pinkerton, sir. When he arrived at the prison, he asked me if the gallows was in good working order. Which I answered it needed a few minor repairs that I'd been meaning to get to, but ... Anyway, Mr. Pinkerton ordered me to ready the gallows post haste, so I have sent the carpenter out to make the necessary repairs. It's *his* hammer you're hearing, sir."

"Ah ... excellent, sergeant. Carry on then."

"Very good, sir. Thank you, sir."

Pinkerton stood and looked out the window. "Yes, I wished them to be prepared. I know it's traditional to hold executions at first light in the morning, but ... I'm tired and have a busy day tomorrow ... no time for such sentimental nonsense. No reason not to just get the business over with tonight.

"Hmm ... perfect view from here ... Perhaps I'll just watch from up here and stay warm. Chilly night out," Pinkerton concluded, and returned to his seat on the bunk.

Against his better judgement, Baldwin stood and looked out the window down toward the yard. Four soldiers stood around the gallows platform holding up torches, as another one pounded nails with a hammer up on the decking.

Baldwin turned and returned to his seat on the bunk, suddenly feeling lightheaded and slightly shaky.

"You wouldn't ..." he said, in a voice barely above a whisper.

"Mr. Baldwin ... I have seen the damning evidence our department has compiled against you and your associates ... There can be no doubt of your guilt. Secretary Stanton has authorized me to hang anyone caught conducting espionage within the War Department—and with the current national emergency, the president has suspended the bother of a trial. So ... as you can see, I *can*, and I *will*."

Baldwin's earlier smirk was gone, and his demeanor had turned deadly serious. And the banging noise outside was making it difficult for him to think clearly. "But I am a high-ranking government official ... I give orders to officers, and they obey ... I order troop movements ... I order the acquisition of arms, and ... if I order you to release me ... *you must do it!*" he said, his desperation now bordering on hysteria.

But Pinkerton just looked at him steadily and said, "No ... I don't think so, Baldwin. Although ..."

"Yes?" Baldwin asked.

"Although ... I might be convinced to spare your neck ... *if* ..."

Baldwin just looked at him wide-eyed, now hanging on to Pinkerton's every word ...

"If you give me something in return for my largesse ... let's say a signed confession, for starters. Followed by a complete list of your associates, and details of all your activities and communications with the rebel government. Then I will only throw you in prison—oh, nothing as nice as this, to be sure, but still ... better than having one's neck stretched, I should think. And who knows ... if you're lucky, once the war's over, and a few more years have gone by, they may even decide to parole you."

"But I'm not ... I didn't—" Baldwin started.

"Oh, *please*, sir," Pinkerton interrupted, "I'm tired, and ready for bed. Surely you're not going to waste my time trying to convince me that the mountain of evidence I've seen with my very own eyes is all false ... that you are entirely innocent of these charges?"

Baldwin gazed at him, eyes now wide and lips trembling, "No ... no, I'll not deny it ... I'll sign a confession, if you'll guarantee I'll not swing. But I'll not give away my compatriots ..."

Pinkerton nodded, then turned to the door and said, "Sergeant ... how are those repairs coming along?"

"Almost complete, I'm told, Mr. Pinkerton, sir. Should be only a few minutes more and then everything will be ready to go. I've taken the liberty of asking the quartermaster to tie up a proper noose, so there'll be no delay in that regard, sir."

"Ah, good thought, sergeant, very efficient of you, thank you."

Pinkerton stood, "Well, Baldwin, since we have nothing further to discuss ..."

"No! Wait!"

Pinkerton paused and turned back toward Baldwin with a raised eyebrow.

"Wait ... wait ... I'll give you the information you ask for ... if you'll sign a document promising not to hang anyone whose name I give you."

Pinkerton thought about this a moment, then said, "Done. Major Smith will produce the appropriate paperwork for your signature, and I will send two of my detectives to gather the other information in the morning."

He turned and moved toward the hallway, calling out, "Sergeant, the door ... if you please."

But as the sergeant opened the door Pinkerton turned around and faced Baldwin one last time. "Oh, and don't think you can cheat me on the information you provide. Assume we already know the names of several of your fellow conspirators — or possibly all — and already have much of the information you have promised to provide. If I find you are being anything less the completely forthcoming with me, I will order your execution after all."

Then he smiled, "And I may even suggest that the warden hold the hanging in the afternoon — I hear we're in for some fair weather ... perhaps he'll let the other prisoners have a picnic while they watch you swing ..."

After Pinkerton had departed, Sergeant Murphy returned to his normal duties downstairs. He immediately ordered the work detail back inside. One of the privates walked up to Murphy and handed him a hammer. "Here's your hammer back, Sarge. I still don't understand why you wanted me to bang on that gallows platform ... and me without any nails!"

But Sergeant Murphy just smiled, and said, "Never you mind that, Phillips ... you've done good, son. Just enjoy the praise and don't think so much. This *is* the Army, after all."

The private returned Murphy's smile, shrugged, and then went back to his regular watch.

Murphy walked back to his office to put the hammer away, but when he entered the room, he noticed something was different. His old, stiff wooden chair had been replaced by a new, softly padded leather one. He chuckled as he moved around the desk, letting out a heavy sigh of satisfaction as he sank down into the soft cushions. *Thank you, Miss Evelyn!*

Chapter 9. Bloody Lane

"The slain lay in rows precisely
as they had stood in their ranks
a few moments before.
It was never my fortune to witness
a more bloody, dismal battlefield."
- **Union Major Gen. Joseph Hooker**
describing the
Battle of Antietam

Wednesday September 17, 1862 – Racine, Ohio:

"I exchanged telegrams with Governor Pierpont this morning, Tom," Nathan said, sitting across from Tom at their camp table just outside the small town of Racine on the Ohio side of the river. They sipped a cup of coffee, enjoying a moment of relaxation before saddling up for the ride to Point Pleasant further south along the river where Colonel Lightburn was now gathering his troops. Nathan had a scowl on his face, so Tom knew it couldn't be *good* news.

"What does his honor have to say?" Tom prompted.

"Well, of course he is pleased with our efforts in helping to rescue Lightburn and all the troops, civilians, and equipment, and he gives his thanks."

Tom nodded, then asked, "*And ...?*"

Nathan snorted, "And it seems our *friend* McClellan is up to his old tricks ..." he answered.

"Oh? How so?"

"He's crowing over crushing a small rebel force at a place called South Mountain in Maryland. But it's another pyrrhic victory ... The governor says McClellan's movements were so sluggish that he's not only allowed Lee to consolidate his previously divided forces in preparation for a major showdown somewhere south of there, but—*here's the part that just boils my blood*, and it will yours too, Tom—he moved so slowly and cautiously that he has allowed Stonewall Jackson to capture Harpers Ferry."

"*What?!* After all we did to keep Jackson out of that town this spring? McClellan just lets him take it without a fight?! *Unbelievable ...*"

"Yep ... and Colonel Miles surrendered his entire garrison there of 11,000 men after enduring a brief artillery barrage from the surrounding heights. *Despicable* ... If only we'd been there again. What could we have accomplished with 11,000 fully equipped men, Tom? We wouldn't have ceded the heights for one, and we would've whipped Jackson for another, that's what ..."

"Well, we could hardly have been in two places at once, Captain," Tom said, "and we were certainly needed here in the Kanawha Valley."

Nathan just shook his head slowly in disgust, "*McClellan!*" he said and spat, as if the name was a curse.

അയ്യോ ഇ അ

Wednesday September 17, 1862 – Sharpsburg, Maryland:

C.S.A. Major Ollie Boyd entered General Lee's command tent to give his report, just as the sun was beginning to lighten the eastern sky. A silence had fallen over the area, as if all of nature was waiting with bated breath to see what the day would bring. Ollie had no illusions that the silence would last, with two vast armies gathered mere yards apart, on the brink of battle.

He stepped right up to the general's table and waited for Lee's attention. Per the general's orders, formalities between the staff officers, such as saluting, had been suspended until the pending engagement was concluded, in order to save time and improve efficiency. But it required an effort of will for Ollie to obey that directive; the habit was now so entirely unconscious.

"Lee glanced up, then back down at the document in front of him, "Oliver ... your report, please," Lee said in a quiet voice. And though he was calm by all appearances, Ollie thought he noted the slightest hint of tension and pent-up emotion in the seemingly unflappable general.

"Sir ... all the intelligence I've been able to gather is in agreement that McClellan commands three large wings under generals Franklin, Sumner, and Burnside—a force of between 75,000 and 85,000 officers and men. We have prepared a reasonably good breakdown by corps, division, and regiment for you—here, sir," he said, handing a sheet of paper across to the general.

"At least ... these were his numbers when he set out from Washington a week ago," Ollie added. "Our sources in Washington—those who provided us the information on ... the *other matter* we recently discussed ..." Ollie said cryptically, referring to the information concerning Lee's battle orders which had mysteriously fallen into McClellan's hands, "... have mysteriously gone silent in the past several days ... I don't know what that means ..." Ollie said, glancing to the side where the other staff officers were busily working, before shrugging apologetically.

"Hmm ... well, nothing we can do about that now. And what about our own counts?" Lee asked.

"Our own forces, discounting those who've not yet arrived, the wounded, sick, and ... *missing* ... are roughly 38,000 at the moment," Ollie announced. A shocked silence fell over the room, and suddenly all eyes were on General Lee.

"You're *sure* of these numbers?" Lee asked.

"No, sir. But they are the best estimates we have ... and I believe the numbers are ... at least in the correct *proportion* between the two armies."

Lee nodded, "Meaning McClellan has us outnumbered at least two to one ..."

"Yes, sir. It would appear so, sir. And likely he will be bringing up more reinforcements as time allows ..."

Lieutenant Colonel Robert Chilton looked at Lee and asked, "Shall I write up the orders for a general withdrawal, sir?"

But Ollie surprised himself by answering the question before General Lee could, "I think it may be too late for that, Colonel.

General Hooker crossed the Antietam last night with a considerable federal force on our left flank. Our scouts expect an attack from that direction at first light, which could come at any minute now. We will at least have to counter that stroke before we can pull back ... assuming McClellan doesn't ... launch ... *a larger* ..." he trailed off, suddenly feeling self-conscious, realizing he may have *way* overstepped his bounds by presuming to answer for the general.

But Lee ignored the indiscretion, bailing him out of his discomfort, by saying, "Oliver is right ... it is too late for a general withdrawal—not without a fight, in any case.

"Besides ... never forget who our opponent is out there: *George B. McClellan.* This is the *same* man whose slowness and timidity allowed us to preserve Richmond after his invasion of the peninsula, despite having us vastly outnumbered, out supplied, and dangerously spread thin in the defense ..."

Then Lee was quiet and thoughtful for several moments, clearly contemplating his next move. No one spoke or thought to offer suggestions; if Robert E. Lee couldn't think of the strategy to save the army, then none of them had any hope of doing so.

After several minutes, Lee sat up straight, shoved the stack of papers he had in front of him off to the side, and spread out a map, gazing at it intently.

"Gentlemen ... our only hope is to use McClellan's weaknesses against him," he began. "We know he is overly cautious and slow to react, along with a propensity for always believing he is outnumbered, regardless of the reality. We must reinforce this belief by swift movement. Being on the defensive, we have the advantage of shortened lines for communication and troop movement.

"Send a message to Generals Jackson and Longstreet straight away. Tell them to communicate *this* to their subordinates; that they must be ready to pick up and move to a new location on a moment's notice, at the double-quick, without thought or hesitation, based on my word alone, as passed through my couriers.

"We may even forgo the normal chain of command, if necessary," Lee continued, "So please inform the generals that I may issue orders to their subordinates directly in order to save time and prevent miscommunication—by which I mean them no disrespect.

"As long as McClellan hesitates to send his entire force at once, and only attacks us piecemeal—as I fully expect he will—we can move our forces to meet each new threat, constantly re-positioning units as needed. This should prevent the federals from breaking through our lines," Lee concluded.

There were nods of agreement around the room; this seemed a sound strategy, until General Long, Lee's military secretary asked, "And ... what if McClellan *does* send his whole force all at once, sir?"

Lee didn't immediately answer. He gazed up at the ceiling of his command tent for a long moment, then sighed, looked back down and said, "Then we shall be annihilated, general."

ಐಹಿಂಜಇಐಹಿಂಜಇಐಹಿಂಜ

Union Captain James Hawkins, of the Seventh Loyal Virginia, was suddenly aware of a great roaring and buzzing noise, and he slowly opened his eyes. Or rather tried to, as only his left eye would open, the other refusing to cooperate. He reached up and felt of it, fearing the worst, but quickly realized the eye was not even injured, simply glued shut by a thick rind of blood that had run down from the top of his head. He felt further up and discovered a ragged, crusty wound that had removed a large chunk of his scalp and hair.

He gave a quick prayer of thanks, suddenly aware that he was alive, but had very nearly *not* been. But this appreciation for his good fortune was short-lived; as he gazed through a thick pall of gun smoke out toward the dug-in rebel position his men had dubbed the "sunken road," a few dozen yards away, he saw that a great battle yet raged.

And at the moment, the rebels were getting the worst of it. After hours of bloody combat, leading to a virtual stalemate with neither side able to gain any great advantage, it appeared that a regiment of Union soldiers had somehow managed to flank the rebel position and now held a piece of high ground that looked directly down the length of the sunken road, making it a horrific death trap for the rebels lying there.

Using what was known in military parlance as enfilading fire, the Union soldiers raked the rebels with volley after volley down the length of the makeshift trench, such that a single rifle bullet could potentially rip through multiple men, to devastating effect. And even poorly aimed shots and ricochets were likely to find a mark.

As Hawkins gazed in horror, rebel soldiers were torn apart by the dozens, falling in heaps, defenseless against the slaughter. After several moments of this, a bugle sounded, and a Confederate officer led a hasty retreat of several thousand men, up out of the road, and off to the south at the double-quick.

Hawkins looked down the lane and saw the Union soldiers turn and follow the retreating enemy, continuing to fire as they went.

And then what had been an ear-splitting, chaotic cacophony of battle just moments before, was suddenly transformed into an eerie, nearly silent charnel house. The bloody, torn bodies of men, both gray clad and blue, lay piled deep on the sloping bank and down on the roadway in front of him. It was a mesmerizing, sickening sight such as James Hawkins had never seen before, despite all the battles he'd previously fought. Nothing could compare to the absolute, stark horror he saw spread out before him as far as his eyes could see …

Hawkins raised himself to a sitting position, groaning from the throbbing pain in his head, then forced himself to stand. Without a clear idea of what he was about, he stumbled forward, down the hill and onto the sunken road. He had a mind to follow the Union soldiers, and join in their attack, but his legs were wobbly, weak, and uncooperative. He quickly realized he had no more fight left in him this day. He turned to retreat back toward the main Union lines, but stumbled on a rebel body lying there. The body groaned, and opened its eyes.

The man sat up. He wore a Confederate lieutenant's uniform, and when he met eyes with Captain Hawkins, he immediately reached down and unholstered his pistol. Hawkins reacted instantly, pulling out his own pistol. But the Confederate had beaten him to the draw, and Hawkins knew with sickening certainty that he was about to die. But even as his own pistol cleared leather, Hawkins heard the *click* of the Confederate's pistol hammer falling harmlessly on an empty chamber.

And if he'd have had a clearer mind, James Hawkins might have stayed his own hand, but his pistol was already moving in a desperate bid to save himself. So before he had any conscious thought of doing anything to the contrary, he had pulled back the hammer and squeezed the trigger, with his gun aimed directly at the young man's face.

But Hawkins pistol also *clicked* on an empty chamber.

The two young men stared blankly at each other, both dazed and bewildered as to what had just happened.

Then Hawkins snorted a mirthless chuckle, and re-holstered his pistol. The Confederate lieutenant gazed at him for another moment, then looked down at his own pistol, shrugged his shoulders, and did the same.

"I reckon this just isn't our day to die, Johnny Reb," Hawkins said, with a wan smile.

The rebel nodded, "Yep ... reckon not, Yank." Then the rebel surprised Hawkins by extending his hand, saying, "First Lieutenant Jubal Collins, Twenty-Seventh Virginia."

Hawkins stared open-mouthed at the proffered hand, before reaching out and shaking it, "Captain James Hawkins, Seventh Loyal Virginia," he answered.

"*Ah* ... we done heard o' y'all," Jubal said. "They call you the *'Bloody Seventh,'* same as us. We've fought y'all before, down in the Shenandoah Valley."

"Yes, that's true. And we've heard of you too ... the *'Bloody Twenty-Seventh,'* part of the infamous Stonewall Brigade we've been battling nearly the whole war. You guys seem to always be around when the fighting is thickest."

Jubal nodded and smiled, then gazed about at the carnage, and his expression immediately darkened. "Reckon we both earned that nickname today down in this-here *bloody lane*, captain."

"Yes ... I reckon so, lieutenant."

They both gazed at the unfathomable scene before them for a long moment before Captain Hawkins turned back to the lieutenant and said, "Well ... good meeting you, Collins. Guess we best be making our way back to our own lines, 'fore someone decides to take a shot at us."

"Yeah, reckon so," Jubal answered.

The two men turned, and started back toward their respective lines, but then Captain Hawkins called out, "Oh, lieutenant ..."

Jubal stopped and turned, "Captain?"

"I'm happy my pistol was out of bullets just now, lieutenant."

Jubal nodded, "Me too, captain. Me too."

☙ℰℭℬℰℰℰℭℬℰℰℰℭℬ☙

Jubal Collins weaved his way between the bodies as he made his way out of the death trap his fellow Confederate soldiers had dubbed the "Bloody Lane." He was looking for any signs of life among the fallen when he recognized a face and suffered a terrible shock. It was his commanding officer, Captain Bob Hill, blood covering a greater part of the front of his uniform tunic.

Jubal stopped and knelt down, respectfully doffing his cap as he said a quick prayer for the man's soul. Then, remembering the captain's habit of writing letters to his lady friend, he carefully opened the captain's tunic, and reached into the inner pocket to see if there was anything there. And then to his shock, he heard a cough, and a soft moan. He reached out, opened one of the captain's eyelids, and saw that his pupils were *not* dilated— Captain Hill yet lived!

Jubal leaned down, grabbed Hill under the arms and lifted, standing as he did. He slung the captain's inert form up over his shoulder and patted him softly on the back. "Maybe it ain't your day to die either, captain. Leastways not if I have anything to say about it!"

He moved out again, this time picking up his pace despite the heavy burden, praying that he might make it back to the surgeons with his captain still alive.

ᔄᘔᘏᘓᘔᘏᔄᘔᘏᘓᘔᘏᔄᘔᘏᘓᘔᘏ

James Hawkins made his way slowly and painfully up the slope that led up out of the sunken road. He had to pick his way through countless dead and mangled bodies, blood, limbs, and entrails strewn everywhere. He looked for any signs of life as he did so, but wondered what he might do if he saw anyone who was only wounded. He was badly wounded himself, and hardly in any condition to carry another man. But fortunately for him, if not for them, he only encountered corpses.

When he reached the crest of the rise and went over the top, he was surprised to see a vast column of Union soldiers formed up there, with a Major General sitting his horse out front. When the general saw him, he spurred his horse forward, followed by his staff officers.

"What's your name, son, and what regiment are you with?" the general asked.

Captain Hawkins saluted, and gave the general his name and regiment.

The general returned the salute, "Seventh, eh? Part of Sumner's army ... I'm General Franklin, what's the situation here, Captain?"

"Your timing couldn't be better, general," Hawkins answered, hardly believing the good luck, "a Union regiment, or maybe two—from New York, I think—has just cleared the sunken road with enfilading fire, and the rebels have fallen back in disarray. The center of General Lee's line is now wide open for your attack. If you move now, you will finish the rebel army, of that I'm certain."

But rather than ordering an immediate advance, as Hawkins expected, General Franklin hesitated.

"What is it, general?" Hawkins couldn't resist asking, though strictly speaking, it was not his place to question a general.

General Franklin scowled, "My column has just arrived at the front, and I have express orders from General McClellan and also from General Sumner—my superior—*not* to attack. I must have them countermand those orders before I may advance."

Hawkins groaned with frustration, "Then, with all due respect, general, I suggest you do so straight away before this golden opportunity is lost and the rebels close the gap."

General Franklin nodded, then snapped a salute at Hawkins, who immediately returned it. The general said a few curt words to his staff officers that Hawkins could not make out, then turned his horse and spurred off at great speed with several of his officers following.

James Hawkins shook his head in disbelief, but knew there was nothing more he could do. So he slowly made his way back to the Union camp, where he was greeted with great joy and relief by his own company of the Seventh, who'd feared the worst when they had not been able to locate his body when they'd been ordered to withdraw earlier in the day.

It wasn't until later that evening that Captain Hawkins learned that both General Sumner and General McClellan had refused General Franklin's earnest request that he be allowed to follow up the breakthrough on the sunken road with an assault to push through and finish off the desperate, beleaguered rebel army of Robert E. Lee.

Instead, the battle raged on for the remainder of the day, costing thousands more lives as the outnumbered Lee battled McClellan's Army of the Potomac to a virtual draw.

∾∾∾∾∾∾∾∾∾

Monday September 22, 1862 – Deerfield, Missouri:

"Whatcha thinkin' Ned?" Sid whispered as they peered through the bushes on a small rise overlooking a village with a general store, post office, and a few other buildings, surrounded by a half-dozen scattered farmhouses. They'd left the road a few miles back so they could reconnoiter the town before passing through.

In the last little town they'd been through, two days earlier, they'd met an old white man with a scruffy gray beard and a worn-looking horse pulling an even more worn-looking wagon, full of pots, pans, and various other odds and ends that the man said he'd repair then sell. He said he was a traveling "tinker," though Ned wasn't sure what that meant.

Fortunately, the tinker was a northerner and sympathetic toward their plight. He gave them directions to Fort Scott, Kansas and explained they could be there in three days' steady travel, crossing the border from Missouri into Kansas on the middle of the third day—*if* they were lucky.

When Ned asked him what kind of *luck* they might need, the tinker explained there was a notorious gang of rebel bushwhackers operating in the area, who might give them trouble. The bushwhackers were led by a cruel, lawless young man named William Anderson, who went by the nickname "Bloody Bill." The tinker said Bloody Bill had a piratical look about him, and acted the part. Though Ned didn't know exactly what that meant, he took it for a bad thing.

Up until this point, they'd been able to keep a low profile, and despite the generally unsettled situation in Missouri, they'd had little real trouble—nothing more serious than some degrading remarks and sour looks from a few town folks. Ned set the tone by looking stern, serious, and tough, without showing any outward reaction to anything negative directed toward them. It was a demeanor he'd spent his entire life perfecting, so it came naturally.

But now, looking down upon the little village, they could see a group of ten or more men lounging about. And these were not typical farmers and tradesmen. Nor did they have the look of common laborers, though their clothing was similar: well-worn and dirty.

For one, these men did not seem to have any particular occupation or reason for being there, despite being young and healthy looking. And for another, all appeared to be armed, with pistols and knives at their belts, and rifles leaning against nearby fenceposts or building walls. But since they wore no uniforms, it was impossible to tell for sure which side they were on.

"Secesh bushwhackers, or I'm a snake ..." Ned said with a scowl.

"What'll we do?" Caleb asked, "Find some other road?"

"Hmm ... the tinker said there was only one road in these parts that lead to Kansas and Fort Scott. We get off the road and we'll get lost in the wilds and maybe never find our way ..." Ned answered.

He turned away from the view and sat on the ground. Pulling his knees up, he leaned his head against them and was quiet for a long time. Though there'd never been any discussion of it, and everyone felt free to give his opinion, regardless of the circumstances, they all looked to Ned to make the hard choices when it came right down to it. So the others said nothing, waiting for Ned to think on what to do next.

It was still early morning. Assuming the tinker's directions had been correct, if they followed the road through this little town, which the tinker had called Deerfield, they would be at Fort Scott, Kansas before nightfall.

Finally, Ned lifted his head, then stood, pulling off his knapsack as he did. He set the pack on the ground, then reached inside and pulled something out. In a moment he was strapping a well-worn pistol holster around his waist. "We're done sneakin' and hidin'. It's time to be *men*. The Captain says, 'A strong show of arms may prevent a fight. If the other'n thinks it'll cost him dear, mayhap he'll back down.' If not ..." he shrugged.

Ned unholstered the pistol, then kneeling down, pulled out a small leather bag that held the lead balls and percussion caps he needed to load it, along with a powder horn.

The others gazed at him a moment, several wide-eyed, but nobody spoke. Caleb and Sid exchanged a look, but then Sid shrugged, and they all unshouldered their packs and dug out their pistols.

After Ned's revolver was loaded, he slipped it back into its holster. Then he walked over to the packhorse and pulled off a long, heavy canvas bag, laying it carefully on the ground. He untied the straps that held the bag closed, and rolled it open, unveiling five rifles contained within. He grabbed one, and loaded it too. The others quickly did the same.

ಬಒಣಅಬಒಣಅಬಒಣ

They walked slowly down the road, right through the center of town. Ned led the way, with Jack in the rear leading the packhorse. All carried loaded rifles in their hands, held across their chests, with pistols in holsters at their hips. Ned had told Jack if the shooting started, to just let the horse go and use his gun—they were close enough to Kansas now that they could get by without it.

He had instructed them to let him do the talking if there was any, and not to make any move to use their weapons unless they saw him do it first, or he was shot dead. They all nodded, and nobody spoke or offered any disagreement.

Then as they began to move out toward the road, he stopped and turned back to them, "One more thing … if they get the drop on us and y'all are thinkin' on surrenderin' … *don't!* They'll just murder us slow. Best to die fightin', gun in hand—mebbe take one or two o' them varmints with you." He was gratified to see serious, hard looks, but no panic or fear, so he turned and led on.

They had passed by the first several of the young toughs, with little reaction, and Ned was daring to hope they'd be able to bluff their way past. But when they'd reached the middle of town, he was disabused of the idea as a lean man with long dark hair, a mustache, intense hard-looking eyes and a wicked grin stepped out in front of them on the road, blocking their way. Ned had a feeling this must be the bushwhacker "Bloody Bill" that the tinker had spoken of, and he now had a pretty good idea what a piratical look was.

Without thinking, Ned held up his right hand in a fist, the army signal for a column to halt. But if the man recognized the significance of Ned's knowing that signal, he showed no sign of it.

"Where y'all think you're goin', boy?" the man asked Ned.

But Ned didn't immediately answer. Instead, he stood and gazed at the man with a hard look. He suddenly realized this man was the very essence of what he hated most in many white men: arrogant, overly confident, cruel, and uncaring. A man who expected to be obeyed for no other reason than the color of the skin he was born with.

It raised Ned's ire, and heated his blood; but he resisted the urge to snap back an insolent response, still hopeful they might get out of this situation without the need of violence.

"Reckon we's just passin' through, headed to Kansas, over yonder. Ain't got no cause for trouble with any o' y'all," he answered, looking the man in the eye even as the Captain had taught him to do, forcing Ned to override a lifetime of doing the exact opposite when addressing a white man.

But if the man was surprised by this, he didn't show it. "Well now … I heard some uppity darkies is fixin' to go over to Kansas and sign up to fight with them cowardly Yankees in their war of aggression again' us freedom-loving men. Don't suppose y'all are some of them types … with your *guns* and all?" he said, in a tone that couldn't be mistaken for anything other than heavy sarcasm.

Ned figured the game was now up and there was no way these men were going to let them past peaceably. He decided to try the Captain's method of a strong show of force, so he said, "If'n we was … then I reckon we'd not be the type who'd let other men tell them whether they could or no …"

The man laughed, and turned to the side, speaking to his own men, who were now gathering around. He said, "You hear that, boys? The darkie boy says he'll not be swayed from his path!" and he laughed again. But Ned noticed either by oversight or overconfidence, most of the bushwhackers had not bothered to gather their rifles from where they'd propped them. Several had pistols at their hips or tucked into their belts, however.

Then the man looked back at Ned and was no longer smiling. He said, "Lookie here, boy … my name's Bloody Bill … You heard o' me?"

Ned just shrugged noncommittally.

"Well, there's a reason they call me that … so if I was you boys, I'd drop them guns, and turn around and go back the way you come. Reckon there's a dozen o' us, again' only five o' y'all. And unlike y'all, we actually know how to *shoot* a gun," he said, and laughed again at his own cruel, demeaning humor.

But rather than answer, Ned immediately lowered his rifle, pointed it straight at Bloody Bill's chest, and cocked the hammer. Almost in sync with Ned, the rest of the freemen snapped their rifles down, aiming at the men surrounding them.

"Reckon I can shoot well enough from this distance," Ned said in answer, staring Bill in the eye. "Y'all may kill us all, but *you* won't live to see it … and I reckon you'll finally earn that nickname … *Bloody.*"

But Ned had to give the man credit; despite the deadly threat, he showed no sign of fear, instead scowling darkly at Ned. But he did raise his hands slowly as if surrendering. But even as his hands reached head high, he snapped his fingers, and a gunshot rang out. Ned's rifle shuddered violently, wrenching itself from his grasp, and spinning to the ground. He realized a bullet had struck the stock of his gun just past the trigger plate, knocking it free and numbing his hands from the shock.

Multiple gunshots rang out around him as he reached for his pistol and instinctively knelt to the ground and ducked to reduce the target he presented. But when he looked up to fire at Bloody Bill, the man was gone, so he turned and fired at a different man who raised up from behind a barrel with a pistol. The man flinched and ducked back down, but hadn't been hit.

Then Ned saw a sudden motion to his left, and the large form of the pack horse was next to him with Jack beside it. And as he passed, Jack reached down and grabbed the back of Ned's shirt and pulled, forcing him to stand and run forward. Gunshots continued to sound as Ned stumbled ahead, trying not to drop his pistol while struggling to maintain his balance.

When they reached a small stand of trees, Jack let the horse go, and pulled his pistol. The two of them ducked behind tree trunks, then turned and aimed their pistols back the way they'd come. Ned was surprised to see their other three, Caleb, Sid, and Sammy running toward them, bent over nearly double while firing their pistols blindly backward as they ran.

Ned and Jack fired their pistols at anyone they saw back toward the buildings as their comrades approached the relative safety of the trees. When the others dived in beside them, Ned took quick stock of their situation. By good fortune, pure chance, or one of the Captain's God-granted miracles, they'd all made it thus far without being hit. But Ned knew from his training they could not hold their current position long, being badly outnumbered. The enemy would soon flank them, and they'd be killed in a deadly crossfire.

"Let's move!" he said, and without waiting for a response, Ned stood and sprinted down the road to the west—the road to Kansas.

For the next five hours, Ned, Jack, Sid, Sammy, and Caleb fought a running gun battle against the bushwhackers, while continuing to retreat toward the west and the Kansas border. Sid and Sammy still had their rifles, but the others were down to only their pistols. From a series of short, breathless, sometimes conflicting explanations, Ned pieced together what had happened after he'd pointed his rifle at Bloody Bill and all hell had broken loose.

Apparently on a signal from Bill, one of the bushwhackers had shot Ned's rifle from his hands. But the sound of the gunshot had startled the rest of the freemen into pulling the triggers of their rifles, unleashing a sudden, devastating volley that had killed several rebels and sent the remainder reeling, scrambling for cover. The shock and surprise had given the freemen the precious seconds they needed to affect their desperate escape. Jack, with great presence of mind, had disobeyed Ned's instructions; rather than immediately dropping the horse's lead and focusing on the gunplay, he'd dropped his spent rifle, grabbed the lead, and run toward Ned, grabbing him and using the horse as a shield.

The others had pulled their pistols and opened fire at anyone who moved, even as they sprinted after Jack, Ned, and the pack horse.

They'd managed to make it several miles west of Deerfield, continuing to move and fight, even as the Captain had taught them to do. But now Ned figured their fight was about done … and not in a good way.

They'd long since finished the water in their canteens. And the pack horse, carrying their spare ammunition, water skins, and other gear, had run off after Jack had dropped the lead to fight, bolting at the sound of the gunfire. Now they were beginning to suffer from thirst in the burning heat of the day, in a land of waist high, dry rolling grass, gullies, and occasional thickets of short trees or bushes—but no water.

But worst of all, they were running short on pistol balls. Ned considered what would happen if they ran completely out of ammunition. The rebels would take them without killing them … then the pain would start in earnest, with only death as an eventual release. Not a pleasant prospect.

He turned to the others and said, "Look here … we're down to our last few shots. Y'all know what they's gonna do to us if they catch us alive. I reckon let's charge 'em, kill as many as we can, but force them to shoot us down so's we die quick."

And then for the first time on their journey, Ned asked, "Do y'all agree?" He figured he ought not be the one to decide on another man's choice of how to die.

He looked from one to the next, waiting until each said, "Yes," or nodded. When he finally got to Caleb, who was the least bold among them, he was surprised to see Caleb looking him straight in the eyes with little fear as he said, "I reckon you's right on it, Ned. I'm tired and thirsty … let's get this over with."

Ned nodded, and pulled his pistol, reloading the empty cylinders. He only had enough balls left to load four of the six. After a few moments, he looked around at the others, and they nodded. Sid and Sammy still had their rifles, so he said, "Go ahead and fire those off when we start, then drop them here and use your pistols," then he smiled at them, one of the few they'd ever seen from him, and he said, "No sense tirin' yourselves out carryin' them heavy guns."

They returned his smile, and Sid chuckled, though there was little humor in it.

"Ready?" Ned asked. *"Let's go!"* he shouted, then jumped up and scrambled out of the ditch they'd been hiding in. He charged ahead, pistol held out front, even as he heard the rifles of Sid and Sammy ring out just behind him, *boom … boom!* He was surprised he was yelling as he ran, a wordless, primal shout welling up from some dark place deep inside him. He glanced to the sides and saw the others running with him, yelling as well, squeezing off pistol shots as they ran. But Ned had not fired his Colt yet. He wanted to wait until he was up close, close enough to see the man he was putting a bullet through, even as the man ended his own life.

And at first the bushwhackers, now only a hundred yards or so away, spread in an arc behind bushes, trees, and berms, returned fire, *pops* of gunfire sounding, and puffs of smoke rising up in the air in the near distance.

But then, for some reason Ned could not fathom, the rebels let off firing completely. Then he heard an entirely unexpected sound; a tremendous volley of gunfire coming from directly behind him, accompanied by the unmistakable sound of galloping hooves from dozens of horses. And in another moment, a horse flashed past him, thundering ahead, even as its rider fired off a pistol shot, aimed out toward where the rebels had been. Other horses passed by off to the sides, following after the first.

And then Ned stopped in his tracks and leaned down, gasping for breath as several shocking realizations hit him in the space of as many heartbeats: first, he was not dead after all, and second, the man who'd just ridden past him wore a dark blue, Union uniform, with a captain's insignia on the shoulder. But then, oddest of all … the man had a *black* face!

꘠꘠꘠꘠꘠꘠꘠꘠꘠꘠꘠

After less than five minutes the gunfire ceased, and Ned looked up to see the Union cavalry soldiers trotting back to where he and the other freemen stood, gazing out toward them. Most of the soldiers were black men, though all but two of the officers were white.

The black man that Ned had first seen galloping past dressed as a Union captain, came trotting up to him. The captain, who looked to be in his mid-thirties, with a long, thick mustache and clean-shaven chin, reached into his tunic pocket, pulled out a cigar, and stuck it in his mouth before lighting it and taking a few puffs. It occurred to Ned that this man was like a black version of Captain Chambers, both in age and in demeanor.

After the captain had taken a drag on the cigar and let it out in a great long puff of smoke, he leaned down in the saddle, looked at Ned and said, "Seems you men know how to fight. Our scouts—as was out watchin' the border—reported back there was one helluva nice little gunfight goin' on out here. So we rode out to have a looksee. Found y'all were holdin' your own against some mighty bad odds … Who taught y'all to fight like that?"

Ned said, "Captain Chambers … over to Virginia way. He was our master … before he done freed us all. They say he was out west fightin' Mexicans and Indians since he was only a boy. Don't reckon there's nothin' 'bout fightin' Captain Chambers don't know."

"Chambers, huh? Well, seems like he taught y'all *well* before he freed you."

"No … he taught us *after*. He was … a good man … for a white man."

"Hmph," the captain said, "Men are men. White … black … don't make no difference. Good is good. And bad … well, bad *ain't*. Color don't make no difference. The sooner you learn *that*, the better off you'll be. What's your name, son?"

"Ned … Ned *Turner*," Ned answered, giving his official "freeman" name that Sergeant Tom had recorded on his manumission papers.

"Ned *Turner* … hmm," the captain said, and took another puff on the cigar, "any relation to *Nat* Turner, Ned?"

"Only in spirit," Ned replied. He found he was already taking a liking to this man.

The captain laughed, "You'n me both, son. You'n me both," he replied. "My name's Mathews. Captain William Mathews. What y'all doin' out here shootin' at rebel bushwhackers anyways, Turner?"

"We come here lookin' for Fort Scott out in Kansas," Ned answered.

"Well, you found it ... or rather, it found you. We're with the First Kansas out of Fort Scott."

"Oh. Well ... we come all this way to join up with y'all," Ned answered.

The captain sat up straight in his saddle and tossed down the stub of his cigar. "Well then, Turner ... seein's how you already know how to fight ... and that y'all's been trained up by a *real* military man ... And me bein' short on non-commissioned officers and all ... Alls I got to say 'bout that is: welcome to the First Kansas Colored Volunteer Infantry Regiment ... *Sergeant* Turner," he said, and grinned.

Ned thought about that a moment, and then for the second time that day, he also smiled.

Chapter 10. Opportunity Lost

*"While we are making up our minds
as to when we shall begin,
the opportunity is lost."*
- Marcus Fabius Quintilianus

Monday September 22, 1862 – Washington, D.C.:

"Mr. President ... fellow cabinet members," Secretary of War Edwin Stanton began, as he stood to give his summation on the Battle of Antietam, "I will omit a dry recitation of the facts you've already seen in the newspapers—horrific casualty counts, General Lee's defeat and subsequent retreat back into Virginia, and so on—and cut right to the matter that most concerns this august gathering: the conduct of Union commanding general George McClellan before, during, and after the battle. Conduct, I submit, that was so scandalously incompetent that it has likely allowed the war to continue when such an outcome was not necessarily a given."

Stanton proceeded to outline all of McClellan's actions, or lack of actions, since departing Washington in pursuit of Lee, starting with his slow, cautious pursuit of the enemy, even after the fortuitous discovery of Lee's lost battle orders. This unnecessarily slow movement allowed the rebels to capture the Union garrison at Harpers Ferry and Lee to consolidate his army at Antietam when the opportunity to destroy it in its separate pieces had been a good possibility.

Then came McClellan's mishandling of the battle, never committing his full strength all at once, allowing Lee with inferior numbers to counter McClellan's attacks piecemeal. Failing to follow through and commit reserves when a breakthrough of Confederate lines was briefly achieved at "Bloody Lane."

And most devastating of all, McClellan's failure to attack Lee the day after the battle, despite Lee's incomprehensible decision not to retreat back across the Potomac with his devastated army under cover of darkness, and McClellan's overwhelming superiority in fresh, unused troops.

Finally, McClellan's continued unwillingness to pursue Lee and finish him off, despite repeated admonishments from the President, General in Chief Halleck, and the Secretary of War.

When he'd finished his summation, Stanton looked directly at the president and said, "Mr. President, with all due respect, I beseech you, sir … relieve McClellan and give the command to someone — *anyone* — who will *fight*, sir!"

Lincoln nodded his head, and gazed down at the table as if seriously considering Stanton's request.

But Secretary of State Henry Seward stood to his feet and said, "*No*, Mr. President," to the surprise of all.

"What's that, Henry?" Lincoln asked, looking up at Seward.

"No, Mr. President … despite all that Secretary Stanton has just reported — and I have no doubt as to its veracity, given McClellan's past performance — you must *not* relieve him."

"Oh? And why *not*, Mr. Secretary?" Lincoln asked.

"Mr. President … if you still mean to announce the Emancipation Proclamation, *now* is the time to do it — who knows when another such opportunity may arise? Whatever our true feelings may be and despite our knowledge to the contrary, we must loudly and enthusiastically declare Antietam a tremendous and unmitigated Union victory … and General McClellan its great and glorious hero. Only *then* can you tell the world your plan to free the slaves …" Seward answered.

Lincoln slowly nodded his head, but Secretary of War Edwin Stanton turned and walked out the door without another word.

ಬಿ೮೦೧೮೮ಬಿ೮೦೧೮೮ಬಿ೮೦೧೮೮

Friday October 3, 1862 – Sharpsburg, Maryland:

Ozias Hatch, Secretary of State for Illinois and long-time Lincoln supporter and personal family friend, had been visiting Lincoln at the White House when the president decided he must personally visit the Antietam battlefield and speak with General McClellan. Lincoln had asked Hatch if he'd like to come along.

Hatch had immediately agreed, though he was unsure of the president's motivation—whether he wanted political advice, as was often the case between them, or he just wanted a friend to lean on and confide in. Either way, Hatch was determined to provide whatever support Lincoln required.

After spending the previous day touring Harpers Ferry, the president's party had set up camp near the site of the battle of Antietam, next to an encampment of Union soldiers. Shortly after the tents were erected, an exhausted Hatch had collapsed on his cot and slept a deep and untroubled sleep.

But then, way too soon for his liking, he heard his tent flap open, even as daylight was just lighting the eastern sky. Glancing up he saw President Lincoln, fully dressed with his iconic top hat, standing in the doorway.

"Come, Hatch, I want you to take a walk with me," Lincoln said in a serious tone.

Hatch sat up, rubbed his eyes, and got dressed while the president waited just outside. As he slipped out of the tent and stepped up next to Lincoln, he was surprised to find they were alone. Even Allan Pinkerton, who'd traveled with them under the guise of a Union major and had been the president's ever-present shadow throughout their journey, was absent this morning.

Hatch gazed around the camp and saw that the soldiers were mostly still asleep in their tents. It was so still and quiet the only sounds he heard were the songs of early birds in the trees, seemingly oblivious to the mass of militarized humanity camped just beneath them.

Lincoln led Hatch toward a low hill overlooking the camp. As they slowly climbed by a gently sloping path, they could view the great city of white tents with their sleeping soldiers, spreading out as far as the eye could see below them.

Hatch, picking up on the president's solemn mood, refrained from initiating any conversation, other than the typical polite small talk about the weather, the birds, and other such innocuous subjects. And the president also seemed disinclined to conversation.

As they walked, Lincoln quietly greeted several guards they encountered, shaking hands and asking after their health, their hometown, families, and other polite niceties.

Finally, the path led them to a place where a ledge provided a commanding view of nearly the entire Union camp. They could see the soldiers were just now beginning their morning duties.

They stood for a long moment in silence, gazing out at the awe-inspiring sight. Then the president turned to Hatch and, gesturing out toward the scene in front of them, said, "Hatch, what *is* all this?"

Hatch was somewhat taken aback by the question. Though the president had asked it in a serious tone, the answer seemed blatantly obvious, so he answered, "Why, Mr. Lincoln ... this is the Army of the Potomac, sir."

Lincoln gazed at the camp below them for a moment, then slowly shook his head. He turned back toward Hatch, and now his thoughtful expression had turned to a dark frown. "No, Hatch ... no," the president said. "*This* is General McClellan's body-guard."

ಬಲಾಣಿಲೀಬಲಾಣಿಲೀಬಲಾಣಿಲೀ

"General, this morning I've been reading through the official reports on your troop strength. Discounting the wounded and infirm, the count of available men I come up with is 88,095. And according to other reports I've seen, the enemy's entire force in this campaign started at something in the neighborhood of 50,000, of which a very large proportion have been lost in the recent battles," the president said.

McClellan gazed across the table calmly and shrugged. "I'm certain the enemy's strength is greatly under-reported, Mr. President—my sources make that number closer to 150,000—while our own troop strength numbers don't take into account the scattered, exhausted, and ill-equipped state of our soldiers. For instance, nearly ninety percent of our cavalry horses are in such poor condition they are entirely unfit for service."

The two men were seated in McClellan's command tent, at the moment decoratively "staged" for a photograph by a man named

Alexander Gardner, an employee of the famous photographer Mathew Brady. Lincoln would have preferred the photo be taken with everything as it normally was, but Gardner insisted that this photo would be historically important—a critical strategy meeting between the two great leaders of the republic—and so it ought to be properly presented. McClellan liked the idea, so they waited while Gardner pinned back the flaps of the tent, neatly arranged the general's cot with a colorful quilt, laid out McClellan's sidearm and other articles on the meeting table, draped the stars and stripes across a smaller end table, and symbolically laid a crumpled captured Confederate battle flag on the ground near their feet. Then the two men removed their hats and sat staring across the table at one another for several minutes while the photograph was taken.

The president had previously endured several hours of posing for photos with various Union officers around the camp. There had even been photos taken with Allan Pinkerton, who had chosen not to wear an army uniform this day, explaining he didn't want his disguise revealed in case one of the photos was published in a newspaper.

But now Lincoln and McClellan were truly alone for the first time since Lincoln's arrival at Antietam—finally free to discuss the issue that was foremost on the president's mind.

Lincoln nodded, "Maybe so, maybe so, general. But regardless of that, I should very much like to see a general advance by this army … across the Potomac as quickly as possible to engage or push back General Lee's army while they are still in northern Virginia. In fact, I expect you to do so as quickly as humanly possible, general. You may consider that an order," the president concluded, giving the general a severe look.

But McClellan seemed unconcerned, "Certainly, Mr. President. I will do everything in my power to get this army ready for a general advance, as quickly as ever it could be done by any man living. In the meantime, I will be working on a plan of campaign to remove the rebel army from this part of the country forever."

"Hmm … please see that you do, sir," Lincoln said, then rose from his chair, replaced his tall hat, and strolled away, with Allan Pinkerton rejoining him a few dozen yards away, then following closely in his wake. But as the president passed by Pinkerton and their eyes met, Lincoln let out a heavy sigh.

ಬಿಟಿಂಚಿಚ್ಞ ಬಿಟಿಂಚಿಚ್ಞ ಬಿಟಿಂಚಿಚ್ಞ

The next day, as the president's entourage was preparing to depart for Washington, a Union Captain stepped up next to Allan Pinkerton, once again dressed as a Union major, and touched him on the sleeve to gain his attention. Pinkerton turned toward the captain, who said, "Sorry, Major … but General McClellan has sent me to ask of you a moment of your time before you depart, sir."

"Oh! Very well … lead on, Captain," he answered.

When Pinkerton arrived back at McClellan's tent, the general was seated at the camp table that served as his desk, going through a stack of paperwork. He glanced up as Pinkerton stepped up to the table and snapped a salute.

"Ah, Pinkerton … please, have a seat," McClellan responded, not bothering to return the salute.

"Uh … I would appreciate you referring to me as Major Allen in the field, if you please, sir," Pinkerton responded.

"What? Oh, yes, yes … of course, of course. Secrets and spies and all that … certainly. Please … have a seat, this won't take but a moment."

"Thank you, sir," Pinkerton said as he sat in a folding chair across from McClellan. It occurred to Pinkerton that it was the very same chair the president had occupied the day before.

"What can I do for you, sir?" Pinkerton asked.

"Pinkerton, I've been reading through the dispatches—"

"*Major Allen …*" Pinkerton reminded him.

"Hunh? Oh, yes, sorry … *Major Allen* … I've been reading through the dispatches this morning … and one in particular caught my attention. It's concerning the rebels' Kanawha Valley offensive."

"Yes, a very unfortunate affair, though I understand our troops were at least able to effect a strategic retreat and salvage a good deal of equipment and manpower in the process."

McClellan waved his hand dismissively, "A retreat is a retreat, Pink ... er ... *major*. What caught my interest was this: the dispatch gives praise to a man sent out from Governor Pierpont's office to help advise and assist with the retreat. A man named Nathaniel Chambers!"

"*Oh!* So, once again the man seems to be in the thick of the action, despite being kept from an army commission. But seemingly once again rendering aid to *our* side ..."

"Oh, do you think so?! You don't find it suspicious he shows up just as the rebels are engaging our troops, and after that there is a general retreat, allowing the rebels to regain nearly half of the western part of Virginia? If he were a rebel agent, that is *exactly* how I'd expect him to behave ... convincing the Union commander that his position was untenable and talking him into an ignominious retreat, handing the victory to the rebels on a silver platter with barely a fight!"

Pinkerton considered this a moment, then said, "Yes ... yes, I can see that *might* be a possibility ... But unfortunately, we have no proof of it. And apparently the Union commander ... what was his name?"

McClellan thumbed through his stack of papers, and found what he was looking for. "Lightburn ... Colonel Joseph Lightburn."

"Apparently Colonel Lightburn thought highly enough of Chambers' actions to praise him in his official report ..."

"Of course he did; he had but little choice after he had followed the man's advice," McClellan answered, with a sneer.

"I see your point, general. But still ... the *proof* ...?"

"Damn the proof! The man's an enemy agent, I'm certain of it. There's a war on, may I remind you; we have no time for the niceties of peacetime ... Remember the president has just suspended the writ of habeas corpus for anyone detained by the military. We don't have to prove a thing."

"But, sir … I believe the president suspended the writ so the army could crack down on people attempting to interfere with enlistments …"

"Yes, and I have gone on record as opposing the president's decision … very undemocratic, certainly," McClellan responded. "But since he *has* done it, we may as well put the decision to good use. Major … I want Chambers arrested for a spy and thrown into the deepest, darkest prison the Union has at its disposal. Do I make myself clear, sir?"

"Yes, general … perfectly clear."

ಬಿ♌ಌ♋ಬಿ♌ಌ♋ಬಿ♌ಌ♋

Joseph, Mary, and Evelyn gathered in the room that the two women shared in a boarding house in Washington City. It was to be their last night in the city; the Employer had arranged another of his typical convoluted-but-brilliant routes back to Richmond, evading both warring armies in the process.

But Evelyn was in a foul humor, a fact not lost on her two companions. So Joseph thought he'd make one last effort to soften her mood.

"I know the Antietam battle wasn't as decisive as we'd hoped, but …"

"Decisive?!" she shot back. "From what I've heard, McClellan barely secured a *draw*, despite us handing him General Lee's battle orders! And he also somehow managed to lose Harpers Ferry in the process, even knowing exactly what the enemy had planned for it. I can scarcely believe it!

"I swear … George McClellan can manage to manifest defeat out of certain victory better than any general I've ever heard of! *Ooooo* … he infuriates me so!"

Well … that didn't work so well, Joseph decided. *Better try another tack …*

"Yes, I agree, but even so, it *was* a Union victory after all, at least enough so as to allow the president to announce his wonderful news about the emancipation," Joseph said.

Evelyn nodded noncommittally, but said nothing, continuing to frown.

"And … you must admit *our* mission was a great success … *missions*, rather, I should say," Joseph continued, "If it weren't for the fact that our activities must remain a secret until the war is over—and likely forever—ours would probably be among the greatest espionage coups in the history of warfare! Stealing General Lee's battle plans right out from under the nose of one of his major generals, then arranging a method to get those plans to McClellan without raising his suspicions? That was no mean feat.

"Not to mention helping to eliminate a major Confederate spy ring within our own War Department in the same journey! Likely such an accomplishment is unprecedented in the annals of the spy craft. There is much to be proud of here, my dear," Joseph concluded, smiling reassuringly.

Evelyn nodded, but remained unmoved. "What good is all that if we are still failing to win the war? And it just … *boils my blood* … to think our failure is almost entirely due to the shortcomings, arrogance, and just plain meanness of one man: *Major General George B. McClellan!*"

Joseph nodded, "I can't disagree with you, Evelyn. But … in the end, there is nothing you can do about General McClellan …"

But Evelyn looked up at Joseph with a scowl twisting her lips, "Oh, *isn't there?!* Just watch me …"

"Why? What do you mean to do, Miss Evelyn?" Mary asked, a concerned look knitting her brow, "What are you thinking?"

"I'm thinking … twice now I've given McClellan information with which he could've taken down the Confederate Army … and twice now he has squandered the opportunity. Perhaps it's time to gain the information necessary to take down McClellan himself … to the betterment of the Union!"

"But … Evelyn … that would mean spying on a *Union* general," Joseph said.

"Well … he has already accused me of that very thing—in fact, he threw me in prison for it—so, I may as well go ahead and do what I've already been falsely imprisoned for doing …"

ᛥᛒᚲᚳᛒᚩᛒᚳᚳᛒᚩᛒᚳᚳᛒᚩᛒᚳᚳ

When Nathan and company finally returned to Belle Meade Farm from their action in the Kanawha Valley, their greeting was enthusiastic and heartfelt by everyone there. All knew, from both the newspapers and Nathan's telegrams, that it'd been a difficult and dangerous fight, despite being overshadowed by the devastating conflict off east in Maryland at the Battle of Antietam. And yet, gratefully, all their men had returned safely—though bruised, battered, hungry, and nearly exhausted from their efforts.

And though they were all given a heartwarming hero's welcome, particularly those with romantic relationships—Tony, Tom, and William—the lion's share of the attention fell on Phillipe. He'd been the only member of their company seriously wounded in the action, and Adilida and Edouard made a big fuss over him, which he only half-heartedly objected to.

When Phillipe removed the bandage to display his healing wound, little Nathaniel was so fascinated by the injury that he pulled his Uncle down onto one knee so he could examine the stitches.

Then Phillipe told the story of how his head was split open and he was nearly killed by an artillery shell burst that knocked all the others to the ground as well. The tale had many fanciful embellishments, and was highly entertaining, so much so that Nathan found himself listening with bated breath to the narrative, even though he'd been there himself.

Most interesting, to Nathan's way of thinking, was Phillipe's bragging on the bravery and heroics of Big George, who'd carried him away to safety, and the gritty, tenacious fighting of the other freemen, along with the soldiers from Texas.

Later that evening, as Nathan, Tom, Jim, and Phillipe sat on the veranda enjoying a cigar and a glass of whiskey, Phillipe looked at Nathan, smiled, and said, "So, Captain ... I must now humbly and shamefully admit I was wrong concerning the black men ... they have served with honor and bravery, and have fought like tigers—with ferocity and great skill. Not to mention that great strong fellow George very likely saving my life, no?

"Will you do me the honor, sir, of accepting my heartfelt apology for doubting your judgement on the matter?"

"No, Phillipe ... I will *not* forgive you, as there is nothing to forgive. I'm a firm believer in everyone's right to state their opinion, even when I vehemently disagree with it.

"But I will admit to feeling highly gratified to see you proved wrong on this occasion. And I admire you for being man enough to admit it." Nathan said, and smiled, raising his glass. Phillipe raised his, and they clinked them together, and took a swallow to formally settle the matter between them.

ༀༀༀༀༀༀༀༀༀༀༀ

Later that evening, as he lay awake in bed, Nathan ruminated on all that had happened in the last month in the wider world. Though it galled him that McClellan remained in command of the Army of the Potomac, despite once again failing to secure an overwhelming Union victory, he had at least forced Lee to retreat back into Virginia, which was all to the good.

And with the president's monumental announcement that he intended to free the slaves in the southern states at the beginning of the next year, Nathan renewed his determination to immerse himself with renewed vigor and purpose in the training of freemen and runaway slaves, knowing the hour of their ascension was quickly drawing nigh.

ༀༀༀༀༀༀༀༀༀༀༀ

Evelyn quickly read through the letter she'd just unsealed:

My Dear Mary Ellen,

Our victory is complete! I feel some little pride in having—with a beaten and demoralized army—defeated Lee so utterly, and saved the North so completely. I am ready to insist that the president remove Stanton, and have Halleck give way to me as General in Chief.

Your loving husband,

George

Evelyn wrinkled her nose in disgust; the arrogance of the man was sickening. Here he'd bungled yet another battle, failing to utterly destroy the rebels as he'd had every opportunity of doing ... and was bragging of his greatness and insisting on being elevated to even higher levels of command as a result.

What a complete and utter fool, she thought. And though the communication was thoroughly conceited and despicable, there was nothing here that rose to the level that she could use for her purposes. Likely President Lincoln was already aware of such shortcomings in the man.

So she resealed the letter, heating the wax seal over a steaming teapot and gently pressing it back down against the paper of the envelope, as the Employer had taught her. She would deliver the letter to Mrs. McClellan as promised, with no sign that the seal had been compromised, nor that the letter had ever been read by another.

Evelyn had been living in the quiet, tree-lined neighborhood of Trenton, New Jersey for two weeks now, trying to obtain the information she needed to convince the president to relieve General McClellan of his command.

She'd remembered how surprised she'd been back in the spring to read Confederate General Joseph Johnston's candor with his wife Lydia in the letter Evelyn's spy had intercepted and copied, back before McClellan's abortive invasion of the Virginia Peninsula. In addition to laying out Confederate war strategy, Johnston had gone so far as to denigrate Confederate President Jefferson Davis, along with General Lee.

Evelyn felt certain that McClellan would not be able to resist saying the same kinds of things—and worse—about Lincoln and Secretary of War Stanton in his letters to his wife. Surely more than enough to get him fired from his command, if not arrested for high treason.

So even as Joseph and Mary were embarking on their return journey to Richmond, Evelyn was enlisting Benjamin Hughes' help in her plot against McClellan. Benjamin, who'd been just as disappointed as she'd been about the Antietam outcome, readily agreed to help her.

Within two days, "Major Smith," their main contact at the War Department—the same who'd been instrumental in the operation against the confederate spy ring led by Assistant Undersecretary Baldwin—provided her with the address of McClellan's wife, Mary Ellen, in Trenton, New Jersey. And even as Evelyn was on her way to New Jersey by train, the Hughes' shipping company was arranging to purchase a house in the same neighborhood—in the name of Evelyn's cover-story *husband*—just a few doors down from the McClellans'.

When Evelyn arrived in Trenton, she was met at the train station by a man whose last name was Smith—of course. The man handed her a house key, and a letter from Benjamin providing her with the address of her new home, and the outline of her cover story.

She would play the role of the spouse of a Union officer, but one stationed out west in General Grant's army, serving as a staff officer for General Rosecrans. Given the enmity between McClellan and Rosecrans, there'd be little chance of McClellan checking up on her "husband," Captain Frederick Adolphus Jones. This time she dared not use the pseudonym *Smith* or the shortened name *Eve* or even Evelyn for fear McClellan might recognize the name and make a connection, should Mary Ellen mention her new "friend" in a letter. So Evelyn would become Emily—Mrs. Frederick Jones.

And the man who handed her the letter told her that Benjamin had also arranged for *Major Smith* to doctor the appropriate War Department paperwork to prove that such a captain did indeed exist on General Rosecrans' staff and that he had a spouse currently living in New Jersey, just in case any of McClellan's War Department allies had any reason to check on her story.

The day she arrived, Evelyn, now *Emily*, set to work meeting the neighbors, and using all her considerable charm to insert herself into the doings of the group of local ladies whose husbands were army officers. Within two days, she'd been introduced to Mary Ellen McClellan at a tea hosted by one of the neighborhood ladies, and the two of them had immediately made a connection. Mary Ellen was attractive, outgoing, and charming—only a few years older than Evelyn—even as Lydia Johnston had been, and Evelyn had no trouble winning her over.

At the end of the tea, Evelyn took the initiative of inviting Mary Ellen to her own house in a few days' time, as they'd "discovered" the happy "coincidence" that they lived only three houses apart from each other on the same city block.

Evelyn had hoped her invitation would be reciprocated in turn, and then once inside the McClellans' home, an opportunity might present itself to search for any letters from the general among Mary Ellen's effects.

But even as Evelyn prepared to host Mary Ellen for tea, fortune seemed to smile on Evelyn's scheme, as Mary Ellen did not arrive as scheduled, instead sending a note via a messenger begging Evelyn to change venues for their tea and come to the McClellan home instead. Of course, Evelyn jumped at the chance.

And then when she arrived, she learned the reason for the change of locations: Mary Ellen was suffering from a flare up of the gout, a condition she suffered from time to time, making it extremely painful to walk. The two ladies once again got along famously, Evelyn finding she actually was enjoying Mary Ellen's company, which triggered the familiar twinge of guilt she always felt when actively betraying someone while pretending to be their friend.

But though no opportunity to search through Mary Ellen's correspondences presented itself, when Evelyn was preparing to depart, she offered to collect Mary Ellen's mail at the local post office whenever she collected her own, so that Mary Ellen need not make the painful five-block walk, or suffer climbing in and out of a carriage. Mary Ellen had gratefully accepted, making Evelyn's operation seem almost too easy.

But Evelyn's initial excitement had begun to wane as she intercepted and read General McClellan's steady stream of letters to his wife; though these letters proved him to be conceited, defensive, and full of grandiose pontification—as one would expect of the man—unfortunately there was nothing in them that was especially damning.

She'd originally feared that she might have only a few days to collect Mary Ellen's mail before the latter had sufficiently recovered from her condition to go back to collecting her own letters. But such had not proven to be the case; Mary Ellen seemed very pleased and content to let Evelyn serve her in that manner, there being a natural hierarchy even among the officers' wives that a captain's wife should, in some subtle ways, be subservient to a general's wife. This, of course, played right into Evelyn's hands.

So Evelyn continued to deliver Mary Ellen's mail, and continued to read General McClellan's correspondence to his wife ...

ᔕᘏᑫᘉᔕᘏᑫᘉᔕᘏᑫᘉᔕᘏᑫᘉ

Wednesday October 29, 1862 – Bates County, Missouri:

Ned and the thirty-seven men of his company lay hunkered down in a shallow, sandy depression at the top of a small rise a few feet above a dry creek bed in a place the locals called Island Mound. Though they'd not yet been overrun, their situation was slowly becoming desperate, as the rebels worked their way to the sides of their position, inexorably enclosing them in what would soon become a death trap. The advantage of their superior Union military rifles, capable of accurate, rifled fire with the .58 caliber Minni ball out to several hundred yards, was not enough to counter the overwhelming numbers against them.

It was the second time Ned had fought rebel bushwhackers in Missouri, but the first time since he'd donned the blue uniform. And it was not lost on him that, once again, he was outnumbered, outgunned, and slowly running out of ammunition. And the odds were even worse this time than they'd been back when it was only the five of them traveling out to Kansas from western Virginia; this time they estimated there were some four hundred rebels out in front of them, comprising a small, irregular army.

Two hundred and fifty men of the First Kansas had been sent out from Fort Scott, Kansas into Missouri to reconnoiter and drive out the bushwhackers three days earlier. But after the first day,

214

the hunters had become the hunted, and they'd been forced to take refuge in a sturdily built farmhouse they'd dubbed "Fort Africa."

Fort Africa had proven stubbornly resistant to the rebels' advances. But after a full day of little fighting, and water and rations running low, Captain Mathews had been forced to send out well-armed foraging parties, including one led by Ned, now known as "Sergeant Turner" to the men of his company. Though he'd been given strict orders to stay within eyesight of Fort Africa, that had proven impractical if they hoped to accomplish anything at all.

And at first, they'd had some success, rounding up a few stray chickens, goats, and a couple of hogs, with no sign of the enemy. But the rebels' inactivity had proven to be a ruse; once Ned and his company were well away from the protection of the fort, they had been attacked with vigor, and had been forced to dig in at their current position. Ned could hear gunfire in the near distance as well, so he assumed the other foraging parties had likewise come under fire, and would be unable to come to their aid.

He leaned up over the lip of the berm, aimed his rifle at where a small puff of smoke was rising up from behind a bush, and squeezed off a shot. Without any conscious thought he immediately slid back down and reloaded. But when he reached into his ammunition bag, he felt only a half dozen lead Minni balls remaining. He cursed aloud.

"What's that Sarge?" Corporal Washington lying next to him asked.

"Nothin' … just a curse for these Goddamned slavers, may they all burn in hell."

Washington returned a rueful grin and said, "Amen to that, Sarge … I just hope we can figure a way to make 'em get there 'fore we do …"

Ned snorted a mirthless laugh, and nodded. He'd begun to consider offering his men the same option he'd given his fellow Mountain Meadows freemen back when they'd been surrounded by bushwhackers before: to launch an all-out attack with the goal of forcing the enemy to shoot them down so they'd not be captured and later tortured to death. It was a grim thought, and a sign of how desperate the situation had become. But he took some solace in knowing that this relatively minor action by the First Kansas Colored Regiment was the first battle fought by a black regiment in the war. Not that he'd live to enjoy the notoriety.

He was mulling this over when he heard a loud noise back toward Fort Africa. At first he couldn't make it out, so he called out, *"Cease firing!"* and stilled his breath to listen. Then he heard it again, a sound that made his heart beat faster—men wildly shouting, the same type of yell he and the other freemen had made when they'd launched their suicidal attack now more than a month ago. Only this time it came from hundreds of voices.

Ned turned to his men, several of whom had also heard the noise and were looking toward him with wide eyes.

Corporal Washington said, "What's it mean, Sarge?"

Ned thought a moment, a slight grin touching the corners of his mouth. "It means … *company will fix bayonets!*" he shouted, then reached down to obey his own order.

In moments, they heard a great volley of rifle fire coming from just behind their little rise, and Ned shouted out, *"Charge!"* His men boiled up out of their hole and down the bank on the other side, bayonets in front, even as streams of black-faced, blue-uniformed soldiers poured past on either side of them in a roiling cloud of gun smoke and dust.

But as he was coming down the bank, Ned tripped over a root and nearly fell. A strong hand caught him by his left arm and jerked him to his feet. He glanced over and was shocked to see the smiling face of Captain Mathews, a cigar clenched between his teeth. Mathews spat out the cigar, raised his revolver and fired off a round, then rushed away shouting, "C'mon … no shirking, Sergeant Turner … we got us some rebs to kill!"

Ned laughed, raised his rifle, and sprinted after the captain.

Chapter 11. Treasonous Acts

"The treacherous are ever distrustful."
- J.R.R. Tolkien
The Two Towers

Thursday October 30, 1862 – Trenton, New Jersey:

On the fifteenth day of her letter-thieving campaign, Evelyn's efforts finally paid off—and in a manner above and beyond her wildest hopes. Her heart skipped a beat, as it always did, when she noticed a letter from General McClellan while flipping through the letters in her hand as she walked briskly down the sidewalk in the neighborhood of her residence in Trenton. Once back in her room, she held her breath as she unsealed and unfolded the letter. Spreading it out on the desk in front of her and sliding the oil lamp close, she read:

> *My dearest Mary Ellen,*
>
> *I don't wish to dishearten you, but I fear my hated enemies are at it again. No, I speak not of the secessionist rebels, but rather those imbeciles in Washington.*
>
> *I can't tell you how disgusted I am with these wretched politicians—they are a most despicable set of men. In their stupidity and wickedness, they continue to do their very best to sacrifice my noble army. I have lost all regard and respect for this Administration, and now doubt the propriety of my brave men's blood being spilled to further the designs of such a group of heartless villains.*
>
> *General Halleck is the most stupid idiot I ever heard of— either that or he drinks hard—for he cannot even comprehend the English language. Stanton is the most unmitigated scoundrel I ever knew, heard, or read of; the magnificent treachery and rascality of the man would*

have caused Judas Iscariot to gasp in holy horror. And the president is nothing more than a well-meaning baboon!

In my present position I am forced to submit to men whom I know to be greatly my inferiors socially, intellectually, and morally. There is not one honest man among them. I fear none of them wish to save the Union. Oh, please do keep these complimentary opinions to yourself or you may get me into trouble.

Lincoln's recent visit to Antietam was an attempt to push me into a premature move into Virginia. The real truth is that my army is not fit to advance. We have been badly cut up and scattered by the overwhelming numbers brought against us on the 17th instant, and the entire army is greatly exhausted, hungry, and in need of rest. I see such insane folly in our government that I feel the final salvation of the country demands the utmost prudence on my part and that I must not run the slightest risk of disaster, for if anything happened to this army our cause would be lost. I feel too that I must not unnecessarily risk my own life—for the fate of my army depends upon me and they all know it.

Despite the continuous pressures placed upon me from the powers at Washington, my present purpose is to hold the Army about as it is now, rendering Harpers Ferry secure and watching the river closely, prepared to attack the enemy should he again attempt to cross to this side.

And the unmitigated folly of the president's announced plan to emancipate the slaves! What is he thinking?! He shall bring ruin and a permanent division upon us all. Instead, the people of the South should be made to understand that we are not making war upon the institution of slavery, but that if they submit to the Constitution and Laws of the Union they will be protected in their constitutional rights of every nature, including their right to own property as their long-honored institutions allow.

It may come as a shock, but I have now come to believe if I had succeeded in taking Richmond (during the late peninsula campaign) or had succeeded in destroying the rebel army here at Antietam, the fanatical abolitionists in the North might have become too powerful and reunion become impossible. I am now sure that it has all turned out for the best.

You may be pleased to hear that I continue to receive letters from men in the North urging me to march on Washington and assume command of the government! Still other good men have promoted the idea of me running for president on the Democratic ticket to unseat the Gorilla in the next election. These are men who appreciate my true worth, and who know if not for the incompetence and mean spirit of the present administration, I would have already won the complete victory I so richly deserve, and the war would be long over.

I must retire now, my dear, and I wish to get this missive in the post before I do, so I will bid you good night.

Yours as always,

George

Evelyn refolded the letter, and slipped it up into her sleeve, as she turned and quickly packed her carpet bag. In moments, she headed out the door without a backward glance. Once outside, she turned and walked briskly down the street toward the rail station, to catch the next train for Washington City. A smile lit her face—not her usual dazzling smile that set men's hearts aflutter and enamored women of her charms—nor yet the soft, friendly kind that warmed the hearts of family and friends. No, this was the wicked leer of a cat who had just eaten the family canary and was now savoring the cruel joy of its ruthless victory.

I have you now, Major General George B. McClellan, she thought as she picked up her pace, stepping purposefully along the wooden sidewalk. *Where I'm sending you will be far harsher than the prison you dumped me in, sir! You will languish for the rest of your days and beyond within the merciless imprisonment of treason, shame, and dishonor! And from this prison, there shall be no escape!*

ॐ๛๛๛ॐ๛๛๛ॐ๛๛๛

Monday November 3, 1862 – Wheeling, Virginia:

"Well, Tom … the good news continues to come in from Charleston," Nathan said, as he sat down next to Tom at the large table in the "War Room" of the Customs House, the unofficial statehouse for the Restored Commonwealth of Virginia. Nathan had just returned from a meeting down the hall with Governor Pierpont, who'd brought him up to date on the latest news on the fighting.

"Oh? Has General Cox completed his re-taking of the valley?" Tom asked. They'd been following events closely via the telegraph wires ever since Cox had returned from the east with a considerable force and joined up with Colonel Lightburn at Point Pleasant on the Ohio River. From there, Cox had launched an offensive eastward up the valley. And unlike the earlier offensive by the Confederates, there had been little fighting this time. C.S.A. General Loring had since been replaced, and Confederate forces depleted in the valley—the fallout from Lee's failed invasion of Maryland.

"Yes, it's official; the entire valley is now back in Union hands. And our old friend Colonel Lightburn has given good service, along with our comrades in the Forty-Seventh Ohio and our own Fourth Loyal Virginia."

"Ah … Colonels Elliott and Parry again, I assume? And Captain Vance of the Fourth?"

"Yes … they are mentioned in several of the dispatches. Though there was but little hard fighting, their competent leadership and swift deployment of Union forces drove the rebels back inexorably until they were forced to abandon the valley altogether," Nathan answered with a grin.

"That *is* good news, sir. And it now makes our strategic retreat — preserving Lightburn's command and all his supplies — seem like more than just a *pyrrhic* victory ... perhaps an actual, *bone fide* victory after all; it kept those forces intact that they might later retake the valley, and preserve the integrity of the new state."

Nathan nodded his agreement, and they shook on it, sharing a satisfied smile.

"Excuse, me, Mr. Chambers ..." Jacob, the young assistant clerk to the governor said, as he stuck his head in at the door of the War Room. "There are three gentlemen from the government at Washington here to see you, sir."

Nathan exchanged a quick look with Tom, then shrugged. Neither had any idea what it might be concerning, so Nathan turned back to the clerk and said, "All right, please show them in, Jacob."

"Yes, sir," he said, and departed. Moments later, Jacob escorted three men into the room. Tom and Nathan stood to greet them. The newcomers were all dressed as gentlemen, in suits with fine hats, so clearly non-military. Each also wore a pistol in a holster at his hip.

"Mr. Nathaniel Chambers?" the one in front said, gazing straight at Nathan.

"Yes, I'm Chambers," he answered, "and this is my associate, Tom Clark. What can I do for you gentlemen? The clerk told me you were from the federal government?"

"Yes, that's correct, Mr. Chambers. I am detective Summers, and these are detectives Mills and Boyd. We come from Mr. Pinkerton's office at the War Department, sir," he answered.

Nathan's first thought was that perhaps Pinkerton had finally come to his senses and dismissed the ridiculous and seemingly interminable "investigation" against him. But his next thought was, *but why send three men to tell me that? And why not just send a telegram?*

The one named Summers then reached behind his back and brought out something metallic and shiny. Nathan's breath caught when he recognized what it was: a pair of wrist shackles.

"Mr. Nathaniel Chambers, in the name of the federal government, we have been sent here to arrest you for conspiracy, espionage, and high treason against the United States and its armed forces. You will submit peaceably and accompany us back to Washington, sir, if you please," Summers stated, matter-of-factly.

Nathan smoothly reached over with his left hand and grabbed Tom's right arm, even as Tom's hand moved toward his gun holster. Nathan turned and looked Tom in the eye, shaking his head. "It won't do, Tom. Not *that* way ... not this time," Nathan said.

Tom was turning red in the face, but nodded and relaxed his right arm.

Just then Governor Pierpont appeared behind the three federal government agents in the doorway. "What is the meaning of this?! I just overheard from down the hall that you think to arrest our good Mr. Chambers?! Well ... I'll not have it! I am the governor of the Commonwealth of Virginia and Mr. Chambers is my trusted military advisor. You have no cause to arrest him, and I won't allow it!"

But Detective Summers turned to the governor and said, "This is a federal government matter, your honor. Please do not interfere, sir."

"By God, I *will* interfere as I see *fit* in my own statehouse! Mr. Wilbert!" he called out to the clerk, "Send for the guards ..."

"Yes, sir," they heard a voice call out down the hall.

The three Pinkerton men backed away toward one wall and put their hands on the guns at their hips, preparing for a possible armed confrontation with the governor's men. Tom's hand strayed back toward the gun at his own hip. Harry the Dog, sensing the sudden tension in the room, crawled out from under the table where he'd been napping, and bared his teeth at the strangers, emitting a low growl.

But to everyone's surprise, it was Nathan Chambers who spoke in a commanding voice, "Peace, all of you!"

All eyes turned toward him as he continued, "There shall be no gunplay in this office. Though the charges against me are false, committing violence now for my sake will only make it look otherwise. No ... the only way to prove my innocence is to submit and accompany these men back to Washington where I can plead my case."

Then he looked back at Pinkerton's men and said, "I will come peaceably, under one condition—that you will allow me a moment once we are outside, to chain up the dog. Otherwise, he will attempt to follow and will never submit to being separated from me."

Summers glanced down at Harry and quickly nodded, "Agreed, Mr. Chambers. We will be more than happy to allow you to chain that animal."

"Are you sure about this, Nathan?" Pierpont asked, still standing in the doorway. "I can ban them from this office ..."

"Then they'll just find me out at my farm. No ... thank you Francis, but no ... It's best to just go and get this thing settled, once and for all."

The governor nodded, but continued to scowl angrily, his face a dark red, as Detective Summers stepped forward once again and reached toward Nathan with the shackles.

But then Tom stepped between them and said, "No!" in a tone that surprised even Nathan. "If you take him, you take him as a gentleman—as a free man who goes of his own free will.

"I will *not* see my Captain shackled as a common criminal. He either walks freely, or I swear by God I *will* use this pistol to prevent it, come what may."

Nathan had rarely seen Tom this fired up and decisive, and it moved him deeply.

Detective Summers thought about it a moment, then said, "Very well. If you will swear on your honor as a gentleman not to escape or to assault us, Mr. Chambers ... then I will allow it."

"I do so swear," he answered, then turned to Tom and patted him on the shoulder, while mouthing, *Thank you.*

Moments later, for the second time in life, Nathan had to endure the heart-rending whining and howling of Harry the Dog, chained against his will, suffering an unbearable parting. Nathan's heart ached for the animal as the carriage slowly pulled away from the Customs House, heading toward the train station.

ಬಿಜಿಂಚಿ೮ಚಿಬಿಜಿಂಚಿ೮ಚಿಬಿಜಿಂಚಿ೮ಚಿ

Secretary Stanton stood next to the president's desk while Lincoln gazed at the folded sheet of paper he held in his hands.

"I have personally compared the hand-writing of this letter to other documents penned by McClellan that we have in the office, and there can be no doubt as to its authenticity, Mr. President," Stanton offered, knowing the president well enough to anticipate the question.

"And how did you say you came by this, Edwin? A man's personal letter to his wife …? I'm not sure I'm comfortable with even *reading* it, let alone using its contents for my own purposes …"

"*I* had nothing to do with collecting it, Mr. President, if that's what you're asking. I left my desk for a few moments, and when I returned it was sitting on my chair with a note saying it had been obtained by a loyal citizen who believed it was imperative that the president should read its contents. I have *never* spied on any of our own officers, your honor … though now that I've read *this*, I am starting to think maybe I *should* have …

"At any rate, now that I *have* read it, I must urge you in the strongest possible terms to read it for yourself, sir. Think of it not as a personal letter between a man and his wife, but rather as a matter of national concern."

Lincoln gazed at Stanton for another long moment, then sighed, nodded his head, and turned back toward his desk. He unfolded the letter, spread it out in front of him under the light of an oil lamp, put on his spectacles, and began reading.

When the president finished, he refolded the letter while slowly shaking his head. He carefully removed his reading glasses and set them aside on his desk, then looked up at Stanton and the two met eyes. Stanton thought the president looked even more haggard and worn than in any of their recent meetings, and that was saying something, considering the man seemed to carry the weight of the world on his shoulders and rarely slept a full night.

"Shall I have him arrested for high treason, your honor?" Stanton asked.

The president didn't immediately answer. Instead, he leaned back in his chair and stared at the ceiling for a long moment. So long, in fact, Stanton feared the president might be nodding off in his seat.

But Lincoln suddenly sat back up and turned to Stanton, this time with a hard, serious look — the type of stern visage the typically easy-going president reserved for his rare moments of righteous wrath, moments when he struck fear into even the stoutest hearted of his advisors.

"As deeply satisfying as that would be, and as much as it is so richly deserved ... *no*, Edwin ... no. We simply can't do it, more's the pity. It would be far too damaging to our cause. Our enemies, both North and South, would ruthlessly use it against us — that we were such poor leaders and judges of character that we would promote a traitor to the highest position in our military — not once, but twice!"

Then he looked down, slowly shook his head, and chuckled — a dry, mirthless laugh. "And the sad truth, Edwin, is ... they'd be right."

Stanton nodded, and resisted the very strong urge to give the president his very most heartfelt *I told you so* lecture. After all, he had personally advocated — hard — for McClellan's dismissal, for months now. But all he said was, "Yes, I think you're correct, Mr. President. In this case, personal satisfaction, and even justice, must be set aside for the sake of the Union."

"Yes. I'm afraid we must simply relieve him of his command of the Army of the Potomac, to await a new command — a command that will *never* arrive ... happily for us," Lincoln answered.

Then the president looked up and locked eyes with Stanton again. "And I would be remiss, Edwin, if I didn't look you earnestly in the eye and say to you that you were right about McClellan all along," Lincoln said. Then he looked back down and chuckled again, this time more sincerely, "and that I recognize—and thoroughly appreciate—the herculean effort it took you just now *not* to say, 'I told you so, Mr. President.'"

Stanton smiled and nodded. Then wishing the president a good night, he turned and headed out the door. But rather than take his awaiting carriage for home, the secretary returned to the War Department to write up the orders himself, to *officially* relieve McClellan from his current command, but *unofficially* to ensure he would never again hold command in the United States Army. Stanton couldn't imagine a more satisfying way to conclude a long, draining day, nor a better way to guarantee a sorely needed good night's sleep.

ഇൽൽ

Wednesday November 5, 1862 – Sharpsburg, Maryland:

"General McClellan, sir ... Brigadier General Buckingham to see you, sir ..." Captain Parker said, then added hesitantly, "he's ... here from *Washington*, sir ..."

This last statement got McClellan's attention, and he looked up from the pile of paperwork he'd been reviewing—the latest requisitions for supplies, uniforms, and ammunition for the Army of the Potomac.

"Oh ... *that* Buckingham," McClellan said, recognizing the name of Secretary of War Edwin Stanton's personal assistant in the War Department. "Very well, Parker ... send him in," McClellan said.

An elderly, lean, stern-looking man with gray hair and beard stepped into McClellan's tent and snapped a salute. McClellan returned the salute, not bothering to rise from his chair.

But before he could inquire as to Buckingham's business, McClellan was surprised when Major General Ambrose Burnside, a younger, more vigorous-looking man, stepped into the tent and stood beside Buckingham. Burnside was always immediately recognizable, even from a great distance, because of his unusual, bushy half-beard that merged the hair on the sides of his face with a thick mustache, combined with a clean-shaven chin.

Burnside also saluted, but was less formal, "George ..." he said.

McClellan just gazed at Burnside open-mouthed, this time not bothering to salute. "Burnside ... what is the meaning of this?"

"I'm sure I don't know, sir," Burnside answered with a shrug. "I was informed that you were meeting with General Buckingham at your tent, and I was asked to join you ... It is all I know."

"I have been commanded to ask you to join us here, General," Buckingham said, looking at Burnside. "My orders are to present you two gentlemen with written orders from Secretary of War Edwin Stanton, and I am to see that you read them in my presence and acknowledge their validity. I am also instructed to tell you that both General-in-Chief Halleck, and the President of the United States have reviewed and have concurred with these commands."

McClellan's mouth dropped open, and he hesitated to accept the document held out to him by Buckingham. But Burnside, snatched his from Buckingham's hand, and said, "I can't see why the secretary would waste a brigadier general's time sending him all this way just to deliver orders ... surely a courier would've sufficed?" Burnside said, opening the seal on the envelope and extracting his orders.

But inexplicably, Buckingham gazed straight at General McClellan when he answered, though it'd been the other general who'd asked the question.

"The secretary wished there to be no doubt about the orders' authenticity, and no possible ... *confusion* ... concerning whether or not these orders should be *immediately* carried out to the letter."

Burnside quickly read through his orders, then stopped and gazed at McClellan wide-eyed. "Sorry, George ... but you must know I had nothing to do with this ... I knew nothing of it until this moment."

"What is it, Burnside?" McClellan asked, still not accepting his own orders from Buckingham.

Burnside continued to gaze at him, then finally said, "Best you read your own orders, George ..."

McClellan nodded, then slowly reached out and took the envelope held out by Buckingham.

He slowly opened it, read through it, his face turning a dark shade of red as he reached the end.

He re-folded the document, carefully inserted it back into its envelope, and set it on the table. Then he stood, looked at Buckingham and said, "My orders are acknowledged, General. And will be obeyed ..."

He then turned to Burnside and said in a quiet, subdued voice, "I suppose ... congratulations are in order, Burnside ..."

But Burnside's face had also turned red, "I had nothing to do with this, George ..."

But McClellan turned, took a quick look around his tent, picked up his sword from where it hung on a hook to one side, then walked out of the tent, leaving the remainder of his personal effects where they were.

And by some secret means, known only to common soldiers, news of Major General George B. McClellan's relief of command by the president spread like wildfire throughout the camp of the Army of the Potomac, such that when he rode away on his horse minutes later, soldiers lined the way on both sides, calling his name, crying, begging him not to leave, and wishing him well as he slowly departed, never looking back.

༄ༀ༃༃ༀ༃ༀ༃༃ༀ༃ༀ༃

"Well, Pinkerton ... you still haven't produced any actual evidence against me," Nathan said, resisting the urge to gesture as he spoke. The heavy, steel shackles on his wrists, joined by a thick chain looped through a steel ring attached to the table of the interrogation room, prevented him from moving his hands freely. Pinkerton sat on the opposite side of the table.

It was the first time Nathan had seen the man since his arrival at the War Department two days earlier. They'd kept him in a holding cell in the basement of the building, with no visitors, and no outings until they'd brought him to this room to speak with Pinkerton.

"As far as I can tell, your whole case is based on the false assumption that '*Miss Eve Smith*' of Richmond, Virginia was a Confederate spy. And the only 'proof' that she was a rebel spy was McClellan's say so, which counts less than *nothing* in my book, nor any more in a court of law."

"Well, I suppose the good news for the government's sake, is there won't be a court of law for you, Chambers … only a swift hanging."

Nathan frowned, "You mean you're willing to hang a man, with no trial and no evidence against him, based on nothing but the word of a general who's clearly afraid of his own shadow? A man who can never win a battle because he's too afraid he'll lose? That I'll have no opportunity to plead my case … to clear my name … to go forth to serve my country in its hour of need?"

"How about we look at it from my perspective, Chambers? The government is able to eliminate a potentially dangerous enemy agent, without tying up valuable resources, and wasting valuable time on a trial."

But Nathan just shrugged, "It'll be your neck as well … though frankly, I'd rather be in my shoes than yours. A few moments of discomfort at the end of a rope versus …"

"What do you mean by that?" Pinkerton asked.

Nathan looked him hard in the eyes, "My men … they're Indian fighters from Texas … Oh, to meet them on the street you'll never find a more polite and kindly crew—true gentlemen all … a testament to the way their mommas raised them, no doubt.

"But if you *cross* them … they are cold, hard killers … and *that* is on account of how *I trained* them. And the Comanche Indians out west taught us—the hard way, I'll admit—all sorts of interesting ways to kill a man very slowly … and under extreme duress.

"What do you suppose, Pinkerton, that *these* men will do to you once they hear you've had me hanged? And I'd hate to think what will happen to your *detectives* should you ask them to guard you. Lambs to the slaughter …" he shook his head in mock pity.

"Are you threatening me, sir?!" Pinkerton said, turning red in the face.

Nathan again shrugged, "Why not? You're threatening me. And the beauty of my threat is, I'll not have to raise a finger; my men will do *that* of their own volition. In fact, I reckon they'd do it even if I told them *not* to," he concluded, this time with a wicked looking grin. Nathan really wished he could stick a cigar in his mouth to punctuate the point, but at the moment he had no means of doing so.

Pinkerton shuddered, and looked down at his hands for a moment. Then he let out a heavy sigh, looked back up and said, "Never mind, Chambers ... I really had no intention of hanging you ... I was just trying to frighten you into signing a confession. But I can see now it was a waste of breath; you don't frighten.

"So ... I'll just have to content myself with dumping you in some God-forsaken hole for the remainder of the war. Let your men occupy themselves trying to figure a way to break you out of *that* ..."

Then Pinkerton pushed back his chair and stood, "I believe we're done here, Chambers ... good day to you, sir ... if that's possible where you're going."

Nathan stood and yanked hard on the manacles, snarling as he lifted the heavy hardwood table several inches off the ground, his muscles bulging under the strain. Pinkerton's eyes widened, and he called out, "Summers! Come take this prisoner away."

Detective Summers appeared in the doorway with the two detectives who'd accompanied him when they'd arrested Nathan in Wheeling. But Nathan relaxed, let the table back down, and resumed his seat. He knew this wasn't the time to put up a fight; he was shackled, and though he knew he could hurt them, in the end they would win, and he would take a serious beating for no gain.

He was starting to regret telling Tom before he departed that the men could come to Washington if they wished—he assumed they would do so whether he forbade it or no—but in no case were they to try to break him out or to use violence on his behalf. But now, knowing he might languish in prison for the duration of the war, a violent breakout was starting to sound much more appealing.

And then, despite the desperate situation he found himself in, he snorted at a humorous thought; what he *really* needed to break out of prison was Evelyn. She'd pulled it off all by herself, with no weapons, and no outside help. Only an unlikely fluke had prevented her from getting clean away.

The detective named Boyd unlocked the ring in the table and gestured for Nathan to stand. He rose and walked out the door of the interrogation room into the hallway, Summers taking the lead, and the other two detectives following behind. Pinkerton stood to the side and watched. But Summers suddenly stopped in mid-stride, nearly causing Nathan to collide with his back.

At first Nathan couldn't see what had caused the halt, but looking around Summers he saw a group of army officers approaching—an armed group of officers, with pistols unholstered, aimed at Pinkerton's men. And then with a shock, Nathan recognized Brigadier General Rufus Saxton as the leader of the group.

The officers—General Saxton, a colonel, and three captains—covered the Pinkerton detectives with their pistols as both parties came to a halt facing each other.

General Saxton spoke first, "Gentlemen, you *will* unbuckle your gun belts and drop them to the ground. And don't think to test me, good sirs—I will not be gainsaid. We are trained and experienced military men and will not hesitate to use deadly force as necessary."

Then Pinkerton stepped up in front of General Saxton, a dark frown knitting his brow, "General ... what is the meaning of this? We are agents of the federal government, doing our duty ..."

"Hmm ... as you say, Pinkerton. But I am also an agent of the government. And I am now doing *my* duty, sir. You *will* unshackle Mr. Chambers immediately, sir. It turns out he will *not* be accompanying you to some God forsaken prison after all."

Pinkerton scowled darkly, "This is *treason*, general ..."

"No, I think *not*, Pinkerton. Rather it is treason to knowingly send an innocent man to prison, and thus deprive the army of one of its finest officers—and in its darkest hour of need too, I might add. I submit it is *you*, sir—and General McClellan, I presume—who are behaving treasonously."

While this conversation was going on, the detectives dropped their weapons as ordered, and Summers stepped up to Nathan, unlocked his shackles, and stuck them back in his pocket.

"You'll not get away with this, general," Pinkerton argued.

But Saxton holstered his weapon and said, "Oh, I think I will, Pinkerton ... You see, we have just received news that you have obviously not yet heard. At eleven o'clock this morning, President Lincoln issued an order relieving General McClellan of all his commands. Your main benefactor has just lost all his power—the president has pulled the tiger's teeth, one might say.

"Now ... I will sit with you while you sign a document clearing our good Mr. Chambers of all charges and freeing him to accept a commission in the Union Army."

"And if I refuse?"

"Look around you, Pinkerton ... we are the professional soldiers ... we know how this War Department works, and how to get what we want—through whatever means necessary, as you have just now seen ... *You* are the outsider who has just lost his major advocate.

"Come, Pinkerton, you're a smart fellow ... answer your own question ..." he said mildly.

As Nathan rubbed his wrists, he turned to Pinkerton and said, "Some unsolicited advice, Pinkerton ... you seem an intelligent and capable man ... but you have saddled the wrong horse. I suggest you return to doing what you are known to be good at—tracking down and apprehending *actual* enemy spies ... and protecting the president. Good day to you, sir."

☙℘ℭ℈Ⅽℬ☙℘ℭ℈Ⅽℬ☙℘ℭ℈Ⅽℬ

When Nathan stepped out the front doors of the War Department, suddenly a free man again, but still rubbing his chafed wrists, he was not surprised to see Tom, Jim, and the rest of his men waiting for him on the lawn below.

What *did* surprise him was his own reaction to seeing them: an unexpected welling of joy and gratitude. It occurred to him his incarceration, and the threat of an indefinite prison sentence that followed, had affected him more than he'd realized in the heat of the moment. He had faced the uncertainty that he would *ever* see any of these men again, or if he did, not for a *very* long time.

So to suddenly see them again, happy and smiling at his unexpected arrival, threatened to bring a flood of tears to his eyes.

Tom was the first to greet him, enthusiastically grasping Nathan's hand with both of his and beaming. The others quickly gathered around, greeting their Captain, and patting him on the back and shoulders. Aside from Tom and Jim, William, Billy, Georgie, Jamie, Tony, Zeke, and even Phillipe were also there. Conspicuously absent was their largest member, Stan.

When Nathan asked about him, Tom said, "Oh, he decided Harry needed a walk, so he took him out across the lawn a few hours ago. To tell the truth, I think it was Stan who needed to *do* something; he was getting a bit twitchy just standing around and waiting."

Nathan had wondered where Harry was, but had assumed he was still tied up back in Wheeling, or else once again out in the wilds searching, as he'd been when Nathan first traveled to Richmond without him, what now seemed like ages ago.

"Speaking of … how did Harry handle this whole thing?"

"Not well at first … as you can imagine, he howled like a trapped wolf that first day, and only Stan could get him to move while still chained so that we could get him home to the farm. But surprisingly, once we all headed out on the train for Washington, he seemed better—like he somehow understood that we were going out to look for you. And when we arrived *here*, in front of the War Department, he suddenly became completely calm and relaxed and laid down on the grass. It's almost as if he *knew* you were inside, so he was content to wait outside. Such an odd and amazing creature …"

"Yes … he certainly is. And what about you men, Tom … what have y'all been doing while I was down in a jail cell, cooling my heels?"

"Well, first Jim and I went to see General Saxton to find out what was going on. But other than Pinkerton having you in a cell, he knew little about it—though to his credit, he was fuming mad about the whole thing and made no secret of it."

Nathan nodded, "Given how it all turned out, I'm not surprised. I'll tell y'all about it later, when we get back to … wherever it is we're staying. So after meeting with the general … then what?"

"After that we've been mostly here waiting, when we weren't debating whether or not to break you out of there under force of arms," he said with a grin.

"Again, not surprised. And … which side of the debate were *you* on, Tom?"

"But Captain … you gave me a direct order *not* to break you out. I have *rarely ever* disobeyed one of your orders, sir. Surely you'd not think I'd go against your wishes now …" he said with a straight face.

"Yes, *surely* … but you didn't answer my question …" Nathan said, giving Tom a stern look, while fighting off a strong urge to grin.

"Oh … so I didn't …" Tom said, then looked up, "Ah, *look* … here comes Stan now … and Harry with him."

Nathan looked over to where Tom was pointing, and saw the two largest members of their crew, the two-legged and the four, walking across the broad lawn between the White House and the War Department, still nearly a hundred yards away, yet unmistakable. The dog suddenly stopped and raised his head as if sniffing the wind. He then made a great noise, something between a bark and a howl, and bounded forward, heading straight at them, Big Stan racing along behind, trying in vain to keep up.

When Harry approached the group he slowed to a trot, then stopped right in front of Nathan, gazing up at him, panting heavily.

"Hello, Harry," Nathan said, and was then nearly knocked backward when Harry stood up on his hind legs, planted his front paws on Nathan's shoulders, and began licking his face. This

Nathan endured for several moments, before saying, "All right ... all right, Harry ... enough."

He grasped Harry's paws and slowly eased him back to the ground. To everyone's surprise, Nathan then knelt on the grass and hugged the animal around the neck, a thing they had never seen him do before. He stayed there a long while, even as Stan came up at a trot, out of breath.

The big man put his hands on his knees, gasping. Then seeing the Captain and Harry together he smiled, snorted a laugh, then stood and turned away to wipe his eyes.

𝄞𝄢𝄡𝄢𝄞𝄢𝄡𝄢𝄞𝄢𝄡𝄢

When Nathan returned to Belle Meade, a spontaneous celebration erupted, and the entire farm family ended up outside in the field, sitting on the grass or in chairs next to a roaring bonfire, or dancing to music provided by William on his "fiddle," Big George on his homemade drums, and several other freemen with various odd instruments.

And to nobody's surprise, Stan and Cobb held a dance contest which ended with no clear winner but plenty of raucous laughter, and much whiskey being consumed.

But to Nathan, the most touching moment of the evening, after tearful greetings by Miss Abbey and Megs, was the reception he received from little Nathaniel. The boy came up to him, held out his arms, and said, "Uncle Nay. Up!" When Nathan picked him up, the child hugged his neck and kissed it.

Once again Nathan had to fight back the tears, and inexplicably an image of Evelyn flashed into his mind, strong and clear, along with the thought of what it might be like to hold his own child one day ... *her* child ...

Chapter 12. Tipping the Scales

*"Each person must see himself
as though the entire world
were held in balance,
and any deed he might do
could tip the scales."*

- Maimonides

Wednesday December 10, 1862 – Wheeling, Virginia:

"Nathan ... the Twelfth Regiment is yours, as I promised ..." Governor Pierpont said, but Nathan detected a note of hesitation.

"But ..." Nathan prompted.

"But ... before you take command, I have a favor to ask."

"Yes?"

"Though Congress has finally passed the West Virginia statehood bill, my sources say the president is undecided about signing it, concerned that it may either be counterproductive to the Union's war effort, or that it may be unconstitutional. And apparently his cabinet is split down the middle on the subject."

Nathan frowned. "This is unexpected news ... I'd never considered that the president might not sign the bill, especially once we agreed to amend the state constitution to include the gradual elimination of slavery."

"Yes, me neither, but apparently such is the case," Pierpont answered, a concerned look knitting his brow.

"Hmm ... not sure what I can do about *that* ..." Nathan said with a shrug.

"I have written Mr. Lincoln a letter; I put a lot of work and thought into how best to persuade him in the shortest number of words, and I am feeling confident I have achieved my aims ... Here, read it for yourself," he said, handing Nathan a single sheet of paper with writing on one side.

Nathan read through it quickly, then handed it back. "This is excellent, you honor ... well argued, both legally and practically. From what I know of Lincoln, it is just the sort of thing that might appeal to him."

"Thank you, Nathan. I think it may work ... if only he *reads* it. My concern is ... if I mail it, it may never reach his desk, and even if it does, he is a very busy man and may not take the time to look at it."

Nathan tilted his head thoughtfully at this, but allowed Pierpont to continue.

"Nathan ... I wish you to deliver this letter to him in person and ensure that he reads it. I know you have certain ... *friends* ... in the War Department; perhaps they can arrange for you to meet with the president."

Nathan thought about this, and his mind immediately went to General Saxton. As far as Nathan knew, the president was still in debt to Saxton for saving Harpers Ferry from Stonewall Jackson back in the spring, despite the fact that McClellan had practically given it back this fall.

"Maybe ..." Nathan answered, "I *might* be able to arrange something ..."

ॐॐॐॐॐॐॐॐॐॐॐ

C.S.A. Major Charles White respectfully removed his neat gray felt uniform hat and accepted a seat as he was ushered into the office of Confederate States Secretary of War James Seddon.

Seddon never rose from his seat, as simple courtesy demanded, nor did he offer any words of welcome to the forty-two-year-old Signal Corps officer. Instead, the secretary gazed at White intently with hard, dark eyes. Beyond his high position in the government, Seddon's thin, hawk-like face, neatly trimmed dark beard, and stern visage added up to a demeanor well suited for intimidation.

White assumed Secretary Seddon was used to dominating other men, and naturally expected to establish that hierarchy upon first acquaintance.

But Major White was *not* intimidated. He was a keen observer of other men and their mannerisms, and he readily discerned their aims and purposes. Because of this, he never felt himself inferior to other men. On the contrary, if anything, his ability to easily analyze their motives gave him a deep-seated sense of superiority.

And so, as Secretary Seddon locked his intense gaze on White, the Major returned the look steadily, never losing eye contact, and purposefully resisting a very strong urge, having nothing to do with Seddon, to remove his spectacles and rub out a smudge on the outside corner of the left lens.

White had no trouble, however, resisting the nervous habit most men had of starting a conversation with some innocuous small talk when feeling uncomfortable. The secretary had sent orders for the major to come to his office in the War Department, and White had come as ordered. Therefore, he believed it was for the secretary to initiate the conversation whenever he was ready to do so. Major White sat upright in his chair and stared across the desk at Seddon, neither man speaking for an entire minute.

Finally, Seddon nodded, and said, "I can see your reputation was not exaggerated."

White tilted his head and briefly broke eye contact, to contemplate what the secretary meant by this statement. White turned back to the secretary and asked, "*Reputation*, your honor?" in a quiet tone that betrayed no emotion, other than mild curiosity.

Seddon nodded again. "Yes, I can see it's not exaggerated in the least … your reputation for being unflappable. Neither intimidation nor charm has any effect, so they say. Is it true you are even impervious to the attentions of beautiful young women, sir?"

White gazed back evenly at Seddon—if he was surprised or offended by this line of questioning, he didn't betray it.

"Your honor, I find myself entirely uninterested in the affections of women … if that's what you're asking," he answered in a flat, matter of fact tone. "I have always been this way. I don't know why, but I consider it a blessing. I observe the trials and tribulations other men go through for the sake of gaining a woman's regard, and I see nothing productive or beneficial in it," he concluded in the same even tone.

For the first time, Seddon smiled, "Hmm ... I can't disagree with you there, major. My own wife, Sarah ..." he sighed and slowly shook his head, finally losing eye contact as he gazed at his desk for a long moment.

When he looked back up, the intense, hard look had returned. "You are *exactly* what I need for a very specific purpose," Seddon announced with no preamble.

"I am gratified, your honor, I'm sure, but ... what purpose would that be, sir, if you don't mind my asking?"

Seddon stood from his desk, turned and walked over to the window at the back of the office and gazed out for a moment, before turning back toward White. "I wish for the Signal Corps to do more than just coordinate battlefield communications. I am led to understand Richmond is virtually inundated with Union spies, giving our enemies invaluable aid. I mean to root the vermin out and put an end to their nefarious doings. I am assigning you to a new counterespionage unit of the Signal Corps. In addition, I am giving you a very specific assignment."

"I appreciate your confidence in me, your honor. And I understand the seriousness of eliminating enemy spies in our midst—nothing can be more insidious and deadly than traitors secretly aiding and abetting the enemy."

"Yes, just so ..." the secretary said, as he retook his seat.

"You mentioned a specific assignment, sir?"

"Yes ... it has come to my attention one of the most successful and diabolical spy rings in the city is actually run by an upper-class lady ... if you can believe it!"

Major White tilted his head and gazed at the ceiling for a moment, finally giving in to the urge to remove and clean his glasses with a handkerchief he pulled from his pocket. He took his time to ensure a perfect cleaning, then replaced the glasses and handkerchief before looking back at the secretary and responding, "Upon reflection, it makes perfect sense, your honor. An upper-class woman would consider herself above suspicion, and yet would have access to the wives of army officers, government officials, and important commercial managers. A productive source of critical government, military, and logistical information, there can be no doubt. It is really quite a brilliant scheme when you consider it. Of course … I would happily bring this faithless harlot to justice, you can be sure of *that*, sir."

"Good, good! That is what I was hoping you'd say … and it is precisely what I *expect* of you, Major White—without fail, sir!"

"It shall be done, your honor. But … what information can you give me about this Jezebel that may help me to track her down?"

Seddon frowned, "I'm sorry to say there isn't much … plenty of stories, but nothing of any substance, I'm afraid. Mostly contradictions and false trails. Only one point seems to be consistent in all the rumors …"

"Hmm … well, anything will be helpful, your honor, no matter how obscure. What is it the rumors are saying, sir?"

"Just this … they say she is the most beautiful woman in Richmond."

"Oh! That being the case, I'm not sure I'm the best officer for the task, sir—having little appreciation for such matters."

"On the contrary, my good fellow—I believe that makes you the *perfect* man for the job," Seddon answered, smiling for the first time since White's arrival.

ಬಿಸಿಆಚಿಬಿಸಿಆಚಿಬಿಸಿಆಚಿ

Major White, of the Confederate Signal Corps, was fighting off a growing sense of futility and frustration in his present assignment, now several weeks in. As an intellectual puzzle, it had at first seemed straightforward enough: identify and arrest an upper-class woman responsible for running a successful pro-Union spy ring in Richmond. But then came the conundrum: he must identify the most beautiful woman in Richmond, a task for which he felt entirely unqualified; having little interest in women himself, he was a poor judge of what features might make a particular woman stand out.

So he set out to tackle the problem in a logical fashion. First, he decided to compile a list of upper-class ladies. This task proved simple enough; he just went through the War Department files and looked for officers and other government officials who's present or pre-war residence was Richmond, and then wrote down the names and addresses of their wives, mothers, sisters, and in some cases, daughters. Although he recognized this would not be a comprehensive list, by speaking with these women individually, he should be able to quickly learn who this mysterious "most beautiful woman" was.

But such had not proven to be the case. Each woman he spoke with had a differing opinion on whom that might be. So he'd been forced to switch tactics. He now asked each lady to compile a list of who they considered the most beautiful ladies in town, thinking there would at least be some consistency there, and that would allow him to narrow the search.

But even this strategy had proven unsuccessful. He sighed as he looked at the stack of papers he had before him, each with an almost entirely different list of ladies.

But mulling over the problem, it occurred to him, *These lists are almost entirely different … "almost" being the key word … hmm … which names are the same?*

He read back through the lists, seeing if there was one name that appeared on everyone's list. Again he came up empty.

So he took out a blank sheet of paper and a pencil, then starting with the first list, he wrote down each name and put a tick mark next to it. Then he took out the next list, and any name that was not on the previous list he added with a tick mark. Any name that was on the previous list he added another tick mark next to it. He repeated this exercise with each list until he had finished the entire stack. Then he went back through and added up each set of tick marks, writing down a score next to each lady.

When he was all finished, he went back through the numbers. Many of the ladies had similar results … but one lady in particular had a score well above all the rest.

☙❧☙❧☙❧☙❧☙❧☙❧

Evelyn sipped tea as she gazed across the room at her odd, unexpected—and uninvited—visitor. His spectacles and quiet manner reminded her vaguely of Nathan's man William, though this man was older with slightly graying hair, and was a bit thicker of build. Another major difference, of course, was that this gentleman wore a gray Confederate officer's uniform, that of a major, replete with butternut embroidery and adornments—ironed and pleated to a perfection that bordered on fastidiousness to her eye.

And despite his unannounced arrival, the major had yet to say a word about his purpose—in fact he'd said nothing at all beyond his name and rank when he was greeted at the door by Evelyn's freeman maid.

The officer sat and gazed intently at her as he blew on his tea. She noted he'd not taken a sip, though the drink was not overly hot to her taste.

"So, major … this is a pleasant surprise," she prompted, gracing him with one or her brightest smiles, attempting to fill the uncomfortable, embarrassing silence.

He broke eye contact for the first time since his arrival, and tilted his head slightly, as if mulling over her statement.

"Is it?" he finally responded, looking back at her. "I can't fathom why it *should* be … after all, you don't know me, nor my purpose for being here …"

Evelyn frowned at the oddness of this response. *Hmm … honest to a fault, I see*, she thought. *Well, two can play at that game, I suppose.*

"I was simply being polite, sir, as decorum and etiquette would demand," she answered, this time toning down her smile to merely warm and friendly. "As you say, I don't know your business here … so perhaps you would elucidate on that matter, sir, if you please."

"Indeed I would, madam. In fact, it is my general preference to get right to the heart of any particular subject and not waste valuable time on … idle small talk … as is the normal manner, I find."

"I couldn't agree more, sir," she answered, resisting the very strong urge to shout, *Sooo … then why are you here?*

"Miss Evelyn, I am an officer in the Army's Signal Corps. Are you familiar with it?"

"*Oh* ... they send messages with flags and such, don't they? Like sailors on ships, only on land for directing troops in battles and whatnot, isn't it? I read something about it in the papers," she said, though that last part was a lie. Jonathan had recently gone over the Signal Corps' operations with her in great detail, including forcing her to memorize all their different methods of signaling, even down to learning all the various flag- or light-based messages—called semaphores—though he couldn't explain to her why he felt it was so important.

Jonathan had also told her the troubling news that the Signal Corps recently had been given a new mission: counterespionage, especially here within the Confederate capital. Though she did her best to act nonchalant, she felt a sudden chill go down her spine at the mention of the corps' name; seated before her, sharing her tea, was potentially one of her most dangerous enemies.

"Yes, that's correct," he answered, "though you may *not* know the Signal Corps has recently taken on a new and entirely different assignment."

"Oh?"

"Yes ... we are now charged with tracking down enemy operatives in our midst."

"How interesting, sir, though I'm not entirely sure what that means. But since you are clearly not here for idle talk, kindly explain to me why you *are* here, if you please."

He smiled slightly, never losing eye contact. "Miss Evelyn, we are currently investigating a rumor of a particular Union espionage ring led by ... an *upper-class woman*."

Evelyn covered her mouth, feigning shock at this announcement. "Surely, sir, you are now jesting with me. I'm sorry, but since we don't yet know each other well I'm having a hard time determining if you are joking ..."

Major White frowned, "I am *not* joking, Miss Evelyn. In fact ... I never joke, so you may assume when I tell you something it is *not* in jest."

"Oh. All right. Then why are you informing me of this odd rumor? Surely you don't believe such nonsense. I have learned over the years you can hear practically *anything* if you listen to enough rumors. But almost none of them turn out to be true, in the end. I am certain that no self-respecting lady of *my* circle would stoop to such indecency—indulging in … how did you call it … a French word, wasn't it? *Espionage?* Is that the correct term?"

"Yes, espionage it is, certainly. Or you may just name it using the crude vernacular: *spying.* And as to whether or not I believe this rumor—it has come to us from too many directions and from too many different sources to entirely discount. So, I am tasked with investigating its veracity."

"Very well. Though I certainly can't bring myself to believe this rumor, how may I be of assistance, sir? Of course, it goes without saying that I would gladly help our beloved country if ever I may."

"I am gratified to hear it, Miss Evelyn. And what I ask of you is really quite simple. I only ask that you take out pen and paper and write down a list of the five or so most beautiful women in the city."

"What? A list of beautiful ladies? Why, may I ask?"

"Because the rumor says the woman leading this espionage organization is the most beautiful woman in Richmond."

"And you want me to provide you with a list of ladies to investigate? Well … I won't do it! It feels too much as if … well, as if I would be accusing any lady I might put on my list of being a spy. No, sir, I refuse to believe this rumor—nobody I know would spy for the Yankees, and I am acquainted with almost every upper-class lady in Richmond. I'll not be a party to bringing undeserved suspicion upon any of these fine women."

But the major's reaction to her refusal surprised her. He did not seem disappointed, nor did he attempt to persuade her to change her mind. Instead, he smiled slightly and again tilted his head in the thoughtful manner he had.

"It's curious you say *that*, Miss Evelyn," he said after a moment. "Fortunately for me, many of your fellow ladies have not been so reticent when it comes to providing names …"

"Oh?"

"Yes. And it has proven to be an interesting exercise. Considering most of you ladies know each other and move in the same circles—as they say—I have been surprised at how different each list has turned out to be. In fact, there is amongst your peers very little agreement on who should be on that list. If it weren't for a dearth of *gentlemen* in town—most of them being off to the war—I'd have to start interviewing *them* as well, to see if *they* had more agreement on the topic between them."

"Oh, so you are admitting defeat in your little exercise? That being the case, why do you wish me to add my own list to the many variations you have already collected?"

White looked thoughtful again, "*Why*, you ask? Not because I especially *want* your list. As I said, it would likely be entirely different from the others anyway. No … rather I came to see your *reaction* to my request, and to hear your answer to it."

Evelyn didn't know how to respond to this, though she was getting a sinking feeling this interrogation was *not* going her way. She could think of nothing to do but give him a questioning look and wait for him to explain himself.

"You see, Miss Evelyn, it turns out there *was* something interesting about the various lists after all. Despite all the differences, one name kept coming up on nearly every lady's list: yours, Miss Evelyn."

"Oh," she said, a frown creasing her brow. Then, after a moments' pause, she sat up … and laughed. She looked back at the major, still smiling, "You had me going there for a minute, Major White. Very flattering, I'm sure … but now either you are teasing me, or joking, I'm not sure which."

But he only smiled, answering, "I am neither a flatterer nor a teaser, Miss Evelyn. And I already told you … I don't joke."

"Oh, my good sir … you can't seriously believe I am … that I am this notorious spy ringleader that you seek?" she asked, a look of incredulity on her face. "Surely *not*, my good sir!"

But he stood and donned on his hat without answering, still holding a slight smile on his lips. He made a quick bow, tipped his hat and said, "Thank you for the tea, Miss Evelyn. It has been … *most interesting*." Then he turned and walked out her front door.

But even as he was stepping out, a young courier, of no more than thirteen years, held the door for him and then stepped inside.

ဢ၄၁ၥ၄ၤၡ၄ၥဢ၄၁ၥ၄ၤၡ၄ၥဢ၄၁ၥ၄ၤၡ၄ၥ

Evelyn distractedly fingered the single folded and sealed sheet of paper the courier had delivered as she stewed over the disconcerting visit by the Confederate Signal Corps major. Her first instinct had been to immediately jump up and run out to visit Jonathan and Angeline so she could discuss this new and disturbing development with them.

But then it had occurred to her the Hughes *must* have already heard about it—with the major conducting interviews with ladies all over town, there was *no way* Angeline wouldn't have caught wind of it.

So, then … why hadn't she contacted Evelyn to warn her? Unless … Angeline no longer felt safe making that contact …

Evelyn thought about this a moment … It very well might be part of the major's scheme to flush out this female spy. Visit a lady, make her think she is a prime suspect, and then watch to see what she does. Angeline must have figured this out, so she intentionally stayed away from Evelyn, not even risking sending a message by courier.

Smart, Evelyn decided, *very smart, and just the kind of thing Angeline would think of. And … she would also trust me to think the same without being told. Yes … and thank you, Angeline for your continued trust in me.*

So, for the moment anyway, Evelyn knew she must avoid the Hughes at all costs. It was galling, but she knew it was necessary until they could figure out some way to counter this Signal Corps major and his new investigation.

And thinking of Angeline, Evelyn sighed. Ironically, the woman the major was seeking was probably not herself, but Angeline—*she* was the true leader of the spy ring, along with her husband Jonathan, a.k.a. the Employer. All the more reason for Evelyn not to give the major her list. And Angeline had probably been the most beautiful woman in Richmond in her younger days, and would still be on Evelyn's list, if she were being honest.

246

But now … Evelyn shrugged. She had to admit that part of the major's veiled accusation was not so farfetched. She had worked hard to charm the upper-class ladies of Richmond, using every feminine trick she had. And it had certainly paid dividends in her scheme to plant freemen spies as domestic slaves in their households. She decided she should not now be surprised if that caused her to be included in multiple versions of the major's "most beautiful ladies" list.

She idly flipped over the letter she held in her hands to gaze at the wax seal. She noticed for the first time that the wax was purple … *Purple? Odd choice, purple … like royalty might use*, she thought. Most people used red, green, or yellow. And then she noticed the stamp was in the shape of a very fanciful "V". *V …*, she thought, *V … V… hmm … who do I know whose name starts with a V? … Oh! Varina! Varina Davis!*

She immediately broke open the seal, suddenly realizing this message was very likely from the first lady of the Confederate States herself. She read:

> *My dear Evelyn,*
>
> *Your powers of persuasion are greater than you imagine, or else your charm is just so overwhelming I can no longer resist!*
>
> *Actually, my darling, it was my dear old butler Hank who persuaded me, in the end, to accept your offer of a highly trained domestic servant to be my personal handmaid.*
>
> *I have decided a servant of this stature is necessary to help train the entire domestic staff so as to uphold the high reputation of this house for the president's sake, especially if he succeeds in convincing European dignitaries to meet with him, as he intends.*
>
> *Please make the necessary arrangements at your earliest convenience.*
>
> *Your friend,*
> *Varina - Mrs. Jefferson Davis*

Evelyn sat still a moment, gazing at the letter, a warm glow slowly rising up inside her.

Oh my dear God! she thought, *I have just succeeded in planting a Union spy in the very house of the Confederate President!*

And then as an afterthought she added, *... and thank you, Hank! I definitely owe you now, my good sir!*

ಬಿಡಿಡಿಡಿಡಿಡಿಡಿಡಿ

Monday December 15, 1862 – Washington, D.C.:

President Lincoln's personal secretary, John Hay, stuck his head in the door of the president's office and said, "Good morning, sir ... sorry to disturb you, but there is a reporter from the *New York Times* here to see you."

"Good morning, John. As you can see, I'm a bit busy ... going over all the dispatches that came in from the battlefield since I went to bed at ... well, whatever time it was in the morning ... I've no time for an interview just now ... and I fear I have but few answers in any case."

"I understand, sir, but he says he doesn't wish to question you, but rather to *report* to you."

"Report to me?"

"Yes, sir ... he says he comes here straight from the battlefield at Fredericksburg ... he wishes to give you an eyewitness account of the action, sir. He says ... well, he is a bit bold if you ask me, sir, but he says he believes you *need* to hear what he has to say."

"*Oh!* Very well then, send him in, John, if you please."

"Yes, sir."

A few minutes later a young man entered, doffing his bowler had, and nodding politely to the president. "Thank you for seeing me, your honor. My name is Mr. Miller ... I am with the *Times*, sir, and have just come back from the battlefield at Fredericksburg, Virginia."

"Yes, so my secretary Mr. Hay has told me, Mr. Miller. I appreciate you coming, but I'm not sure what you can tell me that I haven't already gleaned from the copious reports that have been pouring into the War Department via the telegraph wires for the last two days. The news is … conflicting and ambivalent. Some reports suggest we are close to a breakthrough, and others … seem less hopeful …"

The young man's face turned red, and he frowned, "Please forgive my forwardness, sir … but there is nothing *conflicting* or *ambivalent* about what is happening to the Union Army in Fredericksburg, your honor! It is nothing short of *murder*, sir, that's what it is.

"Your commanding general, Mr. Burnside, has ordered a head-on assault against a well-dug-in, well-defended enemy who controls the high ground. It is … it is … *butchery*. Just *butchery*, plain and simple, Mr. President. If anyone tells you otherwise, they are brazenly lying to you, sir.

"Your brave young men have been sent as lambs to the slaughter, with no hope of victory or even of simple survival. Even now they lie by the thousands in great, bleeding heaps on the field, their youthful lives spent to no purpose on a hopeless, fruitless, suicidal assault.

"This I have witnessed with my own two eyes, sir. I swear as God is my witness, every word I have just told you is true."

Abraham Lincoln bowed his head, and clutched at his heart, feeling as if he might simply die at that moment, or sink into the earth and never reappear. For he knew that he, himself, in his impatience for a victory, and his frustration with McClellan's earlier foot-dragging, had pushed Burnside into attempting the disastrous assault against General Lee, despite adamant military advice to the contrary.

Now the blood of all those loyal, brave young men was on his hands, and he prayed that God would take him instead. But to that prayer he received no answer.

ೞಕಾಚ೮೩ೞಕಾಚ೮೩ೞಕಾಚ೮೩

Saturday December 20, 1862 – Wheeling, Virginia:

"So … what news have you heard out of Washington that I should be aware of before I head out there, Tom?" Nathan asked, as they sat at the kitchen table, sipping a glass of whiskey. The weather had turned icy, with a bitter, biting wind, so they'd been forced to forgo their usual meeting out on the veranda. "I can't imagine anything good coming from the disastrous battle at Fredericksburg ... other than possibly General Burnside being replaced with someone more capable ... if there is such a person ..."

"No good news, sir, that's for certain. I've read through all the papers I could get ahold of, but nobody seems to know for sure what's going on. I've read everything from the president is getting ready to resign, to a coup being staged by radical Republican senators. There's even one report that suggests McClellan will march on Washington with Union troops loyal to him and seize control of the government in his so-called 'righteous wrath'!"

Nathan scoffed, "McClellan couldn't seize control of a schoolhouse, much less the federal government!"

Tom laughed, "Well said, sir, well said ...

"The one report that seems most credible is that a group of senators is pressuring the president to remove Secretary of State Seward. They seem convinced that Seward is the driving force behind the disastrous decision to attack Lee at Fredericksburg, among several other bad decisions, and that Lincoln leans too heavily on his bad advice."

"Hmm ... seems to me they're just searching for a scapegoat," Nathan answered, "I can't imagine the Secretary of State having anything to do with deciding on military strategy, and besides ... Seward has always seemed an intelligent and capable fellow, from all I've heard."

"I agree with you, sir, but *that* particular report was repeated in several papers, along with personal confirmation by several of the senators involved, so it seems the most credible of all the rumors ..."

ಬುಜ್ಞ೧ಚ೮ಜುಜ್ಞ೧ಚ೮ಜುಜ್ಞ೧ಚ

Wednesday December 24, 1862 – Washington, D.C.:

Abraham Lincoln sat slumped in his chair, his long legs propped up on a stool, gazing into the fire. Mary had long since retired to bed, after a long evening of obligatory Christmas celebrations, and even their nine-year-old son, Tad, who had a habit of being wide awake just as everyone else was ready for bed, had finally been persuaded to call it a night—but only after his father had read him several chapters from an adventure book he was immersed in.

Lincoln felt completely drained, physically, mentally, and spiritually. But even so, the relief of a good night's sound sleep evaded him. He felt as if the weight of the world was on his shoulders, and day after day, hour after hour, there was simply no relief from it.

He had pulled himself out of the doldrums and self-pity that had threatened to paralyze him after the horrific Union defeat at Fredericksburg, enough so to have at least staved off an attempted unraveling of his cabinet by a group of angry senators. *Fools wanted me to get rid of Henry Seward*, he groused, *Seward! Of all people, the man I lean on the most for sage advice and a cool head. What a ridiculous notion!*

But he had to admit, the senators' "coup" had very nearly succeeded, egged on by his own treasury secretary, Salmon Chase, who'd had a long-standing rivalry with Seward. It had *so* nearly succeeded that Seward had actually tendered his resignation in order to diffuse the crisis.

Lincoln had refused to accept Seward's resignation, of course, and it proved the tipping point in the crisis. It fired the president's righteous wrath such that he was able to pull himself out of his emotional malaise and call forth all the political savvy and powers of persuasion at his disposal to face the emergency head-on.

In the end, he was able to bend events to his will, so much so that Chase himself felt compelled to offer *his* resignation. This Lincoln had also refused, but it served to put the exclamation point on who was *really* in charge at the White House, and there was no longer any doubt in anyone's mind that was clearly the president, Abraham Lincoln.

And now he was faced with what to do about General Burnside. Though Lincoln had initially accepted all the blame himself for pushing his commanding general too hard, once the initial shock had abated, he recognized that it was not all on his shoulders. He realized that a competent general would have pushed back, even against the direct orders of the president, once he recognized that his attack was doomed to fail, and needlessly cost the lives of thousands of his soldiers. Either Burnside had not recognized the dire situation his army faced, or he had, and had chosen to forge ahead anyway. In either case, he was clearly *not* the man Lincoln needed in command of his armies. But the question remained ... *who, then?*

And perhaps the greatest impact the crisis had had on the president was to shake his confidence in his own decisions. He now actively doubted the wisdom and even the legality of the creation of the new state of West Virginia. He was now leaning toward vetoing the measure, and living with the consequences.

Worse yet, he was now considering once again postponing signing the Emancipation Proclamation—or even calling it off entirely. Coming so fresh on the heels of such a devastating Union defeat on the battlefield, would it once again appear as an act of desperation by the president?

And this tiny seed of doubt seemed to open wide the crack to allow all the old, lingering fears and arguments concerning the measure to come rushing back in: would it trigger a race war? Would it push the border states into the Southern camp? Could white men and black ever truly learn to live together in this country, in peace and harmony, as equals? Or should the freed slaves be re-patriated back to Africa—as some people proposed, including Attorney General Bates—even *forcibly* if necessary?

He continued to gaze into the fire as these worrisome thoughts seemed to spin in his mind in an endless, meaningless circle, until he finally drifted off into a short, unsatisfying, and dream-troubled sleep.

⁊ඞ⁊ඞ

Wednesday December 31, 1862 – Washington, D.C.:

Though General Saxton had assured Nathan he would do all he could to arrange a meeting with the president, he could not promise anything. With the year winding down, and all the business and holiday activities on the president's plate, it was nearly impossible to find a minute that was not already accounted for. But Nathan said he would take any hour of the day or night, if the president was willing.

Nathan had arrived at the capital by train the day after Christmas, but had been forced to wait as Saxton worked to arrange a meeting, and the days of the year ticked away.

This time, Nathan had brought along Margaret, in case she might get a chance to argue the constitutionality of their case, and unexpectedly Megs, though he'd never planned on her coming along.

Even as he was preparing to depart, she had surprised him when she asked to come with him. When he asked her why, she said, "Nathan … they say Mr. Lincoln is going to sign a law freeing all the slaves, come the new year. I'd just like to be there, in Washington City, when that happens. Just to know I was in the same town where this great thing was being done on the very day it was happening," she shook her head, a thoughtful look on her face. "That is a thing I would *never* forget."

Of course, Nathan had immediately agreed, even as he fought down the tears that were threatening to fill his eyes.

He'd decided he didn't need an armed escort this time — there currently being a lull in the fighting — so he'd not brought along any of his men, a decision he immediately regretted when he arrived in Washington and realized there'd be no one to watch Harry the Dog outside if and when he got to meet with the president at some odd hour; he could hardly expect Megs to stand around in the dark outside the White House with the large beast!

So now he sat in a waiting room at the White House at a quarter 'til eleven o'clock on New Year's Eve with Margaret, Megs, and Harry the Dog, waiting to meet with the president of the United States. They were told by the president's secretary, John Hay, that Mrs. Lincoln had already retired to her bed, having had a full evening of entertaining guests for the New Year's celebration, but that the president was still up attending to business, as was his habit.

Surprisingly, they were not the only ones waiting, despite the late hour. A gentleman who appeared to be in his forties sat across from them in the room. He had neatly trimmed hair and a short beard—slightly graying—and was wearing a suit that was simple and businesslike, rather than elegant.

Across his lap he held a case that was closed, but to Nathan's keen eye, the shape was telling—approximately four feet long, but only six inches wide and two deep, the type of box that might hold a rifle.

After Nathan introduced himself and the ladies, the man gave his name as Benjamin Tyler Henry. After the usual polite small talk, Nathan couldn't resist asking, "Tell me, sir, if you would ... Have you a rifle in that case?"

The man's face lit up, and he nodded with enthusiasm. "Well, yes, as a matter of fact I do, Mr. Chambers. I take it, then, you are a man who knows his weaponry?"

"Oh, yes ... you could say that. I'm a long-time veteran ... fought in the late Mexican War, then later out West against the Comanche Indians. And ... I expect to be out in the field again soon, after I ... conclude a little *business* with the president."

"Well then ... I believe you may appreciate my *particular* rifle, Mr. Chambers," he said and opened up the case to display its contents.

Nathan whistled when he gazed at the weapon inside; it was clearly a presentation rifle, with gold plating, fanciful custom engraving, and highly polished stocks. But that wasn't what caught Nathan's eye—this was a *very special* weapon indeed. Though it was shorter of length than most, it had what at first appeared to be a double barrel, with one barrel sitting just under the other, and no wooden foregrip. But on further inspection Nathan saw that it was not so—the second "barrel" on the bottom had no opening on the end. He leaned over and examined the rifle more carefully.

Then he suddenly grasped the significance of what he was seeing and looked up at Henry, with eyes wide. "Did you ... *invent* this, Mr. Henry?" he said, in a voice filled with awe.

Henry nodded with enthusiasm, as a smile spread across his face.

Margaret and Megs exchanged a look, but shrugged. Although the rifle was obviously very pretty, clearly intended as a gift for the president, they had no idea what had suddenly so impressed Nathan.

"Does it work? It's very pretty but ... does the thing actually work?" Nathan asked, again gazing down at the weapon.

"Oh yes, sir. The action is smooth as silk, and highly reliable. And it's accurate out to well over four hundred yards, if well handled."

Nathan slowly shook his head, then looked up at Henry and said, "I can hardly believe it, Mr. Henry ... you've actually invented the *repeating rifle*. This will ... why, this will *end the war*, sir."

ৠৡৰ৩ৠৡৰ৩ৠৡৰ৩

Forty-five minutes later, Mr. Henry had met with the president, presented his gift, and departed. Before he left, he and Nathan exchanged addresses of where they were staying in Washington that they might meet up later to further discuss Henry's miraculous new rifle.

Five minutes after Henry's departure, they were surprised when the president himself came out to greet them, accompanied by his secretary.

"My good ladies and gentleman," Mr. Lincoln said, with a slight bow, "you will please forgive me if I delay formal introductions for just a moment ... my secretary, Mr. Hay here, came into my office a moment ago and made a most curious statement ... He said, 'Mr. President, I know how you have a fondness for ... *interesting* ... creatures, sir. Well, there's an animal out here that is just plain beyond description. But I really can't allow it into this office without your say so, sir. I think you should come see it for yourself, Mr. President,' so here I am ... and here he is," the president said, and sat down in a seat next to Harry.

"His name is Harry, Mr. President," Nathan said, and was about to warn the president not to attempt petting him, when the president did just that. Inexplicably, Harry rolled over on his back, presenting his belly to the president in a clear show of subservience.

"Mr. President … I have to tell you … he never lets *any* stranger pet him, and I've never seen him behave like that before. You must have … a special touch with animals, sir," Nathan said, in a voice that betrayed his surprise.

But Lincoln just chuckled, "Yes, I do seem to have that effect on various odd creatures …" he said, and continued to stroke Harry on the chest.

After another moment he stood and gestured toward the open door to his office.

"Come, ladies and gentleman! Let us remove to my office and discuss the business at hand. You too, Harry. Now that we're friends, you are also now welcome in my office."

Once they'd entered the president's office, Lincoln turned to Nathan and held out his hand, "Nathaniel Chambers, I presume?"

"Yes, Mr. President. It is a pleasure and an honor to meet you, sir," Nathan responded.

"Likewise, Mr. Chambers, likewise. I remembered your name from before … during the first Harpers Ferry incident. You certainly must have impressed General Saxton at the time … he has been tenacious on your behalf, shamelessly using the debt I owed him to press for this meeting."

"For which I am most grateful … to both of you," Nathan answered, returning the president's grin.

"Mr. President, may I present Miss Margaret Chambers, my sister."

She curtseyed, and he took her offered hand, making a slight bow.

"Miss Chambers, it is my great pleasure," the president said, and made a soft chuckle, "and I must confess you have quite confounded my handlers. Whereas your brother, being one of our own army officers, and then a state senator from Virginia, has an extensive record, my people seem to have come up entirely empty when it comes to you, my dear. In fact, there was even some confusion as to whether Mr. Chambers even *had* a sister; the information we had in Mr. Chambers file listed him as an only child! But, I can now see with my own eyes we were most sadly misinformed on that count. And let me say I for one am most delighted to find it is so!"

"Thank you ever so kindly, Mr. President. And may I say, in this thoroughly modern age, it is a relief to know there are still some secrets a lady may keep, even from *you*, Mr. President!"

He laughed, "Well said, my dear ... and I couldn't agree more."

"And may I also introduce Miss Magdalene Chambers ... *Megs*, as she is known at home," Nathan said, "Megs helped raise me from a babe; taught me my letters, kissed my bruised shins when I needed comforting, and whacked my behind when I deserved it. She's ... one of the people I love best in life, Mr. President, and is now a free woman by my hand, I am very proud to say."

"Welcome ... welcome, Megs. It is good to meet you."

Megs bowed low, and for the first time that Nathan had ever witnessed, she seemed humbled and tongue-tied, and would not meet the president's gaze at first. Finally, she looked up at him, smiled, and said, "It is ... it is the greatest honor in my life to meet you, sir ..." and then she nodded once again, and looked down at her feet. The president smiled.

Then Lincoln stepped over toward a small table surrounded by a half dozen businesslike wooden chairs and gestured, saying, "Please ... please, be seated. Can we get you anything? Tea perhaps? No? Ah, very well ..."

Once they'd all taken their seats, the president turned to Nathan and said, "So, now that you have gone to all this trouble to see me, what is it I can do for you, Mr. Chambers?"

Nathan reached into his coat pocket and pulled out the letter from Governor Pierpont. "Mr. President, I am here at the request of Governor Francis H. Pierpont, of the Restored Government of Virginia. He asked that I present you this letter in person, and beg of you to read it in my presence. I believe you will find ... that the governor makes a reasonable, well thought out, and persuasive argument in favor of the new state, sir."

Lincoln took the letter, spread it out on the desk in front of him, and moved the oil lamp closer to better illuminate it. He put on his spectacles, and slowly read through it.

When he was finished, he looked up and met eyes with Nathan, who was taken aback by what he saw. The president seemed both surprised and pleased by what he had just read, and there seemed to be just the hint of wateriness to his eyes that had not been there before. The president slowly nodded his head and said, "Thank you … thank you most sincerely for this, Mr. Chambers. This is … this is most helpful."

Then he was quiet for a moment, gazing back down at the letter as if deep in thought. Then he looked back up and smiled, "Yes, thank you very kindly. And please give my regards to Governor Pierpont when next you see him, and tell him I thank him very much for this excellent, articulate, and well-reasoned letter."

Nathan took this as a *very* good sign, and returned the president's smile. "That I most certainly will, sir. Thank you, sir."

"And now, Mr. Chambers, you will satisfy my curiosity, if you please, as to why you have brought these two lovely ladies with you on what was clearly a political mission."

"Yes, certainly, Mr. President. As you have likely already surmised, Miss Margaret is *not* here on account of her obvious charm and good looks; she did, in fact, play an important part in the founding of the new state. You see, though she has never been a practicing attorney, she has studied law extensively for a number of years, and to our great good fortune, her keenest interest and focus has been … United States Constitutional law. This has been, as you can imagine sir, a Godsend to us under the present circumstances. I brought her along in case you had any lingering questions concerning the constitutionality of the new state."

"Ah, I see … though I believe I have a good grasp of that particular issue, but I thank you for the thought. And Margaret, it appears you are full of many surprises and secrets, my dear!"

"Oh, Mr. President … you really haven't even heard the half of it!" Then she smiled, and shared a knowing look with Nathan, who chuckled, nodding his head in agreement.

"And as for Megs," Nathan said, "well … I think it would be best if she explains in her own words why she wanted to come …"

"Megs? Why have you come to see me?" the president prompted, gazing across at her as he removed his glasses and set them aside on the table.

"Mr. Lincoln, sir … I been a slave almost my whole life, until Mr. Chambers gave me my freedom. But Mr. Chambers' momma, Miss Abbey, who has been my mistress since I was a young girl, offered me my freedom three different times over the years — but I never would accept."

"Oh? And why is that? I don't believe I've ever heard of a slave who turned down an offer of freedom even once, let alone three times."

"Likely not, Mr. President, but it was on account of … it didn't seem right for me to be free while all the others on the farm was still slaves. I was no more deserving of freedom than they. So I always told Miss Abbey I'd not accept my freedom until I was the last slave on the farm."

"Ah … I see … very admirable of you."

"So now … now I *am* free and so are all the others that was on our farm. But still … there are thousands more down South who're just as deserving of their freedom, a thing I pray for every day. So when I heard you was gonna sign a document freeing all those slaves … well, I just wanted to be here when it happened. To be in the same town as you, Mr. President, when you set your pen to that paper and set all those souls free."

Lincoln smiled, and nodded his head, gazing down at his desk for a long time. When he looked up, he had a bright look in his eyes, "I've just had a thought," he said, and stood from the desk. "Stay here, please … I'll just be a moment." He turned and exited out a door in the back of the office. When he returned, he held two sheets of paper with writing on them.

He handed them across to Megs, saying, "Here, my dear. Take this … it's one of the rough drafts of the document. I no longer need it; the final document has been taken out for copying."

Megs stared at the paper, eyes wide, her mouth agape. "This here's written in your own hand, sir?" she asked.

"Yes, ma'am. Though my writing has become a bit scratchy over the years, I reckon it's mostly legible. Anyway, you may have that copy, if you wish, for whatever it's worth."

She held the paper to her breast and gazed at Lincoln, "Thank you … thank you most kindly, Mr. President. I shall treasure this all the days of my life."

A few minutes later, after Nathan Chambers and his guests had departed, and Lincoln's secretary, John Hay had headed off to a well-earned rest, the president sat alone at his desk, his feet now propped up on its surface. He leaned back in his chair, and gazed out the window into the darkness.

For the first time in months, he felt a calmness flow over him; all fear and doubt were suddenly removed. He still could not believe the miraculous, divine hand of providence had chosen to deliver these particular guests at the very last hour of the last day of the year—at the very last moment when he must finally decide on these two momentous decisions before him: creating a new state by carving off half of an old one, and more important, signing a document that would instantly free millions of men, women, and children from a lifetime of bondage.

He'd been prepared to veto the Enabling Act, potentially alienating the portion of Virginia still loyal to the Union, for the sake of preserving constitutional integrity. And he was on the verge of postponing the Emancipation Proclamation—once again waiting for a Union victory, which he now realized was just an excuse for delaying a difficult decision.

Finally, after months of debate and doubt, with both issues still undecided in the president's mind, the simple truth presented in Governor Pierpont's earnest letter, and the reassuring humanness of the former slave woman's personal heart-warming experience—proving that black and white people could not only live together, but could learn to *truly* love one another—had tipped the scales. He would sign both documents come the morning.

As he rose from his chair and stretched, he felt the full weight of a weariness that seemed to reach right down into his bones. But even so, he now felt hopeful that the nation might just survive after all, and that in so doing, it might enjoy a rebirth of the high principles on which it was founded. Gazing out the window one last time before retiring to his bed, he silently rededicated himself to finishing the great task God had set before him.

And that night, for the first time since he could remember, he fell asleep almost the moment his head hit the pillow, and slept a peaceful, dreamless sleep.

⋆⋆⋆⋆⋆⋆⋆⋆⋆⋆

Even as Nathan was meeting with the President of the United States, by pure happenstance, or some odd twist of fate, Evelyn was meeting with the President of the Confederate States, Jefferson Davis.

She'd been invited to a New Year's Eve ball at the Confederate White House by Varina Davis, never suspecting that the president would also be in attendance. As much as she'd wished to meet him, considering it a crucial next step in her espionage activities, she'd never had the opportunity. Though she'd been to a half-dozen or more functions at the president's residence, he'd never been in attendance.

But this evening when she made her entrance, she was pleasantly surprised to see Jefferson Davis himself across the room, standing next to Varina in a long reception line of people waiting to greet the presidential couple. So of course, Evelyn immediately took her place in line.

And when her turn finally arrived a half hour later, Evelyn stepped up and graced the couple with her very best, European-style formal curtsey, in which she offered her hand to the gentleman. Davis seemed surprised at this, but reached forward, took her gloved hand and softly kissed it. Varina gazed at him with an amused expression.

"Jeff, darling ... this is the elegant young lady I have been telling you of, Miss Evelyn Hanson ... you know, the lady who trained our now beloved Mary to run our household." Varina announced.

"Ah! Yes, of course, Miss Evelyn! Well met, my dear, well met. Varina speaks very highly of you, and now I can see why. And we simply adore Mary Jane, and can't imagine how we ever got along before without her; thank you so very much for that."

"I am honored, Mr. President, and very pleased to have been of some small service ..." Evelyn said, as she stood back up and graced Davis with her very most dazzling smile. And then she immediately turned to Varina and bowed, "And it is, as always, an honor and a pleasure to see you as well, Varina," she said.

Varina beamed, clearly pleased that her bragging up of Evelyn, which she had suspected her husband had not entirely believed, was now proven true in front of his very eyes.

For Evelyn's part, she knew this was going well; there was always the risk if one turned on too much charm directed at the gentleman that their spouse would take offense. But Varina seemed to be enjoying the show, so she continued laying it on.

It flashed through her mind how much things had changed since that fateful ball, now more than two years ago—the one where she'd been escorted by the despicable Stanley Finch—when she'd had to wear her mother's hand-me-down, outdated gown, modified to fit her taller, more curvaceous figure, due to their complete dearth of resources.

She now regularly wore the finest gowns available in Richmond, with all the jewelry and accoutrements to match, thanks in part to her thriving business, supplemented generously by Angeline Hughes, who insisted that Evelyn must never be outshone by any lady in attendance at any function—this despite the nagging threat, always lingering in the background, of the mysterious investigation into "the most beautiful lady in Richmond" being conducted by the enigmatic Major White of the Confederate Signal Corps.

And Evelyn had now become an expert at applying the French makeup such that it gave her a subtle, exotic look without any obvious signs of its presence.

The effect, when coupled with Evelyn's natural beauty, figure, and grace, rarely failed to impress both the gentlemen and the ladies. And Jefferson Davis was no exception. She spent several minutes chatting amiably with the president, as if they were old friends, until she finally had to excuse herself from his presence for causing the reception line to stall.

But an hour or so later, Varina sought her out, and invited her to join her and the president at their table, an invitation she gratefully accepted without hesitation. She spent the next several hours in casual conversation with the president and first lady of the Confederate States of America, as the new year, 1863, arrived.

Chapter 13. Then, Thenceforward, and Forever Free

"All persons held as slaves
within any State in rebellion
against the United States,
shall be then, thenceforward,
and forever free."
- Abraham Lincoln
the
Emancipation Proclamation

Thursday January 1, 1863 – Washington, D.C.:

Early in the morning of the first day of the new year, newspapers throughout the north received telegrams from the Lincoln administration announcing that the president had the previous evening signed the Enabling Act, granting statehood to West Virginia, to take effect upon completion of the requirement that the gradual abolition of slavery be inserted into the new state's constitution.

Celebrations erupted in Wheeling and Union-held towns throughout western Virginia, with parades, bands, and fireworks down every major thoroughfare throughout the day and long into the night.

But when President Lincoln went to sign the copies of the Emancipation Proclamation to be presented to congress on new year's morning, he found the incorrect signature section had been inserted in the documents, and had to send them back for recopying, delaying the signing.

While waiting for the copies to return, he attended several previously scheduled public appearances, shaking hands with hundreds of well-wishers. By the time he returned to the White House and prepared to sign the important documents, he found his hands were tired and shaky. He feared future generations might misinterpret his shakiness for uncertainty or indecisiveness. But he took a deep breath and calmed his mind before picking up the pen and boldly signing both copies. He set the pen down, looked up at Henry Seward, smiled, then quoted his favorite line from the document, "… then, thenceforward, and *forever* free."

Even before the official announcement that the president had signed the Emancipation Proclamation, celebrations and prayer services were being held on street corners, in churches, and private venues all around Washington and in cities throughout the Union. Nathan, Margaret, and Megs attended one such gathering at St. John's Episcopal Church, across the street from the White House in Lafayette Square.

And President Lincoln was gratified to hear the reports that many of these celebrations included both black *and* white faces, gathered together in large numbers.

ᏁᏒᏁᏒᏁᏒᏁᏒ

As a courtesy to Miss Abbey, knowing that Nathan was still away in Washington, Governor Pierpont had sent a messenger to Belle Meade Farm on New Year's morning, announcing the good news; that the president had signed both the Enabling Act and the Emancipation Proclamation.

As the word spread like wildfire throughout the farm, a spontaneous celebration broke out much like it had done when Nathan had been freed from his incarceration by the War Department back in the fall.

This time, however, despite the wonderful news, Abbey noticed the celebration was a bit more subdued. She figured that was likely due to a combination of factors: that the Captain was still away in Washington along with Megs and Margaret, that it was midwinter, and that a chilly, biting air forced everyone to bundle up and stay near the bonfire. But most important, everyone understood that the men of Belle Meade Farm, now including the freemen, would soon be marching off to war. That was a sobering thought for all concerned, and put a damper on any overly boisterous activity.

Miss Abbey sat a few feet back from the roaring fire, enjoying a sip of warm brandy. She was pleased to see Adilida sitting across the way next to Rosa, with Tony on Rosa's other side. The two women were chatting amiably like old friends. Conspicuously absent was Margaret; the three young women had formed a bond of friendship based on the threat of their men soon going off to fight, and were often seen together.

But despite all the positive news, Abbey was feeling more than a bit of melancholy due to the absence of her son, her daughter, and her best friend. And of course, ever present, was the knowledge that Nathan would soon be joining the fight in earnest.

But she was *not* surprised that Edouard had chosen to sit next to her and comfort her. As always, he was the warmest, and most pleasant of companions—quick to smile and to laugh, and always there with an empathetic ear. In short, for a woman of her age and in her position, he was the perfect male companion. Then she thought of the "pact" that she and Megs had made concerning him, and smiled. That was a promise she would never break ... never in life.

ᴤᴥᴣᴄᴣᴄᴤᴥᴤᴄᴣᴄᴤᴥᴤᴄᴣᴄᴤ

Ned stood to attention, his dark blue uniform neatly ironed, and his brass buttons polished—gold sergeant's chevrons prominent on the upper arm of his sleeves. A cool breeze stirred the air in a steely blue sky with high, hazy clouds that blotted out the sun. But he ignored the cold and focused on what was going on around him. The men of his company, privates and corporals, all black men, and all dressed in clean, blue uniforms, stood three rows deep behind him.

He knew that somewhere behind him or out to the sides, Sid, Sammy, Caleb, and Jack also stood with their respective companies, sergeant's chevrons also proudly displayed on their sleeves.

The entire regiment stood facing a small, raised wooden platform, just large enough for a half dozen or so men, that'd been built for the occasion out on the parade ground of Fort Scott.

The regiment's commanding officer, a white man named Colonel James Williams, stepped up onto the platform, followed by the regiment's three captains, one of whom was the black Captain Mathews.

"At ease, gentlemen," Colonel Williams called out, and the entire regiment shifted into the formal "at ease" stance—hands behind the back, and feet slightly apart—synchronized as if controlled by a single mind.

"Today is January First, the year of our lord eighteen hundred and sixty-three; so please allow me the honor of wishing you all the best for a happy new year," the Colonel began, and paused to smile at the men. But in proper military protocol, the men's faces remained stoic, and there were no answering smiles.

"I have received, this morning, a very important telegram from the War Department," the Colonel continued. "Some of you may have heard rumors of this ... perhaps others have not. But in any case, this particular telegram contains within it a most monumental and historic announcement which I wish to share with you men, as it affects you most dearly."

He paused, reached into his pocket, pulled out a sheet of paper, and unfolded it.

"The telegram reads, 'Today, January 1, 1863, President Abraham Lincoln, sixteenth president of these United States, set his pen to a document named the Emancipation Proclamation. In said proclamation, the president has declared—based on the war powers granted to him as commander in chief by the Constitution—that as of this day, all slaves held in territories controlled by forces in rebellion against the government of the United States shall be then, thenceforward, and *forever* free.'"

The colonel paused, and looked back at the men, "Gentlemen, this proclamation means that the war will no longer be a mere struggle for conquest of the southern lands, but for you men in particular, this will be a struggle for your own freedom—a determined and, as I believe, *irresistible* struggle for the dis-enthrallment of your people who have long suffered oppression and wrong at the hands of our enemies."

Then he carefully folded the paper, placed it back in his pocket, and said, "Now Captain Mathews would like to say a few words, but before he does, I'd like to say how proud I am of him and of all you black men for stepping up and joining the fight, the first in the nation to do so. And after the captain finishes speaking ... company will be dismissed, after which you have our permission to applaud, cheer, sing ... or indulge in any other such celebrations as you see fit," he smiled, and this time many of the men returned his smile, though no one spoke, and they maintained their disciplined stance.

Then captain Mathews stepped up, saluted Colonel Williams, and said, "Thank you, Colonel."

The colonel returned the salute, and then shook Mathews' hand with warmth and vigor.

"Men ..." Captain Mathews began, "y'all know I'm a man of action rather than words, so as you'd expect, I'll make this brief ...

"Today is the day that I always knew would come ... Now is *our* time to strike!" he raised his fist in the air and shook it.

"When we fight, we're respected. We've already proved we can and *will* fight—that we'll not shirk our duty nor cower in fear when the bullets fly and the blood flows.

"From here on, no man will hold the whip over us! From this day forward, we will bow to no master ... but from now on, our *old* master will learn to respect *us*.

"By our own exertions and our own muscle, we will prove ourselves *men!*"

☙๛ℭ๛☙๛ℭ๛☙๛ℭ๛

Friday January 9, 1863 – Washington, D.C.:

A week after the New Year's celebrations, Nathan was still in Washington, taking care of both some personal business and some West Virginia government business.

He'd sent Megs and Margaret home on the train the day after New Year's, them having little reason to stay, beyond just keeping him company. But of course, Harry the Dog remained behind. Thinking about it later, Nathan had to shake his head in amusement, realizing he couldn't force the dog to leave him if he tried. Even Big Stan couldn't do it.

First, on the personal business side, Nathan again met with Benjamin Tyler Henry to further investigate the intriguing opportunities represented by the man's repeating rifle, which Nathan had first seen in the waiting room at the White House on New Year's Eve.

He arranged to meet with Mr. Henry in a field on the outskirts of town, asking him to bring several examples of the rifle so that Nathan could check the quality of the manufacturing, and test fire several different individual rifles to evaluate their reliability, accuracy, and rate of fire. At the end of several hours, Nathan was so pleased by the rifle's performance that his head was spinning with the possibilities. If the Union Army adopted this weapon and had it mass produced, along with its signature all-in-one cartridge ammunition, it would be a weapon the enemy simply could not hope to match, and it could quickly turn the tide of the war.

He promised Henry that he would do everything in his power to push for the adoption of the rifle by the Army. In the meantime, he could at least acquire a few of the weapons for his own personal use.

So he purchased ten rifles, and a thousand rounds of ammunition for each. He would have purchased more rifles and ammunition, but Henry had to beg off; it was all he could sell him at the moment, as their production capacity was not yet up to full speed. He promised to send more as soon as sufficient quantity was available. Nonetheless, Nathan was extremely pleased and excited about the purchase—more so than anything he could ever remember buying. He couldn't wait to show the weapon to Tom and the other men.

His next order of business was a series of meetings with Rufus Saxton and his subordinates in the quartermaster's office. As Nathan had been promised command of the Twelfth Virginia Regiment—soon to become the Twelfth *West* Virginia Regiment, he reminded himself happily—by Governor Pierpont, he wanted to ensure that the regiment had all the supplies, horses, small arms, and artillery it would need. And he knew from long experience there was no substitute for meeting face-to-face with the quartermaster's department officials in the War Department. He'd long understood that in any endeavor it was much easier to turn down a request on a piece of paper than to tell a person "No" who was sitting across from you at a table, looking you in the eye.

As much as he was eager to return home and start organizing his new regiment, as he was already in Washington, he could not in good conscience forgo the invaluable opportunity to procure the regiment's needs in person. And though it had been a long, grueling ordeal, of the type definitely *not* to his liking, he'd slogged his way through to an outcome that—if not perfect—was likely better than what ninety percent of the other regiments in the field ever attained.

He stepped out of the War Department building and took a deep breath of satisfaction for a difficult—and tedious—job well done. It was a cool evening, so the air was crisp and biting as he sucked it deep into his lungs. His immediate inclination was to pull out a cigar and light up, which he did right there on the steps, even as Harry slipped up beside him from wherever he'd been lounging outside.

As was often the case when he was alone and otherwise unoccupied in the evening, his thoughts turned to Evelyn. Wondering what she may be doing this very night, praying that she was safe and well, and as always, wondering if she might be thinking of him also.

And then, even as he was blowing out the first long, satisfying puff of smoke, he sensed a presence off to his right. He glanced in that direction and noticed a figure stepping toward him, moving up the steps at an angle. Though the figure was cloaked, and the evening light was fading, he could tell it was a woman by the slender build, and the long flowing skirts beneath the cloak.

He tipped his hat toward her and said, "Good evening, miss."

But she did not answer, continuing up the steps toward him. Wondering what this might be about, he pulled the cigar from his mouth, and held it down by his side.

She continued toward him until she was just a few feet away, then she stopped and tossed back her hood.

He gasped, dropping the forgotten cigar to the stone steps.

She laughed, then rushed forward and jumped into his arms, even as she had done at the train station in Harpers Ferry.

"Evelyn!" he cried as he held her, squeezed her, and swung her from side to side in his elation. Then she leaned in and kissed him on the lips, which he eagerly accepted.

After a few moments he set her down and tilted back to look at her face. She was beaming, even as tears of joy streamed down her face. He smiled back so hard he thought his face might crack.

"Dear God, Evelyn … am I going to have to live the rest of the war in fear that you'll show up around the next corner and shock the life out of me?!" he laughed.

She chuckled, "Quite possibly."

Then they embraced and kissed once again.

When they finally pulled apart, he said, "Oh my God, Evelyn … it is just … *indescribable* how wonderful it is to hold you again! I feel like I could burst with joy!"

"Yes … I know what you mean, my love … like half a body becoming whole again … or a great emptiness suddenly filled," she answered in a voice shaking with emotion.

"But, my dear … *how* … *why?"* Nathan couldn't help asking, "Even *I* didn't know I would be here today … how is it you have found me? How are you even here?"

She laughed, "Which shall I answer first?"

He shook his head and laughed with her, "Sorry, I'm just so … excited and flabbergasted, I don't know what to say …"

"To answer your questions, it wasn't really planned at all. I just overheard one of our agents mention that the new West Virginia government was wasting no time using its leverage as a new state to get more of what it needed from the War Department. That they'd sent a man named 'Chambers' to lobby the quartermaster's office for more supplies, arms, and so forth. When I heard the name Chambers, I knew it must be you. So I made the necessary arrangements to sneak into Washington—sorry, I am sworn to secrecy on how that is being accomplished; I'll have to wait until after the war to tell you," she said with a grin.

He laughed, "I don't care if you had to fly, I'm just happy you're here," he said, slowly shaking his head in wonder at the miraculous, unexpected joy of it all.

"But Nathan," she said, now with a more serious look, "before we go any further, I have to tell you ... I absolutely *must* return to Richmond tomorrow ..."

He nodded, and said, "Yes ... I understand ... and I'll not fight it this time. I know it's what you were meant to do. And ... I would be remiss if I didn't tell you how proud I am of you for doing it, and how much I admire you for it."

"Thank you, Nathan; that means ... *everything* to me," she said, and began to tear up. But then she immediately wiped her eyes, smiled up at him brightly and said, "No more tears tonight, my darling. I wish to enjoy every minute we have together ... only joy and happiness tonight ... I think we've *earned* that."

He returned her smile and nodded, "Agreed. No tears tonight, only delight in each other's company. And I wish to hear every detail of what you've been doing since last we parted. I can only imagine the things you've been up to since we last saw each other."

She smiled, "And likewise, Nathan ... I want to know every moment, starting from 'goodbye'..."

He shook his head, and rolled his eyes, but continued to smile. They kissed once again, this time softly, lingering for several long moments.

A few minutes later, they strolled up the street, both her arms clutching tightly to his strong right arm, and her head leaned against his shoulder, as Harry plodded along behind them.

Nathan shared with her his good news about finally being freed from the yoke of George McClellan, such that he could now take command of a regiment for the new state.

She congratulated him on that, but then looked up at him, smiled a mischievous smile, and said, "Nathan, as we walk, allow me to tell you a little story about ... *Mrs.* George B. McClellan ..."

He raised an eyebrow in amusement and curiosity, "*Oh?!* This should prove *interesting* ..."

\<END OF BOOK 7\>

If you enjoyed *Emancipation,*
please post a review.

Emancipation – Facts vs. Fiction

I get asked all the time whether this or that person or event was factual, or invented for dramatic effect. This book in particular contains a good number of interesting historical facts and circumstances that may, at first, seem made up. I thought you might enjoy the following enumeration and explanation of these details (in chronological order per the book.) – *Chris Bennett*

Lincoln's first discussion of the Emancipation Proclamation with cabinet members – the sixteenth president first shared his intention to issue the famous document with Secretary of State Seward, Secretary of the Navy Welles, and Seward's niece Anna during the carriage ride back from Secretary Stanton's infant son James's funeral on July 13, 1862.

Lincoln's first reading of the draft Emancipation Proclamation to his cabinet – occurred as described on July 22, 1862, with Secretary Blair arriving late, and the various secretaries making the arguments presented in the book. Seward ultimately held sway when recommending the announcement be delayed until after a major Union battlefield victory to avoid the appearance of desperation. The meeting was later portrayed in one of the most famous and iconic paintings in U.S. history by Francis Bicknell Carpenter in 1864, who was granted an unprecedented six month's access to the White House by President Lincoln to complete the project. The painting now hangs in the U.S. Capitol building.

Governor Francis Pierpont – was the self-proclaimed governor of the "Restored Government of Virginia" at Wheeling, a pro-Union government in exile, recognized by Lincoln and Congress as the legitimate government over all of Virginia. Pierpont is referred to as the "Father of West Virginia" for his role in the creation of that state. And Lincoln did credit a letter from Pierpont as one of the decisive factors in his decision to sign the Enabling Act, creating the new state of West Virginia.

Brigadier General Rufus Saxton – who is portrayed as Nathan Chambers' friend and loyal supporter in the book, was the real-life hero of Stonewall Jackson's attack on Harpers Ferry in the spring of 1862, as portrayed in Book 6, Invasion, for which service Saxton was later awarded the Congressional Medal of Honor. His primary duties, however, were in the quartermaster's office of the War Department, and later for the South Carolina Expeditionary Corps stationed at Hilton Head. He was eventually appointed military governor of the Union Army Department of the South where he oversaw the recruitment and training of some of the first regiments of black soldiers to fight in the war.

Allan Pinkerton – was in charge of intelligence for the Union Army throughout the war, and also served as Lincoln's unofficial protector, being credited with averting several plots against the president's life. He also courageously went undercover as a Confederate officer on several occasions to gather intelligence, and often went under the guise of Union Major Allen when out in the field. He did, however, apparently have a weakness for following the lead of General George B. McClellan, and for providing the general with the enemy troop counts the general wished to see, as opposed to reality. After the war, Pinkerton formed and ran his well-known national detective agency.

Senator John Carlile – was an adamant anti-secession, pro-Union delegate at the Virginia Secession Convention. He was subsequently one of the driving forces behind the "Wheeling Conventions" that ultimately created the pro-Union "Restored Government of Virginia" which selected Carlile as one of its two U.S. Senators (the other being Waitman Willey, whose amendment to include the eventual elimination of slavery in the new state of West Virginia convinced the U.S. Senate to approve the new state). Despite his energetic and outspoken support for the new state, he inexplicably withdrew his support for the plan midway through 1862. His sudden turnabout remains one of the unexplained mysteries surrounding the founding of the state.

Elizabeth Van Lew and Mary Jane Richard – lived in Richmond during the war, and were involved in pro-Union espionage activities, including the rumored placement of Elizabeth's former slave, now freeman, Mary as a domestic slave (and spy) in the Confederate White House. The rumor was adamantly denied by Varina Davis after the war, however. Elizabeth did promote herself as "Crazy Betty" to divert government attention from her activities.

Forty-Fifth Kansas Colored Regiment – was in fact the first black regiment created on the Union side during the war, even before officially sanctioned by the Army. The Battle of Island Mound was their first action and victory, which caught national attention as it proved black soldiers could fight bravely and with discipline against long odds. **Captain William Mathews** was one of several black officers in the regiment, and gave the speech at the announcement of the Emancipation Proclamation as depicted in this book.

Confederate Brigadier General Albert Jenkins – conducted a cavalry raid into the Kanawha Valley as a reconnaissance in force to determine the viability of an offensive to retake the valley as described in the book. This action was triggered by the transfer of Union General Cox and 5,000 soldiers to the eastern theatre. Jenkin's raid caused consternation among governors Pierpont of Virginia and Ord of Ohio. Jenkins actively recruited pro-Confederate bushwhackers to join him, including those in the Beverly and Rich Mountain areas, where Nathan's long-time nemesis Elijah Walters led his own band in book 5 - Insurrection.

Major General George B. McClellan – was restored by Lincoln to command all Union forced protecting the capital in the face of the devastating defeat of Union General Pope at the Second Battle of Bull Run (Manassas.) Lincoln made this controversial decision in the face of a petition signed by most of his cabinet members to never again allow McClellan command of a Union

Army. Lincoln's answer, "I recognize this seems like a case of curing the bite with the hair of the dog. But we must use what tools we have, and there is no officer in the Army who can man these fortifications and lick these troops of ours into shape half as well as he. If he can't fight himself, he does excel at making others ready to fight," is from accounts of that meeting by his cabinet members. McClellan's subsequent bungling of the Antietam battle and its aftermath is also historically accurate.

Frederick, Maryland – this border state town had mixed loyalties during the war, as depicted in the book, boisterously welcoming Confederate and then Union forces in turn, just days apart during the Antietam campaign.

Special Order 191 – also known as "Lee's Lost Order" is a real historical event, and aside from Evelyn and company's involvement (it was supposedly accidentally lost either by a Confederate courier or general, though exactly how that happened remains a mystery), is depicted in this book exactly as it happened, including its finding by Private Barton Mitchell of the Twenty Seventh Indiana Infantry while stacking rifles in the Union camp outside Frederick, Maryland. The document, wrapped around three cigars and tied with a ribbon, was subsequently passed up through the Union chain of command exactly as described herein (including Union Brigadier General Alpheus S. Williams keeping the cigars for himself.) And witnesses say McClellan did in fact acknowledge the authenticity of the orders, declaring, "Now I know what to do! Here is a paper with which, if I cannot whip Bobby Lee, I will be willing to go home!"

Old Capitol Prison – was a building across from the Capitol grounds, which had temporarily housed Congress after the British had set fire to the Capitol during the War of 1812. It served as a prison during the Civil War, mostly housing inmates such as spies, Union deserters, or female POWs. The prison was exactly as depicted in Books 6 and 7 of the series, including the gallows in the prison yard, which was later used to hang the Confederate captain in charge of the infamous Andersonville prisoner of war camp. The site of the Old Capitol Prison is now home to the U.S. Supreme Court.

Major General James Ewell Brown "Jeb" Stuart – was the commander in charge of Confederate cavalry forces during the Antietam campaign. His battlefield prowess was possibly surpassed by his inclination toward carousing and womanizing, as depicted in the book. The celebratory "ball" he held outside Frederick, even as the Union host approached, is an example of his flamboyant behavior.

Kanawha Valley Campaign – Confederate forces under Confederate Major General William Wing Loring launched an offensive down the Kanawha Valley in western Virginia in September 1862, forcing the retreat of Union forces under the command of Colonel Joseph Andrew Jackson Lightburn. All the events depicted in the book are factual, with the exception of Nathan Chambers' involvement in it. Heroes of the conflict, including Lightburn, Colonel Edward Siber, Lt. Colonel Augustus Parry (and his white horse), Captain Luther Vance, and Colonel Lyman Elliott (with bullet holes shot through his hat and coat) were real men, who actually performed the daring deeds described herein.

Union Seventh (Loyal) Virginia vs. C.S.A. Twenty-Seventh Virginia – these two regiments of Virginians faced off against each other multiple times throughout the war in many of the most significant engagements of the conflict. Both adopted the moniker "Bloody", though in the case of the Union Seventh, the name started out being ironic, as their early war duties were mostly of the mundane guard-duty type. That would soon change, however, especially at Antietam. The Confederate Twenty-Seventh were by contrast "Bloody" from the very start, being part of General Thomas Jackson's famous stand at the first Battle of

Bull Run (Manassas) that earned both the general and the brigade he commanded the nickname "Stonewall."

William "Bloody Bill" Anderson – was a notorious pro-Confederate leader of bushwhackers in Missouri during the war. A contemporary photo showed that he did, indeed, possess a lean, "piratical" look.

Ozias Hatch and Lincoln at Sharpsburg – an historical event, which Hatch recorded almost exactly as described in the book. Their early morning walk was punctuated by Lincoln famously describing the Army of the Potomac as "General McClellan's bodyguard."

Lincoln and McClellan meeting at Sharpsburg – the photographic images by Alexander Gardner have been recorded for posterity, as described in the book. Gardner also photographed various groups of Union officers, and Allan Pinkerton with Lincoln.

McClellan's letters to his wife Mary Ellen – amazingly, despite active and ongoing espionage on both sides, letters from soldiers, including the highest-ranking officers, were sent through the regular mail, entirely uncensored throughout the war. Mary Ellen kept George's wartime letters, and later (perhaps ill-advisedly) had them published after his death, thinking to enhance his reputation. Much of the damning text from those letters, as presented in this book, are copied verbatim from those letters. These letters were *not*, however, McClellan's downfall (via Evelyn) as depicted in the book, rather his lack of action in pursuing Lee after Antietam eventually wore out Lincoln's patience.

Confederate Signal Corps – was initially responsible for coordinating nonverbal battlefield communications via semaphores, either by flag or by light. But later in the war the corps was tasked with counterespionage activities, as described in the book.

Lincoln's cabinet crisis following the Battle of Fredericksburg – after the disastrous, horrifically bloody Union defeat in December 1862 under Major General Burnside, Republican Senators, encouraged by Secretary Chase, attempted to shake up Lincoln's cabinet, which they saw as leading the president astray. The target of their activities became Secretary of State Seward, as he was seen as the most powerful and influential of Lincoln's associates. But Lincoln ultimately outsmarted and outmaneuvered them, leading to the president consolidating his position as the ultimate power and authority within his own party. This gave him the confidence to carry through with his plans to sign the Enabling Act and the Emancipation Proclamation.

Benjamin Tyler Henry and his repeating rifle – Henry did indeed invent an effective and capable repeating rifle in 1862, the longtime dream of forward-thinking military men such Nathan Chambers. The rifle was capable of firing seventeen rounds before having to reload, a revolutionary change that, if immediately implemented by the Union, would have overwhelmed the Confederacy, which had no hope of matching the Union's ability to mass produce the weapon and its signature ammunition. And Henry did present President Lincoln with a gold-plated, highly engraved version of the rifle in the hopes of gaining his support for the Army's acceptance of the weapon (the actual Lincoln Henry Rifle can be seen today in the Smithsonian.) But despite Lincoln's reported enthusiasm for the weapon, the army ultimately rejected it as being too complex to rely on in battle, but mostly because with soldiers firing so many rounds so quickly, it would be a serious waste of ammunition! So its use throughout the war was mostly limited to weapons purchased by private individuals for their own use.

Nathan Chambers and his men are finally dressed in blue and in the thick of the battle as the American Civil War takes a new and deadly turn. Don't miss it:

WAR
ROAD TO THE BREAKING BOOK 8
is coming late 2022.

In the meantime, to show my appreciation for all the loyal readers of Road to the Breaking, please visit my website for a *FREE* **short story** about how Nathan Chambers' particular "Band of Brothers" first came together. I think you'll enjoy it:

ADVENT
A ROAD TO THE BREAKING
SHORT STORY

To download your free copy of **ADVENT** please use the web address below:

https://www.chrisabennett.com/advent

Acknowledgments

Special thanks as always to my editor, Ericka McIntyre, who keeps me honest and on track, and my proofreader and fellow Tolkien fanatic Travis Tynan, who makes sure everything is done correctly!

And, last but not least (at all!), the experts at New Shelves Books, featuring my trusted advisor on all things "bookish," Keri-Rae Barnum. You are the best!

Recommended Reading

For an in-depth look at the uncertainty, doubt, and physical suffering the sixteenth president endured as he wrestled with the ever more devastating Civil War and the issue of slavery, culminating in his most important achievement, the Emancipation Proclamation, read *Lincoln's Gamble: The Tumultuous Six Months that Gave America the Emancipation Proclamation and Changed the Course of the Civil War*, by Todd Brewster.

For a fascinating, thoroughly researched, and tantalizingly controversial theory about Robert E. Lee's "Lost Order," see Joe Ryan's American Civil War website, the article "Special Order 191: Ruse of War."
(https://www.joeryancivilwar.com/Special-Order-191/Ruse-of-War.html)

For an interesting, thoroughly detailed (to the point of possible excess) account of the Confederate offensive in the Kanawha Valley in September 1862, including many firsthand accounts, photos, maps, etc. see *The Battle of Charleston and the 1862 Kanawha Valley Campaign*, by Terry Lowry.

GET EXCLUSIVE FREE CONTENT

The most enjoyable part of writing books is talking about them with readers like you. In my case that means all things related to *Road to the Breaking*—the story and characters, themes, and concepts. And of course, Civil War history in general, and West Virginia history in particular.

If you sign up for my mailing list, you'll receive some free bonus material I think you'll enjoy:

- A fully illustrated *Road to the Breaking* **Fact vs. Fiction Quiz.** Test your knowledge of history with this short quiz on the people, places, and things in the book (did they really exist in 1860, or are they purely fictional?)

- **Cut scenes from *Road to the Breaking*.** One of the hazards of writing a novel is word and page count. At some point you realize you need to trim it back to give the reader a faster-paced, more engaging experience. However, now you've finished reading the book, wouldn't you like to know a little more detail about some of your favorite characters? Here's your chance to take a peek behind the curtain!

- I'll occasionally put out a **newsletter with information about the Road to the Breaking Series**—new book releases, news and information about the author, etc. I promise not to inundate you with spam (it's one of my personal pet peeves, so why would I propagate it?)

To sign up, visit my website:
http://www.ChrisABennett.com

ROAD TO THE BREAKING SERIES:

Made in the USA
Middletown, DE
05 June 2024

55384882R00175